E

England, involv[illegible] ruin of other countries, is face[illegible] financial collapse and revolution, bringing panic, street-fighting and an uncontrolled exodus from the cities to the countryside, where bands of starving people wander, pillaging for food.

Out of the terror and the bloodshed steps Gregory Sallust, to take the leadership of a group of men and women seeking only to survive: to lead them through bitter hardship and terrible hazard to a rural settlement which they fortify against invasion, and which, at first, seems reasonably secure. . . .

BY DENNIS WHEATLEY

NOVELS

The Launching of Roger Brook
The Shadow of Tyburn Tree
The Rising Storm
The Man Who Killed the King
The Dark Secret of Josephine
The Rape of Venice
The Sultan's Daughter
The Wanton Princess
Evil in a Mask

The Scarlet Impostor
Faked Passports
The Black Baroness
V for Vengeance
Come Into My Parlour
Traitor's Gate
They Used Dark Forces

The Prisoner in the Mask
The Second Seal
Vendetta in Spain
Three Inquisitive People
The Forbidden Territory
The Devil Rides Out
The Golden Spaniard
Strange Conflict
Codeword—Golden Fleece
Dangerous Inheritance

The Quest of Julian Day
The Sword of Fate
Bill for the Use of a Body

Black August
Contraband
The Island Where Time Stands Still
The White Witch of the South Seas

To the Devil—a Daughter
The Satanist

The Eunuch of Stamboul
The Secret War
The Fabulous Valley
Sixty Days to Live
Such Power is Dangerous
Uncharted Seas
The Man Who Missed the War
The Haunting of Toby Jugg
Star of Ill-Omen
They Found Atlantis
The Ka of Gifford Hillary
Curtain of Fear
Mayhem in Greece
Unholy Crusade

SHORT STORIES

Mediterranean Nights

Gunmen, Gallants and Ghosts

HISTORICAL

A Private Life of Charles II (*Illustrated by Frank C. Papé*)
Red Eagle (*The Story of the Russian Revolution*)

AUTOBIOGRAPHICAL

Stranger than Fiction (*War Papers for the Joint Planning Staff*)
Saturdays with Bricks

IN PREPARATION

The Ravishing of Lady Mary Ware (*another Roger Brook story*)
The Devil and all his Works (*Illustrated in colour*)

Dennis Wheatley

Black August

ARROW BOOKS

ARROW BOOKS LTD
178–202 Great Portland Street, London W1

AN IMPRINT OF THE  HUTCHINSON GROUP

London Melbourne Sydney
Auckland Johannesburg Cape Town
and agencies throughout the world

First published by
Hutchinson & Co (*Publishers*) Ltd 1938
Arrow edition 1960
Second impression 1963
Third impression 1965
Fourth impression 1971

Made and printed in Great Britain
by The Anchor Press Ltd,
Tiptree, Essex

ISBN 0 09 004500 9

To

JOAN

With all my love and thanks
for help and encouragement
during a hard but magnificently
successful year

Contents

Author's Note

This story was written in 1935 and its action was envisaged to cover a period of forty days many years hence.

All mentions of 'Queen Elizabeth', 'The Prince', 'Ministers', 'War Lords', 'Clergy', 'Inn-keepers', and others, have therefore no reference to Her present Majesty—long may she reign—or any other living person.

DENNIS WHEATLEY

1

The Prophet of Disaster

The bright July sunshine gave the ultimate degree of brilliance to the many coloured flowers in the stationmaster's garden. From a field not far away the sweet scent of clover drifted in through the windows of the waiting train, and in the drowsy heat the hum of insects came clearly to the man and girl seated in one of the third-class compartments.

They were strangers and had not spoken, yet he had been very conscious of her presence ever since she had scrambled in, just as the train was leaving Cambridge.

For a time his paper had absorbed him. It seemed that the curtain had gone up on the last act of that drama entitled: 'The Tragedy of Isolation,' which the United States Government—forced by the pressure of their less educated masses—had produced in the middle 1930's.

From that time onwards America had been driven more and more in upon herself, while Europe rotted, racked and crumbled. Now, faced with critical internal troubles of their own, the States had finally closed the door upon the outside world by a sweeping embargo; prohibiting all further exports to bankrupt Europe which could no longer pay, even in promises; refusing entrance on any terms to all but their own nationals, and enforcing a rigid censorship on their news.

The girl was staring out of the window at a placid cow, which ambled down a lane beyond the station under the casual guidance of a ragged boy, who swished now and then at the hedgerows with his stick. As the young man glanced at her his quick blue eyes took in the headline of the paper lying at her side:

'FURTHER SABOTAGE BY POLES—MORE GERMAN GARRISONS WITHDRAWN'

and his mind leapt back to the previous summer. With superb generalship, the veteran officers of the German army had carried out a classic campaign, subduing the whole of Poland in the short space of ten weeks while the French army looked on, biting their nails with fury yet impotent to help their allies, being themselves in the throes of that revolution which terminated the nine months' reign of the Fascist puppet-king, Charles XI of France.

And now Poland was slowly driving out the conqueror compelling the Germans to concentrate their forces in the larger towns by interference with supplies, the destruction of waterworks, electric plant, railway lines and bridges.

'Where will it all end!' he speculated for the thousandth time; starvation rampant in every city in Europe—millions of unemployed in every country eking out a miserable existence in so-called Labour Armies on state rations; Balkan and Central European frontiers disintegrating from month to month, while scattered, ill-equipped armies fought on broken fronts, for whom, or for what cause, they now scarcely knew; Ibn Sa'ud's dynasty dominant in the near East, gobbling up the Mesopotamian kingdoms created by Britain after the first Great War, and, with the simple, clear-cut faith of the Koran for guide, turning their backs contemptuously upon their protests of the Christian powers, now impotent to stay their Moslem ambitions.

France was rapidly becoming Communist; Germany in a desperate plight, her commerce at a standstill, and only kept from open Bolshevism by martial law.

England had kept out of the strife for the last ten years; the will of the people for once dominating the folly of the politicians, but creeping poverty was driving her horribly near the precipice, and if the United States could no longer help, another month might see her too in a state of anarchy.

Looking out upon the little wayside station and the country all about it flooded with sunshine, serene and peaceful, it seemed impossible—yet he knew it to be true.

The clang of a couple of milk-cans farther down the platform shattered the silence, a whistle blew, and the train—an unhurried local—chugged on in the direction of Ipswich.

Weary unto death with his thoughts of folly, bloodshed and disaster, the young man glanced again at the girl and caught her eye for a second. The thought that she might be willing to talk offered a most pleasing distraction. He pulled off his soft hat and flung it on the seat beside him, disclosing a crop of auburn hair; then he leaned forward, his hands clasped between his knees and smiled at her:

'I see you've finished your paper—am I being rude, or would it amuse you to talk for a bit?'

She regarded him steadily for a moment from beneath half-lowered lids. He looked a nice young man—blue-eyed and slightly freckled; he wore a suit of brown plus-fours, ancient but still retaining the cachet of a good tailor—and his hands were well cared for.

'Why not?' she said lightly; 'being a lazy person I left it to the very last moment to get up this morning and forgot my book in the rush to catch the train, so you may fill the gap and entertain me if you like!'

'Splendid! My name's Kenyon Wensleadale—what's yours? That is unless you'd rather remain anonymous?'

She shook her dark head: 'It is Ann Croome.'

'What a nice old-fashioned name,' he said, 'and may I ask if Mistress Ann Croome often travels on this antiquated line?'

'No, only I've been staying with a friend in Cambridge —one of the four year students at Girton, and I'm spending the rest of my holiday at Orford; the air-buses were full, so I thought it would be quicker to come this way than via London.'

'It is too; though not much since they've fitted the main lines with the mono-rail. Were you at Girton yourself?'

'Yes, came down last year—I'm a full-blown secretary now!'

'And how do you like it?'

'It's a bore sometimes, especially on the sunny days; but at least it means independence. The only other alternative is a life of good works on a microscopic allowance with an aged uncle at Orford; in fact, if my firm crashes I shall have no choice, and I'm afraid they may before long.'

'Things are pretty bad, aren't they?'

'Bad?' Ann's dark eyebrows lifted, wrinkling her broad forehead, 'they couldn't be much worse!'

'I don't know,' he said thoughtfully, 'I'm afraid they *are* going to be before we're very much older. This American business . . .'

'Oh, I'm sick to death of America! The whole of my

young life the papers have been crammed with what America is going to do—and what America hasn't done—and what the jolly old Empire is going to do if America doesn't!'

'Yes, that's true. Still, this embargo is going to be the very devil; it looks like the last straw to me.'

'I don't know; if we took a leaf out of their book and stopped lending money to the bankrupt countries, things might improve a lot.'

'Ah, that's just the trouble. England isn't self-supporting, and if we can't keep our trade with the outside world—we're done.'

'I wonder? Germany is sticking to her moratorium, and so is Spain. People are dying by the thousand every day in Central Europe!—they can't buy bread, let alone the things *we* are making, and the Balkans are in such a mess that the papers say we have even refused to supply them with any more munitions to carry on their stupid war. So what *is* the good of all this commercial nonsense if there are no customers left who can pay for what they buy?'

'There is still the Empire—the Argentine—Scandinavia—Belgium, Holland, Italy—lots of places.'

She frowned. 'They say the Italian state ration just isn't enough to live on.'

'I know, but Mussolini laid the foundations of the new Italy so well that they will pull through somehow. He is one of the few who will survive when the history of this century comes to be written.'

'*And* Lenin.'

He laughed. 'Lenin, eh?—you know, you don't look like a Bolshevik.'

'Don't I?' she smiled mischievously, 'and what do Bolsheviks look like? Are you one of those people who imagine that they all have straggly hair and dirty finger nails?'

'No—not exactly—' he wavered, 'still . . .'

'Well, as it happens I'm a Marxist, and I think Lenin was a greater man than Mussolini.'

'Really?'

'Yes, really,' she mocked: the set of her square chin with its little pointed centre showed an unusual obstinacy in her otherwise essentially feminine face.

Kenyon Wensleadale smoothed back his auburn hair and made a wry grimace. 'Anyhow, Lenin made a pretty hopeless mess,' he countered. 'Things were bad enough in Russia when they were running their last Five Year Plan, but since that broke down it has been absolute chaos.'

'Things would have been different if Lenin had lived.'

'I doubt it—though they might have taken a turn for the better if the Counter-revolution had come off two years ago.'

'Thanks.' Ann took a cigarette from the case he held out. 'I wonder what's happening there now?'

'When the Ogpu had butchered the remnant of the intelligentsia, they must have gone home to starve with the rest of the population, I imagine, and the whole country is gradually sinking back into a state of barbarism. The fact that their wireless stations have been silent for the last six months tells its own story.'

'I think that the way the capitalist countries strangled young Russia at its birth is tragic, but perhaps it would be best now if the Japs did take over the wreck.'

He shook his head impatiently. 'Japan's far too powerful already with the whole of the Pacific seaboard in her hands from Kamchatka to Malaya. The new Eastern Empire would be the biggest in the world if they were allowed to dominate Russia as well.'

Ann gave a sudden chuckle of laughter. 'Ha! ha!—afraid of the old Yellow Peril bogey, eh?' With a little jerk she drew her feet up under her and leaned forward—a small, challenging figure, framed in the corner of the compartment.

'Yes,' said Kenyon. But he was not thinking of the Yellow Peril—he was studying her face. The broad forehead, the small straight nose, the rather wide mouth, tilted at the corners as if its owner constantly enjoyed the joke of life—and her eyes, what colour were they—not green or brown, but something of both in their dark background, flecked over with a thousand tiny points of tawny light. They were very lovely eyes, and they were something more—they were merry, laughing eyes.

She looked down suddenly, and the curve of her long dark lashes hid them for a moment as she went on. 'Well, who's going to stop the Japs?—we can't anyway.'

'No, but it's pretty grim, isn't it?—the whole thing I mean. The world seems to have gone stark, staring crazy. Ever since the end of the 1920's we've had nothing but crashes, and revolutions and wars and dictatorships. God alone knows where it is all going to end.'

'International Socialism,' said Ann firmly, 'that's the only hope, but ever since I've been old enough to have any fun some sort of gloom has been hanging over the country. Half the people I know are living on somebody else because their firm has gone broke or their investments don't pay. I'm sick of the whole thing—so for goodness' sake let's talk of something else.'

'Sorry,' he smiled, 'one gets so into the habit of speculating as to what sort of trouble is coming to us next! Do you live in Suffolk?'

'No, London—got to because of my job.'

'Where abouts?'

'Gloucester Road.'

'That's South Kensington, isn't it?'

'Yes, it's very handy for the tubes and buses.'

'Have you got a flat there?'

'A flat!' Ann's mouth twitched with amusement. 'Gracious, no! I couldn't afford it. Just a room, that's all.'

'In a hotel?'

'No, I loathe those beastly boarding-houses. This is over a shop. There are five of us; a married couple, a journalist, another girl and myself. It is run by an ex-service man whose wife left him the house. We all share a sitting-room, and there's a communal kitchen on the top floor. It is a queer spot, but it is cheap and there are no restrictions, so it suits me. Where do you live?'

'With my father, in the West End.'

'And what do you do?'

'Well, I'm a Goverment servant of sorts, at least I hope to be in a few weeks' time—if I get the job I'm after.'

'I wonder how you'll like being cooped up in an office all day? You don't look that sort of man.'

'Fortunately I shan't have to be—a good part of my work will be in Suffolk. Do you come down to Orford often?'

She shook her dark curly head. 'No, only for holidays. You see, I like to dress as nicely as I can, and even that's not easy on my screw—so it's Orford with Uncle Timothy or nothing!'

Kenyon smiled. He liked the candid way in which she told him about herself. 'What is Uncle Timothy like?' he inquired.

'A parson—and pompous!' the golden eyes twinkled. 'He's not a bad old thing, really, but terribly wrapped up in the local gentry.'

'Do you see a lot of them?'

'No, and I don't want to!'

'Why the hate—they're probably quite a nice crowd.'

'Oh, I've nothing against them, but I find my own friends more intelligent and more amusing—besides the women try to patronise me, which I loathe.'

He laughed suddenly. 'The truth is you're an inverted snob!'

'Perhaps,' she agreed, with a quick lowering of her eyelids, the thick dark lashes spreading like fans on her cheeks; 'but they seem such a stupid, vapid lot—yet because of their position they still run everything; so as I'm inclined to be intolerant, it is wisest that I should keep away from their jamborees.'

Kenyon nodded. 'If you really are such a firebrand youre probably right, but you mustn't blame poor old Uncle Timothy if he fusses over them a bit. After all, the landowners have meant bread-and-butter to the local parson in England for generations, so it is only part of his job.'

'Church and State hang together, eh?'

'Now that's quite enough of that,' he said promptly, 'or we'll be getting onto religion, and that's a thousand times worse than politics.'

'Are you—er—religious?' she asked with sudden seriousness.

'No, not noticeably so—but I respect other people who are—whatever their creed.'

'So do I,' her big eyes shone with merriment, 'if they leave me alone. As I earn my own living I consider that I'm entitled to my Sunday morning in bed!'

'How does that go in Gloucester Road?'

'Perfectly—as we all have to make our own beds!—that, to my mind, is one of the beauties of the place.'

'What—making your own bed?'

'Idiot!—of course not, but being able to stop in it without any fuss and nonsense.'

'Yes,' he said thoughtfully, 'you're right there—rich people miss a lot of fun, they have to get up because of the servants!'

The train rumbled to a halt in the little wayside station of Elmswell. The carriage door was flung open, and a queer, unusual figure stumbled in. Kenyon drew up his long legs with a barely concealed frown, but he caught the suggestion of a wink from Ann and looked again at the newcomer.

He was very short, very bony, his skinny legs protruded comically from a pair of khaki shorts and ended in a pair of enormous untanned leather boots. He carried the usual hiker's pack and staff, and a small, well-thumbed book which he proceeded at once to read. The close print and limp black leather binding of the book suggested some religious manual. Its owner was of uncertain age, his face pink and hairless, his head completely bald except for a short fringe of ginger curls above his ears.

As the train moved on again Kenyon turned back to Ann. 'What were we talking about?—getting up in the morning, wasn't it?'

'Yes, and how rottenly the world is organised!'

'I know, it's absurd to think that half the nicest people in it have to slave away at some beastly job for the best years of their lives when they might be enjoying themselves in so many lovely places.'

'Would you do that if you had lots of money?'

'I might. . . .'

'Then I think you would be wrong.' The tawny eyes were very earnest. 'I'd love it for a holiday, but everybody ought to work at some job or another, and if the rich people spent less of their time lazing about and gave more thought to the welfare of their countries the world might not be in such a ghastly state.'

'Lots of them do work,' he protested, 'what about the fellows who go into the Diplomatic—sit on Commissions—enter Parliament, and all that sort of thing?'

'Parliament!' Ann gurgled with laughter. 'You don't seriously believe in that antiquated collection of fools and opportunists, do you?'

'Well, as a matter of fact I do. A few wrong 'uns may get in here and there, but it is only the United British Party which is holding the country together. If it hadn't been for them we should have gone under in the last crisis.'

'United British Claptrap!' she retorted hotly, 'the same old gang under a new name—that's all.'

'Well, you've got to have leaders of experience, and there are plenty of young men in the party.'

'Yes, but the wrong kind of young man. Look at this Marquis of Fane who's standing in the by-election for mid-Suffolk.'

'Lord Fane?—yes, well, what about him?'

'Well, what can a Duke's son know about imports and taxation? Huntin' and shootin' and *gels* with an "e" and *gof* without an "l" are about the extent of his experience I should think. It is criminal that he should be allowed to stand; Suffolk is so hide-bound that he'll probably get in and keep out a better man.'

Kenyon grinned at the flushed face on the opposite side of the carriage, and noted consciously how a tiny mole on her left cheek acted as a natural beauty spot. It was amusing to hear this pocket Venus getting worked up about anything so dull as politics. She had imbibed it at Girton, he supposed. 'You think this Red chap, Smithers, is a better man than Fane then?' he asked.

'Probably—at least he is in earnest and has the good of the country at heart.'

'I doubt it. Much more likely he is out for £400 a year as an M.P. It's quite a decent income for a chap like that, you know.'

'Nonsense—that's just a little childish mud-slinging, and you know it. Anyhow, things will never get any better as long as these hoary old conference-mongers cling to office.'

'Yes, I agree with you there, and that's probably what Fane and all the younger men think too—but nobody can just *become* a Cabinet Minister—they've got to get elected and work their way up.'

'Oh, that sort of pampered imbecile will arrive all right,' she prophesied grimly. 'He'll get an under-secretaryship by the time he's bald and there he'll stick.'

For a second he felt inclined to laugh at her bitter antagonism to the existing order, but it was growing upon him every moment what an unusual little person she was. Not merely pretty as he had thought at first—although her eyes would have made any man look at her a second time; but with her dark curling hair, clear healthy complexion and firm little chin, she was virtually a beauty. Not striking perhaps, because she was so short, but her figure was perfectly proportioned and her ankles were a joy—yet above all it was her quick vitality, the bubbling mirth which gave place so quickly to sober earnestness, that intrigued him so much.

'Well, you may be right about Fane,' he said after a moment, 'but the United British Party is the one hope we have of staving off Revolution. It stands for everybody who has a stake—either by inheritance or personal gain—in this England our ancestors have made for us; and that applies to the tobacconist with the little shop, or the girl who has fifty quid in the bank, every bit as much as these titled people you seem to think so effete. The Party is fighting for the continuance of law and order here at home while the world is cracking up all around, and that is why I think a girl like yourself should put aside your theories for the moment and use any influence you've got at Orford to help Fane win this election.'

'There will be no election!' came a sudden harsh interruption from the far end of the carriage.

They turned to stare in amazement at the small, bony man. His pale eyes glittered strangely in his pink, hairless face as he glared at them.

'The time is come,' he cried in accents of fierce denunciation. 'The money changers shall be cast out of the Temple—the wine bibbers shall be choked with their excess—the women shall die filthily in the chambers of their whoredom. Those who have read the wisdom of the Pyramid shall see the light. Praise be to the builder for he was the architect of the Universe; but few shall survive, for the third Era of Azekel is at hand. As the great middle Empire of the Egyptians went down into Choas—as Rome fell before the hordes of the Barbarian—so shall the strength be sapped from the loins of the people in this day. The Moon of Evil cometh with the openings of the month—and that which is written in the stone must be accomplished in human blood. Man shall be chastened yet again for his ungodliness. Nation shall war against Nation—Brother against Brother—and the Strongest shall go down into the Pit.'

He ceased as abruptly as he had began and, apparently oblivious of their startled stare, reverted to the contemplation of his little book.

Further conversation seemed impossible in such circumstances and after a quick exchange of significant glances, Ann and Kenyon fell silent until the great block of indrosteel dwellings, which had recently sprung up outside Ipswich, came into sight. Then he leaned towards her again:

'Will there be anyone to meet you?'

'Yes,' she replied softly. 'Uncle Timothy, I expect, with the slug on wheels.'

'With what?'

She smiled. 'His ancient car I mean.'

'I see, well can I help you with your luggage or anything?'

'No, I've only got one suitcase—but it is nice of you to ask.'

'Not a bit—but look here. There's one thing I would like to know.'

'Yes?'

'What is the number of the house in Gloucester Road?'

'Why?' she hesitated for a moment, 'do you mean that you want to see me again?'

'Of course—may I?' His blue eyes were very friendly. 'How soon will you be back in London?'

'On the thirtieth.'

'All right—if I drop you a line will you dine with me one night?'

'I don't know,' she spoke doubtfully, and a little wistfully, he thought, 'you see, in some way that I can't explain you are rather different to most young men that I know—so I might!'

'Tell me the number then.'

'Two seven two,' said Ann, but he only just caught her words for as the train pulled into the station the strange man closed his book and burst into speech once more.

'By numbers did the Architect build, and by numbers he shall destroy. The third Era of Azekel is at hand, and with the coming of the New Moon his reign of destruction shall begin. That which is written in the stone must be accomplished, and man chastened yet again for his ungodliness.'

As Kenyon pulled Ann's suitcase from the rack some queer superstitious current in her mind compelled her realisation of the fact that the new moon was due two days after her return to London. Two days, in which she might have seen this tall, auburn-haired, blue-eyed man again. . . . Would life hold a new interest for her by the coming of the August moon?

They had hardly stepped down on to the platform when

a newspaper placard caught their eyes:

'FIRST RESULT OF THE AMERICAN EMBARGO—GOVERNMENT TO RATION VITAL SUPPLIES'

With a little nod of farewell to Kenyon, Ann turned to wave a greeting to the scraggy-necked clergyman who was hurrying through the crowd towards her. Yet even as they moved apart both had caught the tones of a harsh voice in their rear—crying out from the depths of the carriage.

'Nation shall war against Nation—Brother against Brother—and the Strongest shall go down into the Pit.'

2

The Tramp of Marching Men

Ann Croome lay back in the largest of the three arm-chairs which, with a dilapidated settee, constituted the principal furniture in the sitting-room of 272 Gloucester Road.

Opposite to her stood Mr. Rudd, the landlord of this strange caravanserai. His yellowish hair was close-cropped and bristling at the top of his head, but allowed to grow into a lock in front which he carefully trained in a well-greased curve across his forehead. A small, fair moustache graced his upper lip, but as he always kept it neatly trimmed it failed to hide the fact that his teeth badly needed the attention of a dentist. His eyes were blue, quick, humorous and friendly.

'It's this way, Miss,' Mr. Rudd twirled a greasy cap in his hands—the only headgear he had been known to use during his twelve years' tenancy in Gloucester Road. 'White's white, an' yeller's yeller—if you take my meanin'. It wouldn't be fair to you an' the others ter take a Chink inter the 'ouse—so Mrs. P. can say wot she likes abart 'is art an' all—but the second floor front remains empty.'

Ann knew that Rudd's slender income was the shadowy balance between what he received from his tenants and the rent he paid for the house; and that he found it necessary in order to make both ends meet to act as storekeeper, loader, and occasional vanman to Mr. Gibbon—the grocer whose shop occupied the ground floor.

'It means a serious loss to you,' she said.

'Maybe, Miss—but my old lady sez to me afore she died: "Ted," she sez, "seeing' this ain't egsactly a posh 'otel, it's *recommendations* wot counts—so, if you're ever in any quandairy, think of the comforts of the lodgers wot ye've got, an' you'll be orlright." '

'Well, personally, I'd much rather not have to share the sitting-room with a Chinaman.'

'Now that's jus' wot I sez ter Mrs. P.—"you're married wiv an 'usban' an' all, Mum—but there's Miss Croome and Miss Girlie ter be thought of. Wot'll *they* feel like when their frens come ter see them wiv a Chink in the place?"—tho' she took me up proper when I called 'im a Chink to 'er. But I'm scared now she may take the needle an' 'op it to another 'ouse.'

'Mr. and Mrs. Pomfret won't move because you've turned their yellow friend down,' Ann assured him; 'they're far too hard up.'

'That's so, Miss—seven week 'e owes me for, an' not that I likes to discuss one person's business with another, but I don't get no credit with me rates. Still, 'is new book's comin' out on Friday 'e tells me—so we'll soon be touching the spondulicks now.'

'It's a rotten time to bring out a new book.'

'Yes, business is that bad everywhere, it's a poser ter me 'ow any of 'em carries on at all. Did you 'ear about poor old Mr. Watney darn the street?'

'No—do you mean at the dairy?'

'Yes—put 'is 'ead in the gas oven 'e did—'im an' 'is missus as well!'

'How terrible!'

'Crool, wern't it?—but as I said ter Mr. Gibbon—"wot can you expect?—an old chap 'oo's conscientious like, an' owin' all them bills!"—'e owed Mr. Gibbon close on forty pound. An' when you bin livin' respectable all yer life it aint nice to owe people money—it 'urts—but wot's a man to do if people won't pay 'im?'

'But you wouldn't take that way out yourself, would you?' Ann inquired. Rudd's views on life amused her, so she always encouraged him to talk.

'Wot, me?—no fear, Miss!' his broad grin displayed the ill-kept teeth. 'I'm an old soldier I am—an' you know wot they say—"*Old Soldiers Never Die—They Only Fades*

Away," but that 'ud be a bit before your time I reckon. Lumme! come ter think of it, you couldn't 'ave bin born when we went an' put the Kibosh on the Kaiser—yet it seems like only yesterday ter me.'

'Was it really so terrible as the war-books make out?'

'Well,' he scratched his head thoughtfully, 'I don't know about no war books—not bein' a great reader meself, but I used ter get the wind up proper when Jerry 'ad one of 'is special 'ates on, an' the little visiters used ter make yer itch somethin' crool. Still, the War 'ad its compensations as yer might say. The grub was a treat—far better'n wot most people 'ad at 'ome—an' if you could nobble a bottle or two of that vin rooge from the estaminay ter push around the Crown an' Anchor board in the billet of an evenin'—the War weren't none so dusty!'

Ann laughed. 'It doesn't sound very romantic as you put it, but I expect you did all sorts of brave things as well.'

'Brave?—me?—not likely!' Mr. Rudd's kind blue eyes twinkled. 'I wouldn't never 'ave seen a Jerry if it 'adn't bin fer Mr. Sallust.'

'Mr. Sallust? Ann repeated with a puzzled note in her voice, as Rudd named the loose-limbed journalist with the perpetual stoop, who occupied the big back room on the first floor.

'Why, yes, Miss—'e was my officer in the War, an' that's why 'e lives 'ere tho' 'e could well afford a better place. It's just 'is bein' a bit Bo'emian like, an me knowin' all 'is little ways. Now 'e was a reel tiger—"Rudd," 'e used ter say ter me when we was in the line—"what abart makin' some little h'addition to h'our collection ter-night?" "Very good, Mr. Sallust, sir," I used ter say—since seein' I was 'is servant I couldn't say nothin' else, but I knew what that meant orlright—orlright. A couple of hours a-crawlin' round in No-Man's-Land till 'e'd coshed an 'Un wiv 'is loaded crop—an' took 'is pistol or binoculars orf 'im!'

Ann had always been interested in Gregory Sallust, although his caustic wit and avowed cynicism sometimes repelled her. Now she was trying to absorb this new view of him. But it was difficult to reconcile the lazy self-indulgent man she knew with Rudd's picture.

'I suppose that is how he got his scar,' she remarked, thinking of the short white weal that ran from the outer corner of Sallust's left eybrow up into his forehead.

'That's so, Miss, one of them little Gurkhas give 'im that, mistook 'im in the dark for an 'Un—an' 'is langwidge!—strewth!—I thought they'd 'ear 'im in Berlin an' put Big Bertha on us before I got 'im 'ome.'

'Berlin!' Ann touched the evening paper with her foot, bringing the conversation abruptly to the latest news. 'Isn't it terrible about this fire. Nobody seems to know if it is organised by Poles or Jews but it seems to be breaking out in a fresh place every hour or so, and they say it has gutted thousands of houses and shops in the last two days.'

Rudd shook his yellow head. 'They've 'ad a shockin' time an' no mistake. But it's Glasgow as worries me! It ain't in the paper o' course but I 'ad it on the Q.T. from Mr. Sallust this mornin'. The troops was firin' on the crowd lars' night—an' when it comes to that in *this* country. . . .'

'If that is true it is utterly shameful!' Ann's eyes blazed with partisan indignation. 'The workers have every right to meet and voice their grievances when the Government is so hopelessly incompetent.'

'Ah, yes—the workers, but if you'll pardon me, Miss—this riff-raff ain't the workers. It's all them youngsters wot never done an 'and's turn in their lives.'

'Well, is that their fault?'

'Yus—why don't they volunteer for the National Army of Labour wot was started lars' year? I'd conscript the lot o' them if I 'ad my way. Not that I 'old with armies mind you, but a bit o' discipline is what them sort wants, an' one of those old walrus-faced sergeant-majors to tickle 'em up a bit.'

'How could we keep an army of five or six million men?'

'Well, ain't we feedin' 'em all at the present time—an' they still gets a dole that's bigger than the army pay—so why shouldn't they do a bit o' work?'

Ann was saved from the necessity of replying by the sudden entrance of Mrs. Pomfret—large-bosomed, untidy, breathless and agitated as usual.

'My dear!—Hildebrand?—isn't he back?' she exclaimed, ignoring Rudd.

'I haven't seen him,' Ann replied, 'did you want him for something special?'

'No, oh! no,' Mrs. Pomfret sank on to the settee, 'but we promised to see Zumo Kriskovkin's drawings this evening, and dear Hildebrand—he has *no* sense of time!'

Rudd shuffled his heavy boots uncomfortably. 'Well, if there's nothin' you're wantin' I'll be gettin' along, Miss?'

Mrs. Pomfret turned on him quickly. 'Mr. Rudd, I do hope you have reconsidered what I was saying about Mr. Choo-Se-Foo?'

'No, Mum,' Rudd backed swiftly towards the door, 'you won' take it unfriendly, Mum—I 'ope—but it's a rule of the 'ouse in a manner o' speakin'.'

'Oh, dear, oh, dear—' the large lady settled her skirt over her ample thighs, 'you are a most unreasonable man,' but a sharp click of the latch informed her that Rudd had made his escape and was now half-way down to the insalubrious gloom of the basement where he dwelt in mystery and disorder. She turned on Ann.

'The prejudices of the working class are too absurd—don't you agree? Mr. Choo-Se-Foo is the most charming man, and yet, just because he is Chinese, Rudd won't have him in the house. It would be a real distinction to have a genius like Choo-Se-Foo among us, but the masses have positively no appreciation of the arts. Sometimes it makes me wonder if it is worth while to go on.'

Ann had a quick mental picture of a small, smirking Oriental, cunning and insincere, deprecating his own presence with wearisome false modesty, and sneaking in and out like some large yellow cat. Living at such close quarters made one cautious of offending the other occupants of the house however, so with a show of interest she said:

'You know I'm afraid I'm terribly ignorant—but just what does Mr. Choo-Se-Foo do?'

'*Do*!—my child!—but there, once again we see the tragedy of souls pinned down to earth because they are compelled to earn their daily bread. How can you have time for the beauties of life, and for your work? Choo-Se-Foo is, perhaps, the greatest sculptor of our time.'

'Has he had any exhibitions of his work?' asked the practical-minded Ann.

'Well, now, isn't it strange that you should ask *that,*' Mrs. Pomfret's false teeth showed in a wide smile. 'Only the other day I was saying that we simply must arrange an exhibition for him, but of course he is like a child, my dear—so simple—so unspoiled! Our hard, western commercialisation of beauty is quite beyond the understandings of his delicate mind.'

Ann felt an intense desire to giggle. She thought it highly probable that the Chinaman was a clever little rogue who made an excellent thing out of the enthusiasms of his arty-crafty European friends; but she was saved the necessity for comment; Mrs. Pomfret had heaved her bulk off the settee and was dragging a heavy parcel from the corner of the room.

'My dear, I must show you,' she exclaimed—fumbling with her small useless hands at the wrappings. 'He lent me this because I know a dealer—really an unusually clever man for his class—and I thought he might be interested. Look, my dear, his Infant Jesus—don't you think it *quite* remarkable?'

Remarkable was the word Ann agreed as she gazed with astonished disgust at this monstrosity in stone. A large ball covered with every variety of human face, the expressions varying from benign to mercilessly sadistic; it stood upon two short, splay feet, and two puckered, feeble hands protruded from its upper surface.

'It is clever, I suppose,' Ann remarked doubtfully, once more forbearing to offend.

'Clever!' Mrs. Pomfret cried, her pale blue eyes bulging at Ann's lack of enthusiasm, 'but it is marvellous—it has such atmosphere—such rhythm!—help me to lift it on to the bookcase, dear, I simply must keep it for just one day.'

'Rhythm!' thought Ann impatiently, 'what utter rot!' but she helped to lift the figure, and then curled up in her chair again while Mrs. Pomfret stood back to admire this product of a distorted mind, her small hand clasped in an ecstasy of adoration.

'It makes me feel . . . so . . . Oh! how hard it is to put one's emotions into words. I wonder if you understand?'

Ann did not care two kicks what the woman felt, but at that moment Mr. Pomfret limped into the room.

He was a tall, cadaverous person, moody and silent—which his wife attributed to his great artistic gifts. Unfortunately the British public did not share her appreciation of Mr. Pomfret's genius, so although he had been writing for some twenty years it was a constant struggle for him to induce his publishers to renew their contracts and actually put into print those long dissertions upon the hesitations of the human soul which he evolved so labororiously.

'My love,' he said, smiling wanly at his Junoesque spouse.

'Hildebrand!' she swayed towards him—they kissed.

To Ann, there was something incredibly grotesque about the performance; the fat, emotional woman in her too highly coloured clothes, the lank, disappointed man who, despite the August weather, still wore a thin dark overcoat which dangled far below his knees.

'Hildebrand—my treasure, we must hurry!' exclaimed Mrs. Pomfret with a quick return to the practicalities of life.

'But where?' the man turned sad, dark eyes upon his wife.

'Zumo, my darling—had you forgotten?—and Chitterson Phlipper will be there, perhaps we can persuade him to take your article on the sex-life of the cryptogam.'

'Ah, yes. Let's go then' He held the door open for her with the elaborate courtesy of an old-fashioned actor, but her exit was momentarilly impeded by the hurried entrance of Miss Griselda Girlie.

Griselda tossed a heavy satchel on to a nearby chair as the Pomfrets left the room. She was studying for her medical degree, and still taking student courses through the long vacation. Striding over to the hideous plush-covered mantelpiece, she looked quickly through the letters. 'Oh dear,' she sighed to Ann. 'He hasn't written—he won't now, I don't think.'

Ann nodded sympathetically; she knew that Griselda had tasted one glorious evening of romance when a young traveller in medical implements had made love to her at a students' dance. For a few days Griselda had been almost beautiful—but that was a fortnight ago, and now once more was bony—plain. Ann felt that it was unkind to encourage her to hope. She knew that Griselda was desperately, tragically, anxious to be loved—but how could any man in sober earnestness desire to caress that gaunt unprepossessing body, or kiss those pale bloodless lips.

'Perhaps it is just as well, dear,' she said softly, 'an affair would handicap you terribly in your work.'

'I'm sick of work,' Griselda threw herself angrily into the second-best arm-chair.

'That's because you've been doing too much,' Ann soothed her. 'Take a day or two off, and you'll feel better.'

Griselda shrugged despondently. 'Oh, what's the good, Ann—why are we cursed with sex I wonder?'

'Who is cursed with sex?' asked a quick voice behind them. Gregory Sallust had entered unobserved.

'I am,' cried Griselda fiercely, to Ann's amazement.

He laughed, not unkindly. 'Blessed, you should say, my dear. Sex is the one great escape we have from the incredible dreariness of daily life. It only becomes a curse when you haven't the courage to get it out of your system in the normal way.'

'Shut up!' said Ann sharply. She was feeling acutely for the other girl, and wondered how Gregory could be so wantonly cruel.

'You're a medico,' he went on blandly, ignoring Ann. 'Be sensible then, put aside your stupid little suburban prejudices and make the young man happy. No harm could come to you, and it would probably cure your indigestion.'

'What a brute you are!' Griselda flung at him. 'As though any girl could go out into the street and offer herself to the first comer.'

Gregory ran his hand over his dark, smooth hair. 'Dear me, I thought you had a man in tow already—but never mind, the other is just as good—clinically!'

'How revolting! I couldn't!' gasped Griselda.

'Why not?' his voice was sharp—imperious. The scar which lifted the outer corner of his left eyebrow gave his long, rather sallow face a queerly satanic look. 'There are a hundred thousand lonely men in London—go out then, wait till some strong, healthy-looking blighter tries to pick you up—be coy if you like, but grab him. Then, once you get down to brass tacks, throw your inhibitions overboard; men always fall for that because it's rare in Anglo-Saxon countries. He'll ask you to meet him again—certain to, and when you do—don't look at his Adam's apple, gaze into his eyes and tell him he's a new Sir Galahad! Then with any luck the poor fish will get all sentimental, and you will at least have secured someone to fend for you in the trouble that is coming to us all.'

'You filthy beast!' Griselda sprang to her feet, and rushed from the room in a futile endeavour to hide the tears which welled up in her small tired eyes.

'Gregory, you are a cad.' Ann flung a half-smoked cigarette into the grate, and gave him an angry look beneath half-closed lids.

He swung upon her quickly, his shoulders hunched, his hands thrust deep into his trousers pockets.

'Why?—don't be silly, Ann. God knows who'd look at her, but some fool would. There are lonely men—lots of them, and her one asset is that she's a young healthy woman, but of course she hasn't got the guts to do it. She's the stupid, inefficient sort who go under in every war and revolution.'

Ann's eyes fell before his glance. 'What is the latest, Gregory?—are things getting very bad?'

'Glasgow is under Martial Law. The troops were compelled to fire on the rioters last night. There were seven killed and sixty wounded. In Hull, during the early hours of this morning, an organised raid was made on the principal banks; a number of police were injured, the safes were dynamited and the contents carried off in fast cars. It is said to be the work of international crooks who are taking advantage of the disturbances. In a village of the Merthyr valley an income-tax collector was pulled out of bed at four in the morning, saturated in petrol, and then set on fire; he was burnt to death while the crowd cheered as if it had been Guy Fawkes' night. The crews on some of our biggest ships are giving trouble because it is the leave season, and all leave has been cancelled. Three pawn-brokers—Jews, of course—were dragged from their shops and kicked to death in the East End this afternoon. Troops are being moved into the dock areas now, because they fear rioting here tonight.' Sallust paused, and then added cynically: 'Want any more of the gory details?'

She shivered slightly. 'No! it's all too horrible—but do you really think the whole system is breaking up?'

'I don't think—I *know,*' he laughed harshly, as he crushed out the butt of his cigarette. 'I've been watching events for months and it's only a question of days now. There is not a single strong man in the whole of the Government—and this time next week the people will be fighting for food in every town in England.'

'What do you mean to do?' she asked him curiously.

'I,' he shrugged; 'oh, don't worry your little head about me. The traditional bad man of the party may get killed in the play, or in that poor boob Pomfret's novels—but not in real life. Luckily, I'm not handicapped by any illusions or scruples, and so, my dear—I shall come through; a little drunk perhaps on looted gin, but otherwise unscathed. The thing is—what about you?'

'I . . . I hadn't realised that things were quite so desperate,' Ann confessed.

'Well, you'll survive—you're too damned good-looking for anyone to want to do you in. But you'll have to pay the price unless you slip off now. What about those people of yours in Suffolk?—I should get out of it if I were you while the going's good.'

'Perhaps I ought to have stayed down there. A man I met the other day wrote and urged me to, but the letter only reached me just as I was leaving because it was forwarded from here.'

'Who is he? Anybody who's really in the know, or just some chap who is anxious for his lovely's safety?'

'He's a civil servant, I think; he told me that he was after some post to do with the Government.'

'Then he probably had some good reason for his warning. Take his tip, Ann—and mine. Quit the party . . . God! what's that?' Gregory Sallust had suddenly caught sight of the monstrosity on the bookcase.

'A masterpiece by Mrs. Pomfret's *protégé* Choo-Se-Foo,' Ann chuckled. 'The Infant Jesus, I believe.'

'How utterly blasphemous!'

'Dear me,' she mocked him. 'I thought you were an atheist.'

'He turned on her swiftly. 'Perhaps I am—but Christ was a great man—I hate to see Him mocked at by these filthy pseudo artists.'

A new sound came to them above the casual noises of the street. The rhythmic tramp . . . tramp . . . tramp of marching men. They both moved instinctively to the open window. As the head of the column came level, the door opened and Rudd joined them:

'Wonder where the boys are off to,' he remarked thoughtfully; 'we don't often see 'em darn this way.'

'They are *en route* for the East End, I expect,' Gregory told him, 'and they are probably taking the side streets in order to avoid comment as far as possible.'

It was a full battalion in war equipment. Steel helmets—packs—gas-masks—overcoats, bandoliers and rifles. Company after company swung by. The dust on their boots showed they had come in from the country and evidently their Colonel did not consider that they were far enough into the heart of London to call them to attention.

They marched at ease, their rifles slung or carried at the trail, many of them smoking, chewing sweets, or talking.

'They might give us a bit of a song,' said Rudd.

'That's just the trouble,' murmured Gregory Sallust, 'they are not singing—and that's a damn bad sign.'

3

'Eat, Drink, and be Merry, for . . .'

The sound of marching feet died away in the distance, and they drew away from the window.

'I wonder whether Clarkson's is still open?' Gregory remarked as Rudd left them.

'Why?' asked Ann.

'Want to get a fancy dress for the party,' he answered absently.

Her tawny eyes were filled with sudden mirth. 'How like you, Gregory, to go fiddling while Rome burns.'

'You, I suppose, prefer to pray?' he countered in quick derision.

'No, as a matter of fact I'm going out myself this evening.'

'Good for you—"business as usual", eh? and "Keep the home fires burning". All the old gags will come out again—you see! . . . Got a new boy-friend?'

'I shouldn't be going out alone, should I?'

'No,' he eyed her critically, 'by some amazing stroke of good fortune for you the proportion of proteins, hormones and vitamins which make up your body vary slightly from the proportions allotted to Griselda—owing to the result of the blend you don't have to. All the same, what I said to her goes for you too and, if you've got a man, you'll be doubly wise in these days to make it worth his while to stick to you.'

'Thanks, but the proportions vary in men as well, and so thank goodness they're not all like you. The decent kind don't need to have it made worth their while to stick to a woman if they're in love with her.'

He gave a sudden shout of laughter. 'God! what fun you

are, Ann—I love to see you get all romantic, I've a good mind to take you out myself one night!'

'If that's an invitation it comes a little late,' Ann smiled.

'Ah! well,' he shrugged his stooping shoulders, 'Fleet Street keeps me busy six nights out of seven, so work shall serve as an anodyne to my broken heart!'

'Idiot!' she laughed. 'You haven't got a heart.'

'No, perhaps I haven't, unless it's in my stomach. The ancients believed the stomach to be the seat of all emotions, you know—and they were right about so many things. In any case it is time for me to feed it and then go forth to grasp the nettle of my nightly toil.' As he moved towards the door he flung a smile at her over his shoulder. 'Bye-bye, little pansy face—good hunting to you!'

For a time she sat alone in the lengthening shadows debating with herself the advisability of taking Gregory's advice and scuttling back to Orford the next day, but there was her job to be considered; supposing all this pessimism proved a false alarm?—there had been isolated acts of violence and occasional rioting for the last eighteen months. If she once cleared out she could hardly expect her firm to take her back—besides she was going to see Kenyon again that evening! And unless he proved disappointing at this second meeting, she somehow felt that she would not want to leave London for the present. Still undecided, she went up to dress.

An hour later, as she was being carried swiftly towards Charing Cross in the Underground, she wondered why Kenyon had asked her to meet him at nine o'clock. It seemed absurdly late to her—yet his letter had clearly said dinner. She wondered, too, how he would be dressed—tails or a dinner-jacket. Most of the young men she knew could not afford two sets of evening clothes, and favoured the latter as more economical for their laundry bills. She assured herself that it did not matter twopence really, but as he had suggested the Savoy it meant dancing afterwards, and she preferred not to go to pretentious places unless her escort was properly dressed.

At Charing Cross she hopped into a taxi, since she had no intention of arriving at the Savoy on foot. As she walked through the lounge of the hotel she found that she had timed her arrival admirably, the clock showed two minutes past nine, and there at one of the small tables below the stairs Kenyon was waiting to greet her.

In one swift glance she saw that no woman could cavil at his appearance. White tie, and a double breasted waistcoat making a sharp line across his trousers-top, his rebellious hair brushed smoothly back, and a flower in his buttonhole. 'Really,' thought Ann as she walked towards him, 'he looks terribly distinguished, almost as though he wore dress-clothes every evening.'

He rose as she came up. 'My dear, you're looking ravishing; have a cocktail?'

'Thanks, I'd love one,' she smiled serenely as she settled herself in the chair he held for her.

So he thought her ravishing—what fun—and really, she had never felt better than she did tonight. How fortunate that she'd decided to blow the extra twenty-five bob and have the prettier frock—it had seemed a horrible extravagance at the time but now she had no regrets. Ann's face flushed to a delicate pink, her eyes bright with excitement as she raised her glass in response to him across the little table.

'Your friends the Communists are making a fine to-do about the shooting in Glasgow,' he remarked with a grin, 'threatening all sorts of reprisals against the Government.'

Ann reddened; somehow her Socialistic theories seemed rather futile and childish in the atmosphere of this luxury hotel. It ought, she knew, to have strengthened her conviction in the rightness of her cause. But being honest with herself, she knew that she was enjoying every minute of it; so she shrugged her rather plump little shoulders under the flimsy frock, and smiled, 'Shall we give politics a miss this evening—just pretend we're living in normal times—I wish you would?'

'Why rather—I'd love to. What about another cocktail?'

'Yes, er—that is . . .' She hesitated a second, used as she was to practising consideration for young men's pockets. 'Don't think me rude—but can you really afford this sort of thing?'

'You stupid child, of course I can,' he laughed, 'still—it's sweet of you to think of it. Waiter—two more *Forlorn Hopes*.'

Ten minutes later as he followed her down the broad, shallow stairs towards the restaurant, his thoughts were chaotic. What a skin she's got—and those little dark curls on the nape of her neck . . . I'd love to kiss them . . . By jove I will, too. There's not a girl to touch her in this place . . . I'm thundering glad I wrote to her after all . . . but that was a little queer, thinking I might not have the price of a second cocktail. Damned decent though . . . and *how* refreshing!'

'How goes the job?' Ann inquired, after he had ordered what she considered to be an almost criminally expensive meal.

'I think it will be all right, but I shan't know for about a fortnight.'

'I do hope you get it; would they give you a decent screw to start with?'

'Oh, not too bad, about eight quid a week. Here's to it!' he added, lifting his glass; 'and long life and happiness to Mistress Ann Croome.'

'Thank you,' she smiled quickly as the bubbles of the champagne tickled her tongue. 'Well, eight pounds a week is nice, but not a fortune,' she was thinking, and if they were going to be friends she meant to teach him to be economical. It was terribly nice of him to give her such a marvellous evening, and perhaps it was excusable just this first time, but there must be no more dinners at places like the Savoy.

'Of course I get an allowance from my father,' he cut in, almost as if he had read her thoughts.

'I see,' she coloured slightly, 'and is he a civil servant too?'

'Well, hardly,' Kenyon's blue eyes shone with sudden humour, 'he's a farmer really—although fortunately he has a few investments as well.'

'Investments are so uncertain these days, aren't they?'

'They are, indeed—did you hear that Vibro-Magnetic crashed this afternoon?'

'No! That means another slump in the city, I suppose?'

He nodded. 'Bound to, they're such a tremendous concern, and they'll bring down dozens of smaller people with them, so goodness knows how many more poor devils will be hammered on the Stock Exchange next settling day.'

'If things go on like this there won't be any Stock Exchange left.'

'Not unless the Government decide on a moratorium, they've been talking about it for the last week.'

'What effect will it have if they do?'

'No one will have to pay anyone else except for a new transaction.'

'I hope they do then—it would give all the firms that are in difficulties a chance to carry on.'

'Perhaps—but it almost means an end of credit. People wouldn't be able to get any more goods unless they were in a position to pay for them.'

'Well, it would keep my firm from going under—I'm terrified every day that they'll close down and that I shall lose my job.'

'Ann,' he said gravely; 'why did you come back to London?—delighted as I am to see you, I did write and warn you not to. There's going to be real trouble here very soon.'

'I thought it terribly sweet of you to write as we'd only met just that once—would you really like to know why I came back?'

'I would.'

She leaned a little forward across the table, a mischievous smile lurking in the depths of her golden-flecked eyes.

'Then I'll tell you! . . . It was because I wanted to see you again!'

'Really! Do you mean that?' he bent eagerly towards her, stretching out one of his large, freckled hands to take hers, but she laughed and shook her curls.

'No, not *really*,' she mocked, then seeing the sudden look of disappointment that clouded his face, she added quickly: 'At least . . . I did want to see you again, but the principal reason was my job.'

He nodded to a waiter who held a roast Aylesbury duckling for his inspection, then he turned back to her: 'You hadn't quite forgotten all about me when you got my first letter?'

'No—I'd thought about you quite a lot.'

'Had you?'

'Of course if I'd been anywhere but Orford I should never have given you a second thought—but in a place like that there is so little to think about at all!' The dark fans of her lashes fell demurely on her cheeks.

'Ann! you're a perfect little beast!'

She glanced up swiftly. 'Have you only just discovered that? Most of my young men find me out at once . . . and they all find me disappointing when they get to know me better!'

'I don't believe a word you say!'

'Oh, I mean it—' she stuck her chin out challengingly. 'I'm selfish—conceited of my looks, and I'm sullen when I don't get what I want—so now you know!'

'Then it's quite time someone took you in hand,' he said firmly, 'and I'm applying for the job.'

Her eyes dropped beneath his steady gaze, but he was forced to look up as a tall, thin man paused by their table on his way out.

'Hullo, Akers?' he said with evident annoyance. But he did not introduce his friend to Ann.

' 'Lo, Kenyon,' said the tall man lazily. 'Government's taken special powers for a three months' moratorium—just had it from the House and thought you'd like to know.'

'Have they? Well, perhaps it's a good thing on the whole. At least we shall know where we are in a day or two now.'

'Optimist!' grinned Akers.

'Pessimist!' countered Kenyon. 'Have they had any news from the States yet?'

Akers's pale blue eyes went suddenly blank. 'My dear boy—how should I know?'

'Well you ought to, you're in the F.O.'

'Not my department,' Akers smiled blandly as he fingered his long moustache.

'Well, have they managed to check the fire-raising in Berlin then?'

'Heaven Knows!—but I shouldn't worry your young head—make hay my dear boy, hay—while the sun shines!' Ann could not see his face and without turning his head he swivelled his eyes in her direction.

'Good night,' said Kenyon pointedly.

'God bless you—we shall all meet on the steps of the guillotine, I don't doubt.' With a dry chuckle Akers sauntered slowly away.

Kenyon looked after him thoughtfully. 'How like a Foreign Office man,' he said. 'Always ready to tell you everybody else's news, but never any of their own!'

'Is he really in the Foreign Office?'

'Yes, he's a first-class civil servant.'

'Like you will be one day?'

'Well, not exactly. He's quite an important person—I only hope to be a minor cog in the Government wheel.'

'I couldn't help overhearing what he said. Do you think his story about the moratorium is right?'

'Certain to be, the information of men like Akers is always reliable. Have some raspberries—sorry there is no cream but it is this wretched rationing of dairy produce and butcher's meat.'

'No thanks—Kenyon?'

'Yes,' he looked up quickly, it was the first time she had called him by his Christian name.

'He was only joking when he talked about the guillotine —or its equivalent, wasn't he?'

'Why, of course—there's nothing to worry about really.'

'But I am worried—*now*. There was something about that man's horrible cynicism that brought things home to me as nothing else has done . . . and you see I live on my own, so if things get really bad . . .' She paused with the sudden realisation that she was doing exactly as Gregory Sallust had suggested—appealing for the protection of a man she hardly knew. 'Oh, I suppose I'm being silly,' she finished awkwardly.

'No, I understand,' Kenyon hesitated, not wishing to go back on his own urgent warning of a few days before but longing to reassure her. He ended by adopting the latter course. 'Just look at all these people, Ann—you can see that there is no immediate cause for alarm anyway.'

She glanced round the crowded restaurant. Not a single table seemed unoccupied, and yet the floor was already packed with dancers. Everybody was drinking champagne. Waiters hurried to and fro clutching two, three, four bottles or magnums in their strong fingers, whisking away the empties and plunging the new supply into the silver buckets which held the crackling ice. Above the soft music of the band came the unceasing murmur of the thousand guests. The shaded lights drew out the rainbow colours of the women's dresses, but hid their faces, kindly for the most part, in a softer light as they smiled and laughed, fingering the pearls that took life from the bare flesh of their bosoms and playing the eternal game of make-believe with their respective men.

The whole scene breathed such an atmosphere of tranquil, prosperous solidity among the ruling caste that Ann was momentarily reassured. It seemed impossible that in one awful cataclysm they might be swept away. The band lilted slowly into an old-fashioned Viennese waltz set to the new rhythm. She smiled across at Kenyon.

His thoughts had been very different. He knew that this seeming prosperity was an empty, tragic sham. Two-thirds of these well-dressed people were already on the verge of ruin, or bankrupts; striving to forget their crushing anxieties for a few hours by reckless expenditure and forced gaiety. If the crash really came they would be swept away like thistledown, the great hotel left empty—deserted—a prey to prowling thieves; those ragged outcasts who now slept fitfully on the hard seats of the Embankment would take possession of the soft beds in the rooms upstairs. What would happen if the rioters proved too much for the troops he wondered; supposing a gang of roughs burst in at this moment—armed Communists—what then? This crowd would stampede like any other. A few gallant fellows who put up a fight would be shot down—the rest scramble wildly for the entrances—and the women!—he could almost hear them scream as they fled down the corridors, and the rip of the silk and the satin as the invaders clutched at their dresses in a brutal endeavour to grab their jewels.

Kenyon sipped his brandy and looked at Ann. She was smiling at him. Mechanically he smiled in return; then with an almost superhuman effort lest she should sense his forebodings, he cried: 'Come on—let's dance!'

The floor was crowded, but somehow they managed to edge their way into the slowly-revolving mass. Kenyon's height was an advantage, Ann's head barely came up to his chin, so to steer her was easy, and her weight was so slight that he could hardly feel it unless he pressed her to him. As he glanced down he caught a glimpse of the little mole on the curve of her left cheek, and the sight of it thrilled him curiously.

'Happy?' he asked almost curtly.

'Oh, need you ask!' came the swift reply, and she seemed to cling more closely to him.

'Ann?' he whispered a few moments later. She heard him even above the throb of the band, and turned her face up to his in quick response:

'Yes, Kenyon—yes?' Her eyes seemed enormous, limpid yet sparkling in the reflected light.

For once Kenyon found himself tongue-tied. 'Just . . . just Ann!' he breathed; 'just *Ann*!'

How long they danced Ann could never afterwards remember. She had a vague recollection of Kenyon ordering an ice for her and a brandy-and-soda for himself. They did not say anything particular, and in that swaying throng waltzes or one-way-walks made little difference—only a slower or a faster time.

Quite suddenly it came to her that the great room was two-thirds empty, and she was saying that she simply *must* go home. He settled his bill while she got her coat and then led her out into the street.

'I shall be all right,' she said as he helped her into a taxi, 'please don't bother to see me home.'

'Nonsense,' he laughed. 'Taxi—272 Gloucester Road,' and in a moment they were seated side by side speeding along the almost deserted Strand.

As he reached out and took her hand she made no pretence of trying to avoid the gesture, but let it rest for the remainder of the journey, warm between his own. Almost impossibly soon, it seemed to her, the cab stopped—she was getting out, and Kenyon was paying off the man. 'But don't you want to take him on?' she heard herself saying.

'No, pick up another later.' He stood tall, purposeful—looming above her in the semi-darkness as she inserted her key in the lock.

'You can't come in, you know!' she said.

'Can't I?' he squeezed her arm. 'Don't be silly, Ann—I want to carry away memories of the place where you live so that I can call up pictures of you in my mind. I know there's a sitting-room—you told me so. You trust me, don't you?'

Somehow his quiet, almost mocking assurance made a refusal seem stupid and childish. She turned the key and felt him behind her in the close darkness of the tiny hall.

'This way,' she whispered, stretching back one hand to guide him as they reached the landing and, with the other, softly opening the sitting-room door.

In the faint light that penetrated through the half-drawn curtains the arm-chairs and settee were just visible as outlines of a deeper blackness. She put out her hand to press the electric switch, then hesitated, remembering suddenly the worn shoddiness of the room—but Kenyon's fingers closed over hers and bore them swiftly downwards as he drew her to him.

Her arms stretched up and closed round his neck, drawing his face down to to hers. Something outside her consciousness seemed to impel her movements. She closed her eyes, her heart hammering in her breast as her soft mouth melted into his; standing on tip-toe, straining to him, she returned his breathless kisses with almost savage passion.

As in a dream she found herself lifted—held in the air—and then laid gently on the long settee. He was kneeling beside her, fondling her hands, and repeating over and over again, 'Ann—Ann—Ann.' Then his arms were tight about her once more.

How long they remained fast in each other's arms, while the silent night wended its way towards the dawn, Ann did not know or care. Her mouth was sore with the strain of repeated kissing yet his fevered lips seemed insatiable of her caresses.

With a sudden devastating unexpectedness the light was on—Gregory Sallust stood, framed in the doorway, returned from his night's work. His paper was even now thundering from the presses, going North, South, East and West, to carry the news of the moratorium to the breakfast tables of the millions.

'Hullo!' he said. 'So sorry—had no idea you were still up—only came in for my nightcap—won't be a second.' Then he walked over to the cupboard where he kept his whisky.

Ann noticed through a sort of haze that Kenyon was standing up with his back to the mantelpiece. His hair was rather ruffled, but he looked remarkably self-possessed.

'It is I who should apologise,' he said. 'I've been rottenly ill—ate something at supper that didn't agree with me I think. Anyhow, Miss Croome insisted that I should come in and lie down in the dark for a bit, and I'm feeling ever so much better now.'

'Oh?' Gregory nodded. To Ann's relief he showed no shadow of disbelief in this preposterous story; 'how rotten for you—may I suggest that a whisky-and-soda wouldn't do you any harm—buck you up a bit before you go home!'

'Thanks, that's nice of you.' Kenyon drew his tongue quickly across his burning lips, 'I could do with a drink!'

'Good, here we are—say when.' Gregory squirted a siphon into an extra glass he had already filled a quarter full with whisky, and Kenyon picked it up. Ann stood there marvelling at their quiet, easy behaviour, as they talked casually of the moratorium for a moment. By some mysterious freemasonary they already seemed to be on the best of terms, although she had forgotten even to introduce them.

'Well, I must get along,' Kenyon set down his glass.

'You'll find a taxi at the end of the road,' said Gregory affably.

'Thanks—thanks too for the drink. I'll give you a ring, Ann, if I may—sorry to have been such a nuisance to you.'

Kenyon was standing by the door, but Ann felt that he might have been a thousand miles away. By the time she had reached the landing he was half-way down the stairs.

'Don't bother to come down,' he called. 'I can easily let myself out.'

The front door banged while she was still upon the second step. 'He might have waited,' she thought, 'but of course the darling was trying to make it seem ordinary and natural. Anyhow Gregory couldn't have seen much!' She yawned, suddenly realising how tired she was and went back into the sitting-room to fetch her coat.

Gregory stood there grinning like a fiend. 'Ann,' he said, 'Ann—how could you be such a little idiot?'

'What do you mean?' she cried, her eyelids lowering angrily.

'I never meant you to go and overstep the mark like that!'

Misunderstanding his meaning completely she flushed scarlet. 'Thank you, Gregory, what I choose to do is entirely my own affair.'

'Of course,' he was serious now, 'but why in God's name pick on a man like that?'

'He's worth a thousand like you!' she snapped.

'Perhaps, but he won't be any earthly good to you if we all have to get out in a hurry—and that's what it is coming to, you believe me!'

'Why?' Ann demanded truculently.

'Because he'll be too busy with his own crowd.'

'What exactly do you mean?' she said slowly.

'Well, you're a typist-secretary aren't you?'

'What about it? He knows that.'

Gregory set down his glass with slow deliberation; his mouth hung slightly open. 'Does he? Well, do you seriously think he'll give a damn what happens to you when the crash comes? You've just been an excellent amusement for the evening that's all. A little quiet fun which will be forgotten in the morning. Surely you realise that, unless . . Good God! perhaps you don't know who he is?'

'I do—his name is Kenyon Wensleadale. I was telling you about him only this evening, and that he was getting some sort of Government job.' Ann shivered slightly, feeling for the first time the chill of the night air.

'Government job, eh?—that's pretty rich.' He shook his head whimsically. 'You poor little fool, hadn't you the sense to realise that Wensleadale is the family name of the Dukes of Burminster? The young man is the candidate for mid-Suffolk, Ann—and he is known officially as my Lord the Marquis of Fane!'

4

Love, Cocktails, and the Shadow of Fear

'Darling! How divine of you to come!' Lady Veronica Wensleadale was stretched at full length on the comfortable sofa in her private sitting-room. It was on the third floor of the Burminster house in Grosvenor Square, a friendly, well-lit and exquisitely furnished room.

'My dear! I've been simply dying to see you.' Fiona Hetherington stretched out both her hands. She was Veronica's closest friend and from their greetings one might have imagined that they had met after a separation of months. Actually they had seen each other less than ten days before, exchanged letters, and held two long conversations on the telephone in the meantime.

'Sit down, my sweet, and tell me *everything*.' Veronica pulled the other girl down beside her. She was darker than her brother Kenyon, but a suggestion of red lit the almost black hair on her small and shapely head. As she lay back her slim body was half-buried in the cushions and her pale oval face only just appeared above her knees. A thin spiral of smoke rose from a cigarette in her slender jade holder.

'I suppose you've heard all these ghastly rumours which are floating round,' Fiona said.

'Yes, too nauseating, my dear—why don't they have their absurd revolution and get it over!—but tell me about the Tweekenhams' dance?'

'It was an awful flop, half the people failed to turn up!'

'But, darling, they were completely loppy to give a party in August, anyhow.'

'I don't know,' Fiona remonstrated, 'as Parliament is still sitting everybody has stayed on in London this year, but even Peter tried to back out at the last moment—said it was such damned bad taste with the King ill and everything—but we had to go in the end, I couldn't let Angela down.'

'Poor Angela! she is a complete nit-wit, but such a sweet. It was hellish to have to refuse her, but I couldn't get away from Holkenham until yesterday.'

Fiona pulled off her hat and shook back her fair hair. 'Was it amusing?'

'Grim, my dear—grim.' Veronica cast her eyes up to the ceiling. 'The house was Strawberry Hill Gothic, not enough bathrooms, and a vast brown-tiled hall—real Neo-Lavatorial!'

'How depressing. What were the Bronsons like?'

'Quite too terrible. Of course it's a bit of luck for Kenyon that he was at Magdalen with the son. Old Sir George is practically fighting the election for him, but the old woman was appalling. It is one of those ghastly places they keep up the prehistoric customs of the men sitting over their port, and as Juliana Augusta went up to bed early the first night the Bronson cornered me in the drawing-room. She third-degreed me about Juliana Augusta's little whims and she must have said "the dear Duchess" forty times in the hour. I think she thought that to say "Your Mother" would have been *lèse majesté*.'

Fiona smiled. 'And what about the young man?'

'Oh, he was quite a nice little cad—played a decent game of golf and made sheep's eyes at me of course, but the poor lamb was dragged off to do this filthy electioneering most of the time—Hell's bells—that's done it.' Veronica grabbed frantically at the end of her cigarette which had fallen from the holder into her lap. When she had succeeded in rescuing the glowing stub she surveyed her light summer frock angrily. Two large yellow burns showed right in the middle of it.

'Ruined, my dear—ruined!' she exclaimed wildly in her rather high-pitched voice. 'How absolutely *too* maddening—and the rag's not even paid for!'

'Poor darling,' Fiona consoled her, 'but you can have it

dyed, I've got quite used to that sort of thing since I married Peter.'

'I know, sweet—you've been an absolute angel, but I just can't wear dyed clothes.'

'I do wish you'd be sensible. How you can keep on running up these awful bills, I can't think.'

'Madness, isn't it. *Maria* threatened to writ me last week!'

'Did she? My dear, if I were in your shoes I shouldn't be able to sleep a wink.'

'I don't, darling, at times I squirrel terrifically, but let's face it—if you're not a beauty, clothes do count.'

'What nonsense—you're lovely!'

Veronica tapped her high, arched nose. 'Good old mountain goat, lovie.'

'How absurd—who wants stupid doll-like prettiness anyhow. You've got the most shapely head I've ever seen, a figure like a sylph and the loveliest pair of legs in London. Besides you're the most amusing person in the word to talk to and the men adore that!'

'Oh, I can get away with murder among the males.'

'Well, what are you grumbling about then?'

'Clothes, dearie, clothes, an' 'ow ter pay me bills!'

'Must you have so many?'

'Yus! All part of the gime, lovie.'

Fiona nodded. 'I don't blame you really because you've got such marvellous taste. I expect I should be the same if I looked so devastatingly *chic*. But can't you get papa to increase your allowance?'

'Not a hope, darling; Herbert is broke to the wide. I cornered the old boy at Holkenham after he'd been at Bronson's '96 port, but it wasn't any earthly use.'

'But he must have a pretty big income still.'

'He swears he hasn't a bob. It would be different if we could persuade him to close down Banners. That place positively eats money, but he won't. He says it is unfitting that he should add to the number of the unemployed.'

'It's a pity that some of these beastly Communists can't hear him!'

'Oh, it's not only that, my dear, he gets all Ducal too! "As long as there has been a Burminster, Banners has been the centre of life for three counties. The Monarch would be most displeased, I'm sure." Then I hoot with laughter. You know what a little round fat man Herbert is, and he's just too comic for words when he starts to take himself seriously. No, darling—I'm afraid it's got to be the Purple Monkey in the end!"

'You *can't,* Veronica.'

'Darling, why not? He's got a delicious wit, really artistic taste, and we could have a bedspread sewn with diamonds. What more does any girl want?'

'Someone to be really fond of—don't you think?'

'What rippling rot, Fiona. Everybody gets divorced after two years these days.'

'Ugh!' Fiona gave a little shudder. 'Just to think of that blue chin pressed against my neck makes me sick—and he's old enough to be your father—you simply couldn't!'

Veronica leaned back and gave a shout of laughter. 'You pet!—how gloriously serious you are!'

'I detest lecherous old men.'

'I don't—they amuse me. Besides he's no age really—forty-five perhaps, but he looks more because he's dark and a foreigner. Anyhow I should *trompée* him and have dozens of handsome young lovers!'

'How's Alistair, as mad about you as ever?'

'Yes, poor lamb—and I thank you, my love, Major Hay-Symple is in excellent health. He was with us at Holkenham.'

'To help Kenyon with the campaign or to flirt with your ladyship?'

'Both!—but my ladyship was rather unkind I fear. Holkenham is no place for parlour games. If we'd been rumbled by the Bronsons they'd have spread the most ghastly scandal about me in ten ticks. I simply didn't dare risk it, so Alistair had to console himself by punishing the port. He was a great success with the children though.'

Fiona looked puzzled. 'I didn't know there were any.'

'Oh, in the house?—thank God, no! that would have been the last straw. I mean the young Britons. We made him tell them "What I did in the Great War, Daddie!" He simply hated it, of course, and he was only some sort of junior dogs-body at the time, but he got crossed fig-leaves or something for some act of idiocy he performed when he was tight as an owl—they lapped it up! He had to leave us on Saturday though, he was recalled by telegram.'

'Yes, all leave has been cancelled. Peter says the Government have got the wind up to the eyebrows—but about Alistair. Why don't you marry him, Veronica?'

'My sweet, you know perfectly well that he hasn't got a cent.'

'But he'll come into the place when his father dies.'

'Yes, when he's ninety—and I've grown a lovely long dewlap, thank you, darling—No!'

'Oh, Veronica, don't be absurd.'

'I mean it, lovie—these 'ere surgeons is that 'andy wiv their h'instruments nowadays they keeps all the old crocks in the 'untin' field until they're h'octogenarians!'

'You'd be very happy with Alistair.'

Veronica stretched her slim arms above her head and smiled indulgently. 'You think of everybody in terms of Peter and yourself—and, little sentimental fool that you are—I adore you. But I always have been attracted by queer men—and I shall always be liable to go off the rails with any new man who comes along if he's got brains and guts.'

'Well, you can't say that Alistair lacks guts, and he's got brains as well—he's been through Staff College.'

'Yes, with a kick in the pants!—as for guts, darling, he keeps them filed away in the War Office to be taken out when wanted, so they're not the kind I care about. Tell me, is Peter coming in to booze with us this evening?'

'Yes, about six I expect, it's nearly that now.'

'Marvellous—I tried to get several chaps but they are all in their little uniforms playing at Special Constables, or busy joining Llewellyn's comic opera Greyshirts. Still, Alistair is coming in for half an hour, and Kenyon will be in any moment so they'll be able to tell us all about Auld England on its last legs. I suppose you haven't seen an evening paper, have you?'

Fiona shook her head. 'No, but I believe that there's been awful trouble in the north. Dorothy—you know, the girl who does my hair at Ernaldé's, told me that Glasgow is completely cut off, and a railway bridge blown up so that no trains come through.'

'My dear! these filthy Communists.'

'Terrible, isn't it, but I suppose we shall pull through somehow—we always seem to!'

'Of course, darling. Everything would have been straightened out years ago if it hadn't been for those pompous old lunatics in the Cabinet. Half of them are absolutely gaga.'

'I suppose they do their best, but really Gladnor ought to have retired æons ago. How he has had the face to hang on to a post in each successive Government is a mystery to me.'

'My pet, don't you know?—he can't help himself, it's Mrs. Gladnor. She locks him up in the schoolroom and puts him on bread and water every time he threatens to retire!'

'Do you mean the old trout who wears a kipper instead of a hat?'

'Yes, lovie, she thinks he's a reincarnation of John Bull!'

'Well, if somebody doesn't do something soon we shall be in a fine mess. Lots of people are so scared they are leaving for the country.'

Veronica blew out a thin spiral of smoke and nodded. Herbert said something last night about packing Juliana, Augusta and me off to Banners.'

'That sounds rather grim.'

'Quite shattering, my dear, just think of mother and me cooped up at Banners without a soul to separate us when we fight. The thought appals me.'

Fiona turned as the door opened behind her. 'Hullo, Kenyon, my dear. How are you?'

'Splendid, thanks. Electioneering can be almost as good exercise as polo. How's Peter?'

'He's very fit, but so swollen-headed I hardly know what to do with him. Last Sunday he got round the Red course at the Royal Berks in 82. He'll be here in a moment and then you'll have to hear all about it.'

'Good for him—but all the same, I flatly refuse to listen to any more golfing stories except from registered voters in my own division.' Kenyon glanced at his sister, 'Well, long-legs—what about a drink?'

'Brute!' she flung at him, 'how many times have I told you that I absolutely forbid the use of derogatory terms in connection with my delicious limbs. The drinks are in the cupboard, *and*, my boy—may I remind you that it is your turn to pay?'

'But hang it, we were away all last week,' he protested as he opened the cupboard. 'Still there's lots here—some fresh bottles, too!'

'Yes, my love—I ordered them this morning.'

'Oh, well that was decent of you—I take it all back.

Vernonica suddenly guffawed with laughter, 'And I put

them down to your account at Justerini's! Tra-la-la! . . . tra-la-la!'

'The devil you did! I owe them quite enough already.'

'Never mind, Herbert pays his bills regularly so they won't worry you.'

'I dare say not, but I hate running up big bills. Electioneering is the most expensive pastime I know after yachting.'

'You forgit the lidies, dearie!' mocked Veronica. 'All the same I think Herbert is a mean old pig to make us pay for our own tipple.'

'Does he?' exclaimed Fiona. 'I thought he was supposed to have one of the best cellars in England?'

Veronica nodded. 'Yes, sweet, and sherry, if you like it, is "on the 'ouse" as they say. But Herbert doesn't approve of cocktails so that great lumping *rasta* over there and I pay for our three pen'oth of gin in turns.'

The door opened again and a footman in plain livery announced 'Major Hay-Symple.'

'Hullo, Veronica—Fiona, how are you? How's Peter, eh? —Hullo, Kenyon, old boy!' The rather thickset soldier with lively blue eyes threw a quick succession of smiles at them all. For a moment they stared at him in mild surprise. His immaculate khaki tunic with its little row of ribbons, wide breeches and shining field boots seemed strangely alien upon this intimate friend. That he should arrive at a cocktail party in uniform brought home to them more than any newspaper placard the gravity of the situation.

Then Veronica jumped up, and flinging her arms wide, kissed him with a loud smack on the forehead. 'Alistair, my hero! come and sit here by me. What news out of Flanders, laddie? Stand the King's colours where they stood—spare not the gruesome details for we women of England. What news of the War?'

'Eh—what's that? What war?' Hay-Symple looked vaguely astonished at her onset.

'The rioting or whatever you call it, stupid—in all these horrid places that no one ever goes to!'

'Oh, well—there's been a spot of bother in the North.'

'God! what a man!' Veronica sank back on the sofa, her hands clasped dramatically to her head. 'Details, my good fool—details are what we want.'

He grinned good-humouredly and took the cocktail that Kenyon held out. 'Well, there's trouble in Glasgow; the wires are down and some of these blackguards have sabotaged a bridge, but it's nothing to worry about. Three battalions of the Highland Division have been concentrated there, and they're great fellows—know a lot of 'em myself. They'll soon put things right.'

Veronica shook him gently by the shoulder. 'You divine person, we heard all that hours ago from Fiona's hairdresser. Do you really mean to tell us that you don't know anything more?'

'Not much,' he smiled at her affectionately. 'We're just standing by. Have to give a telephone number if we leave barracks for more than half an hour—that's all.'

Kenyon filled up Fiona's glass from his shaker, then he looked across at Veronica. 'Why waste your breath, sweet Sis?' he inquired with gentle sarcasm. 'Don't you realise that Alistair rides one of the King's horses and is one of the King's men. If he did know anything he wouldn't tell *you* in a thousand years. It's his job to keep his mouth shut.'

'That's true.' Hay-Symple ran the back of his hand under his upturned moustache, 'but honestly I know little more than you can read in the papers. Only odds and ends about what to do in the event of an outbreak of plague and that sort of thing.'

'Gadzooks! these men—what children they are,' Veronica exclaimed to Fiona. 'Let's all play robbers—but don't tell the girls, they'd spoil everything!'

'The children must have their fun, darling!' Fiona smiled, 'they are all going to be so important now. Alistair will run up and down in a nice brass hat before he's much older. Kenyon will be given a purple ribbon for his buttonhole, so that everyone will get off the pavement knowing him to be an M.P.—and Peter—well poor Peter will have to put up with a little red, white and blue shirt just to show he's on the right side in the General Strike.'

'It's all very well for you young women to scoff, but you may be almighty glad we've got an Army before this business is through.' Hay-Symple held out his glass, 'Here, Kenyon, old man, give me another, will you?'

'Why do you compare this with a General Strike?' asked Kenyon curiously.

'Well, isn't it?' Fiona parried. 'They've been having the most ghastly trouble up at Peter's works in Sheffield since they stopped supplying the Balkans with munitions, and he's always said that when steel went down the drain, everything would go too.'

'I agree that all these strikes and stoppages have helped to bring it about, and the Communists have played an enormous part in aggravating the situation; they are so much stronger now, but that's where the resemblance ends. The Trades Unions and the working men are no more responsible for the present state of things than we are. It is the effect of colossal bad debts made through other countries cracking up—taxation of industry out of all proportion to the profits made, and the complete stranglehold which the banks have acquired on every form of property and business. As long as they maintain their policy of refusing further advances without adequate cover more and more people are bound to go under, and every crash gets us nearer to six million unemployed—which in turn means more taxation for the poor devils who are still striving to carry on. That is the vicious circle we are up against.'

Fiona nodded. 'Yes, the rations for the unemployed have got to be paid for somehow of course, but I don't see why the banks should lend money without security all the same.'

'They are getting it in the neck today,' observed Hay-Symple, 'half London was queuing up this morning to get their money out.'

'Effects of last night's moratorium.' Kenyon patted his breast pocket. 'I was on the doorstep round the corner when they opened today and drew out a couple of hundred. The bank was chock-a-block with people then.'

'But why the panic, lovie?' inquired Veronica.

'Well, I knew there would be a rush, and it's just possible that they may not be able to stand it.'

Hay-Symple swallowed the remainder of his second cocktail, 'I don't see why—we're not on gold.'

'Gold has nothing to do with it. The loans made by the banks are always bigger than their deposits—which is a queer situation anyway, but if they can't collect their loans they are stuck—whatever they are paying out in. They need time to realise their stock just like any other business.'

'I should think it will put the lid on it if they do close down.'

Kenyon's reply was cut short by the reappearance of the footman, 'Mr. Hetherington, milady.'

'Hullo, Peter—Hullo!—Hullo! . . .'

'Hullo, darling . . . Hullo, Kenyon . . .' the greetings flew round.

Hetherington smiled affectionately as he took Veronica's hand, 'Look here, my dear—I've only come in to collect Fiona—you must forgive me if I don't stay.'

'Why the hurry, Peter my love, someone chasing you with a writ?'

'Perish the thought! No, but I want to take her back to pack.' He turned and stooped over his wife's chair; 'I've just left your old man at the club, my sweetheart, and we both agree that it will be best if I motor you up to Scotland tonight.'

'My sainted aunt!' shrieked Veronica. 'Am I tight or have we all gone mad?'

Hetherington turned to her with a grave face. 'Honestly, my dear, we're in for trouble, and I mean to have Fiona out of it. Up in the Highlands among her own people on the West Coast she'll be safe—whatever happens in the towns.'

'You stupid darling!' Fiona smiled at her large husband. but the protest was a caress and the sharp eyes of Lady Veronica Wensleadale, which never missed a trick, caught anxiety and adoration in the quick glance of the man as he bent over his wife.

Kenyon broke the momentary tension. 'Well, there's always time for a drink—do you really know anything, Peter?'

'Yes. I had it over the private wire half an hour ago that the Reds have dynamited the Bradfield and Redmires dams. So Sheffield will be half under water by now.'

Veronica stared at him blankly. 'But, darling, Sheffield's nowhere near the sea!'

'Of course not—I'm talking about the reservoirs. When Dale Dyke burst in 1864, nearly three hundred people were drowned and half a million pounds' worth of property destroyed. This will be even worse with two dams gone—and they've probably blown up the Ewden dam as well by now.'

'Oh, just think of those poor people,' Fiona sighed. 'What is going to happen to us all?'

'God knows,' said Hetherington grimly. 'Anyhow I mean to have you out of it. The result of the Admiralty decision looks like the last straw to me.'

'Need we talk about that?' Hay-Symple stiffened slightly. His voice was sharp, and his eyes had suddenly gone cold.

'It's—er—common knowledge, isn't it?' Hetherington hesitated.

'What is it—do tell us!' came the excited chorus.

The soldier shrugged. 'All right—if it's got out already, may as well tell 'em. It's a pity though that these things can't be kept quiet. They only make people panic.'

'Come on, big boy—spill the beans!' Veronica broke into the Americanese she sometimes affected as an alternative to her proficient Cockney.

'Well, you know all leave was cancelled last Saturday by the mobilisation telegram. It seems that quite a big proportion of the men failed to rejoin their ships. Fearing further trouble the Admiralty ordered the fleet out of its Home ports to rendezvous twenty miles south of St. Catherine's Point—off the Isle of Wight. When they got there it was found that several of the capital ships were so seriously undermanned that, instead of sending them up to Scapa or some place where the malcontents could be dealt with, they ordered them home again; and now the sailors are deserting by the score.'

'By Jove!' Kenyon whistled. 'Then things are a jolly sight worse than we thought.'

'Well, anyway the Army is all right,' said Hay-Symple grimly. 'But I must be getting back to barracks.'

As he stood up the footman reappeared. This time with a letter on a silver salver. He presented it to Kenyon and spoke in a low voice. 'A messenger boy has just delivered a large bunch of flowers, milord, and this note was with them. He said there was no reply.'

'Thanks, William—excuse me, chaps.' Kenyon's face turned a deep shade of crimson as, angry and embarrassed, he turned away to open the letter. It was from Ann and read:

Dear Lord Fane,

It was not until this morning that I learned by accident of your identity. You chose to conceal it, no doubt on account of the fact that we move in such different circles —and since that is the case, no possible good could come to either of us by continuing our acquaintance. I must apologise for the rather stupid remarks which I made about you in the train on the way to Ipswich, as I realise now that they were quite unjustified, but I am returning the flowers you sent me since I prefer to forget the whole episode as soon as possible.

Yours sincerely,
ANN CROOME.

The others had been discussing the effects of the moratorium and Hetherington was confirming the rumours of an approaching bank crisis when Kenyon turned back to them.

'Who's been bunching you, Kenyon?' Hay-Symple inquired with a grin, from the door.

'Oh—er—some flowers that I sent have come back—went to the wrong address, I think,' he finished lamely.

Veronica suddenly hooted with laughter. 'Wrong address my foot! Just look at him, darlings—do! The poor fish has been turned down by some wench. His face is as red as his hair!'

'Oh, shut up!' snapped Kenyon savagely. 'It's nothing of the sort.'

A general titter of amusement ran round the room, but after a moment it sank to a hushed silence. They had caught the voice of a newsboy calling in the square below. Faintly at first—then louder, the harsh cry was wafted up to the strained ears of the listeners.

'Speshul edition! Speshul! . . . Speshul! . . . Decision by the Big Five . . . Banks Close Down!'

5

The Structure Cracks

The morning after she had returned Kenyon's flowers Ann put off getting up till the very last moment and lay thinking about him.

Perhaps she had been a fool to dash off that note. So many of her thoughts had centred round him since their first meeting, and now she had ended the affair by her own impulsive act. But he had deceived her about himself, and it rankled badly that he had allowed her to say those stupid things about him in the train. Still, she had apologised for that and Gregory was right of course; Kenyon would only regard her as a fit companion for a few evenings' amusement. No, she had taken a line, the right line, and she must stick to it even if he tried to open the affair again. She turned over on her tummy and nestled her dark head into the crook of her arm; then a sudden annoying thought struck her. She had forgotten again yesterday to give her ration card to Rudd. That meant no glass of milk for breakfast, and no butter for her bread. The wretched thing had been quite useless to her so far except for her light lunch in the City, although she had taken it out immediately on her return from Orford. If only she could get back to the sleepy peace of that little Suffolk village, but it was impossible unless she sacrificed her job. She had spoken of it the day before to her immediate superior, the fussy, pot-bellied Mr. Crumper, and she could hear his sharp rejoinder now.

'Nonsense, Miss Croome—nonsense. Business as usual will be our motto. The rioting will not affect us in the City you may be sure and we shall weather this crisis just as we did the one last winter.'

It would have been useless to argue with the man and most of the other members of the firm seemed to share his view. Who would prove correct she wondered, Mr. Crumper and the office staff or Gregory Sallust and Kenyon—Damn Kenyon!—anyhow if the trouble blew over after all she would never get another job with things in their present state, so she must cling on to this one.

'A life on the Ocean Wave,' chanted a husky voice which she recognised as Rudd's, and a moment later he knocked loudly on her door. 'Yer wanted on the 'phone, Miss.'

Ann rolled over. 'Who is it?' she called.

'Gentleman—name of Fane.'

'Tell him I do not wish to speak to him.'

' 'E said as 'ow I was to say it was urgent.'

'I don't care—do as I tell you, and say I shall be grateful if he will not bother me by ringing up again!'

'Orlright, Miss.' Rudd's heavy boots clumped away, and Ann turned over again with a set expression on her face. She hated weakness in other people and scorned it in herself. It was bad enough that she was half in love with the man already. To go on with the affair would only be to pile up endless misery for the future. Far better cut it out altogether.

Rudd obediently delivered her message, and Kenyon, wrapped in a thin silk dressing-gown, hung up the receiver with an angry grunt.

The night before they had told him that she was out, and now she refused even to speak to him. In his bath he thought the matter over and admitted that he had not quite played the game. To talk of himself as seeking a Government position at £400 a year might be accurate, but it was certainly misleading, and to describe his father as a farmer with few investments was hardly in accordance with Debrett. His quick decision to conceal his title had been governed by his comparatively small experience with girls of the upper middle class. He had discovered in his Oxford days that they were apt to affect strange mannerisms which they believed to be socially correct as soonas they knew that he was heir to a Dukedom; whereas if they remained in ignorance they continued to be natural and amusing.

He wondered how she had found him out, and put it down to her seeing one of his photographs in the illustrated papers. Hardly a week passed without his appearing in one of them—grimly smirking in a flashlight snap at some party, or with one enormous foot stretched out as he made for the paddock at a race-meeting.

His mind leapt back to the darkened sitting-room, visualising again fragmentary episodes of that unforgettable hour. His pulses quickened at the thought—he had got to see her again somehow—there wasn't a doubt about that. The best way would be to slip down to Gloucester Road and catch her before she left for the office. He scrambled out of his bath.

Breakfast, he decided, could wait, and having hurried through his dressing he telephoned for his car to be brought round.

In Gloucester Road, Rudd answered his ring, and with a quick grasp of his business clumped upstairs to the communal sitting-room, leaving him below.

Two minutes later he came down again, shaking his yellow head: 'I'm sorry, sir, but Miss Croome sez she don't want ter see yer—an' yer ter go away at once.'

Kenyon produced a pound note from his pocket book and displayed it to Mr. Rudd. 'Look here,' he said, 'I want to see Miss Croome very badly indeed, and I'm sure you've got a lot of work to do, so slip along and get on with it while I run upstairs . . . there's a good chap.'

'No, sir. This bein' my 'ouse as it were, I can't do that—but I tell yer wot—if I perswides the young lady ter see yer I earns it, eh?—but if I don't you keeps the quid?'

'Splendid—that's fair enough.'

Rudd ascended once more with new vigour in his step, and this time Kenyon had a longer wait, but his ambassador returned—alone!

'No go, Guv'nor,' he said sadly. 'She sez she don't care if you do look 'orribly un'appy like I told 'er—an' I'm ter mind me own blinkin' business. But there's no accountin' fer wimen and their ways.'

'Never mind, keep this for your trouble.' Kenyon thrust the pound note into Rudd's hand. He liked the fellow's quick intelligent sympathy and felt that he might prove a useful ally later on.

'Now that,' muttered Rudd to himself, as Kenyon walked swiftly back to his car, 'is wot I calls a gentleman.'

It was not until Kenyon was sitting down to breakfast that he realised what a fool he had been to hurry back. If he had waited in Gloucester Road he would have caught Ann for certain on her way to work and might have made his peace. However, it was too late to think of that now.

The paper was full of the previous evening's decision by the banks. The suspension of payments was only a temporary matter, necessitated by the withdrawals of the day before which were estimated at the colossal figure of forty million. *Assignats* were now being printed and would be issued on demand to depositors when the banks reopened, which it was hoped would be on Monday. In the meantime patience, mutual help and 'our British sense of humour' were suggested to carry the population over the intervening days.

His Majesty's illness was referred to at some length. He had suffered a relapse on the previous day and his condition was causing the gravest anxiety. The physicians at Windsor insisted on all news being kept from him and would not allow even the Prime Minister to see him on the most urgent business.

The Prince had gone down to the Dockers' mass meeting the night before without any previous intimation of his intention. Some hostility had been shown, but this had been speedily drowned by a tremendous ovation from the majority, and his appeal for the maintenance of law and order had met with an excellent response. He had asked all those who could do so to enrol themselves as special constables or join the Greyshirt organisations in support of the existing Government, and had secured a thousand volunteers before he left. His courageous action had resulted in allaying unrest in the Dockland area.

The news from Glasgow was confined to a short paragraph. Disorders had occurred in certain sections of the city, but a number of Communist leaders had been arrested by the military and it was hoped that order would soon be restored. The train service would not be renewed, however, until after the week-end.

'Not too good,' thought Kenyon, and the brief mention of the Navy was even less reassuring. A number of clashes had occurred between the police and the Communists at Portsmouth, and parties of sailors were stated to have been among the latter.

After breakfast Kenyon considered his supply of cigarettes. He had a few hundred left but if things became worse it might be difficult to get more since he smoked a particularly fine brand of Turkish made for him, at a very reasonable price, by an importer in Manchester. If he wired at once asking them to send him triple his usual order by passenger train they should arrive, with luck, next day. Kenyon was one of those people who never minded taking a little trouble to ensure his future comfort.

He walked round to the post office, dispatched his telegram, and then strolled on to his club. It was unusually crowded and the members were gathered six deep round the tape-machine. 'What's the latest, Archie?' he asked an acquaintance on the edge of the group.

'Devilish difficult to say, old man,' Archie made a pessimistic grimace, 'the news is so heavily censored that very little really important stuff is allowed to come through.'

'Heard anything about this Glasgow business?'

'Have I not?' the other grinned. 'That old tiger who is commanding in the north bagged twenty Communist leaders last night, erected a nice old-fashioned gallows on Glasgow Green, and hung the lot. He's keeping the bodies dangling too as a warning to the rest!'

'The devil he did! What will the Cabinet have to say to that?'

'Lord knows! They'll recall him, I expect, just like they did poor old Dyer in India after the Amritsar trouble years ago.'

Kenyon nodded gloomily. 'It'll be a rotten show if they do. It seems to me that our only hope now is a few stout fellows with real guts like that. By hanging twenty he's probably saved at least a hundred from being killed in street fighting.'

'You haven't heard anything from South Wales, have you?'

'No—why?'

Archie lowered his voice. 'Well, that's one of the worst danger spots, and I had it from a man I know that there was an organised rising there last night. He says that some sort of Soviet have seized control in Cardiff.'

'Do you think his information is reliable?'

'Ah, that's where you've got me. I wondered if you'd heard anything, that's all.'

'Nothing except that business about the income tax collector, and that the miners are sabotaging the pits, but they've been doing that on and off for months past.'

They wandered into the smoking-room and ordered a couple of dry sherries. Then Archie began to give his general views on the situation. They were not cheerful views and after a little Kenyon asked him what he meant to do.

'Well, I've got a little place in Gloucester—only a glorified cottage, you know, but my cousin is Chief Constable of the county, so I thought I'd go down there for a bit, and take on any job of work he cares to give me; London will be no fit place to live in for the next few weeks.'

Kenyon nodded. It looked as if they would all have to get out soon if they meant to save themselves. His thoughts flew to Ann. How would she fare in London if the food supply broke down and there was really desperate fighting? He simply must get hold of her somehow, if only to persuade her to chuck her job and go back to Orford while there was still time.

Preoccupied with these thoughts, he said good-bye to Archie rather hurriedly, but on his way through the hall old Lord St. Evremond stopped him.

'Have you heard?' he asked.

'No, sir—what?

The old man nodded portentously and sank his voice. 'The King is dead—died at five o'clock this morning.'

'Good heavens, sir! that is bad news—especially at a time like this.'

'Yes, he was a great man too. Far greater than the bulk of the nation realised. He devoted his whole life to the service of his country and did a tremendous lot of good. It is an incalculable loss.'

'It is,' Kenyon agreed, 'and its effect on the public is bound to make things worse.'

'Oh, they won't let it out until this business has blown over. That would never do—my information is strictly private, of course.'

'I see—but they can't hold the funeral over indefinitely—and how do we know that this business is going to—er, blow over?'

Lord St. Evremond gave an indignant grunt. 'Why, of course it will, my boy. We're British, ain't we? I hope you don't suggest that we should let a lot of out-at-elbows Communist fellahs run the country—eh? We'll jug 'em. Yes, sir! jug 'em, and if necessary shoot the lot!'

'Well, I hope you're right,' said Kenyon mildly, and the old peer shambled away to spread his strictly private news elsewhere.

As Kenyon made his way up St. James's Street his thoughts were mixed. The King's death—Communists—and Ann. She was a Communist herself theoretically, but that was only stupid nonsense gleaned from the adolescent debating societies at Cambridge. One of half a dozen ways of blowing off excess of youthful steam. Probably, though, it partially explained her turning against him. How the deuce could he get hold of her again?

A familiar figure caught his eye as he crossed Piccadilly to Albemarle Street. Veronica sailing gaily along with a swing that displayed her supple figure and enchanting ankles to the admiration of the passers-by.

'Hi!' he called. 'Hi!' as he hastened after her. A sudden inspiration had flashed into his mind.

'Hells bells! it's you!' She turned as he caught her up 'I thought it was a street accident at the very least.'

'Where are you off to?' he asked.

'Home, lovie—to fill my foul carcass with whatever cooked meats the *chef* offers us for lunch.'

'Well,' he paused opposite the entrance of the Berkeley, 'what about a cocktail first?'

'Angels defend me!' she exclaimed in a loud voice, apparently to the street at large. 'The Millennium is come—my brother offers me a drink!'

'Do try not to be such an ass—I want to talk to you.'

'Ha, ha! I thought there was a catch in it somewhere. But a drink's a drink, and talking costs nothing, so lead me to it, my most noble lord.'

In the lounge the *maître d'hôtel* himself, imperturbable as ever in this crash of empires, hurried up to them.

'We are not lunching today,' Kenyon told him, 'but you might send the cocktail man and some writing-paper—will you?'

'I take your order myself.' His teeth flashed in a quick smile. 'The cocktail man—he is gone!'

'Gone where?' demanded Veronica with surprise.

The man gave an expressive shrug. 'I do not know, m'lady—many of my waiters become frightened and they run away to Italy—but I tell them they are fools. If they are not safe in England they are not safe anywhere. What cocktail would you prefer?'

Kenyon gave his order and turned quickly to Veronica. 'Look here—I want your help.'

'Now, Kenyon darling, let's be quite clear. If it's money, for goodness' sake cancel the drinks—I haven't got a cent.'

'It's not,' he reassured her. 'But you remember those flowers that came back last night?'

'Tra-la-la! Do I not, my red-headed Lothario.' Veronica rocked backwards and forwards in an ecstasy of mirth.

'Yes, I know you thought it devilish amusing—anyhow, you were right—the girl turned me down.'

Veronica's mirth changed to a quick sympathy. 'Poor sweet!'

'You see, she's found out about the handle to my name, and she's sore that I didn't tell her in the first place.'

'And why didn't you, pray?'

'Because she's only somebody's secretary . . . oh, I know that sounds rottenly snobbish . . . but I picked her up in the train going to Ipswich.'

'Kenyon, you idiot! Why can't you confine your affairs

to women in your own set? I know half a dozen who are dying to have an affair with you.'

'I dare say you do—but that is beside the point as I happen to be crazy about this particular girl.'

'Don't tell me we are going to have prayers in the village church "to guide the footsteps of our young master" and, "HEIR TO DUKEDOM MAKES A RUDDY FOOL OF HIMSELF" in all the papers?'

'Certainly not—I haven't gone quite mad. But I do want to get on speaking terms with this girl again.'

'Then it's the young suburban Miss who must be batty, my dear—most of them would give their eye-teeth to be ruined by a real live lord—she must be a queer——!'

'She's not a queer, or a suburban Miss—on the contrary, she is damnably attractive, and I want you to be a darling and meet her.'

'What!' Veronica sat up as though she had been stung. 'Lord love us! the man *is* mad!'

'Shut up!' said Kenyon sharply, 'that piercing voice of yours can be heard from here to Leicester Square.'

'All right, darling—don't get irritable, send for a spot more gin to help me to recover from the shock.'

'Sorry, my dear—I'm a bit nervy, I'm afraid!' He gave the order and turned back quickly. 'Will you write a note saying how much you'd like to meet her, and ask her along to cocktails tomorrow night?'

'What, at home? Herbert would have a fit!'

'No he won't, he's too damned busy packing up the art collection and rushing if off to the bank.'

'Are you really serious about this, Kenyon?'

'Yes, honestly. It's the only way I can think of to break down this absurd class-consciousness of hers—in every other way she's a perfect darling.'

'But is she really presentable?'

'Absolutely—I promise you. She wouldn't be at her best among a lot of smarts, because she has not acquired the gift of chattering like a parrot, and her Billingsgate is definitely poor—but I wouldn't dream of asking you if I thought there would be any sort of *gêne*. Her uncle is a country parson—you know the sort of thing.'

'Do I not!' Veronica sighed resignedly. 'But I thought better of you, Kenyon. I expect she is the most deadly bore—dull, dowdy and dumb!'

'No, she isn't. You'll find her charming if you'll only show a little bit of that nice generous nature that you persist in hiding under a flow of trashy wit.'

'Hark at the boy!' she mocked him; 'never mind, give me the paper. Now what do you want me to say?'

'Oh, anything you like, provided that you make it clear that you really want her to come. Her name is Ann Croome, by the way.'

Veronica nibbled the end of her pen for a moment, and then covered two sides of a sheet of paper with her rapid scrawl.

'How's that?' she asked, handing the result to Kenyon.

'Marvellous!' He folded the sheet of paper and thrust it into an envelope. 'Now just address it and we'll send it off right away.'

'There!' exclaimed Veronica when it was done, 'see how I cover your shameless amours with the cloak of my spotless purity—come on, let's eat.'

When Ann received the letter some nine hours later she was on the point of going to bed after a long and tiring day. Mr. Crumper lived at Teddington, and for some reason unexplained, although it was rumoured that there had been sabotage in one of the principal power-stations of the line, the electric trains were only running at half-service. He had taken the delay and discomfort of his morning journey out of Ann.

She read the letter through slowly, and then something impelled her to glance through the window.

'Nation shall fight against Nation—Brother against Brother and the Strongest shall go down into the Pit.' The harsh words of the strange man in the train came back to her with renewed force, for there through the clear glass, low in the heavens and curiously misty, hung the slender curved sickle of the fateful August moon.

6

The Exodus from London

The following morning Kenyon received a summons to the headquarters of the United British Party, and there at twelve o'clock he interviewed certain prominent members of the House. Two Cabinet Ministers were among them.

They informed him of the Government's decision that the Mid-Suffolk by-election was to be called off—at least for the time being. Kenyon naturally protested, as his recent tour of the constituency had convinced him of the certainty of his election; but they told him that the Government was determined to prevent meetings of any kind which might lead to riots and disturbances—and an election without meetings was unthinkable.

Forced to accept their decision, Kenyon informed them that as he was now a free agent he would volunteer at once for the mounted branch of the Special Police, but they asked him to refrain. Owing to the enormous pressure of business his services would be much more valuable in some administrative capacity. So he agreed to hold himself at their disposal.

Other business was discussed by the Party Chiefs before he left the meeting, so he found himself in the privileged position of attending the deliberations of a little group of men who, if not the actual Cabinet, were perhaps the most potitical body after it. The information which he gathered was first-hand and authoritative.

The King's death was baseless rumour. The banks would definitely reopen on Monday, and the *assignats* which they proposed to issue would receive Goverment backing, thereby converting them into legal tender.

A serious split had occurred in the Cabinet over the question of Martial Law. A strong minority were for proclaiming it immediately throughout the Kingdom, but the Labour, Liberal and weaker Conservative elements were averse to placing such power in the hands of the military. They instanced the high-handed action of the Scottish Commander and even suggested his recall. At that the Secretary of State for War had intimated grimly that if the old Tiger went, he would go too.

Glasgow had then been thrown on the television screen in the Cabinet Room, and except for the sentries and Special Police the principal streets were seen to be quiet and orderly. The Minister for War had pointed out that the General's action, together with a rigid enforcement of the curfew, had been solely responsible for the restoration of order; and urged a general proclamation of Martial Law in view of the desperate situation in South Wales.

Television had then been switched on to Cardiff, but the receiving screen remained blank, and it was evident that the transmitters there had been damaged, yet the Prime Minister would not give way and they had adjourned at eleven-thirty without reaching any decision on the point.

The naval situation was also causing bitter controversy, and the Secretary for the Dominions had stigmatised the action of the First Sea Lord in recalling the disaffected ships to their home ports as 'H'ay cowardly compromise calculated to do endless 'arm.' Nor was his truculence pacified by the specious reasonings of the lawyers and schoolmarms among his colleagues who assured him that the ships were under-armed and that they feared a general mutiny in the Fleet.

The affair of Canvey Island made the Home Secretary irritable and nervy. The previous night he had ordered the Special Branch to round up three hundred and fifty of the leading Communists in London and intern them there, but the Reds had proved to be better organised than he knew. In the early morning the big convoy of police vans had been ambushed in the marshes when nearly at their destination. A horrible *mêlée* had ensued, and after a desperate fight against automatics, razors and sawn-off shotguns, the police had only succeeded in getting about half their prisoners on to the island. The rest had got clean away, and the Home Secretary was acutely conscious that only his personal jealousy of the War Minister had prevented him applying for the proper escort of troops and armoured cars which would have prevented such a disaster.

The Prime Minister likewise had a special worry of his own, for, without consulting him, the Prince had paid a visit to the Air Ministry and arranged for the dispatch of about forty planes to unknown destinations. The Minister of Air refused all explanations and offered his resignation, but as he was one of the few really popular figures among the masses the Prime Minister felt that this was no time to accept it. His Royal Highness's action was in the highest degree unorthodox, and the Prime Minister resented it accordingly, but faced with the duty of reprimanding him he felt an exceedingly strong desire to postpone the interview.

His Royal Highness was proving difficult in other ways too, apparently. With tireless energy he motored or flew from place to place, and wherever he went they knew him to be in constant consultation with important people who represented every shade of feeling. The only potentates whom he resolutely refused to interview were the principal members of the Government. He declared that authority had not been delegated to him, and therefore he was not prepared to take the responsibility of lending his countenance to their decisions. On the other hand the Prime Minister, the Chancellor of the Exchequer and the Home Secretary knew that he was in constant touch with the Secretaries of War, Air and the Dominions. The situation rankled.

Another nebulous but potent figure outside the Cabinet hovered on the Prime Minister's horizon. Lord Llewellyn with his great private organisation of Greyshirts, formed it was said without political aims, but for the maintenance of law and order under established Government. The Prime Minister detested the autocratic Llewellyn, and had the gravest suspicions regarding his middle-class volunteers though it was denied that they were in any way associated with the Fascists. However, Llewellyn having offered his legions as additional Special Police the Prime Minister had been compelled to accept them under pressure from his more belligerent colleagues, and official status was to be given to the Greyshirt army that evening.

The last and most disquieting piece of news which Kenyon learnt before he left the meeting was that the mutinous sailors from Portsmouth were now marching on London, not as a mob, but in well-disciplined formation, determined to lay their grievances before the Government.

The information had come through just as the Cabinet were breaking up after a five-hour session, and the Dominions Secretary had made the cynical but practical suggestion that the Prime Minister and First Lord should go to meet them. ' 'Ave a word with 'em,' he had urged as he lit a fresh cigar. 'Talkin's your big line—and the boys are only a bit excited, they don't mean no 'arm!'

The Prime Minister, however, preferred that troops should be ordered out from Aldershot to head the sailors off and there, for the moment, the situation rested.

As Kenyon drove back to Grosvenor Square he was struck by the strange, unusual aspect of the streets. It might have been Sunday or some queer little semi bank-holiday.

Less than half the ordinary number of buses were running, and there was hardly a trade van to be seen. Many shops were closed, and in front of others little knots of assistants stood chatting on the pavement. Some people were hurrying to and fro with unusual energy, others occupied the street corners in small groups—evidently swapping the latest rumours. There also seemed to be an unusually large proportion of a class alien to the West End in normal times. Gaunt, pale-faced workers in threadbare clothes, slouching along in little batches. Blue-coated police and Specials dotted about in couples every hundred yards or so.

When he entered the residential district he was astonished by the activity which had invaded the quiet streets of Mayfair. Large private cars were being loaded up with trunks and boxes, and from many houses the more valuable possessions were being stowed into furniture vans.

In Grosvenor Square he found two great pantechnicons drawn up outside his home and sweating men staggering down the steps under the burden of a large Van Dyck. The short, fat, rubicund Duke was personally superintending the removal of his treasures.

'Damnable, but understandable!' was his comment when Kenyon told him of the decision to postpone the election. 'Heard about the sailors? They seem to be out for trouble.'

'Yes,' Kenyon nodded. 'I should think the balloon is due to go up in about two days' time now.'

'Less, my boy, less. The troops had to use the butts of their rifles on the crowd in the East End this morning. I have ordered the cars for three o'clock to take your mother and the staff down to Banners.'

'Hell!' thought Kenyon, 'that puts the lid on the cocktail party,' for even in the stream of startling events his mind had never been far from Ann and he had persuaded himself that she would accept Veronica's invitation. Now, if Veronica had to go down to Banners with his mother, Ann would find him alone in Grosvenor Square and probably imagine the whole business to be a put-up job. His father's next words reassurred him.

'I suppose you can fly Veronica down tomorrow?'

'Oh, rather!' Kenyon agreed with relief.

'She had a fine rumpus with your mother—said she must go down with you tomorrow because she's got some party on this evening that she doesn't want to miss. What it can be at a time like this, heaven only knows—but you know how impossible she is, and I can't force her, much as I should like to have her out of London tonight. They are going to proclaim martial law you know.'

'I don't think so, sir.' Kenyon reported the latest news from Westminster.

The Duke grunted irritably. 'I bet you a pony they will, whether the P.M. likes it or not. I saw J. J. B. this morning.'

'Did you?' exclaimed Kenyon, much interested, for 'J. J. B.' was the First Sea Lord who had undergone a serious operation only ten days before. 'I thought he was *hors de combat* in a nursing home.'

'So he was, or they would never have got away with that fool decision about the big ships. They've been keeping everything from him because he was so ill, but Jaggers broke through the cordon of medicos this morning and told him the whole position. He said J. J. B. ought to know even if it killed him!'

'I'd love to have heard his language!' Kenyon had a vivid mental picture of the red-faced, autocratic sailor. 'What did he do?'

'Had himself carried out in his dressing-gown there and then. He was still in it when I saw him. He said he'd choke the life out of that whimpering rabbit of a schoolmaster they'd had the impudence to foist on him as First Lord—and do it with his own hands if they hanged him for it afterwards!'

'Good for him! I bet the fur is flying at the Admiralty now.'

The Duke chuckled. 'Yes, but he's a wily old fox. He went to the Air Ministry first. That's where I saw him—I'd dropped in to offer them the cars as soon as they'd taken your mother to Banners.'

'What was the idea?'

'To get behind the Government, I think. Llewellyn was there and what's-his-name—the War Office chap, and Badgerlake. It looked to me as if they were forming a kind of Junta. Jaggers told me that if the P.M. refused to declare martial law by midnight they meant to do it themselves, and Badgerlake will bring it out in all his papers tomorrow.'

Arm in arm father and son walked into lunch. Veronica and the high-nosed Duchess were already there. A strained silence hung over the first part of the meal, punctuated by a wearisome little monologue of complaint from Juliana Augusta regarding Veronica's obstinacy—folly—and lack of feeling in refusing to accompany her to Banners that afternoon.

'Well, father's going with you,' Kenyon attempted to pacify her.

'You are wrong, dear boy, it seems that I am to be packed off alone with the servants; your father is going to Windsor.'

'Windsor! Whatever for?'

'Well,' the small red-faced Duke spoke with unusual decision. 'We are faced with a national crisis of the first magnitude, and these Parlimentary people are all very well in their way, but they are a mushroom growth entirely. The whole basis of the throne is a loyal and responsible aristocracy. It is older, better, and more fitted to govern by centuries of practice than these—er—lawyer people. I do not suppose for one moment that I shall be called upon, but I feel that it is my duty to place myself at the disposal of whoever is acting for the monarch.'

Veronica was mildly amused. She thought it incredibly comic to see her fat and livery parent mouthing the phrases of a knight at arms, but for Kenyon the little man was invested with new dignity in claiming this ancient privilege of his order.

Directly the meal was over Veronica stood up. 'Well, darlings,' she declared. 'I'm going to have a L. D. on the B. without my B. and C.'

'What *is* the girl talking about?' muttered the Duke.

'A lie down on the bed without my bust bodice and corset,' she laughed, kissing the bald spot on the back of his head. 'Don't be rash and get yourself strung up to a lamp-post or anything while we're away.'

As the two women left the room the Duke pushed the decanter over to Kenyon. 'Have some more port.'

'Thanks.' Kenyon filled his glass.

'Wish to God you'd got a son,' was His Grace's next rather unexpected remark.

'*Son*, father? I don't quite understand.'

'Don't you? You're a fool then. To carry on, of course. Three generations stand more chance than two. Surely you realise that you and I will probably be as dead as doornails before the month is out.'

'Do you really believe that?'

'I do. The whole system is cracking up. Tomorrow is Friday, isn't it? Do you realise what that means to the millions? It is the day on which nine out of ten people draw their weekly wage—and the banks are shut. This Government rationing scheme can only be a stop-gap because, now that the pound has gone to blazes, they won't be able to pay for the food cargoes which are coming in from the only stable countries that are left. London will be starving in a week!'

'Yes, I'm afraid you're right.'

'As a natural consequence the people will turn and rend their leaders. You can't blame 'em after all. How can you expect them to understand the terrible series of shocks our finance has sustained. The man in the street judges by results after all, and if he can't get food for himself and his family, he'll go out to burn and rob and wipe out the upper classes that he thinks have been responsible for landing him in such a mess.'

'That won't do him any good!'

'Of course it won't, that's the tragedy of it. But he will do it all the same, and you can take it from me that people like us are going to be hunted like hares before we're much older.'

The Duke pushed back his chair. 'Well, I may as well go and see about the rest of the pictures. Directly they are packed and your mother has gone I shall leave for Windsor.'

'Then—er—I may not be seeing you again for some little time?' Hesitantly Kenyon held out his hand.

'Bloody fools, aren't we?' His Grace of Burminster gave a stiff, unnatural grin. 'Keep out of it as much as you can, Kenyon—don't shirk anything, I wouldn't ask that—but your elder brother went in the War and you are the last of the hatching, so I'd like you to see it through if you possibly can. They may consider us effete, but England wouldn't be England without a Burminster in the background.' He squeezed his son's hand and let it drop.

By half-past three the great house was empty and deserted, dim from drawn blinds and comfortless now with covers over all the furniture. The removal vans had gone with their freight of pictures and old silver. The Duke was on his way to Windsor, and Juliana Augusta had departed with the staff for Banners.

Having seen them off Kenyon began to make preparations for his own departure. He rang up Selfridge's roof garage where he kept his helicopter to give instructions that it should be overhauled and made absolutely ready for an early start the following morning, but he received an unpleasant shock. All private aircraft had been commandeered, and his helicopter with the rest.

That meant motoring down, so he went through to the garage in the mews at the back of the house, and spent half an hour tinkering with his car. E. C. G. was the next thing, every ounce that he could carry, so he ran her round to the nearest filling station. A long line of cars stretched ahead of him, all bound on the same errand. Many of them were stacked high with the weirdest assortment of luggage. The great exodus from London had begun, and everybody who had any place to go to in the country was making for it.

In the queue strangers were talking together with unaccustomed freedom and exchanging the wildest rumours. The news of the sailors' advance on London was now common property. A story was current that the Scottish Commander had been assassinated, another that one of the principal power-stations on the Underground had been wrecked that morning. Certainly trains were only running on two of the lines, and those had curtailed their services. When at last Kenyon reached the cylinders he asked for 5,000 atmospheres, but the man shook his head. One thousand was the limit for any car, irrespective of its size, and the price of gas ten shillings a thousand.

'But the price is controlled,' Kenyon protested.

'Can't help it,' said the man, 'if the rush continues it'll be a couple of quid termorrer—do I renew your cylinders or not?'

Kenyon promptly parted with his money and drove away, but the episode made him more thoughtful than ever. Events seemed to be moving now with such terrifying speed. What would London be like in another twenty-four hours with all these people abandoning the sinking ship, and the services breaking down? He began to feel guilty about detaining Veronica for another night, but it had never occurred to him that the trouble would accelerate so rapidly, and the more he thought of Ann the more determined he became not to leave London until he had satisfied himself about her future safety.

He was neither rake nor saint, but had acquired a reasonable experience of women for his years, and he could remember no one who had aroused his mental interest and physical desire to the same pitch as Ann. Now, in the customary manner of the human male when seized with longing for the companionship of one particular female, he was endowing her with every idealistic and romantic perfection.

Back at Grosvenor Square he decided that he ought to discuss the increasing gravity of the situation with Veronica at once, but her maid, Lucy, informed him that she had gone out.

At the sight of Lucy's trim figure—a pert young hussy he had always thought her—it occurred to him that she and his own man ought to be given the opportunity to rejoin their own families if they wished, and he put the proposition to them.

Lucy tossed her head. 'That is a matter for her ladyship, milord, though I wouldn't leave her with things like this even if she wished it. She'd never be able to manage on her own.'

'If it please your lordship I would prefer to carry on with my duties.'

'Well, that's nice of you both.' Kenyon nodded. 'Unless I receive instructions to take on a job of work I propose to leave for Banners first thing tomorrow morning. You can drive a car can't you, Carter?'

'Yes, milord.'

'Then Lady Veronica will come with me, and you can take Lucy with you in her ladyship's two-seater. Better do any packing tonight. I take it His Grace has sent the rest of the staff down to Banners?'

'There's Moggs and his wife still here, milord.'

'I see—well, I'll have a word with them.' Kenyon went downstairs to the grim gloomy basement. He paused to look into the store-room and satisfied himself that although tinned goods and luxuries had been difficult to procure for months past, the chef, with the ducal purse behind him, had not allowed his reserves to become depleted. The contents of the shelves would have stocked a fair-sized grocer's shop. Then he went on to the house-keeper's room where he found Moggs, and his wife, the laundry woman of the establishment, enjoying a large pot of very black tea. He told them that the situation was growing worse from hour to hour, and suggested that they might like to make other arrangements.

Old Moggs, who cleaned the boots and apparently spent most of his day in the area, jerked a grimy thumb at his wife.

'Me and the missis 'ad better stay 'ere, milord—can't leave the 'ouse empty, can we?'

'I don't like to,' Kenyon replied, 'but I'm thinking more of you than the house at the moment.'

'Very good of your lordship, I'm sure, but we'd just as soon stay 'ere as I told 'Is Grace, if it's all the same to you—ain't that so, Martha?'

'I'm willin', Tom,' said his wife.

'All right,' Kenyon agreed, realising suddenly that the couple might have no home to go to, but thankful not to have to leave the house untenanted. 'Take what you want from the storeroom, but I should go canny with it if I were you—there is enough there to last you a couple of months if you're careful.'

'Thank you, milord, an' my best respects.' Old Moggs touched an imaginary forelock.

'Good-bye then, and good luck to you both!'

'Same to you, milord, same to you,' came the quick response as he left them in the eternal half-light which perpetually envelops the dwellers below stairs in most London houses.

Up in his own study once more he began to pack a few of his more precious possessions into a couple of suit-cases. He was growing more and more certain that if they ever got back to Grosvenor Square they would find it sacked and looted. With a regretful glance he ran his eye along the bookshelves, faced in reality now with the old problem: 'What books would you choose if left on a desert island?' Windwood Reade's *Martyrdom of Man,* that wonderful survey of the history of every civilisation. Magee's great new achievement *Time and the Unconscious,* enough suggestive matter there to keep the most able brains speculating for a lifetime; and John Cowper Powys' *Glastonbury*

Romance with its half-million words. These were Kenyon's choice for the open boat, bound he knew not whither.

It occurred to him that he ought to ring up the Party Office and see if they had decided on any job for him. If they had, Carter would have to run Veronica down to Banners; but the man he wished to speak to was not in, and the secretary had no message for him.

Restlessly he wondered now if Ann would turn up, even if she had meant to in the first place. He could not expect her before seven anyhow, but would she come at all in this state of crisis and with transport breaking down? He began to hatch fresh plans in case of her non-appearance, but he needed Veronica's help and she had not yet returned.

It was nearly six, so he switched on the wireless to hear the latest bulletin. The Sappers had performed miracles with the wrecked bridge and the trains were running to Glasgow. Negotiations were proceeding which it was hoped would pacify the sailors. There was now reason to hope that the United States would lift their embargo as far as Britain was concerned, and extend further credits to ensure an adequate food supply. The Government were taking active measures to cope with the situation.

Kenyon turned off the instrument in disgust. Why was there no news of Cardiff or of the trouble in the East End that morning? The Goverment were trying to stay the panic by suppressing the most vital facts. Impatient now for Veronica's return, and unable to settle down to anything, he went out on to the front doorstep to watch for her.

A low-built powerful Bentley roared out of Carlos Place at a hideously dangerous speed, but the driver, catching sight of Kenyon, pulled up a few yards past him with screaming tyres. Kenyon knew the car and ran down to meet him. It was young Bunny Cawnthorp, dressed as an officer of Greyshirts. There was a nasty gash across his forehead and his face was smeared with blood.

'I say! Are you bad?' Kenyon asked.

'No, nothing serious; we're having hell in the East End with these ruddy Communists. I can't stay though, only stopped to tell you to get out; London will be Red tomorrow.'

'I'm off first thing in the morning.'

'You go tonight, my boy—I am!'

'But aren't you still on duty?'

'Duty be damned, Kenyon. I've slogged a few of these blokes and I'll slog a few more before I've done; but you know my mother is a cripple, and she's the only thing in the world that matters two hoots to me. My first duty is to see her safe out of it—then I'll come back to the other if I can—take care of yourself, old scout. So long!'

As the Bentley roared away Veronica pulled up in her two-seater. Kenyon hurried over to her. 'Where the deuce have you been all the afternoon?'

'With Klinkie Forster; the poor sweet's due to shed an infant this week. Ghastly for her, isn't it?'

'Yes, filthy luck. I'd forgotten about that, and you're paying for the nursing-home, aren't you?'

Veronica went scarlet. 'How the hell did you know that?'

'Oh, her husband told me, ten days ago. The poor devil was almost weeping with gratitude, and I know they've been down and out for months. I don't wonder you're always broke!'

'Well, that's my affair,' she snapped, angry and embarrassed as she fumbled with the door of the car.

'Steady on,' he soothed her. 'It's nothing to be ashamed of, and I meant to offer you a bit myself towards it, only I've been so busy I forgot; but don't get out. I want you to run down to Gloucester Road and pick up Ann.'

'She's coming, then? I had no answer to my note.'

'I think the post has gone groggy, like everything else; there's been no delivery yet today!'

'She may not have meant to come, anyway?'

'Perhaps not, but I simply must know what has happened to her, and if she is there I thought you could persuade her into coming back with you. I'll wait here in case she is already on her way.'

'My dear! You *have* got it badly!'

'Yes,' said Kenyon grimly, 'so badly that I've made up my mind to take her with us.'

'What! To Banners?'

'That's the idea; why not?'

Veronica exclaimed, protested, and talked wildly of Juliana Augusta's possible reactions to his project, but finally agreed to assist her brother when he had fully outlined his plans.

'But say she doesn't want to go with us; you can't keep

her here all night against her will?' was her final protest.

'Got to,' said Kenyon tersely. 'You get her for me if she's there and think up some idea to delay her departure once she's here till nine o'clock; I'll do the rest! Off you go!' A quarter of an hour later Rudd showed her up to the sitting-room in Gloucester Road.

Ann was there, and with her the Pomfrets who, apparently oblivious of the crisis which was shaking Britain, were busy addressing postcards to their friends asking them to get Pomfret's new book, *The Storm of Souls,* which was to be published next day.

Veronica sailed into the room, her small neat head tilted in the air. 'Miss Croome?' her smile was almost bewildering, 'I do hope you don't mind my coming in, but I've been simply dying to meet you because I've heard so much about you from my brother Kenyon. I spent the afternoon with friends in Queen's Gate, and as you were so near I thought I could give you a lift back?'

Ann was taken completely by surprise. She had decided not to go to Grosvenor Square but to write a letter of apology. 'How . . . how very nice of you,' was all she could murmur, a little breathlessly.

'Poor child,' thought Veronica. 'It must be horrid for her to have me butting in like this with these squalid people about.' Mentally she wiped the Pomfrets from her consciousness like flies from a window pane: the girl hadn't meant to come, of course—a stubborn little piece, but damned good-looking, all the same. Yes, Kenyon knew his oats all right, and like it or not she was coming back—Veronica meant to see to that.

'Ye Gods! what marvellous eyes you've got,' she exclaimed. 'I don't wonder Kenyon is crazy about you. Am I being terribly personal? I've got into such an awful habit of saying just what I think; do you mind if I smoke?' She whipped out an onyx cigarette-case and dropped on to the settee.

'Oh, no; please do.' Ann's eyes showed interest and a flicker of amusement.

'Isn't that fun?' Veronica rattled on, thrusting the case at Ann. 'Carter, my dear—Miss Croome, I mean—an American gave it to me; sheer blackmail, of course, but I simply had to have it.'

'I think it's lovely, and so are you!' Ann riposted neatly, as she returned the cigarette-case.

Veronica launched swiftly into a series of incidents which had occurred to her during the day. Things always happened to Veronica that never happened to anyone else—absurd, trivial things, but in the quick dramatic telling, punctuated by bursts of infectious laughter, they gained the status of incredibly humorous adventures.

It was impossible to be mulish in the face of Kenyon's magnetic sister if she laid herself out to charm, so when, after ten minutes' incessant talking, she exclaimed: 'My dear! It's a quarter to seven—we must positively fly!' Ann found herself standing up too.

She had been laughing uproariously only a second before and the attack had been so sudden, so swift. How could she possibly say now that she did not wish to go, and begin an argument with the listening Pomfrets in the background; two minutes later she was sitting beside Veronica in the car.

The stream of chatter flowed on. Veronica had no intention of allowing her captive time to think of belated excuses to make on the doorstep. The body of Ann Croome must be handed over to Kenyon in good order and good humour. Veronica took a pride in her achievements.

'Looks like a doss-house, doesn't it?' she cried, as they entered the wide hall now stripped of its old masters. 'But we shall all be murdered in our beds, I expect, so what does it matter?'

Kenyon came down the stairs to meet them. 'Well, Ann,' he said, 'it *is* nice of you to come with all this upset going on.'

'I didn't mean to,' she said frankly, 'but I found your sister irresistible!'

They went up to Veronica's sitting-room. Kenyon shook the drinks while his sister talked, and an hour sped by unnoticed, but Veronica had her all-seeing eye on the clock. The guest must not be allowed to say that she was going!

Suddenly, as though struck by a lightning thought, she cried: 'What a bore, with the servants gone we can't possibly ask you to stay for dinner; but wait, I've got it! We'll picnic up here on what's left in the larder; come on, let's beat it to the basement!'

'Splendid!' Kenyon laughed. 'Ann shall cook us an

omelette; she told me the other night that she could!'

What could Ann do against the enticements of these charming people? Only follow Veronica through the door that Kenyon smilingly held open.

Half an hour later she was seated on a table in the vast, empty kitchen, where in the spacious days of lavish entertaining twenty men and women had laboured at the preparation of ball suppers. She was gobbling a large slab of omelette which she had helped to make, and laughingly protesting that she was quite unfitted to give Veronica the cooking lessons which were for the moment that tempestuous lady's most earnest desire.

They opened champagne and drank it out of tea-cups, scorning to call Moggs or Carter to their aid when they could not find the glasses; then carrying more bottles they proceeded upstairs into the silence of the great empty house.

Back in her sitting-room, Veronica, with Ann beside her, curled up on the floor and began to tell the cards. There were journeyings across water, meetings in tall buildings, love, treachery, imprisonment, and in Ann's cards—death!

When the last round was finished Veronica drew the pack quickly together with her slim fingers. 'Darlings, I must leave you,' she declared. 'Lucy is a perfect saint, but she simply cannot pack; don't go, Ann, please; give me a quarter of an hour and I'll be back.'

Alone with Ann, Kenyon wasted no time in fencing. He stooped to take her hand but she withdrew it quickly. 'Ann!' he protested, 'you're still cross with me?'

'Not cross—but I only came this evening so as not to be rude to your sister. It doesn't alter anything I said in my letter.'

'What nonsense! I'm terribly sorry I didn't tell you my full name in the first place; but what difference does it make? I haven't got three legs, or a tail, or anything!'

'I see,' a glint of humour lurked in Ann's tawny eyes, 'you're just like any other man, and you're in love with me. Is that it?'

'I am.'

'A lot?'

'Yes, Ann, a lot.'

'Do you realise the logical conclusion then?'

'N . . . no,' he hesitated, fearing some kind of trap.

'In such circumstances it is usual for the man to want to marry the girl: do you want to marry me?'

The question was so direct that Kenyon hesitated again, floundered, and was lost. 'Marry? . . , well, you know . . . I hadn't meant to . . . yet!'

'Please don't go on, my dear.' Ann was smiling now. 'Of course you don't; I didn't expect for one moment that you would. I'm not suitable and I know it. If you were really going to get a Civil Service job at £400 a year I might be—but you're not!'

'But Ann——'

'What?'

'Well, I do care about you—terribly.'

'Perhaps.' She stood up. 'I like you too; you must know that.'

'Then can't we—carry on?'

'Listen,' she said slowly, fingering the lapel of his coat, 'it's this way. I might live with a man who wanted to marry me and couldn't—if I liked him enough; but I would never live with a man who did not love me enough to *want* to marry me. I wonder if you understand. Anyhow, I'm going home now. Say good-bye to that nice sister of yours for me, and tell her I liked her an awful lot—and I *have* enjoyed this evening.'

'I understand, Ann; but you're not going home; I am not going to let you!'

'What do you mean?' Her eyes grew hard, and the heavy lids came down, half-concealing them.

'Just this. I warned you to stay in Orford, but you wouldn't listen. It may be too late now for you to reach there safely on your own. I'm going down to the country tomorrow and I mean to take you with me.'

'No, Kenyon. I can look after myself; I'm not going with you.'

'You are.' His eyes were hard though he was smiling.

'I've had a room prepared for you and you'll sleep here tonight.'

'No!' she snapped, filled with sudden fury by his dictatorial manner.

'You will,' he repeated firmly.

'No!'

'I say *yes*! I've put you next to Veronica, so you will be quite comfortable—and quite safe.'

'No! You've got no right to keep me here against my will!'

'Nobody will have any rights in a few days' time. I'm anticipating the movement, that's all!'

'No! You'll let me go now—*now*! D'you hear!'

His only reply was to take her firmly by the arms. For a second she tried to wrench herself away but realised immediately how powerless she was against his strength.

He let her go for a moment and pulled open the door. 'Come on; do you walk or do I carry you?'

Beneath the lowered lids her eyes were blazing with anger as with sullen tight-shut mouth she walked slowly past him. He piloted her down the corridor and pushed her gently into a spacious bedroom.

A tiny fire burned in the grate although it was early August, and the sheets had been carefully turned back in the great four-poster. A nightdress—Ann supposed it to be one of Veronica's—lay across the bed. A dressing-gown, slippers, and everything else she could possibly require also seemed to have been provided, but there was no other exit than the door by which she stood with Kenyon.

'I'll never forgive you for this,' she said slowly. 'Never!'

He smiled slightly. 'We're making rather an early start in the morning, I'm afraid, so you will be called a six o'clock. Good night, Ann—sleep well!' He shut the door softly behind him, and with renewed fury Ann heard the key turn in the lock.

Kenyon went along to report to his fellow conspirator.

'Well?' asked Veronica curiously. 'How did she take it?'

'Damn badly. I had to lock her in!'

'Phew!' Veronica let out a peculiarly vulgar whistle. 'You'll find yourself in Bow Street, laddie, if these troubles blow over.'

'I don't care. She comes with us if I have to carry her all the way now. I love that girl like hell!'

Nevertheless, when Kenyon decided to call Ann himself in the morning, he found the door still locked but the bed unslept in and the window open. Ann Croome had gone.

7

Nightmare Day!

Kenyon walked over to the window. There was an eight-foot drop to the leads of the music-room, then a short fire-escape down to the empty garage, from which it was easy to get into the Mews. That was the way she had gone.

'Damn!' he said briefly, and striding back into the passage he knocked on Veronica's door.

'Yes, who is it?' came a petulant voice. Veronica was never at her best in the early morning.

'Me—Kenyon.'

'You can't come in, darling, I'm naked!'

'All right, but look here—Ann's cleared out.'

'More fool you for letting her. Where were you—in your bath?'

'No; in my room, of course!'

'Ye Gods—the man *is* crazy.'

Kenyon laughed angrily. 'I'm perfectly sane, thanks; we'll talk it over at breakfast, then.' He strode off to his room.

Veronica did not prove helpful or particularly sympathetic when they met over the bacon and eggs and tea. 'You had your chance last night, my boy, and if you mucked it you've only yourself to blame,' was her somewhat cynical comment.

'What did you really think of her?' Kenyon asked.

'Oh, she's quite a sweet and too devastatingly bedworthy for words!'

'Veronica! Why must you drag that in?'

Her eyes opened wide. 'Snakes and ladders! Why not, my poor fool. You don't want to discuss higher thought with the wench, do you?'

'Of course not . . . but . . .'

'But what?'

'Oh, nothing.'

Veronica put down her teacup with a deliberate bang.

'S'welp me Gawd, but I believe 'e is thinkin' of makin' an honest woman of 'er after all!'

'No,' said Kenyon 'I'm old-fashioned enough to feel that I do owe something to the family and it would pretty well break old Herbert up.'

Veronica shook her head sadly. 'My dear, you *are* loopy, there's not a doubt about it. You don't want to marry the girl, you don't want to discuss the state of your soul with her, and you don't even want to play slap and tickle—at least you say you don't. What the devil *do* you want?'

'I want to get her safe out of London; after that we'll see. Are you game to put off our departure till after I've been down to Gloucester Road?'

'Yes, my quixotic numskull, if you like. Let's start after lunch. That will give me a chance to see Klinkie again; she may have brought another infant into this world of sin by now.'

'All right. I'll go straight away.'

'Oi!' she called after him, 'chuck us the piper, lovey.'

He picked it up and glanced quickly through it. 'My hat! It's down to four pages now; that's bad.'

'Anything in it?'

'No, nothing new that matters; martial law declared last night. . . . Train derailed at Peterborough. . . . Further trouble at the London docks, and lots about a new scheme for rationing all commodities, but it's all fill-up; bound to be now that the Press is muzzled by the Government censorship. Well, I'll be off; see you at lunch if not before.'

Although it was only just past eight a considerable number of people were about. Little groups of servants, from the big houses and blocks of flats which were still occupied, stood talking together. As Kenyon passed the Dorchester he noticed that some wag had chalked up the words: 'To Let—Furnished' in large letters on the wall, but the big commissionaire still stood impassive and important at the front entrance. The Park displayed a bustle of activity. Troops, Special Police and long lines of lorries moved up and down between the food dumps, and sentries were posted on the gates. At Hyde Park Corner Kenyon saw half a dozen khaki figures, and some black blodges which he knew to be machine-guns, high up on the great arch that spans Constitution Hill; an admirable strategic position commanding three main thoroughfares—one side of Buckingham Palace, and the two Parks. In Knightsbridge there was quite a crowd, yet the streets looked empty, and after a moment he realised that it was because there was not a single bus in sight. The crowd thinned again, and he sped down Cromwell Road.

Mr. Rudd received him on the doorstep. 'Sorry, sir, Miss Croome ain't in—not likely to be for that matter.'

'Why?' demanded Kenyon, with a sudden sinking feeling. 'Did she sleep here last night?'

'Yes, sir, same as usual; but she asks to be called at six when she come in lars' night. In a rare state she was too, that dirty! an' a temper! Well, I ain't never seen 'er like it before. Then she ups an' packs this mornin'; give me me money, an' 'ops it, rahnd abart a quarter of an hour ago.'

'Where to?—do you know?'

'Liverpool Street—I 'eard 'er tell the taxi. Don't know fer sure but I think she's got relations down Suffolk way.'

'Right. Thanks!'

'You're welcome, sir.'

Kenyon was already back in his car. Liverpool Street was the other end of London so he ought to be able to beat her to it if she only had a quarter of an hour's start. He was determined to see her again before she left.

Knightsbridge was more crowded now. Still no buses on the streets, but many cars loaded with luggage and streaming westward out of London. He raced up Piccadilly, wondering at his swift progress, then he saw the explanation. The traffic signals were not working, but farther on he paid the price; at the Circus there was a solid jam which took him twenty minutes to get through. In Trafalgar Square a crowd was collecting, but the police moved steadily through them, breaking up the groups. When he reached the Thames Embankment he was able to put on speed again, but had to pull up momentarily for a full battery of Field Artillery—horses, guns, and limbers—which was reversing preparatory to parking along the roadway under the windows of the Savoy. Blackfriars was almost deserted, and as he entered the City by Queen Victoria Street, he was reminded of a Sunday when he had attended a special service at St. Paul's. The place was dead, empty, desolate. Long rows of closed offices and shuttered shops without a pedestrian in a hundred yards, and this was Friday.

Within a quarter of a mile of Liverpool Street he was brought to a halt. A long line of taxis and private cars, all heading for the station, barred his way; several thousand people, like Ann, were making for the Eastern Counties.

Kenyon fumed and fretted. He dared not leave the car

in case it was stolen. Then he had an inspiration. If he took a side turning he could work his way round to the Bishopsgate entrance; it was a risk, for Bishopsgate borders on the East End, but there would be nothing like the traffic, and after a few moments of twisting in and out through narrow streets he reached the eastern entrance of the station.

There was no sign of any crowd hostile to car-owners such as he had feared, and a loafer in a battered hat stood nearby on the pavement. Kenyon beckoned him over.

'Can you drive a car?' he asked

'Not me, Guv'nor—no such luck.'

'All right,' said Kenyon. 'Come and sit in this one. I may be half an hour or so but there's a quid for you when I get back.'

'Strite?'

'Yes, I mean it.'

'Orlright, Guv'nor,' grinned the loafer.

Kenyon hurried into the station. From the top of the staircase he could see the wide platform spread beneath him. It was one black seething mass of humanity; it seemed utterly hopeless to try and find Ann in such a crush, but he went down and shouldered his way in amongst them.

After a few moments he reached the footbridge and crossed it, knowing that the departure platforms were on the other side. The space there was even more densely crowded, but he managed at least to edge his way through the crush to the gates, beyond which lay the trains. There were a number in the sidings but to his surprise all that he could see were empty, and not one showed any sign of imminent departure. A tired-looking porter who sucked at an unlit cigarette leaned over the barrier, and the nearest members of the crowd were bombarding him with questions. He only shook his head.

'It's no use blamin' me,' he kept on saying. 'There won't be no more trains till further orders.'

Kenyon questioned the people who stood around him and learned that the provincial towns had become very alarmed at the influx of visitors in the last few days. Now they were employing their local police to prevent any but permanent residents in their municipalities from alighting. Thirty or forty trains had returned to Liverpool Street during the night, still loaded with their human freight, and the railway company, not unnaturally, refused to sanction the departure of any more.

Obviously Ann could not have left London then. Kenyon turned and looked at the closely-wedged mass of people who stood there, speechless for the most part and waiting in the hope that the Company might reverse its decision. She must be somewhere among them if only he could find her, so he buffeted his way back towards the booking office. That too was crammed with patient careworn humanity.

For ten frantic minutes Kenyon squeezed and pressed his way through the throng, standing on tiptoe at every second step to peer above the heads of the surrounding people. Then he gave it up as hopeless and made his way back to his car.

His new acquaintance uncurled himself from the seat, and Kenyon handed him the promised pound. The fellow grinned sheepishly.

'Don't seem fair to tike it reely—does it? Still, h'easy come and h'easy go, as they say. Well, so long, Guv'nor—I only wish there was a h'upset like this every day!'

Kenyon sped back through the deserted City and along the Embankment, but he passed the end of Northumberland Avenue, thinking it better to cut out Piccadilly and Trafalgar Square. Yet near Victoria Street he got caught again. This time by a long religious procession. It was headed by priests from the Cathedral who carried Crosses and an image, while they chanted an age-old hymn. Dozens of little boys in surplices followed meekly in their train. Free of it at last the rest of the journey was easy, and he pulled up once more ouside 272 Gloucester Road. The door was open so he went straight up, not expecting to find Ann, for he did not think she could have returned so quickly, but determined to wait for her. Rudd was in sole possession of the sitting-room and he was busy. Two large automatics lay on the floor in pieces, and he was polishing their parts with loving care.

'Hullo!' said Kenyon. 'Where did you get those things?'

Rudd grinned. 'Mr. Sallust give them to me, sir—told me to clean 'em up—just in case like.'

Kenyon did not ask 'in case of what.' He knew, so he sat down to wait for Ann, and Rudd meanwhile entertained him.

Eleven o'clock chimed from the hideous pale bronze clock on the mantelpiece, then twelve, and he began to wonder what had happened to her. If only she had been reasonable the night before they might have been out of London by this time. He found himself taking cigarette after cigarette out of his case until it was exhausted; Rudd, who had long since reassembled his dangerous-looking battery, but continued to bear him company, came to the rescue with a packet of Gold Flake.

Kenyon sat on, but by the time the clock struck one he was thinking of Veronica. To delay much longer would not to be fair to her, and he must get her down to Banners somehow, yet every moment he wanted more desperately to see Ann. At twenty minutes past he pulled himself together, and stood up to go.

Rudd promised faithfully that he would telephone the very second that Ann returned, and with that slender comfort Kenyon descended to his car.

He took the by-ways to Hyde Park Corner, but there he found a block; thousands of people and several hundred police. The sailors from Portsmouth with the aid of commandeered vehicles had completed their march, and were due to arrive any moment. Arrangements had been made for them to camp in the Green Park. A dozen people, cheerful but unapologetic, immediately occupied the bonnet and back hood of his car, so Kenyon, knowing it would be useless to protest, took the invasion without comment and stood up in the driver's seat.

Over the heads of the crowds, from the corner of St. George's Hospital, he saw the bluejackets go by. Shepherded by mounted police and cheered by a considerable proportion of the people, they passed quite peaceably to their temporary encampment. With them were quite a number of soldiers, sympathisers Kenyon supposed, from the Aldershot Command which, rumour said, had failed to head the sailors off.

He looked meditatively again at the tall arch. The men up there were hidden now, but at the first sign of trouble they could mow the malcontents down like ripe corn.

The crowd suddenly thinned, overflowing into the street. His uninvited companions who were using his car as a grandstand smilingly descended, and at a foot pace he edged his way towards Hamilton Place. A few minutes later he was back in Grosvenor Square.

Veronica had started lunch without him, and she felt quite shocked as she gave a quick glance at his drawn face.

'What *is* the matter, darling?' she asked.

'Oh, nothing,' he said wearily, and sitting down, told her the events of the morning.

'I see,' she said slowly. 'Well, as a matter of fact, Alistair rang up. He wants me to meet him this afternoon at a tea-shop behind Wellington Barracks; and I said I would if you were agreeable to postponing our departure till this evening.'

'That's not true, Veronica! You thought of that story to give me another chance to see Ann.'

'My sweet, I may be an habitual liar, I am with most people, but I don't have to be with my own brother!'

'Honestly?'

'Yes, honestly!'

'No, I've got to get you down to Banners this afternoon; perhaps I'll come back tomorrow, we'll see.'

'I suppose you're worried stiff about her?'

'The fact that I don't know where she is, and the thought of what may happen to her, if she is not out of London by tonight, is driving me half-crazy.'

'I like your little Ann, Kenyon.'

'Do you really?'

Veronica thought him almost pathetic in his eargerness for her approbation. 'Certainly I do,' she said firmly. 'She's got guts, darling, guts. And I adore the way she hopped out of the window; I've been thinking about her all the morning.'

'Thanks, Veronica; you've been damn good about this business.'

'Don't be a fool! I'm never good about anything unless it suits my book. Now I'm going to leave you to finish your lunch alone.'

'Right. We'll get along in half an hour's time.'

When he had finished he rang for his man and asked: 'Did you go up to Euston this morning, as I told you?'

'Yes, milord, and the cigarettes from Foyer and Co. had arrived. I had an awful job to get them, though.'

'Had they, by Jove! Good old Yorgallidis! What a performer not to let us down, even at a time like this. Were the crowds very bad?'

'Shocking, milord, no trains running, and by the time I left the people were that angry they were wrecking the booking offices.'

Kenyon nodded gloomily. 'It's about time we cleared out. Pack a good-sized picnic basket, and put it with the cigarettes and luggage in the car.' Carter's usually impassive face showed sudden surprise.

'Am I to take it that you are going without her ladyship?'

'Of course not; she's upstairs getting her things.'

'Excuse me, milord, her ladyship left the house about ten minutes ago, and I was to tell you that she would be back round about half-past six.'

'I see. We must wait till she gets back then.' Kenyon did not believe the story about Alistair for one moment. With quixotic disregard of danger to herself, Veronica was giving him a few more hours to try and get in touch with Ann; between the two of them he was now at his wits' end with anxiety and worry.

There was no alternative but to take advantage of her generosity so he decided to telephone to Rudd. When he dialled the number there was no reply. He dialled it again and a man's voice spoke:

'Number, please?'

'I dialled it,' said Kenyon.

'If you will give it me, I will ring you as soon as I can,' said the voice.

Kenyon gave the number, thinking as he did so how greatly it would add to the Government's difficulties if the telephone service broke down. For half an hour he sat beside the instrument, then the call came through. Rudd had no news of Ann, nor could he suggest any place that she was likely to have gone to. He promised to telephone if she did return to Gloucester Road.

For an hour Kenyon paced the library in growing desperation. He tried to read but could not settle to a book. Where, in all this vast stone wilderness of London's streets, could Ann be at that moment, was the thought that racked his mind; and what would become of her in the days ahead if he could not make certain of her safety.?

At half-past four he rang up again, waited half an hour,

rang up the supervisor, and was begged by the much harassed operator to be patient. It was a quarter-past five before his call came through—still no news of Ann.

With a sudden feeling of guilt he remembered that he had not been in touch with Party headquarters that day. They might have work for him in connection with rationing or some emergency committee, so he put through a call to the office. After another long wait he got through to his immediate Chief, but the man was worried, irritable.

What did he want? Why didn't he get off the line? They were expecting important news. . . . It was essential that incoming calls should not be blocked. . . . Kenyon rang off quickly, praying that he had not blocked a call from Rudd. In nervous exasperation he put through another. The wait seemed interminable, and he felt now as though he had been sitting beside the instrument for days. It was nearly seven o'clock before his call came through.

'Rudd speakin', sir. Bin tryin' to get you this last 'arf hour. Miss C. come in at a'pars'six. Bin ter see 'er cousin in Muswell 'Ill, I gather, but 'er cousin weren't there; she's gone out again now. . . . When'll she be back? . . . That's more 'an I can say. Gone out wiv Miss Girlie she 'as—ter get a bit of food, I reckon.'

'All right, I'll come right along,' said Kenyon.

He dashed up to Veronica's room only to find that she had not yet come in. Downstairs once more he paced restlessly up and down the hall—now furious with impatience to get away. Carter appeared, silent-footed and efficient as usual with a cocktail shaker and glasses on a tray. He poured one out and offered it to Kenyon.

'Can I help you in any way, milord?' he asked quietly.

'Yes—er—thanks.' Kenyon swallowed the drink and seized gratefully of this offer of assistance. 'Get Lady Veronica's car and load it up; directly she returns bring her and Lucy down to 272 Gloucester Road; understand?'

'Very good, milord.'

'Right, and now come and give me a hand with the picnic basket and my own things. I'm going on ahead but I'll wait there until you turn up.'

Directly his car was loaded he headed once more for South Kensington. Hyde Park Corner was still alive with people eddying slowly backwards and forwards in the evening light. Agitators were haranguing large sections of the crowd, but the police seemed to be in sufficient force to prevent any hostile demonstration. It took him twenty minutes to get through the press, but once he reached the top of Sloane Street he was able to slip away.

A square grey motor-truck stood outside 272, stacked with boxes, barrels, and every variety of tinned goods; Rudd was on top of it arranging a tarpaulin to cover the load.

'She ain't got back yet, sir,' he called cheerily to Kenyon, 'but don't you worry, she won't be long.'

'Thank the Lord for that!' As Kenyon got out of his car he glanced through the grocer's window. The interior of the shop looked as though a hurricane had swept through it; empty boxes, paper, and cardboard cartons littered the floor, while the shelves were practically denuded of their stock. Then he noticed that the name on the lorry had been blacked out, and just below the driver's seat a small W.D. with a short broad arrow, the mark of the War Department, stood out in fresh white paint.

'Hullo!' he exclaimed, 'have they commandeered your stock?'

'Yes, commandeered; that's what it's bin, sir!' With quick efficient fingers Rudd jerked tight the last knot; 'I should wait upstairs if I was you.'

Kenyon took the hint and left him. In the sitting-room he found the Pomfrets peering excitedly out of the window at the doings of Mr. Rudd below.

'I do think we should do something about it, Hildebrand,' the woman said sharply.

'My love, what can we do?' the lanky man protested.

'Can't you go for the police?'

'Good evening,' said Kenyon; 'what's the trouble?'

Mrs. Pomfret turned on him and waved her small fat hand appealingly.

'They've taken all poor Mr. Gibbon's groceries; really, they ought to be stopped.'

'Why?' asked Kenyon. 'Surely the Government has the right to commandeer things in times of emergency like this?'

'But it's not the Government; I'm sure it's not! Mr. Gibbon knows nothing about it, and the very moment he'd gone home they started to loot his shop. I wouldn't be surprised if that van they've got isn't stolen too!'

'Really? But who are "they". Are there others in it besides Rudd?' inquired Kenyon with astonishment.

'Oh, its that Mr. Sallust, of course. Rudd only does what he tells him—treats him like a kind of god—though why I *cannot* think; a cynical, *heartless* man!'

'My love, you are prejudiced on my account,' Pomfret said mildly.

'Well, he could have got you some marvellous notices in his paper if he had wished, but he was positively rude when I suggested it!'

'Not rude, my dear; he only said that fine work was always bound to make its mark, and that overworked reviewers were apt to become irritated if pestered for complimentary notices.'

'He did not mean that *kindly*, Hildebrand; it was a sneer. But can we do nothing to prevent him stealing all those things?' She looked hopefully at Kenyon.

Sorry,' he said. 'I'm only waiting for Miss Croome, and directly I've seen her I must get away.'

There was a clatter of footsteps on the stairs. Griselda Girlie poked her head round the door and then came in. Ann was behind her.

'My dear!' exclaimed Mrs. Pomfret as Ann pulled off her hat, 'where have you been? You look half-dead!'

'I am,' she said wearily. 'I must have walked twelve miles and all for nothing; I've had a filthy day. The book's not out, I suppose?'

'No; isn't it infuriating? Hildebrand went down to his publishers this morning but they were shut.'

'What rotten luck for you.' Ann sensed the tragedy of the thing for this struggling couple by the hunted look in the man's eyes, but the next moment she had caught sight of Kenyon standing half-hidden behind Griselda and the open door.

'Good evening, Ann,' he said. 'Can I talk to you for a moment—I mean alone?'

'No! How dare you come here after last night?'

'I'm sorry.' Kenyon was horribly embarrassed by the presence of the Pomfrets and Griselda. 'Look here,' he hesitated, 'I only came to find out what you are going to do?'

'That does not concern you in the least!' The other three moved over to the window.

'Why, here's that awful woman again!' exclaimed Mrs. Pomfret.

'What woman?' asked Griselda.

'She came here yesterday; the most vulgar, ill-bred person I have ever . . .' Mrs. Pomfret broke off suddenly, remembering that Ann was in the room.

Kenyon had overheard her. Mrs. Pomfret might well apply such a description to Veronica. A swift glance out of the other window confirmed his guess. There she was, seated in her car with Lucy beside her, and Carter, bored but dignified, clasping the most unsuitable of headgear, a bowler hat, upon the dicky. She saw him and waved a greeting as he turned back to Ann.

'Look here,' he repeated, 'there are no trains running from Liverpool Street—you know that—and you must get out of London somehow. How do you propose to set about it?'

She stared at him angrily. 'I don't. I shall probably stay here—lots of people will have to!'

'You're mad! and I won't have it.' All Kenyon's pent-up anxiety from his long day of worry was coming out with a rush.

'You!' she snapped. '*You* won't have it?'

'No. Since you are incapable of looking after yourself I'm going to do it for you! I refuse to leave you here.'

She laughed then shook her head. 'I'm afraid you'll have to—this isn't Grosvenor Square—and you can't take me by force!'

'Can't I? I can and I will!'

Ann drew quickly away from him, a little scared by the hard light in his blue eyes. 'Go away!' she said. 'Go *away*!'

'No,' he gripped her by the arm, 'not without you—don't be a fool, Ann. It's madness to stay here. If you had other plans I wouldn't interfere, but you haven't so you've got to come with me.'

'I *won't*! Oh, Mr. Pomfret—Griselda—stop him!' Ann cried as he pushed her towards the door.

'May I ask . . .' Pomfret stepped forward while the two women beside him stood with wide, excited eyes.

Kenyon dropped Ann's arm and advanced on the novelist with a threatening glare. 'You go to hell! Keep out of this, do you hear?—unless you want to get hurt.'

Pomfret backed hurriedly away, but Ann had seized the

opportunity to rush out of the room, and the door crashed to with a resounding bang. Kenyon tore it open and dashed after her across the landing. She had slipped through the further door, but he threw his shoulder against it before she had time to lock it on the other side, and she was sent flying to the floor while he came sprawling on top of her.

'Now!' he panted, seizing her again, 'we've had enough of this.'

'And so have I,' cried an angry voice. It was Gregory Sallust, a bricklayer's trowel in one hand—a large brick in the other.

Kenyon stumbled to his feet and looked round with amazement. Sallust's room presented an extraordinary spectacle. The bed had been moved out of a large alcove, and in its place were stacked hundreds of books, boxes, bundles; apparently all the worldly possessions which Gregory Sallust could not carry with him, but held dear. He was busy bricking them up and a three-foot wall already separated the alcove from the rest of the room. Rudd stood nearby mixing mortar on a board, and the two big shiny pistols which Kenyon had seen earlier in the day reposed behind him on the abandoned bed.

'Gregory!' Ann ran forward, clutching at the mason's arm, 'stop him! Oh, don't let him, please?'

Sallust shook himself free impatiently. 'Let him what?'

'Take me away! He's trying to force me to go to the country with him against my will!'

'Is that true? Sallust looked sharply at Kenyon.

'Yes, more or less—but if she stays here she'll starve.'

'That's so. I'm clearing out tonight. Why don't you want to go, Ann?'

'I won't! not with him. Gregory, if you're going, take me with you—please?'

'Sorry, my dear—it's quite impossible.'

'But why—why?'

'Because I'm too old a soldier to want to have a woman hampering my movements at a time like this.'

'Don't be a brute, Gregory. You can drop me directly we get into the country. I'll manage somehow—then.'

'Don't *you* be a stupid little fool. If Fane is ass enough to want to take you—let him! and thank God for giving you such damn fine eyes!'

'Thanks,' Kenyon cut in. 'If ever we meet again I'll stand you the best magnum of champagne we can find for giving her that sound piece of advice. Come on, Ann!'

'Gregory—please?' she begged.

'Oh, shut up, and get out—I'm busy. And for God's sake keep what you've seen to yourselves, otherwise someone will come and break this wall before I get back.'

She turned on Kenyon, her eyes blazing. 'I'm not going with you—I won't!'

'You are,' he said, 'and now!' Then stooping suddenly, he picked her up in his arms. She kicked and fought, but it was useless. In stature she was hardly taller than a well-grown girl of fifteen, and still struggling ineffectively, he carried her down the stairs.

'Darlings!' shrieked Veronica as they appeared on the pavement. 'Romance at last! How too thrilling!' She flung open the door of Kenyon's car while Carter and Lucy, now seated side by side in her own, endeavoured to hide their interest and astonishment under masks of gravity.

Kenyon dumped his burden in the centre of the car. Veronica slipped into the near side, and slammed the door while he ran round to the driver's seat.

Ann wriggled into an upright position as Kenyon touched the accelerator. 'Let me get out,' she cried fiercely. 'Let me get out! Help!'

'Shut, up, damn you,' snapped Kenyon. He was furious that he should have let himself in for such a scene, but determined now to go through with it. The car slid forward.

'Help!' shouted Ann again, while the residents who remained in Gloucester Road began to fling up their windows to learn the cause of the excitement; but Veronica put a restraining hand on her shoulder.

'Listen, my sweet,' she said firmly, 'if the police or anyone stop us now I'm going to tell them you are loopy. Your poor little baby died last night—and the shock has temporarily turned your brain, so your nice kind cousin Veronica is taking you to the country. I've got away with worse stories than that in my time, so you needn't think they won't believe me—understand?'

'Yes,' sobbed Ann. 'I believe you'd get away with murder!'

'I would,' said Veronica, 'if it was for anyone I was fond of!'

8

Nightmare Night!

Ann let herself relax into a more comfortable position between them, realising suddenly that she had been acting like a fool. All day she had been striving to leave London, really frightened now as to what might happen in the capital, and here was a heaven-sent opportunity. If it had not been for Kenyon's high-handed treatment of her the previous night—if he had only tried persuasion instead of bullying—and if she had not been so wretchedly tired after her long and disappointing day, she would have come quite willingly. He could not prevent her leaving him at the journey's end if she wished.

Kenyon was angry with Ann, and with himself. If only she had been reasonable the night before this ridiculous scene would not have occurred, but he ought, of course, to have been more patient with her—actually to kidnap her was pretty stiff—it was the impulsive nature which went with his red hair, he thought ruefully, which led him into scrapes like this. Anyhow, the thing was done, and he had her safely beside him in the car, which meant a lot. He turned his attention to the best way of getting out of London.

'Why this gaiety by night?' asked Veronica. They were coming into Grosvenor Place, and the sound of many voices raised in a swinging chorus came to them from the direction of Piccadilly.

'Sailors in the Green Park, I expect,' muttered Kenyon, 'looks as if they had bonfires going too,' he added glancing eastwards at the red glare that lit the dying twilight.

'Poor Queen Elizabeth—all her nice furniture at Buck House going up in smoke.'

'Oh, no, I don't think so,' he disagreed as he swung the car in the direction of Victoria—but Veronica was already thinking of other things.

'What sort of a reception would they have a Banners?' she was wondering. 'It was one thing to arrive there according to their plan of the previous evening with Ann as a willing adjunct to the party. Juliana Augusta might prove a little awkward, but Veronica had prepared a story to fit the case, and at the time she had counted on Ann's co-operation in putting it over. Now it was a very different matter. This small, pink wildcat with the tawny eyes was apparently guaranteed to blow up on the slightest pretext. What asses they would look if Ann spilled the beans about her forcible abduction!'

By the tram terminus at Victoria there was a considerable gathering of people. The trams, like the tubes and buses, had now ceased running altogether, but the crowd appeared to be waiting there on the off chance that something might happen. A news van drew up just ahead of the car and the people swarmed towards it, so they were compelled to pull up, while bundle after bundle of the thin sheets were distributed to eager hands. The man on the van would give no change. 'No time,' he kept on repeating and many a shilling or half-crown reached his ready palm in addition to the coppers of the multitude, which seemed to grow every moment. Within four minutes the van was empty and the disappointed members of the throng sullenly dispersing.

Kenyon had no chance to secure a copy, but a bystander gave him the leading items of news from the single-sheeted edition which he held.

The Government had resigned . . . the Communist minority in the House had made a bid for power, but the Committee of Imperial Defence had temporarily taken over the control of the country . . . there was a stirring appeal by the Prince for fair play and the maintenance of law and order. All loyal citizens were asked to refrain from hoarding food, and adding to the difficulties of the police by congregating in the streets.

The crowd thinned, and Kenyon was able to proceed slowly through it. Soon they were running at a good pace down Victoria Street, which was almost deserted; long lines of shuttered shops, gloomy and lifeless in the shadows, for there had been more trouble at the power stations and only one side of the street was lighted.

At Westminster there were crowds again—also apparently waiting for something to happen. The great bulk of the Parliament Houses loomed up grim and silent, deserted after the last momentous session. The strong iron gates were closed, and police mounted guard at the entrances. In the yard, which is habitually the parking-place for Members' cars, Kenyon saw groups of soldiers sitting about or leaning on their rifles.

By sticking close behind a police van, he managed to get through the square without difficulty, and round the corner to Westminster Bridge, but to his surprise he found the bridge-head guarded. A large tank stood in the middle of the road, chains had been drawn across from side to side and detachments of police stood on either pavement. An inspector came forward.

'Can't I go through?' asked Kenyon.

'No, sir. I'm sorry, but this bridge has been closed to traffic and pedestrians.'

'But why?'

'Well, it's not that we mind people going south, sir, but to prevent them coming over from the other side. If we took the barrier down they might rush us.'

'Good gracious, who?' smiled Veronica looking at the empty bridge.

The inspector grinned. 'You'd soon see, miss, if you was on the other side. That's where the real barrier is; this is only a sort of second line. They're a real ugly lot over by the County Hall tonight.'

Kenyon nodded. He had meant to avoid the worst districts on the south side by going out of London via Brixton and Herne Hill, then through Bromley into Kent. Now he would have to rearrange his plans. 'Are all the bridges closed?' he asked.

'No, sir, it's just the Houses of Parliament and the Government offices round Whitehall that we're anxious about at the moment. It's important that there should be no trouble round here.'

'I want to get on to the Maidstone Road,' Kenyon confided, 'but I thought it would be a bit risky to take the ordinary way.'

'It's a pity you didn't go yesterday, sir. So much has happened these last twenty-four hours, and in some places the people are a bit out of hand—we can't be everywhere at once you see. I'd cut back as far as Putney Bridge if I were you, and make a big circle—you'll be out of all the trouble then.'

Kenyon frowned. The plan was a good one, but he was anxious now about his supply of gas. He had not been able to fill up to capacity the previous day, and had used a lot in the last twelve hours. A circuit by Putney Bridge would increase his mileage enormously and if his pressure failed they would be stranded by the roadside. It occurred to him that if he telephoned to his Party headquarters they might be able to tell him of a place in the neighbourhood where he could pick up some more, so he nodded to the Inspector and backed his car. 'There's a call-box in the Underground Station, isn't there?' he asked.

'There is, sir, but there are only skeleton staffs on the exchanges now, and they're too busy to put through any but official calls. The military take over at midnight.'

'Thanks, Inspector.' Kenyon turned to the faithful Carter who had now pulled up behind him: 'You'll be all right for gas with the small car, so you'd better leave us here—go out round Putney. I'm going to the office, it's only just round the corner, and I'll follow you if I can, but get out of London as quickly as possible and don't worry about us.'

'Very good, milord—just as you wish,' Carter touched the absurd bowler hat, Lucy smiled brightly, and the small car backed away.

When he reached his office he looked at Ann doubtfully. 'You won't make trouble or anything, will you?'

'No—I'm sorry I made a fuss. I'll come with you to the country, but no further—you understand that, don't you?'

He smiled at her downcast face as he got out. 'An armed neutrality, eh?—well, just as you like.'

In the office he found everything in confusion. Not being actually a Government department its continuance was in no way vital, and most of its principal executives being people with some sort of official position, they had abandoned it to attend to more urgent affairs. Normally it would have been closed hours before, but owing to the crisis a certain number of clerks and typists who had congregated there during the day now displayed no intention of even endeavouring to get home. Kenyon could find no one in authority and, after refusing half a dozen cups of tea from female members of the staff, went out into the street again.

A commissionaire was on duty, but when questioned about gas, shook his head. 'Thirty bob a thousand, sir, it was today, but I doubt if you'd get any anywhere now. Most of the gas-filling stations have been cleaned out.'

Scotland Yard was only just across the square, so Kenyon thought he would go there. He did not expect that they would be able to help him in the matter of gas, but they would probably know about conditions on the other side of the river, and if there was any real danger in taking the direct route over London Bridge and down the Old Kent Road.

Whitehall was a thick jam of people right up to Trafalgar Square and more seemed to be flooding in every moment, despite the fact that the bridge was closed and the tubes and buses not running. Up near the Horse Guards the crowd was singing, and Kenyon recognised the tune as the Red Internationale, so things did not look too good in spite of the squads of police who kept the people moving.

The car crept along at a foot pace but after he had gone about fifty yards he was forced to bring it to a standstill. A mob of roughs were eddying round a big Daimler. Inside, gaunt—impassive—monocled, sat a grey-moustached General, apparently on his way to the War Office. They were booing him but he appeared quite unconcerned. A detachment of mounted police rode up, edging their horses through the crush with the skill born of long practice. The hooligans dispersed, the Daimler moved on, and Kenyon followed.

The gates at the entrance of Scotland Yard were closed, but they were opened for a minute to admit a lorry on which was mounted an enormous searchlight. Kenyon caught a glimpse of motor-cars, reserves of mounted and foot police, and the steel helmets of soldiers in the court-yard. Every window of the great building was brightly lighted and the shadows which moved constantly across them told of an intense activity within. Kenyon was directed to the entrance further down, at Cannon Row Police Station; there he had to wait some little time. Half a dozen rioters were being brought in and a wounded police-man. A little batch of sad-eyed aliens stood in a corner of the room; they had no knowledge of what was happening in their own countries, but now that England seemed to be on the verge of Revolution, they were anxious to get away, and turned with pathetic confidence to the police.

A hysterical woman was loudly insistent that the Sergeant should find her husband, who had gone out the evening before and failed to return. 'There would be plenty of that,' Kenyon reflected, 'in the next few days.'

At last he managed to get a few words with the harassed officer. Gas was out of the question. Even if he could find a supply he would not be allowed to buy it without a permit. All stocks had been comandeered by the Government. The bridges were open except for Westminster and Waterloo. As far as the Inspector knew there had not been any serious rioting in Southwark or Bermondsey. Isolated cases but nothing more, and cars had been going through up to the last hour.

The Sergeant attributed the comparative quiet in the South-Eastern area to the fact that the majority of roughs had come up to the West End. There had been considerable looting in the Strand earlier in the evening he said, but the mob had been dispersed by baton charges and the situation was well in hand. 'If things get worse we've got plenty of tear gas inside,' he ended up jerking his thumb over his shoulder. 'We'll have to give 'em a real lesson.'

Considerably cheered to think that somebody who possessed real resolution was handling the situation at last, Kenyon fought his way back to the car, and taking the short cut down Cannon Row to Westminster Bridge again, turned left along the Embankment.

Night had fallen now but no sky-signs illuminated the tall buildings on the south bank of the river, and owing to the lack of traffic a strange hush seemed to have fallen over London, yet there was something sinisterly menacing about that unusual silence broken only by the deep drone of patrolling aeroplanes as they passed now and then low overhead.

The City was quiet as the grave, only an occasional knot of men tramping westward and a few policemen standing on the street corners.

At Cannon Street a flying squad car hurtled past them at breakneck speed—the whine of its siren making the night hideous.

Kenyon turned south over London Bridge. On the far side he was called on to halt. A group of Greyshirts with an officer at their head came towards him. 'Where for?' asked the officer.

'Kent—Maidstone Road,' said Kenyon.

'Right—got any food in the car?'

'No—why?'

'Orders to stop any supplies leaving London—d'you mind getting out?'

'Look here!'

'Sorry to trouble you, but I've got to search your car.' The man was polite, but firm. Obviously the only thing to do was to look cheerful and obey.

They climbed out and a swarm of lusty Greyshirts began to rummage in the car. Out of the back came the picnic basket.

'Here—what's this?' exclaimed the officer.

'Supper,' said Kenyon. 'You're not going to pinch that are you—we've had no dinner as it is!'

The basket was opened up, and it was obvious that Carter had done his job thoroughly. He had removed all the gadgets for picnic teas and stuffed every available inch of space with provender.

'Take it inside.' The officer jerked his head towards the Bridge House Hotel, which had been converted into a depot. The hamper was carried off and the search renewed with vigour.

Under the seat the Greyshirts discovered Kenyon's cigarettes, two bottles of hock and one each of Port and Brandy.

'Here! that's not food!' Kenyon protested as he saw these items about to follow the picnic basket.

The officer grinned. 'Sorry—but I'm afraid they come under the heading of supplies. You can have your hamper back when it's empty if you like.'

'No, you can keep the damned thing,' Kenyon said angrily as he climbed back into his seat. 'How are things further South—down in the Old Kent Road, I mean?'

'Might be worse—they were making a bonfire of a big Rolls just past the Elephant and Castle half an hour ago, but they are more playful than vicious—only took the gold watch off the old boy that owned it and let him go. He's back here in the Bridge House now.'

'That doesn't seem too good.'

'No, I should take the side turnings if I were you—down Tooley Street and then strike into the main road further along.'

Veronica leant out. Her smile was seraphic—enchanting. 'You don't think *really* that we shall all be murdered, do you?'

The officer smiled. 'I—er—sincerely trust not!'

'But it is rather shattering isn't it—for a woman I mean—if only we had you with us I should feel absolutely safe.'

'I'd love to see you through.' The young man's chest broadened perceptibly under Veronica's gaze, 'but I can't possibly leave my job—be here all night I expect!'

Veronica had noticed the long line of cars parked outside the Bridge House. She glanced towards them now. 'Haven't you someone you could leave in charge?' she wheedled, 'just for ten minutes, while you took us through the worst part by the docks?'

'Well,' he hesitated. 'I couldn't go myself, of course, but I've got dozens more men than I actually need and I could send a car-load to convoy you as far as Greenwich Park—that would get you through the most troublesome area anyhow.'

'Oh, how perfectly splendid!' she loosed again the battery of her seductive smile.

With sudden embarrassment, cursing the presence of Kenyon and Ann, both interested spectators, he turned away and blew his whistle. The Greyshirts came tumbling out of the hotel, and he hurried over to them.

'How clever of you,' murmured Ann.

'Easy dearie!' chuckled Veronica. 'The conceit of women is nothing compared with that of men!'

The officer was calling for volunteers and there was no lack of them. Ten minutes later a dozen Greyshirts had clambered into an open car and Veronica's new friend returned with another officer.

'This is Mr. Harker,' he said, by way of introduction.

'Silas Gonderport Harker,' corrected the lieutenant of Greyshirts with the faintest intonation that declared an American origin.

Ann gazed at him almost in awe. He was a good head taller than his senior, broad of shoulder, and magnificent in girth. Yet on that vast body he displayed no trace of superfluous fat. His face was round, flat-nosed and cheerful. There was an undeniable hint of humour about Mr. Harker's tight-shut mouth and twinkling eyes. 'If you'll stick as close as you can behind my car,' he said slowly, 'I'll see you through.'

'Thank you—thank you a thousand times. *And* you!'

Veronica momentarily dazzled the Captain again with her bewitching smile.

Harker squeezed his elephantine bulk into the Greyshirts' car and moved off into the darkness with Kenyon following.

'All the luck!' shouted the slim Captain, and the last they saw of him was a saluting figure silhouetted against the light which streamed from the open door of the Bridge House Hotel.

Tooley Street was a cavern of silent blackness. They raced down it and into the gloom beyond. At the crossing by Tower Bridge they met the first sign of trouble; it was a still warm night, and a hundred and fifty people were standing out in the open road in front of a public-house. Immediately they saw the Greyshirts an angry murmur ran through the throng and one man hurled an empty beer bottle. The leading car tore on and hurtled round the bend into Dockland, they young Greyshirts cheering derisively at the mob.

'Good thing I've got you an escort, lovie!' said Veronica quietly.

'I'm not so certain,' Kenyon muttered. 'The people down here hate these Greyshirts like hell. I've a good mind to catch them up and send them back—we'd probably be safer on our own.'

Ann shook her head. 'It's too late now. If you try and overtake them at the speed they're going you will probably knock someone down.'

'That's the devil of it,' Kenyon agreed.

Through ill-lit Dockland the cars roared on, past more public-houses, then swerving sharply entered Parker's Row. Every hundred yards or so a fresh crowd surged out into the roadway, yelling abuse and throwing missiles. A rotten tomato thumped and spluttered on the windscreen of Kenyon's car. He thanked his gods that the glass was shatterproof, the next bull's-eye might be with half a brick.

In Jamaica Road the crowd grew thicker, even the Greyshirts were afraid to rush it, and pulling up, signalled to Kenyon to turn back.

As he reversed his car up a turning they passed him again and sped down a side street lined with small, grim, poverty-stricken houses. A moment later he was after them. The headlights of the cars threw the women and children huddled in the doorways into sharp relief. One harridan shrieked foul epithets as they rushed past—another hurled a flower-pot. Ann shuddered, realising suddenly that if the car stopped for a moment she would be at the mercy of these harpies.

The Greyshirts' car turned again and Kenyon followed through another dark canyon of decaying dwellings, where squalid garbage littered the gutters, and another contingent of frail, half-starved, wolfish humanity lifted shrill voices against the flagrant opulence suggested by the powerful private car. Another turn, and they were back in the main street once more, but forced to slow down by the stream of people who overlapped the narrow pavements. Ahead, in the uncertain light which flickered from a public-house, the crush was denser, and in an open space before it they caught a glimpse of serried rows of people. Perched on a barrow above his head, a short squat bare-headed man was gesticulating violently; they could not catch a word he said, but as he struck his open palm with his clenched fist a moan went up from the crowd. The Greyshirts had been forced to halt again; a black-haired boy perched on the back of their car was making violent signals to Kenyon, who stopped and put his car into reverse.

'Hi! Where yer goin'—blast yer!' came angry cries from the pavement. An empty egg box hurtled into the body of the car. It caught Ann on the head, but it was light and fortunately did no serious damage. With admirable presence of mind she turned, made a wry grimace in the direction whence it had come, and smiled. The man who had thrown it saw her, and the result was electric. He looked astonished—crestfallen—then all at once he grinned.

'Sorry lidy—I didn't mean to 'urt yer.' He was a big burly chap, and forcing his way to the front of the crowd he pushed the onlookers right and left from in front of the bonnet.

'Come on, mates,' he shouted. 'Aht of the way fer the Duchess o' York—she ain't done no 'arm, and lor blimey, ain't she a daisy?'

The people good-humouredly gave way and for a moment Ann had saved the situation, but as Kenyon glanced over his shoulder he saw that the Greyshirts were in trouble. They were only a few yards behind them, but in turning they had knocked down a man; a threatening mob surged round their car. The black-haired boy was being dragged off the back, the others were using their long heavy sticks freely upon their assailants.

Ann's new-found friend was swept away from them in a sudden eddy of the crowd. A red, angry, drink-sodden face was thrust over the side of the car, its owner glared at Kenyon.

'Bleedin' torf,' yelled a voice from the rear. 'Look at 'im wiv 'is ruddy chorus girls.'

'Chorus girls? Tarts, yer mean!' screamed a shrill-voiced woman; 'an' honest people withart food in their stomachs—I'd learn 'em if I was a man!'

Kenyon glanced round desperately. How was he to get Ann and Veronica out of this? The crush was ten deep on every side. Above their heads he caught a glimpse of the Greyshirts; the black-haired boy had been hauled back into their car, but blood was streaming from his face, his eyes were flashing, and his mouth drawn down into a cruel vindictive snarl. With sudden venom he jerked a gun from his hip-pocket, and blazed off with it into the crowd.

For a second there was absolute silence, then a howl of fury went up from the maddened mob. An irrestible wave like the surging of a stormy sea almost submerged the Greyshirts' car. Kenyon caught a glimpse of Ann's face, white now and terrified. Veronica sat, sneering almost, her eyes angry and flashing, but her hand trembled upon his knee—and he knew that in the next few moments he must fight—fight for his life unless they were to be torn limb from limb and trampled under foot in the blind, vicious fury of a starvation-maddened mob.

9

'Burn Them! Burn Them!'

'Quick!' cried Kenyon to the girls, 'out you get—no good staying here!'

Veronica slipped on to the pavement and Ann after her. It was only a matter of seconds, but before Kenyon could join them a little rat of a man had snatched at Veronica's necklace. It snapped, she grabbed at it, and the thread parted again, leaving a string of twenty knotted pearls between her fingers; someone jogged her elbow and they were jerked from her hand into the gutter. A wild scramble ensued, and Kenyon seized the opportunity to hustle the girls nearer to the Greyshirts. They, too, had abandoned their car and were fighting—a small compact group—on the pavement ten yards away.

Howling obscenities, a lean hag seized Ann by the hair and tried to pull her down. Kenyon abandoned all ideas of chivalry and hit the woman a smashing blow in the face. Her grip relaxed and she sank from sight with a little moan. The crowd surged over her, trampling her down into the gutter.

Veronica was struggling desperately with a sinewy lascar. He had her round the body, but years of outdoor exercise had given her slim form far more strength than might have been supposed. She beat her small, clenched fists furiously against his face, and after a moment he staggered back, half-blinded by her blows.

Kenyon had turned to help her, but before he had a chance another woman had kicked him on the shin. Her boot was man's size and the pain excruciating. A fellow wearing a red sweater rushed in and began to hammer him with his fists, but Kenyon had been a boxing blue. A left to the jaw and the red sweater disappeared from view.

A few yards away the lights of a cheap eating-house caught Kenyon's eye. It was of the type usually run by Italians; polonies and tarts covered with course coconut decked the window beside a water-bottle with a lemon stuck in the top. If they could reach its shelter they would be safe for the moment. The Greyshirts evidently had the same idea; they were fighting their way towards it in wedge formation, the gigantic Mr. Silas Gonderport Harker at their head. Kenyon pushed Veronica in their direction and dragged Ann after him.

The lascar rushed in again, but Kenyon put out his foot and the man crashed to the ground; another dashed in—ducked as Kenyon lashed out—and grabbed him round the middle. They swayed together, locked in each other's arms up and down the pavement. Kenyon gave his assailant a quick jab behind the ear, the man grunted and staggered back, but as Kenyon thrust his way towards the lighted window of the little restaurant, he suddenly missed Ann—she had disappeared.

A second later he saw her, still on her feet but out in the roadway, separated from him by half a dozen people. Her dress had been ripped away at the neck, showing the bare flesh of her shoulders, but she had snatched a short, thick umbrella from a woman in the crowd, and was beating wildly with it at the faces of the people who surrounded her. Kenyon dashed back into the road striking out right and left, irrespective as to whether his opponents were men or women, and the mob shrank away from the menace of his powerful blows. Ann had slipped to her knees by the time he reached her, but he used his long arms like flails and, clearing a space, lugged her to her feet again; yet it seemed that it could only be a matter of seconds before they were both dragged down, for his back was unprotected now and the mob was closing in again, snarling and angry.

Suddenly there was a resounding crash. A group of people had fastened on Kenyon's car with senseless fury, and tilting it, had thrown it over on its side. In the brief silence that followed Ann glanced wildly round. A mad animal blood-lust glared from the mean faces that ringed them. Hundreds of cruel merciless eyes seemed to devour her in anticipation, and a multitude of clawlike hands reached out to rip her shrinking body, but momentarily they were drawn back, and Kenyon seized her by the waist, half carrying, half dragging her towards the lighted doorway.

They were nearly there. The Greyshirts were already clustered in the entrance, and the big American was thrusting Veronica behind him when a well aimed brick caught Kenyon on the head. He staggered and fell.

The mob rushed in again, but Ann stood over him. She remembered having heard somewhere that to lunge at people's faces with the point of an umbrella was far more effective than to beat them about the head. As in some ghastly nightmare she prodded fiercely at the head of an aged crone who was bearing down on them. The point caught the beldame on the mouth, and her stream of hideous blasphemies ceased in a sudden whine. A chimney-sweep, his face begrimed with soot, his red-rimmed eyes gruesome in the flickering light, dived at her from the other side; she jabbed at him and he clutched his eye with a scream of pain.

'Well done, Ann—well done!' It was Kenyon who had

stumbled to his feet, blood streaming down his face, but grasping in his hand a short length of wood which he had found on the pavement. It was a Communist weapon and had two ugly nails driven through the heavy end.

He gripped Ann round the shoulders with his left arm and began to savage the people nearest to them with the bludgeon. A moment later they were hauled into the cook-shop by the Greyshirts.

Ann sank fainting and exhausted to the floor, but Kenyon picked her up and barged his way towards Veronica, who stood half-way up a narrow flight of stairs at the back of the restaurant. The whole place was a struggling *mêlée* of people. The Greyshirts were endeavouring to throw the customers and occupants out into the street.

Veronica pulled Ann beside her and Kenyon jumped back into the rough and tumble. It was short and sharp, only one big man who looked like a professional bruiser was giving serious trouble, but a china mug caught him on the side of the head, the Greyshirts closed in on him, and he was flung out in a heap, on to the pavement.

A bottle filled with stones hurled through the window, shivering the glass in all directions, and a slab of stone came whizzing through the open door. It caught the foreign-looking youth who had started all the trouble on the foot, and flushing with pain and rage he whipped out his automatic again.

There was a sudden crash of shots as he poured its contents deliberately into the nearest of the crowd. The carnage at such short range was terrible, some of the bullets penetrating two or more people apiece in the close-packed mass. Kenyon saw them fall right and left, gripping their wounds, vomiting blood, and howling with agony while the unwounded turned on their companions, fighting desperately to get out of range of the murderous weapon.

A temporary lull ensued while the Greyshirts stood, gasping and panting, dabbing at their wounds and trying to staunch the flow of blood.

'Don't waste time!' bawled Harker. 'Get that door shut and make a barricade.' He knew that they had only secured a most doubtful sanctury. The mob still swayed—angry, threatening, dangerous—outside.

The door was slammed and a couple of marble-topped tables piled against it.

'Let's use the counter, that looks solid,' suggested Kenyon.

'Can't,' said the youth with the gun. 'It's nailed down.'

'Oh, pull the damned thing up!' Kenyon seized one end of it in his strong arms. The American grabbed the other end. 'Come on now!—all together—heave!'

The counter came away with a loud splintering of wood. The coffee urn fell to the floor with a ringing thud. Plates, glasses and cakestand crashed and jangled. Pushing and panting they slewed the mighty piece of wood across the window and the door, pulled out the tables and piled them on the top, then the chairs and stools. In an incredibly short space of time they had formed a solid barricade which it would not be easy for the mob to force.

'Wonder if there's a back way out,' gasped Kenyon to the American.

'Good for you! I wish you'd look,' was the terse reply.

Kenyon ran to the rear of the shop, through a door and into a small kitchen. One narrow window looked out on to a dark well, enclosed on three sides by sheer blank walls. No hope in that direction!

He dashed back and up the stairs to the first floor. In the front room overlooking the street he found Veronica quietly making up her face in the central mirror of an ornate overmantel, and Ann dialling away at a telephone.

'What's the idea?' he asked.

'Trying to get help, of course.'

'No good, my dear. The Inspector told us that only official calls were allowed.'

'Well,' she protested, 'the police are official aren't they?'

'Yes, but I shouldn't think there's a policeman within a hundred miles of here.'

'Why not?' asked Veronica, carefully darkening her eyelashes.

'Because they have to concentrate in the West End; what good could they do scattered in twos and threes all over London at a time like this?'

'How too shattering!' Veronica inspected her handiwork with care.

'Hadn't you better cut that out?' Kenyon suggested. 'It only angers the crowd to see you painted up like Jezebel!'

'Darling, I'm sorry, but if we're going to meet God face to face in the next hour I must look decent. Besides it gives me moral support, like boiled shirts to Englishmen in the tropics. Tell me! If there is no chance of help what does A do now?'

'Get out—if we possibly can. I'm trying to find a way now; if we can't—God knows! Anyhow, keep away from that window both of you or they'll start throwing things in here.' Kenyon slammed the door behind him.

The back room he found was a frowsty bedroom, and the windows only showed the blank-walled well again. Above there were two more bedrooms, stale-smelling and horrible, the beds unmade, and the tumbled sheets filthy with stains and grease. He had hoped to find a trap-door in the ceiling of the top landing, but he was disappointed. After a hasty search he gave it up and hurried below to report to the American.

'That's bad,' nodded Harker. 'We've just beaten off an attack, but how long we'll be able to keep them out, Lord knows!'

'Give me a couple of your men and the next time they rush you we'll chuck things on them from the upstair windows,' suggested Kenyon.

'That's an idea.' The American tapped two of his Grey-shirts on the shoulder. 'Bob—Harry—get upstairs and lend a hand to Mr. Whatshisname.'

Although all the men round him were sweating and dishevelled, the gigantic Mr. Harker remained as cool and unruffled as if he were seated in his favourite bar playing a game of poker dice.

Kenyon and his assistants collected all the plates and other useful missiles that they could carry and staggered up to the front room. Veronica and Ann were peering cautiously out of the window.

'Oh, look!' cried Ann as he came in. 'They've got a battering ram!' Then he saw that a dozen burly fellows had shouldered the shaft out of a large wagon, and were making ready to stave in the door of the shop.

He threw up the window and seizing a hideous china vase from the mantelpiece, hurled it at the men below.

Bob and Harry took the other window while Veronica and Ann kept all three supplied with plates, and a rain of clattering china descended on the heads of the besiegers forcing them to drop their ram, but the mob on the far pavement were quick to retaliate. Bricks, stones, bottles and potatoes came from all directions, smashing through the windows and thudding into the room. Harry's face was so badly cut that he had to retire, and Veronica stopped half a brick with her elbow, which temporarily put her out of action.

The mob howled and shouted, urged on by a blue-chinned man who had climbed on to the Greyshirts' derelict car. He waved a Red flag in one hand and pointed at the windows with the other. Kenyon picked up an aspidistra plant from a nearby table and hurled it at him, but it fell short, the pot obliterating the scared face of an old woman who saw it coming but had no time to get out of the way.

The agitator yelled derisively at the men with the battering ram. They picked it up and came on again. There was a rending crash as the door gave way, Bob staggered to the open windows with an old shiny, black, horse-hair covered arm-chair. With Ann's help he tipped it out; yells and curses from the street told that it had found at least one mark, but for every casualty the mob sustained there were a hundred infuriated, fight-maddened people pressing forward to fill the gap.

'One, two, three.' The battering ram was flung with the weight of twenty men behind it against the barricade. The flimsy shopfront had been completely demolished now. In the parlour above, the ammunition was almost exhausted; every ornament had gone, the oleographs and photos from the walls, and most of the furniture. Kenyon turned to fetch more missiles from the bedroom and found Harker behind him.

The big man was grinning but he shook his head. 'We can't keep it up, and they'll be through below-stairs in a moment; barricade's half-down already.'

Kenyon groaned as he wiped his grimy, bloodstained face. 'Where has that fellow with the gun got to? Can't he pick off the agitator and the other ring-leaders?'

'He's run out of shot, but don't worry. I'll bring the boys up here. The crowd will never be able to pass us on those stairs in a month of Sundays.' With his leg-of-mutton hands thrust deep into his breeches pockets the Greyshirt officer strolled out of the room.

The battering ram found its mark again with a terrific thud, the whole barricade was shifting, chairs and tables tumbling to the floor. With a howl of triumph the mob surged forward, thrusting the remaining obstacles inward through the shattered shop-front, and clambering wildly over the top. The Greyshirts retreated to the rooms above and hurriedly erected a new rampart on the landing with beds and bedding; the fight at the windows was renewed with increased vigour.

Suddenly there was a lull. A motor horn was hooting insistently further along the street, and the crowd, scenting fresh and easier prey, began to stream in that direction.

The hooting grew louder, and there were angry cries as a big closed car zigzagged down the street. The people drew hastily back on to the pavement, but one small urchin ran out and threw a broken teacup at the chauffeur. Next second the mudguard caught him, and he fell under the near front wheel. There was a howl of execration, and a dozen men flung themselves in front of the long bonnet. Two, three, four were sent spinning, and then the car pulled up.

'How about trying to break out now?' Kenyon suggested.

Silas Gonderport Harker shook his cherubic head. 'Not a hope; we'd never get a hundred yards.'

Over the heads of the crowd they watched the occupant of the car, a tall, lean, elderly man with a lined aesthetic face. He showed no trace of fear or excitement but produced an automatic and with the utmost calmness fired three times, once to the front over his chauffeur's shoulder, then swiftly once through each side window of the car. The bullets drilled neat round holes through the glass, and each one killed a man. The mob snarled with rage but gave back instantly, cowering with fear one against the other. With a sudden jerk the car bumped over two more of the bodies and sped on.

Almost before it was out of sight another car came in view, and the crowd greeted it with a roar of savage hate; the driver, a young man in a soft hat, hesitated and slowed down. A woman stooped and picking up a small bronze ornament from the gutter, hurled it at him. It struck the young man full in the face; his head lolled stupidly for a second and then the car swerved violently, ran on to the pavement, and crashed through the window of a shop. A man was pinned between the bonnet and the framework, his head gushing blood from the cuts of the splintered glass; his screams, and those of the other people who had been run down could have been heard half a mile away, yet no one paid any attention to them; they were dragging the occupants from the back of the car; an old man, a fat woman, and a girl.

'Oh, can't we help them?' Ann clutched at Kenyon's arm, but almost before she had finished speaking the girl had disappeared, thrown down and trampled upon by a hundred feet. The old man went next, struck on the back of the head by a bottle. His eyes goggled stupidly, staring out of a fleshy white face for a second, then he sank from view; but the fat woman survived for three or four minutes. She swung a weighty bag, driving her aggressors from her by striking them with it in the face, but hands clawed at her from all sides and her clothes were ripped to ribbons; a malicious urchin kneeling behind her lugged at her skirt, the fastening broke and it descended to her ankles revealing a bright blue petticoat. He seized that too and wrenched it to the ground.

Suddenly she kicked herself free of the clothes around her feet and leaving a large portion of her pink silk blouse in the hands of a vicious shrew, broke away from her tormentors. With amazing swiftness for her bulk she pelted down the street, naked to the waist, her legs encased in a pair of frilly calico drawers; she presented a ludicrous, but pathetic and terrifying sight. Rivulets of blood coursed down her shoulders and tears gushed from her eyes; before she had gone twenty yards she was tripped and fell. The mob closed in on her and kicked the great unwieldy body into shuddering immobility.

'Hunted like hares!' whispered Kenyon.

'What say?' asked the American.

'Nothing.' Kenyon was thinking of his father's prediction and wondering where he was now; safe at Windsor, or already fallen a prey to the blind resentment of the people against the ruling caste which had allowed things to drift into this terrible pass.

The car had been pillaged before the fat woman fell, and now the sullen, angry faces in the street were turned up to the windows again. Like a savage inhuman herd they stampeded across the road and into the shop below. Fighting began on the stairway while Kenyon and Bob tore down the over-mantel and curtain rods to hurl from the windows.

'Burn them!' yelled a shrill-voiced woman suddenly. 'Why don't yer burn 'em.' The cry was taken up; the street seemed to rock under the reiterated howling of the mass. 'Burn 'em—burn 'em! The blasted Greyshirt swine!'

Kenyon caught a glimpse of Ann's face, drawn and haggard with unnaturally bright eyes. He fumbled for her hand and pressed it. 'I'm sorry, Ann, terribly sorry that I bought you into this.'

She smiled, frightened, but trying to remain courageous. 'It wasn't your fault. I'm quite all right.'

Veronica joined them. She held an unlighted cigarette between her fingers. 'Kenyon,' her voice was quite even, 'got a match?'

He produced a lighter. 'How long,' she asked, 'do you think we've got?'

'Not long,' he confessed. 'If they do set fire to the place we'll have to try and fight our way out, but——Anyhow, I wish to God I'd taken you out of London last night.' The moment he had spoken he regretted his words, for the delay of course was due to Ann, but she still held his hand and now she pressed it.

'I'm sorry, Veronica; I've been an awful fool,' she said.

'Darling, I could not have borne it without another woman!' Veronica announced, puffing at her cigarette; which was a lie anyhow, since she hated the presence of other women if there were men about.

Silas Harker hurried in from the landing. For the first time his placid cheerful face showed real anxiety. 'We're sunk!' he exclaimed to Kenyon, 'they've just set the staircase on fire!'

'Turn on the tap in the bathroom and flood the house,' suggested Veronica.

'There is no bathroom in a place like this,' the American answered tersely, 'and we're for the golden shore unless we can think of something quick!' Without waiting for a reply he left them again and as he opened the door a cloud of smoke billowed into the room.

The acrid fumes caught Veronica in the throat; she coughed and spluttered. 'What shall we do, Kenyon? For God's sake say something; we can't stay here to be burnt alive!'

Wreaths of smoke were creeping under the floor, filtering into the room so quickly that it was already difficult for them to see out of their smarting eyes. It could only be a matter of minutes before they would be driven into jumping from the windows to be seized upon and kicked to death by the frantic crowd below.

At his wits' end Kenyon moved back to the windows; as he leant out a lump of coal sailed past his head. It was not more than a twelve-foot drop to the ground, but the mob stayed there—angry, expectant.

'Hark!' he exclaimed, drawing in his head. As they listened a faint rat-tat-tat came to their ears. 'Machine-guns!' he added suddenly.

'Soldiers!' supplemented Bob. 'If only they're coming this way.'

A low sullen roar like an angry sea came to them from the distance; then the staccato rattle of a machine-gun again, clearer now; a sudden hush had fallen on the crowd outside.

The machine-guns barked again, the sound coming sharp on the night air. Harker came running in. 'The Tommies! he cried, 'd'you hear them?—and they're coming down the street.'

Then Kenyon, craning out of the window, saw the first lorry. It was packed with khaki figures, their bayonets glimmering in the uncertain light as they stabbed at the boldest of the rioters who were trying to cling to the sides and back of the van. It rumbled below the window. Ann, Veronica, and Kenyon leaned out and shouted. 'Help! Hi! Help!'

One soldier looked up and grinned, but they did not stop. At a steady pace the big grey wagon thrust its nose into the crowd and pressed on. A second appeared, apparently loaded with supplies; half a dozen Tommies sat on the top and back systematically prodding with their rifles at any member of the crowd who tried to gain a foothold.

Next to the driver sat an officer, and Kenyon saw at once that he was no ordinary A.S.C. lieutenant, but a member of the General Staff; the peak of his cap bedecked with golden oak leaves and the red tabs on his tunic proclaimed it from the house-tops. He lolled back puffing at a cigarette, but a riding crop lay across his knee, and he used it without hesitation on the faces of anyone bold enough to climb on to the step.

'Help!' they yelled again. 'Help!' But although the officer must have heard them he took not the slightest notice. Then the driver looked up casually at the window, his face changed suddenly, he spoke to the officer and brought the lorry to a halt. The latter glanced up and muttered a quick order, the lorry reversed and bumping its rear wheels on the kerb, pulled up with a jerk on the pavement beneath them.

The crowd welled up against the now stationary vehicle, and brickbats began to fly again, but a third lorry had come into view carrying another load of troops; and a machine-gun was mounted on the driver's seat.

The officer stood up and waved his crop. There was a sudden spurt of flame, and a horrible clatter echoed through the narrow street. For a second the crowd hesitated, but even as they did so the watchers at the window saw the front ranks drop, mown down by the blast of flying lead into a horrible shambles. The gun rattled and coughed, spluttering forth its message of death; the third lorry had drawn up beside the second now, and Kenyon could see the face of the man crouched behind the gun; it was a mask of malicious glee; he was shooting to kill and glorying in the fun, as mad with blood lust as any of the crowd he was executing.

The street cleared with extraordinary rapidity, but in every direction bodies lay huddled in grotesque attitudes, or wounded strove frantically to drag themselves clear of this hellish tornado.

'Come on, cried one of the Tommies. .'What are yer waitin' fer—Christmas Day 'an a well-filled stockin'? Jump, an' we'll catch you.'

Bob led the way, landed on his feet and tripped on the uneven surface of the load under the tarpaulin. The soldiers pulled him to his feet. Then Ann and Veronica were lowered by willing hands until their ankles were on a level with the heads of the troops below.

The officer had climbed down and stood on the pavement superintending the evacuation. The Greyshirts followed one another out of the window; then Kenyon, his eyes smarting abominably from the smoke, looked at the American. Only the two of them remained.

'Go to it!' called Harker, flinging a leg over the window-sill. 'I felt certain we'd get out of that jam some way!' then he let himself drop.

Kenyon was perched on the ledge of the other window, below him on the pavement stood the officer. 'Coming,' he shouted, and jumped. He landed with a thud, the officer caught him with a quick grip of the arm, and as he pitched forward, his nose came in sharp contact with the crossed sword and baton of his rescuer's shoulder.

'Brigadier-General in full war paint,' flashed into his mind, then he heard a quiet voice say: 'I hope you've brought the promised magnum of champagne,' and looking up, found himself staring into the amused face of Gregory Sallust.

10

The Mysterious Convoy

'Keep your mouth shut,' snapped Gregory with a sudden change of face, 'and thank your stars that Rudd spotted Ann at the window; up you go.'

As Kenyon was hauled up he recognised Rudd, under the thin disguise of a khaki uniform, grinning at him from the driver's seat, and suddenly realised that the loaded lorry was the same that he had seen in Gloucester Road that afternoon. Silas Harker was perched on one side of him and Ann on the other.

'Did you see,' she gasped. 'Gregory! What *can* it mean?'

'God knows!' He shook his head. 'But better say nothing.'

'Wasn't that just marvellous luck?' The American slapped his enormous thigh and then waved cheerfully to some of his men who were climbing into the rear lorry. The leading vehicle had halted a hundred yards further along the street and its complement of troops were out in the road dragging the wounded and killed on to the pavement so that the convoy could proceed.

Except for a few of the mob who had crowded back into the scant protection of the doorways, Jamaica Road was almost deserted now. Gregory jumped up into his place, waved his crop and the three lorries got under way again.

A woman on the opposite side of the street hurled a chamber pot from a second floor window. It crashed harmlessly to pieces in the road but without waiting for any order a soldier raised his rifle. There was a loud report, a scream and the woman disappeared. One of the men laughed.

'That was pretty brutal—and unnecessary,' said Kenyon angrily to the sergeant who was sitting back to back with him.

'Can't blame them, sir,' the man replied. 'If you'd been standing by for days on end, while the blighters chucked things at you and not allowed to raise a finger, I reckon you'd do likewise. It's made a power of difference to the boys, having an officer who believes in tit for tat. They'd follow the General anywhere—already.'

'*Already.*' Kenyon turned the word over in his mind. Evidently Brigadier-General Sallust had not been in command of the detachment long; and what the devil could he be doing with them now, anyway? Could he have been posing as a journalist while actually employed by the Military Intelligence? The term journalist could be made to cover a multitude of strange activities. Perhaps that was the explanation, and now that the balloon had gone up he had come out of his chrysalis into his natural splendour of scarlet and gold. But where were they off to convoying Mr. Gibbon's store of groceries under the protection of a platoon of troops? It was all so strange and mysterious that Kenyon had to give up the riddle.

'If only I was not so thin,' Veronica moaned, 'my chassis will be black and blue,' and the hard edges of the cases upon which they were sitting allied to the jolting of the springless lorry was already proving the acme of discomfort.

' 'Alf a sec', miss, we'll soon make you comfy.' A grinning soldier folded his greatcoat into a cushion and utilised those of his comrades as pillows for her back.

'Oh, thanks—thank you most awfully. But are you quite sure you don't need them yourself?'

'Not me, miss; and maybe we're in for a longish run.'

'How too thrilling. I adore motoring at night, but do tell me, where are we going?' Veronica stretched out her slim legs and wriggled comfortably down into her khaki nest.

'Ah! Now you're askin' something.' The man closed one

eye with a knowing wink. 'I can't say fer certain but——'

He settled himself beside Veronica and they continued the conversation in low voices. Kenyon, knowing her so well could imagine the grave face with which she hid her amusement while she led the soldier on to talk.

The lorries rumbled down Union Road but at the corner where Albion Street leads off to the docks and the Blackwall Tunnel, they were forced to slow down. In front of the low dilapidated houses where the street market is held there was a dense mass of people.

Harker touched Kenyon on the shoulder and pointed to the opposite side of the street. 'That's a cheery poster, isn't it?'

'PREPARE TO MEET THY GOD' stood out in letters a foot high on a great hoarding. For the moment it looked as if the crowd meant mischief. They booed and cat-called, but the set faces of the soldiers as they trained their rifles on the mob, obviously only waiting for an order to open fire, overawed even the boldest roughs, and they passed the danger point without a clash.

In the long length of Evelyn Street there were fewer people, only huddled groups gathered here and there on the steps before the dilapidated but still lovely Georgian doorways; yet when they reached its end, it seemed that the whole population of the neighbourhood had gathered in the open space at the entrance of Creek Road. The crowd had evidently broken into the public-house on the corner earlier in the evening, and now they reeled about the pavements, fighting drunk after their unaccustomed orgy of strong spirits.

A black mass of people packed the street from side to side making it impossible to pass, and immediately the leading lorry appeared one or two youths began to throw broken glasses and beer bottles. Without hesitation Gregory Sallust blew his whistle and the machine-guns started their horrid stutter again.

Kenyon noticed that a strange look of blank surprise seemed to come over the faces of the people who were hit, then like puppets whose limbs could not support them, they sagged and fell. With incredible speed the mob faded away, scattering in all directions. One great fat man who was evidently too drunk to stand, remained seated on the pavement, a comical air of fright on his round face as he feebly flapped his hands in a futile endeavour to wave away the bullets; with drunkard's luck he escaped destruction, and was still there hiccoughing and flapping—the only unwounded person in the street—when the lorries moved on again.

Ann had buried her face in the cool tarpaulin directly the shooting began. She felt that she would be physically sick if she witnessed any more slaughter, and she stopped her ears to shut out the screaming of the wounded.

Turning up Church Street and over Deptford Bridge they left the Dockland area for the quiet peacefulness of Blackheath. At a steady pace the lorries forged through the night up the long hill past Woolwich Hospital and on through Welling and Bexley Heath; yet although it was well past midnight every public-house in these outer suburbs had at its doors a little gathering of people wrought to such a pitch of excitement by the events of the last few days that, obviously loath to disperse to their homes, they had forced the landlords to keep open for fear of looting.

At last when they had passed Crayford they were out in the open country, and were able for a few miles to drink in the clear night air purified by its passage through the wooded glades and Kentish gardens; but all too soon they rumbled past scattered houses again, and then down the hill into Dartford.

Here too the people seemed to have no thought of bed, but stood on the pavements eyeing them curiously as they passed, and when they reached the main street they found it crowded. From the way the men began to handle their rifles Kenyon feared that there would be further bloodshed, and when the lorry drew to a halt he peered forward anxiously.

He soon saw that it was not the crowd which caused the delay but a solid barrier of empty cars and vans drawn purposely across the street. A group of men stood near it armed with cudgels, and their leader, a plump, prosperous-looking individual, came forward. Sallust got down to meet him.

'What's under that tarpaulin?' asked the man pompously.

'Supplies,' said Gregory briefly.

'Right! Drive into that yard on the left, will you?'

'What the devil for?'

'To unload. I'm on the Food Committee here, and I have

orders to commandeer everything which is brought into the town.

'Hardly army rations, I think.'

'Yes, everything. The Government is down and out so it's up to each town to fend for itself now. Why should the soldiers be given preference when there are hundreds of starving families within a mile of where I stand?'

'Not to mention yourself, eh?' Sallust's tone had grown suddenly harsh.

'Now, look here, I'd have you know I'm acting on behalf of the Mayor and Corporation.'

'Ho, ho!'

'Yes, and I've plenty of people to support me.' The man jerked his head angrily in the direction of his newly enrolled Civic Guard.

Sallust raised his right eyebrow in symmetry with the left. 'You don't seriously suggest that these people would stand a chance against the rifles of my men, do you?'

'Of course not.' The pompous man drew himself up stiffly. 'But English soldiers would never fire upon law-abiding citizens. If you refuse I shall address them and I have no doubt that they will agree to their food being distributed among the starving women and children of Dartford.'

'Sorry—but I've no time to argue. Tell your people to get that barrier aside at once.'

'Nothing is allowed to pass without permission from the Mayor.'

'To hell with the Mayor!' snapped Gregory, and jerking out his automatic he jabbed it hard into the fat man's stomach. 'Get that barrier moved, d'you hear?'

The Mayor's representative paled and stepped quickly back, but Sallust followed. Several of the Civic Guard advanced with threatening faces, but a good-humoured voice came from the lorry:

'Just a little to one side, if you don't mind, gentlemen; these things is apt to go off sudden, an' somebody might get 'urt.' Mr. Rudd leaned negligently from the driver's seat, a cigarette stuck behind his left ear and a very modern looking pistol dangling loosely from his right hand.

'This is an outrage,' exclaimed the offended citizen.

Sallust ignored him, turning swiftly to the others : 'Do I shoot this bird—or do you move those cars?'

'Better let them through,' said a thin-faced fellow in a bowler hat.

'Right!—get busy then.' Gregory returned his pistol to its holster and smiled suddenly at his late victim; 'Give my love to the Mayor, will you? If I survive I must drop a line to him and recommend you for the Freedom of Dartford—you'd make a good Mayor yourself.'

Veronica let out a hoot of laughter, and glancing up, Sallust gave her a quick, apprising look before clambering back on to the front of the lorry.

Ten minutes later the obstructions had been dragged aside. The convoy moved on its way; another brief sight of the open country beyond the last houses of Dartford, and they were running under the railway bridge into the single street which composes the old waterside village of Greenhithe. No one except Sallust was aware of it, but half a mile beyond the hamlet lay their immediate destination.

He had chosen it for a number of reasons. It was more or less in the direction in which he wished to go yet an oasis off the beaten track, where it was highly improbable that he would find trouble, and thus he could be reasonably certain of securing a few hours' uninterrupted sleep for his men before proceeding further; moreover, having once been a cadet on H.M.S. *Worcester*, which lay off the shore, he knew the country round about which might prove advantageous.

He had even made up his mind as to the quarters he meant to occupy. A large old-fashioned house called Ingress Abbey, said to have been built out of the stones of old London Bridge, which stood sequestered in a dip midst forty acres of its own grounds looking out over the Thames estuary. He had stared at the house so often during the years he had spent in the *Worcester*, wondering who lived there and if they had cakes for tea. It would be amusing now, he thought, to eat the cakes and stare at the old wooden battleship. Of course the house might not be occupied, for who with sufficient income to keep it up would care to live overlooking the mud flats of the Thames—their only neighbours longshoremen and the riff-raff of the seven seas cast up by the world's shipping.

Once through Greenhithe he halted the convoy and took the lead himself—up the steep hill which joins the main road, then round a hairpin bend down the curved black darkness of the Abbey drive shut in by the swaying tree-tops. Out into the open again, the river shimmered dully on their left and the big square house loomed up gaunt and stark among its shrubberies to the landward side, against the pale starlight of the summer night.

The lorries turned and parked with military precision, their bonnets towards the gate, ready to set off at any moment. Gregory sent the sergeant to reconnoitre the house and told Rudd to get enough food out of the lorry to provide a good meal for the troops; then he paraded his force, numbered them off by sixes and selected a guard by making every sixth man take a pace to the front. He posted one sentry on the lorries, and one each to the front and back of the house, then sent the remainder, in charge of a corporal, up to the lodge at the entrance to the drive with instructions that another should be posted on the gate and the balance used as relief every two hours throughout the night.

The sergeant returned to make his report: 'The house is empty, sir, but furnished—might be a school or something from the look of things; I was h'obliged to force an entrance.'

'Very good, sergeant. March the men in. They can occupy the whole of the ground floor. Pick any men you want for fatigues from the Greyshirts.' He swung quickly on Harker: 'You've no objection to that, have you? My men are doing guard.'

'No, that's fair enough,' the American nodded.

Sallust turned to Kenyon, Ann, and Veronica who were standing just behind him; 'We may as well go in. Rudd will have some food for us presently, but I will take a little time to get the fires going, I expect.'

Inside, the soldiers had already flung off their heavy accoutrements and were busy securing the best corners in the downstairs rooms for the night. As Gregory glanced about him he remembered how he used to come down by an early train on rejoining ship the first day of the term, in order to bag the softest mattress, and he smiled good-naturedly at the men. One room on the ground floor, he noted, was a chapel, panelled with lovely old Flemish carving; in the left hand corner by the altar stood a War Memorial. He glanced at it and saw the long list of names, all *Worcester* boys, and the sight stirred a chord of memory in his mind. Of course the whole estate had been taken over years before by the Trustees of the Ship. There was a new fellow commanding too, a V.C., who had gingered up the whole concern; seeing to it that the little pink-faced cadets, who were later to pass into the Navy or officer the great ocean-going liners and British Airways, had, in addition to their seamanship every bit as good an education as could be offered by any public school.

He looked into another room converted into a sick bay and saw with approval that one of the Greyshirts had opened up the medicine chest and was busy treating the cuts and bruises of the wounded.

Rudd had already annexed the Greyshirt, Bob, as his assistant, and they were busy lighting the fire in a room filled with working models of aeroplanes, upstairs, He stood up as Gregory came in.

'Issued the rations?' asked the General.

'Yes, sir! Tinned 'am and beans is wot they get ternight, but I got a little something speshul fer you and the ladies.'

'Good! Did you tell the Corporal of the Guard to keep an eye on that lorry?'

'Yes, sir! Told 'im 'is own muvver wouldn't know 'im termorrer mornin' if there was so much as a pineapple chunk missin' aht of a tin.'

'That's the spirit,' Gregory agreed, as Quartermaster-Sergeant—batman to the General—Lorry Driver—Mr. Rudd left the room. Then he undid his Sam-Browne belt and flung it into a corner while the others sank wearily on to the stiff-backed chairs.

Harker came in. 'I've been having a chat with the boys,' he announced. 'Told them that they'd better muck in with your crowd since we may be together for some little time.'

'Good, we shall be.' Gregory stretched his feet to the blaze. 'What's your name, by and by?'

'Silas Gonderport Harker. What's yours?'

'Gregory Sallust. Do you know these people here—by name, I mean?'

The American shook his head.

'Well, the lady with the big eyes is Ann Croome, and this tall chap is Kenyon Fane.' He looked at Veronica and hesitated. 'I'm not quite certain about you myself?'

'Veronica Wensleadale. I'm Fane's sister,' she added.

'I thought so.' He grinned. 'Well, now we all know each other.'

'You are a queer bird for a British General,' said Harker thoughtfully.

'Any complaints?'

'No, none at all.'

'Right. Do you accept my absolute and unquestioned command of this party, or do you wish to clear out with your men?'

'It suits me to stick to you for the time being if you're willing.'

'Good, then let's get below and see if the men are getting their rations.'

Gregory buckled on his belt again and the American followed him out of the room.

'What *is* he doing in that get-up?' asked Ann directly they had gone.

'Do you know him then?' inquired Veronica.

'Of course. He was living in Gloucester Road. He *said* he was a journalist then.'

'Why worry,' Kenyon shrugged his shoulders wearily. 'He's damned efficient, anyhow.'

Veronica raised her eyebrows. 'But you must admit it's queer.'

'Not really. He must have been doing Secret Service work before.' He sank his head between his hands; it was aching abominably now that the excitement was over.

When Sallust returned he found them sitting in silence, the flickering light of the fire the only relief to the shadows of the room; in another few moments they would all have been sound asleep. Behind him came Rudd, who switched on the lights and began to clear the big table of its charts and models. Ann looked at Gregory and marvelled. His lean face seemed ten years younger and he showed no trace of weariness despite the long day.

Silas Harker appeared carrying a couple of bottles. 'All I could find,' he said. 'The cellar's as dry as a bone so I had to rob the sanatorium.'

'Better than nothing,' Gregory agreed looking at the bottles, 'although I'd give the earth for a quart of champagne.'

Rudd left them again and came back with a steaming dish of sausages and macaroni. 'Sorry, sir,' he apologised, 'but we're out of spuds. There's tinned goosegogs an' a bit of cheese to foller—will that be all right?'

'Excellent.' Sallust drew his chair to the top of the table. 'Let us go in to dinner,' he observed dryly; 'Harker, will you take the bottom of the table and act as Mr. Vice?'

The American's plump face wrinkled into a smile. 'Just what does that mean?'

'Quite simple. After we've fed, Rudd will serve the Invalid Port, I shall stand up and say "Mr. Vice, The King!"—you will then spring smartly to your feet and say: "Ladies and Gentlemen, The King!" upon which we shall all drain a bumper to His Majesty. That clear?'

'Sure,' Harker grinned.

'Right, we shall then, ladies and gentlemen, return the compliment to my second-in-command by drinking the health of the President of the United States—after which we shall sink into a drunken slumber. Let's eat the sausages while they're hot.'

His queer ironic humour had the effect of rousing the others from their lethargy. They had eaten nothing for the best part of twelve hours, and once they tasted food they fell to ravenously.

For twenty minutes they laughed and ate, forgetting for the moment their strange situation. The toasts were drunk as the General had directed, then he lit a cigarette and sank back in his chair.

'We'll get some sleep in a minute,' he announced, 'but first I want to talk to you. I suppose you realise that we are all in an appalling mess?'

A succession of nods greeted his statement.

'Good. Well, quite frankly, I don't want you with me. Women are a handicap at such a time, but when Rudd spotted Ann at that window I couldn't very well leave her to be burnt alive—and my sentimentality having got the better of my common sense, I had to save you all. Having gone so far, if you wish to stay with me I'll take you along, but it's on the understanding that you take your orders unreservedly from me, otherwise you must clear off tomorrow morning and face whatever is coming on your own.'

'I've always adored soldiers,' said Veronica brightly, 'and I should feel so safe under your protection, *Mon Général*.'

'Thank you,' he smiled, 'and since your request, Ann, of a few hours ago to take you with me, seems to have been granted by Providence despite my refusal, I know your answer already. What about you, Fane?'

'My first duty is to the girls. If they are agreed about it I am quite prepared to take my orders from you.'

'Good. Had you any military experience?'

'O.T.C. at Eton.'

Sallust nodded. 'I'm glad of that. You see, present conditions are quite exceptional. Here am I, with the rank of Brigadier and entitled to the command of about four thousand men, stuck in charge of these lorries and a miserable platoon, without even a subaltern under me. But the whole Military Organisation is upside down so it's up to me to act on my own initiative and make the best arrangements that I can. If you travel with us you will have to do your whack, so I propose to appoint you as temporary officer under Harker, who has some sort of claim to the job already, and the two of you can help me run this outfit.'

'Well, I'm a little rusty on my drill, but I'll do my best,' Kenyon agreed.

'That's settled then.' Gregory stood up. 'Now you'd all better get what sleep you can—you two,' he looked swiftly at the girls, 'will occupy the first room that opens on the gallery over the hall. We move off at six-thirty tomorrow—or rather this morning, I should say.'

'Where to?' asked Kenyon.

Gregory Sallust drew a big, official-looking packet from his pocket and smiled at the party. 'Sealed orders,' he said abruptly. 'That's why I'm only in charge of a platoon—but you'll all know more about it this time tomorrow. Good night.'

11

The Taking of the *Shark*

They were all up with the dawn—cold, miserable and still sleepy, their bruises from the night before giving renewed pain, their limbs stiff after the inadequate rest.

The weather had turned. The sky was overcast, and a gentle but persistent drizzle saturated everything. From the windows of the big house the grey sweep of the Thames, rolling towards the sea between the low mud flats, showed a cheerless and uninviting prospect.

After a hurried breakfast Gregory Sallust surveyed the scene through his binoculars. The sloping meadows of his boyhood had been levelled into fine playing fields, but the shipping was almost nil and the only sign of life in the near distance a small tug, about a quarter of a mile from the shore, which seemed to be in difficulties. He could make out two men and a woman on the bridge, but the vessel did not seem to be under power. It floated swiftly, broadside on in the sweep of the tide, turning a little—first to this side, then to that—as fresh eddies caught it. 'Somebody trying to escape to the Continent,' thought Gregory, 'but unable to handle the machinery, or perhaps their supply of fuel has already run out.'

He turned his glasses on H.M.S. *Worcester*, lying at her permanent anchorage just off the foreshore. The old wooden battleship, with her bulging sides neatly painted in longitudinal stripes of black and white, looked silent and deserted. The cadets would be on summer leave, he reflected, and only a skeleton staff of instructors left in charge, hence the tenantless condition of the Abbey.

'All present and correct, sir.' The sergeant saluted stiffly at the door.

'Very good, I'll come down then.' Gregory snapped his binoculars back into their case and glanced at the others. 'We must move off in five minutes, so you'd better come too.'

They followed him meekly downstairs, and stood in a little group on the terrace in front of the house while he walked slowly down the ranks of his men, inspecting each rifle with meticulous care. He then addressed the whole platoon and the detachment of Greyshirts.

'Now men, your own officer has failed to rejoin us, and as I cannot be elsewhere at the same time it is important that I should have assistance in your leadership. Owing to the events of last night the services of one officer—of perhaps unorthodox, but commissioned rank—are available. I refer to Lieutenant Harker of the Greyshirts. We also have Lord Fane, who has been through the O.T.C. Unusual circumstances demand unusual steps, and therefore it is my intention to delegate authority over you to these two gentlemen for, shall we say, the duration!'

The sergeant's mouth twitched and one or two men tittered, Sallust smiled and went on evenly:

'You will treat them in every respect as you would your own officers, so should any unforeseen accident occur to me you will take your orders from Lieutenant Harker, and failing him, from Lord Fane.' He paused, and turning strode towards the others with his curiously unmilitary slouch: 'Mr. Harker, you will take the leading lorry please—Lord Fane, you will take the third and your sister will go with you. Miss Croome, you will come with me. Prepare to mount.' He waved his crop at the detachments; 'Mount!' The lorries jolted their way slowly up the hill, past the lodge, and so out on to the road to Rochester.

Most of the inhabitants of Gravesend were still sleeping after the late night which they had shared with the rest of England. Strood was waking to the dreary day, and as they entered it Ann, who was seated between Gregory and Rudd, asked if they could stop for a moment when they passed a dairy so that she could buy a bottle of milk.

'Do you wonder that I didn't want women on this trip?' said Gregory, but his tone was mocking rather than unkind, and when they passed a creamery he ordered Rudd to pull up.

The shop was open and a short man stood in the doorway; a light brown overall, several sizes too large for him, dangled to his boots.

'Hi! Bring me a couple of quarts of milk, will you?' Gregory called, leaning from his seat.

The short man shook his head. 'Wish I could sir, but I haven't got a drop.'

'All been commandeered for rationing, eh?'

' 'Tain't that, sir, I'm afraid. The farmers won't send it in no more—lots o' people is going to miss the milk bottle from their doorstep this morning!'

'Sorry, Ann—let her go, Rudd.' Gregory was waving a farewell to the dairyman when Ann gripped his arm and drew his attention to a pillar-box on the the other side of the road. The slit had been pasted over and a square, white placard stood out in sharp relief against the red paint. In bold black letters it bore the legend:

'SERVICE TEMPORARILY SUSPENDED.'

In Rochester they tried to secure a paper but none were available. No trains had arrived since the previous afternoon; however, there were plenty of rumours; 'The King was dead again . . . the King was quite recovered . . . the discontented sailors had volunteered in a body as Special Police . . . they had also attempted to burn down Buckingham Palace . . . the Lord Lieutenant of the County had been hanged from the porch of his own house by rioters . . . bombs filled with mustard and chlorine gas were being dropped by aeroplanes on the East End of London . . . the Bank of England had been blown up by International Crooks. . . .'

The last man they spoke to declared that he had it on the very best authority that Field-Marshal Lord Plumer had been assassinated by the Reds.

'You fool!' snapped Gregory angrily, 'he died years ago. Let her go, Rudd.'

They rumbled on under the ancient castle of Bishop Odo, across the Medway Bridge, and so, while it was still early morning, into Chatham.

Sallust's lorry then took the lead and he piloted them straight down to the dockyard's gates. A Marine sentry called on them to halt—then catching sight of Gregory's hat—turned out the guard.

The General dismounted and spoke to the Marine Police sergeant who appeared to hesitate about letting them through without instructions, but Ann caught the words 'with the country in a state like this' and saw Gregory produce his bulky official envelope. The sergeant saluted and had the gates thrown open. Gregory climbed back into the lorry and they jolted down the hill between the lines of cheerless barrack buildings, workshops, and offices.

Leaning forward in his seat Gregory peered sharply from side to side as they advanced, his keen eyes taking in every detail of the naval township which lies hidden behind the high dockyard walls. One big battleship lay seemingly deserted in a far basin, two destroyers in another, and a group of submarines in a third. A sudden swift smile of satisfaction twitched Gregory's thin lips for a second as he caught sight of a single destroyer lying in the lock by the furthest quay—the haze from her funnels showing that she was apparently ready for sea. He ordered Rudd to drive towards her.

A few moments later they pulled up, and Gregory, dismounting, strode over to the gangway. The Quartermaster who stood there came quickly to attention.

'Where's your Commanding Officer?' asked the General.

'He's ashore sir, shall I fetch the officer of the watch?'

'Yes, General Sallust's compliments and he would like to see him at once.'

The sailor disappeared and returned with a short, fair, square-faced naval lieutenant.

'This is the *Shark*, isn't it?' Gregory questioned, although the name was inscribed in bold letters on the lifebuoys.

'Yes, sir.'

'Your Commander is ashore, I understand, but how soon can you be prepared to sail?'

'Sail? Well, I don't know, I'll ask the Executive Officer to speak to you.' The N.O. turned, and sent a messenger for his superior, and a few moments later a Lieutenant-Commander came on deck.

'This is Brigadier-General Sallust,' the Lieutenant introduced Gregory.

The new-comer smiled as they exchanged salutes. 'My name is Fanshawe. What can I do for you, sir?'

'I was inquiring when you will be ready to sail?'

'Sail, sir! But why, may I ask?'

Gregory frowned. 'Didn't you know that you were to act as transport for my men?'

The Lieutenant-Commander looked a little astonished. 'No, I've had no instructions, and the Owner's ashore at present, so is our Engineer Officer. Of course, we are more or less standing by expecting to be ordered up to London, but we were told we should have a couple of hours' warning, and they may not be back for some time.'

'I see, but the matter is of the gravest urgency.'

'We are to take you up the river with us, I suppose?'

'I've no idea.' Gregory drew the bulky packet from his pocket and showed it to the sailor. 'OFFICIAL SECRET—Not to Be Opened Until Out of Harbour' was scrawled across it under the bold lettering, 'O.H.M.S.'

'Sealed orders, eh? Well, sir, the crew is complete, so we could get under way in half an hour, but we must wait for the return of the Captain.'

Gregory frowned. 'That's awkward—I thought you would be expecting us and ready to leave immediately. Anyhow, I'd better get my men on board at once—that will save a little time.'

'We've had no instructions about you here,' demurred Fanshawe, 'but as you say it's so urgent perhaps that would be best.'

'I've got some stores, too—mostly tinned stuff—I wonder if one of your people would be good enough to show my men where to stow them?'

'Certainly, sir—Mr. Broughton!' The Lieutenant-Commander turned to the officer of the watch. 'Show the troops where to stow their stores, please—better use the foremost mess-deck.'

Gregory stepped over the gangway and beckoned Harker to him. 'Tell the men to unload the lorry, and get the stores on board, will you?'

Harker grinned: 'What's the big idea, General? Are you standing us all a Mediterranean cruise?'

'In the interests of discipline, Mr. Harker,' said Gregory with studied coldness, 'I should be glad if you would confine yourself to a prompt execution of orders when on parade. In the Mess, of course, you can express any opinion that you wish.'

A queer look came into Silas Gonderport Harker's eyes. First anger, then surprise, and finally amusement tinged with a flicker of respect. 'As you say, sir.' He brought his heels together with a click and marched back to the waiting men.

The lorry was speedily unloaded, and the supplies carried on board, the sailors giving every assistance. Veronica with Ann behind her came up the gangway.

'Er—excuse me,' the Lieutenant-Commander spoke in a rapid, low-voiced aside to Gregory, 'these ladies—are they —er—to be in the party?'

'Yes, worse luck,' Gregory's tone was bitter and the stare with which he regarded the women left no doubt in the naval officer's mind as to his extreme disapproval of their presence.

'It's a bit irregular, isn't it, sir?' he hazarded.

'Damnably so, but instructions were passed from M.I.5 to take them along, so I had to lump it—better send 'em below somewhere, hadn't we?'

The sailor accepted the glib lie with an understanding nod and cocked an appreciative eye at Ann. He did not appear to share Gregory's apparent misogyny. 'I'll take them below to the wardroom,' he volunteered.

As Fanshawe turned away Gregory gave a swift glance along the jetty. No sign of the Captain yet—Broughton was busy with the stores and troops—the quarter-deck free of officers for the moment. He caught the eye of Rudd, who was standing near, and strolled casually up to the starboard ladder to the bridge. Rudd followed.

For two very fully occupied minutes Gregory was in the wireless room, while Rudd lolled close to its entrance. By the time the Lieutenant-Commander returned from below, the General was standing once more by the rail on the quarter-deck watching the approaches to the lock.

'Look here,' he addressed the sailor anxiously—'how soon can we move off?'

'I've got to wait for my Captain, sir.'

'Yes, yes, I know, but you don't seem to appreciate the urgency of the situation. This ship should have been ready and waiting to take me and my men to sea at once. If you've had no instructions someone's made a bloomer at the Admiralty and they will get it in the neck.'

Fanshawe smiled: 'That's hardly my fault, sir.'

'Of course not, but I must carry out my instructions—can't you get her ready to move off directly the Captain does turn up?'

'Yes, there's no reason we shouldn't do that.' He turned to his petty officer: 'Quartermaster, call the hands, stations for getting under way—ask the engine-room to tell me how soon they will be ready—it's urgent, so skip!'

Broughton, who was standing near them hurried forward. Gregory kept an anxious eye on the jetty while preparations were being made but there was still no sign of the Captain, when, some twenty minutes later, the Lieutenant reported to the Lieutenant-Commander that the ship was ready to proceed.

Gregory, who was standing near shook his head with a worried frown: 'If that Captain of yours doesn't turn up soon,' he observed quietly, 'we shall have to leave without him.'

'But we can't possibly do that, sir,' said the Lieutenant-Commander in a shocked voice.

'Why?' asked Gregory, 'surely you can navigate the ship yourself?'

'Oh, yes, Broughton and my other lieutenant and I can do that between us, it's not that.'

'I see, but of course your Engineer Officer is ashore as well, isn't he? Is that the trouble?'

'No, not exactly, but——'

'Well, what is it then?' Sallust cut him short impatiently. 'I understand you to say that you had a complete crew.'

'Yes, nearly eighteen of them are in irons at the moment, we had rather a bother with them last night—demonstration in sympathy with those bad eggs in the Battle Squadron; normally they would be in prison on shore, but instructions were to keep them here for the time being. We had a bit of bad luck with our Gunner this morning too—the front wheel of his push bike got in a tramline and he went over the handlebars—they've detained him in hospital on shore, but of course I could manage easily with the rest.'

'Then for goodness' sake let me get on with my job.'

'I'm sorry, but I've already told you, sir—I can't sail until my Captain turns up. I have no official order—unless you've got one you can show me from a Naval Authority?'

'Of course I haven't.' Sallust spoke with unusual heat. 'I received my orders verbally from Eastern Command when they handed me the packet I showed you, but you should have had your instructions from the Naval people here in the early hours of the morning.'

'Quite, sir, but you do see my position, don't you?'

'Now look here, Commander,' Gregory had suddenly become very amiable again, 'I quite appreciate that it is an awkward situation for you, but there's a war on you know—or its equivalent at all events. The Goverment seems to have got the country into a ghastly mess and now it's looking to the Services to pull it out. It's my job to get my troops wherever they're ordered at the earliest possible moment—you must understand the urgency of the matter. I appeal to you as a brother officer to get this ship under way without any further delay.'

The Lieutenant-Commander smiled, obviously sympathetic towards the General's anxiety to be off. 'I'm sorry, sir, it's quite impossible—I can't put to sea without my Captain. I tell you what though! I'll slip over to the signal station and try and get him on the telephone; it's not a long job, and if I can't get in touch with him I'll ring up the Secretary's office at Admiralty House and ask if any instructions have come through.'

'Splendid!' Gregory grinned suddenly. 'That's awfully good of you—I wish you would.'

'Righto! I won't be five minutes.' With a friendly wave of his hand Fanshawe disappeared over the side.

Gregory paced slowly up and down the quarter-deck. His lean, rather wolfish face showed a nervy satisfaction, but his sharp eyes were never off the jetty for more than a moment, and when the Lieutenant-Commander reappeared he walked quickly over to the gangway to meet him.

'It's all right, sir,' came the cheerful hail, 'I haven't found my Captain but I can explain why those orders never came through!'

'Can you? That's good,' Gregory nodded.

'Yes, all the wires are down and the private line's been cut, so they are sending dispatches by road and one of the cars was wrecked outside Strood round about two o'clock this morning. The Secretary at Admiralty House seemed to think instructions about your party must have been among that bunch.'

'I see, but he agreed to our sailing at once.'

'Well, he could hardly do that himself, and when he went in to see the Admiral the old man was so up to his eyes in it that he couldn't get anything very definite, but he says General Instructions are that where communications have broken down officers will be expected to act on their own initiative, rather than remain idle, and that every opportunity should be taken to act in conjunction with the sister services—so in an emergency like this, I think that lets me out.'

'Good for you. Then I'll slip down to the wardroom for a moment if you don't mind.'

A pleasant smile spread over Fanshawe's face. 'Rather, sir, and I think we'd better make you an honorary member of the Mess.'

'Thanks,' Gregory tapped his pocket. 'When we're clear of the lock I'll come up again and we'll open these orders.' Then he went below.

The orders when opened caused Fanshawe considerable surprise. They were not destined for London after all but ordered to proceed to a point some miles east of the Goodwins, and there to lie-to until nine o'clock the following morning, at which hour a second set of sealed orders, enclosed in the first, were to be opened.

The naval man thought it devilish queer—so apparently did Gregory, but he suggested that possibly they had been detailed to act as escort to some personage of importance who was leaving the country in a yacht, and who intended to rendezvous with them there.

However, the orders were definite, so His Majesty's destroyer *Shark* proceeded down the Medway, and making her pendants to the signal station at Garrison Point put out—under these somewhat strange conditions—to sea.

It was now obvious that the troops would have to spend at least one night on board, so arrangements were made by which that portion of the crew quartered on the lower mess deck handed it over to the soldiers, and mucked in temporarily with their shipmates on the upper. Ann and Veronica were allowed to occupy the absent Captain's cabin, and Gregory that of the Engineer Officer; Kenyon and Silas Harker that of the Gunner.

The weather clearing they were able to spend most of the afternoon on deck, and the Tommies seemed already on the friendliest terms with the men of the sister Service.

Fanshawe excused himself from dining that evening by saying that he had an urgent matter to attend to on deck, and Broughton was again officer of the watch, so Mr. Cousens—a tall, freckle-faced lieutenant with a pleasant smile, played host in the wardroom.

They discussed the many rumours and catastrophic events until, the port having gone round the table, Cousens stood up and bowed to the girls. 'I hope you'll forgive me, but I go on at midnight, so I must snatch an hour or two's sleep.' He smiled round in the others; 'Please ask the steward for anything you want.'

When he had left them Gregory signed to Rudd, who had been helping to wait on them, to shut the wardroom trap hatch which communicated with the pantry, then he lay back in his chair at the bottom of the table.

'Filthy port, isn't it?' he remarked casually, 'still, that's no fault of the Navy; just hard luck on the poor devils that they can't take vintage wine to sea, the constant rocking breaks the crust and turns it into mud.'

Kenyon shrugged. 'It's not too bad, I like a wood port

for a change; but I was wondering where we shall be this time tomorrow.'

'This time tomorrow!' the General echoed. 'Well, I can give you a very good idea. If the weather is reasonably favourable we shall be heading westward—a hundred miles or more south of the Isle of Wight.'

'My hat!' exclaimed Veronica, 'we're not going out into the Atlantic in this cockleshell, are we?'

'We are, my dear; so you'd better make up your mind to it.'

'Ye Gods! But I shall die.'

'I trust not.'

'Tell us, General,' Harker leaned forward across the narrow table, 'just how do you happen to know what's in that second set of secret orders?'

'I ought to,' Sallust replenished his glass with a second ration of the despised port, 'since I was responsible for planning this expedition.'

They all regarded him with quickened interest as he went on slowly: 'I realised that these Naval birds would never swallow the whole draught at one gulp, that's why I allowed for a twenty-four hour interval before opening the second lot. Fortunately, as it turns out now, that gives me a chance to put you wise concerning my intentions.'

'*Your* intentions?' inquired Kenyon with peculiar emphasis.

'Yes, *my* intentions; which are—with due respect to oil consumption and the hazard of picking up fresh supplies —to run this hooker down to the West Indies just as soon as ever I can.'

'The West Indies!' Kenyon frowned. 'The War Office must be crazy to send troops out of the country at a time like this.'

'Oh, the War Office had nothing to do with it,' said Gregory mildly. 'I'm acting entirely on my own initiative.'

'What! You had no orders about proceeding somewhere in this ship!'

'No—none at all.'

'But—damn it, man, you boarded her and ordered the ship to sea; do you mean you had no authority to do that?'

'None, my dear boy. None whatever, I assure you.'

'Good God, Sallust! You can't be serious!'

'I was never more serious in my life.'

The eyes of the whole party were riveted on Gregory's face in amazement, anger and alarm, then Kenyon suddenly burst out: 'But you can't do this sort of thing, you simply can't. Using your own initiative is one thing, but this is nothing less than running away. You're a soldier, and if you've no right here you ought to be on duty somewhere else.'

The General sipped his port, then the furrows round his mouth deepened a little as he smiled: 'Dear me, no. When I got out of the Army last time I determined that nothing should ever induce me to enter it again. This outfit—' he patted his buttoned tunic—'and Rudd's were supplied by my old friend the theatrical costumier—Willie Clarkson.'

12

Piracy

For a moment there was absolute silence while they all stared a little stupidly at Gregory, dumbfounded by this staggering revelation, and endeavouring to assess what effect his criminal proceedings might have upon themselves. Kenyon was the first to recover. 'This is piracy,' he announced abruptly, getting to his feet.

'Is it? Yes, I suppose it is.' Gregory calmly lit another cigarette.

'And you can be hanged for it; do you realise that?'

'Perhaps; but they've got to catch me first.'

'That won't take long directly Fanshawe learns the truth.'

'Oh! You seem to have forgotten the presence of my troops.'

'Yes, I've been wondering about that,' said Ann softly. 'How did you get hold of them, Gregory?'

'Would it amuse you to hear?' Sallust grinned openly with a certain pride in his achievement.

'I think it's more important that we should get this situation cleared up without delay.' Kenyon spoke sharply.

'Why worry?' the American cut in lazily. 'The ship's only cruising round—has been for hours, so we're not going further away, and this sounds like a great story to me. 'Let's have it—er General.'

'All right.'

Kenyon sat down again reluctantly.

'Well, if Fane can bottle up his desire to have me hanged for five minutes, I'll tell you.' Gregory puffed at his cigarette and smiled round at them. 'You see I made up my mind years ago that in the event of a real break up, the only road to safety lay in assuming the outward trappings of authority. Of course there was the sporting chance that the mob might single me out for an immediate hanging—but if I could once get going the world was mine—or at all events everything which happened to be left of it.'

Harker grinned appreciatively, as Sallust went on: 'Having planned the whole show so far in advance it wasn't difficult really. Rudd and I knew of a small garage in Elvaston Place that housed several lorries. We knew too that the owner lived down at Brighton, and he couldn't get up to London. We snaffled three of them in the afternoon and made a few alterations with a couple of pots of paint. Some of you saw one of them I think loaded up outside Gloucester Road. After that we changed into our uniforms, took one of the empties up to some barracks that I had in mind and parked it a little way down the street. We had to wait there for nearly three hours, but at last some troops marched out—a company, as luck would have it, although I only needed a platoon. I tackled the Captain. Told him I had to have a certain number of his men immediately. Naturally he was a bit doubtful what to do at first, just like our friend who is taking his exercise up on the bridge, but you know what it was like in London last night—everybody a bit excited and pulling too quick a stroke. I utilised the name of his own Colonel which I made it my business to find out and of course he imagined that I was a full blown Brigadier, so after a very short discussion he gave way and I went off with the boys crammed like sardines in the lorry. At Elvaston Place we distributed them among the other two vans, then we proceeded in accordance with plan to advance on Chatham.'

'Good God!' Kenyon sat back suddenly. 'But wasn't there an officer with the platoon? What happened to him?'

'Oh, certainly.' Gregory gave a chuckle of enjoyment. 'I kept him with me for half an hour, and then packed him off with an urgent message to the War Office—he's still there, for all I know.'

Silas nodded. 'It was a great performance, but I wonder at you being able to pull the same bluff twice.'

'What, Chatham you mean? Yes, that was the crucial point of the whole campaign, but as a journalist I got myself taken round the Dockyard some time ago, and the visit gave me a knowledge of the regulations which are observed before a ship is allowed to put to sea, so I had half a dozen different lines of bluff ready to meet the most probable emergencies. I banked very largely upon their being in a state of chaotic muddle, the appearance of troops giving weight to my request which it could never have had from a single man—and the staff at Admiralty House being dead-tired after such a night. That's one reason why I delayed my arrival until this morning.'

'I wonder we haven't been recalled by wireless by this time though,' Kenyon remarked.

Gregory laughed suddenly. 'No, it's not working. That was a really masterly touch. I managed to remove some of the essential parts within ten minutes of coming on board.'

'Fanshawe must have thought that pretty queer when it was reported.'

'He did, but I persuaded him that it must have been one of the mutineers last night, or a sympathiser early this morning.'

Two bright spots of colour had appeared in Veronica's usually pale cheeks. After a moment's silence she said suddenly: 'And you have the face to sit there and tell us quite calmly that you have taken all these men away from their duty when the country's on the verge of revolution?'

'I have, dear lady. These troops and this destroyer are at the present time engaged solely upon the very important duty of securing the safety of Brigadier-General Gregory Sallust—' he paused for a moment with his chin stuck out as he looked challengingly round the table '—and that of those friends whom he delights to honour.'

'My hat, what a party!' Veronica flung her hands above her head and did an excellent imitation of a faint.

'I wish to God you'd told me this before,' said Kenyon seriously.

'Why?'

'Well, naturally I should never have dreamt of lending myself to such a scheme. It's not only criminal—it's treason. Nothing less than stabbing the Government in the back when they need every man they've got to keep order.'

'Stop talking hot air and be honest with yourself, Fane. The Government has ceased to exist already. How could they hope to survive with the machinery of supply and control cracking up in every direction? Surely you don't suggest that a few thousand troops could keep a population of fifty million starving people permanently in subjection, do you? And as a matter of fact, the troops themselves are starting to give trouble. There was a mutiny at Aldershot yesterday. That was the last piece of authentic news I had from old Jolliat, the editor, before I left the office of my paper. Actually this particular platoon should thank their stars that I've got them out of it along with myself.'

'Perhaps—but even if you're right there is such a thing as principle.'

'I see, and so, my noble squire of dames, you think I should have taken my chances of starvation or death with the rest of the fools, and have left these poor devils of soldiers to turn into a gang of bandits—roaming the countryside and adding to the general misery, eh? I wonder where you would be now if I had.'

'Dead,' Kenyon admitted, 'I haven't a doubt about that, but all the same I don't see how we can go on wrongfully detaining Government troops and a ship.'

'Well, what do you propose to do about it?'

Kenyon looked wretchedly uncomfortable. 'I don't know,' he confessed. 'I hate ingratitude and since you saved us all it would be a pretty bad show to get you put under arrest, especially in view of what's likely to happen to you; but unless you are prepared to order the ship back to port I feel that it is up to me to let Fanshawe know where he stands.'

Gregory smiled amiably. 'Before you actually send the balloon up I think it would be interesting to hear a few other views. What does Lady Veronica feel about it?'

She looked at him steadily and then she said: 'I agree with Kenyon that apart from the question of our personal gratitude you ought to be shot for what you've done, but there is a sort of half truth in your specious excuses about the troops being useless where they were with the whole country in chaos; the great point is, that right or wrong you've done it now, and I for one have no desire to be dumped back on the quay at Chatham. Last night was quite enough slumming for this child. I shall probably die of seasickness, but I'd rather chance that and take a trip to the West Indies with you.'

Sallust nodded. 'A most sensible summing up of the situation. What about you, Ann?'

'I agree with Veronica. What you've done may be frightfully wrong theoretically, Gregory, but fifty soldiers and one destroyer aren't going to save England from anarchy, and since you've saved us once already I think we can't do better than trust in you again.'

'A delightful vote of confidence, my dear.' He grinned and turned to Silas. 'Do you want to beat your little drum, Harker, and see me clapped in irons?'

The American's large humorous face had grown very grave as he replied: 'I think I'd like to have a word with Fane alone before I give any answer to that.'

'All right, go ahead; you'd better use the lobby, but wait—' Gregory held up his hand as they both rose from the table. 'I'd be glad if you will remember that I personally have not the least intention of returning to England, and that I only brought you along as a kindness. Moreover, I have the best part of sixty men under my command; they, at least, would never believe your story, and are prepared to carry out my orders to the letter. If through your interference Fanshawe cuts up rough there's going to be blue hell on this ship—get that?'

'Do you really mean that you would go to the length of ordering your troops to fire on Fanshawe's sailors?' asked Kenyon horrified.

'That's it; and Fanshawe wouldn't stand a chance against me even if he had twice the numbers, but in the meantime the ship would become a shambles, and after, unless I could persuade sufficient sailors to come over to my side, we should probably be wrecked. Worst of all I just might be killed myself. I say worst of all, not out of any personal conceit, but because as long as I remain alive there is a reasonable prospect of discipline being maintained. Without me—well, you've got a half-mutinous crew already, and I'm not altogether satisfied about one or two of my own men. Now—out you go, and just consider the sort of thing that might happen to your sister and Ann here in such circumstances, then come back and tell me if you still think it's up to you to go putting a match to the powder barrel.'

The conference in the lobby was brief. 'He's got us,' said Kenyon shortly. 'At least he's got me. Principles or no principles I can't run the risk of exposing the girls to any horrors like that.'

The American loomed immense and lofty even over Kenyon's height. 'He means it too,' he said seriously. 'He'll loose hell on this ship if he meets with any opposition, and he's right about the possibility of mutiny. I'd been counting that in myself.'

'Yes. He seems to be one of those exceptional egoists who really have the courage to throw all established ideas overboard and carry their theories into practice regardless of the cost.'

Harker's blue eyes twinkled. 'He's a proper blackguard, but I like the man; this sort of thing needs guts.'

'It does. He's just the sort of chap I'd follow anywhere if only his authority were legitimate.'

'What's the odds?' Silas's full-lipped mouth crumpled into a smile. 'We're either for him or against him, and if it's "for" we'd best back him for all we know, and put our scruples right behind us.'

'Yes. If we go to Fanshawe now things will blow up for certain, and if we don't we'll be liable anyhow to the same penalties as Sallust if his plans break down; so the sensible thing seems to do our damndest to help him pull this mad venture through.'

'Sure, I'm glad you see it as I do. Let's get back, shall we?'

Kenyon nodded. 'Righto! I only hope we don't have trouble with the sailors after all.

'Don't worry.' Silas ducked his head quickly as he stepped through the wardroom door. 'If we stick together we'll see this party through.'

'Well?' Gregory raised his left eyebrow with cynical inquiry.

'Having registered our protests we are going to forget it,' said Kenyon, 'and accept your leadership without further question.'

Silas squeezed himself back into his chair. 'That's so, General, and for the duration, as you call it, you can count on us.'

One of those rare smiles lit up Sallust's face. 'I'm glad,' he said slowly. 'It makes a world of difference to have your voluntary support, although I don't mind telling you now you would never have got as far as Fanshawe. The sentries in the passage outside the lobby had their instructions before we sat down to dinner.'

Kenyon smiled. 'I see; that's why you had them posted, eh? Although Fanshawe seemed to think it a mad idea to put sentries outside a mess.'

'A General Officer is entitled to his guard, my friend,' Sallust replied lightly. 'But now we're all agreed, what about some more port? A toast to a happy and successful voyage.'

Rudd hastened forward with a new decanter, and the toast was drunk, then Veronica leaned towards Gregory: 'Were you serious about taking us to the West Indies?'

'Perfectly, have you any preference for any particular island?'

'I've always wanted to go to the West Indies,' Ann announced unexpectedly.

'Good,' he nodded. 'Well, I favour Haiti myself, it's native owned—or one of the smaller islands. Dominica perhaps—I've friends there; you see complications might arise if we turned up at Jamaica or Cuba.'

'But why the West Indies?' Veronica protested. 'Think of the voyage in this armoured speed-boat. There's so much engine to it they haven't even room for a bathroom.'

He shrugged. 'Europe is impossible, and the African coast presents all sorts of unpleasant problems. In the Indies there is an excellent climate; very few poisonous reptiles in the better islands, an abundant variety of fruit, and excellent deep-sea fishing. What more do you want?'

'But my dear man, you don't expect us to live on the beach, do you?'

'Why not? All towns will be dangerous for a year or two to come—until the world settles down again with a considerably reduced population. Even after the bloodshed stops there will be starvation and every sort of ghastly pestilence. Our only hope as I see it is to find a garden of Eden for ourselves and sit in it playing contract for shark's teeth.'

'What! live in the woods like savages?'

'Not quite. My reason for commandeering troops was not only for my own protection. I don't doubt that I could have got out of England on my own, but I should hate to live on a desert island, however fruitful, in complete solitude, and with organised labour one can do anything. Build houses, dig gardens, assure oneself an adequate and regular supply of food, and protect oneself from possible hostility of the inhabitants—if any. These Tommies are to act the role of numerous Man Fridays to my Crusoe.'

'My God, you've got a nerve!' exclaimed Veronica.

'But surely,' Kenyon cut in, 'they're bound to realise that you are not acting on instructions once you get them on the other side.'

'Of course, but I shall offer them a choice. To return to England in the ship with Fanshawe or to stay with me. These chaps are not fools, Fane. They will have been under my orders for three weeks or a month by then, and since a natural gift for leadership has been thrust upon me by a kindly and all-seeing Providence, nine-tenths of them will stay under their self-appointed Commander rather than face a return to the uncertainties of England. In fact, I expect most of the sailors will stay too, perhaps this ship will never go back. If not we'll see if we can't find some method to refine crude oil or perhaps convert one of the engines. If we could we'd turn her into a private yacht.'

'As I see it you're out to start a brand new Colony,' remarked Harker. 'And I think it's a great idea.'

'That's it, "Hesperides" we'll call it. The Golden Isle where all is peace under the benign reign of King Sallust the First—that's me. You will form my natural aristocracy and the lads shall be the population.'

'I've a notion that you'll have a spot of trouble with one ot two of them first.'

'I expect so. That's why in a way I would rather that the ship went back. It would take any discontented elements with it. As it is I anticipate having to make a few drastic examples. That red-faced fellow Brisket is a bad egg, I'm sure, so is the bird with the protruding teeth. Sanders, I think his name is, but I'm not certain. I haven't been with them long enough to get all their names pat yet.'

'What is the drill tomorrow?' asked Kenyon.

'You'd better take Orderly Officer, Fane. First parade six-thirty. Inspect their turn out and create hell if any of them are unshaven or slipshod in their dress. Then run 'em round the deck for ten minutes, follow-my-leader fashion, to get their circulation going. After that an hour's physical drill. Second parade nine o'clock, rifle inspection. I'll take that myself.'

'Very good, sir.'

'I'll rough out some sort of plan this evening for the day's routine, then we must put our heads together as to how to vary it a bit. The men must be kept busy, interested and amused during the voyage. That will keep them fit, help to preserve discipline and enable all of us to get to know each of them personally. Besides, regular healthy occupation is the strongest antidote against discontent.'

Harker gave his slow smile. 'You certainly have the right idea how to handle a job like this.'

'Then amusements,' Gregory went on with a little nod. 'We'll arrange a sing-song for tomorrow night I think. You might attend to that, Harker. Find out what local talent we've got amongst our own men, then get Fanshawe or Broughton to co-operate and rope in some of the tars as well—excellent way of getting the two lots on a friendly footing. We might try and fix a gymkhana for the following afternoon, high jumps, obstacle race round the deck and all that sort of thing—then a boxing contest the following night.'

'Thank goodness I'm not a man,' Ann murmured to Veronica.

'I know, darling, I detest organised games.'

Harker's curiously musical accent covered the aside. 'When do you mean to open these marvellous secret orders—officially—General?'

'After nine o'clock inspection. All my men will be on deck and under arms then.'

'You've a feeling that the naval bird may not stand for it, eh?'

Gregory smiled slightly. 'Well, as Fane said a little time ago, it's hardly rational that the Government should send troops to the West Indies with a Revolution going on at home—and if they did it's not usual to send them in a destroyer. However, I've got quite a good story in my head for Fanshawe because I thought this whole party out a very long time ago. I only hope for his own sake that it convinces him.'

'*Himmel*!' cried Veronica suddenly.

'What is it?' came a chorus of surprised exclamations.

'I've just thought, darlings, what in the world shall we do for clothes?'

With the exception of Gregory they all burst out laughing, but he eyed her gravely. 'I thought you told me this afternoon that you were a devil with a needle.'

'So I am, what of it?'

'Well, we can't afford to carry passengers on a trip like this, everyone must earn their keep in some way. Ann's quite a useful cook, so with Rudd's assistance and a couple of orderlies to do the dirty work she'll be able to pull her weight, but your only accomplishment being sewing I'd thought of you as seamstress for the party; there will be several score socks to mend.'

'Take him away somebody or I shall faint,' Veronica covered her eyes with her hands as though to shut out this nightmare vision, but they only laughed the more as Gregory went on: 'When the socks give out you shall make a sweet little grass skirt for each of us; decency, like discipline, must be maintained.'

As the laughter subsided Kenyon found Ann smiling at him for the first time since she had visited Grosvenor Square.

'You know,' she said, 'I'm looking forward to life on an island. I think it's all going to be wonderful fun.'

'Do you, Ann. I—' but his sentence was cut short by the sudden entrance of Lieutenant-Commander Fanshawe. He looked more square-jawed than ever and there was an angry light in his eyes as he flung at Sallust:

'I've been busy on the wireless and now we've got it going again.'

'Have you? that's splendid.' Gregory's tone was mild as milk but his eyes suddenly narrowed and his hand fell casually to his belt, just above the pistol holster. Mr. Rudd appeared, silent and watchful in the doorway of the wardroom, behind the Lieutenant-Commander. His hand slipped under a newly-acquired apron.

'Yes,' said Fanshawe harshly, 'and we've picked up Chatham. They say that no orders have been passed to C.-in-C. Nore, and that they've never heard of Brigadier-General Sallust. My instructions are to return to port at once.' As he finished speaking they felt the engines beginning to throb. The destroyer had leapt from cruising to full speed ahead.

13

The Bluff is Called

'I gather that you have already given the necessary orders,' said Gregory.

'Yes.'

'Without consulting me?'

'I don't have to.' The Lieutenant-Commander's voice was grim.

Sallust nodded. 'All right. Still, I want to talk to you and it might as well be now; sit down and join me in a glass of port.'

'Thank you, no! I have to return to the bridge.'

'Why; is there no one up there now?'

'Yes, the officer of the watch, Broughton.'

'Then there is no need for you to return at once; sit down for a minute.'

Fanshawe regarded Gregory with an angry stare, his chin thrust out, his bushy eyebrows drawn together. 'Look here,' he replied, 'I don't know what your game is. A Brigadier in charge of a platoon, with a couple of officers who aren't officers at all and two ladies attached; but one thing's clear—you've got no right on board this ship. You jollied me into leaving port against my better judgment and I'll be lucky if I'm not court-martialled for this trip; anyhow you'll have the chance of explaining to the authorities directly we arrive, but in the meantime I and the officers under me do not propose to hold any further communications with you at all. Understand?'

'That's a pity,' said Gregory affably; 'because we are going to be cooped up in this ship together for quite a little time.'

'What the devil do you mean?'

'Simply this. We are going to adhere to our first instructions and if you think it over you will see why.'

'I'm hanged if I do!'

'Don't you? Then it has obviously not occurred to you that these orders you have just received by wireless may be faked. It is highly probable that the Communists have taken over at Chatham by now.'

The sailor made an angry noise; half-grunt, half-laugh. 'What rot! Besides they wouldn't be able to use the Admiralty code even if they had!'

'Oh? What about the mutineers in the fleet?'

'We're not all fools, you know; they will have been dealt with by now.'

'All right then; in that case your new orders can only be the result of some blunder on the part of Higher Command.'

'Thank you, they are quite plain, and in these waters it would be difficult to get higher authority than C.-in-C. Nore.'

'Perhaps.' Gregory rose slowly to his feet and stood, passing the tip of his tongue backwards and forwards between his lips while he eyed the sailor with a queer meditative look; then he added suddenly: 'But he's not quite high enough for me. I don't want trouble but I intend to carry out my mission.'

'Trouble?' the Lieutenant-Commander picked him up: 'I shouldn't advise you to start it! I left instructions with the officer of the watch exactly what to do if I failed to return to the bridge ten minutes after I left him.'

'Did you? How thoughtful.' Gregory was almost purring now. 'Well, time is nearly up so you had better beat it, hadn't you?'

'*I'm* going all right—but you and your party will kindly remain here until we get in.'

'Am I to understand that you are placing us under arrest?'

'Understand what you like, but I am in command of this ship and those are my orders.'

'All right; Rudd!' Gregory's voice was curt. 'The door, for the Commander.

'Yes, sir.' Rudd's eyes had never left Sallust's face, now he forced his way quickly in front of Fanshawe and gripped the knob of the wardroom door; as the sailor turned he was between them.

The whole thing was over so quickly that the others, seated at the table behind Gregory, hardly saw what happened. His arm seemed to shoot out with a vicious jab, his fist thudded on the flesh below the naval officer's ear, and Rudd, with a muttered 'easy now,' caught the body as it fell.

'You brute!' Veronica was on her feet, her eyes blazing,

but Ann was first beside the unconscious sailor, kneeling by him and pillowing his head in her lap.

'Shut up!' snapped Gregory. 'You didn't want me to shoot him, did you? Rudd, nip into the pantry quick, and get that steward out of the way; send him forward to get some rum or some damn thing. Fane, take charge of the two men in the passage, let no one pass. Harker, give me a hand to get this bird on the settee.'

Between them they carried Fanshawe over to the side of the wardroom and propped him up with cushions. Gregory rolled up one of his eyelids and gave a grunt of satisfaction. 'He won't give us any trouble for a bit.' Then he stood thoughtfully rubbing his own knuckles while the girls fussed over the unconscious man.

'What about the officer on the bridge?' asked Harker. 'That ten minutes is back with Omar Khayyam's seven thousand years by this time.'

'I know; we've go to do something pretty quick. Slip up on to the bridge will you, Harker; tell Broughton that Fanshawe sent you; that we are discussing the situation quite amicably down here and that he is to take no action for the moment.'

'Do you think he'll believe me?'

'Got to chance it; come back as soon as you can and let me know how he takes it. If they try to arrest you, you must use your gun; we've gone too far to turn back now.'

Silas opened his round eyes with a comically rueful look, then shrugged and left them.

Rudd reappeared in the door of the wardroom. 'I sent the steward to find the brandy out o' Mr. Gibbon's stores,' he reported.

'Brandy? I didn't know old Gibbon had a licence?'

'Nor 'e 'ad, sir; that's why 'e lorst most of 'is customers to 'Arrods.'

'Then—?' Gregory frowned, his mind on the bridge with Silas.

Rudd grinned at him. 'Finding that there conyak's goin' ter take the steward a bit of time!'

'Good boy. I wish to God though that we had got a bottle of good brandy, especially as I've got to be up all night!'

'Plenty o' whisky in the pantry, sir; can I get you a peg?'

'Yes, do; then take over from Lord Fane in the passage and ask him to come in here.'

While Rudd was getting the whisky Gregory paced slowly up and down, ignoring the two girls whose whisperings by the sailor was for the moment the only sound other than the hissing of the waters, as the destroyer ran on into the night. He gulped the drink down when it arrived and drew a deep breath of satisfaction. A moment later Kenyon appeared; his face was unusually grave and he spoke sharply. 'Look here, Sallust, I've had about enough of this business; outing Fanshawe like that was a rotten trick.'

'Swallow a camel and strain at a gnat! Is that the idea?' Gregory swung round on him with an angry look. 'Don't be a fool, Fane. I haven't hurt him seriously and it was the only thing to do. Anyhow I'm not going to argue about it with you now.'

Suddenly Ann gave a quick, nervous laugh.

'What is it?' snapped Gregory.

'I was only thinking how funny it is to hear Kenyon lecture you after his own performance in Gloucester Road.'

'All right,' Kenyon's mouth tightened grimly. 'We're all in it up to the neck now, so I suppose we'd better get on with it. What's the next move?'

'We've got to deal with the other officers before they have a chance to start in on us with the crew; knock them out or lock them up somewhere. Once they're out of the way I'll manage the men.'

'How can you?' cried Veronica. 'Your Napoleonic act was great fun in its way, my dear, but even Boney would have found himself up against it if he had tried to run a ship!'

Sallust raised his only movable eyebrow. 'A poor comparison, I fear, unjust to both Bonaparte and myself. I could never have drafted the Code Napoleon, but I can certainly navigate a ship.'

'You don't really mean that, do you?' said Ann.

'I do; it happens that I was educated in the *Worcester*, so although my navigation is a little rusty, I shall manage well enough with the aid of common sense and the Admiralty charts.'

'Darlings! the man's a genius!' exclaimed Veronica.

'No, only a jack of all trades; and your sincere admirer, Madam!' he countered quickly.

Veronica lowered her eyes and fumbled with the

matches. She had caught him studying her with a queer look on his face twice that day, and this quick, half-humorous compliment left her for once without an apt reply.

'You'd have to have help,' remarked Kenyon.

'Of course, I must sleep sometimes; however, I can stick it for another twenty-four hours, till I get her clear of the Channel. Then you and Harker will relieve me turn and turn about.'

'Good Lord, man! I don't know the first thing about a ship; it would be madness to give me such responsibility.'

'Not a bit of it. Once we are out in the open sea it will be the simplest thing in the world. I shall set the course before turning in so all you will have to do is to keep an eye on the helmsman; see that he sticks to it, and watch out for any other shipping. I will sleep in the bunk in the chart-house, so in any emergency you'll only have to bellow down the voice pipe and I shall take over again immediately.'

A groan from the settee drew their attention back to Fanshawe; he showed signs of coming round.

'We'll have to truss him up,' said Gregory, 'and put a light gag over his mouth so that he can't shout for help. Come on, Fane.'

They tore the table napkins into strips, and before the sailor regained consciousness he was neatly bound. Then Gregory got hold of him under the armpits. 'Take his feet, Fane; we'll put him in the pantry, he'll be out of sight there.'

'What are you going to do about the engine-room?' Kenyon inquired when they had deposited their victim.

'I'll fix that somehow. They must know that if the ship ceases to be under power it is only a matter of hours before we become a wreck, and none of us want to drown!'

'Supposing they refuse to take your orders?'

A hard note crept into Gregory's voice. 'I think I shall be able to persuade most of the engine-room staff to join us.'

Kenyon nodded; 'Well, I give you full marks for letting nothing daunt you, but I'd like to know what's happening on the bridge. For all we know Broughton may be dishing out cutlasses to his jack-tars while we're standing here talking, and we don't want to give any excuse for a pitched battle or find ourselves arrested before you've had a chance to get your men on deck. Hadn't we better do something about it?'

'I believe you've got the makings of a good officer, Fane.' Gregory smiled his appreciation. 'As a matter of fact I'm only waiting for Harker to return. Then the three of us will get the troops together and tackle the situation.'

There was the sound of steps in the lobby and Silas poked his head in at the door.

'Well?' inquired Gregory.

'It's all quiet for the moment,' he reported, 'Broughton's busy with his own caboodle. The Chief Petty Officer has just been handing out a yarn that there's a spot of bother with the men forward, so Broughton asked me to pass his compliments to Fanshawe and request that he go up to the bridge right now. Sergeant Thompson's here with me, he wants a word with you.'

'Right, let him come in. Take over from Rudd in the passage and tell him to bring in that whisky bottle.'

Harker beckoned over his shoulder. 'Come in, sergeant, the General will see you now.'

The red-faced sergeant saluted and stood to attention.

'What is it, sergeant?' asked Gregory affably.

'If you'll h'excuse me, sir, I thought you should be h'informed as to the state of things on this boat.'

'Ship, sergeant, ship!' Gregory corrected gravely.

'Well ship, sir, there's doings amongst the crew that I don't like, wrong talk about the h'officers, an' the discipline is something awful. They laugh, sir, just laugh, at the orders of their own N.C.O.s.' The sergeant's face was nearly purple with suppressed indignation.

'I see. Of course the whole fleet is in a state of unrest but I imagined that the destroyers were comparatively unaffected.'

'H'in my opinion, sir, these sailors are ripe for any mischief, even the mess steward's just joined them, 'an worse than that, they're connivin' with our own men now.'

'That so?' Gregory looked up sharply. 'We must prevent them contaminating the troops at all costs. Have you taken any action?'

'No, sir, I held me 'and thinking it best to report to you, though there's one or two of them I'll be bringing up before you at h'orderly room tomorrow.'

'Where are they at the moment?'

'With the seamen, sir. There's a sort of meeting bein'

held h'on what they call the Lower Deck, and quite a number of our men's among them.'

'Very good, sergeant, I'll deal with the matter in a moment. Care for a glass of whisky?'

'Well, sir—' Sergeant Thompson's eyes brightened perceptibly; 'I don't mind if I do, sir.'

'Rudd, a glass for Sergeant Thompson.'

'Ay, ay, sir!' Mr. Rudd in his new role of sea-going steward hurried forward. With his usual tact he produced an outsize glass. The sergeant lifted it and removed his cap.

'My best respects, sir, and to the ladies'; swiftly the big tumbler went up to his mouth, tilted, and like a conjuring trick the golden spirit slid gently into his mouth. He smiled, coughed politely and set down the empty glass. Gregory more slowly drained his own.

'Harker!' the General looked at Silas; 'Get back on the bridge will you. Tell Broughton that Fanshawe and I are going forward to tackle the trouble among the men. Take the sentries on the door with you—if anyone attempts to come aft challenge them, and failing a satisfactory reply, fire at once. Fane, Sergeant Thompson, Rudd, you will come with me, and you—' Gregory glanced swiftly at the two girls, 'will remain here. You will be perfectly safe this end of the ship, but lock the door and don't open it except to one of us. Lead on, sergeant.'

The small party filed out and up the ladder to the deck; the night was dark and the sea rising. Away on the beam flashed the North Foreland Light, and—Fanshawe's orders still remaining unchanged—they were forging ahead at full speed. Gusts of spray came over the bows of the destroyer as she met the bigger waves, and she was already pitching slightly.

'Looks like a dirty night, sir,' said the sergeant as they made their way forward in the dark, stumbling now and again over chains or into torpedo tubes.

'Yes,' Kenyon agreed, 'I'm afraid the women don't know what they're in for yet.'

'Silence,' said Sallust curtly.

Two dark figures were seated near the forehatch. A beam of light from the North Foreland caught the braid on Gregory's hat and they stood up.

'Who's this?' he asked, peering at them.

'Chief Petty Officer Wilkins, sir,' said the nearest figure, 'and Petty Officer Sims.'

'Oh, what are the two of you doing sitting on the deck here in the dark?'

'Just talking, sir.'

'I see,' the cynical note crept into Gregory's voice; 'You think it safer to remain up here than to go to your bunks, eh?'

'The men's not themselves tonight, sir,' Sallust caught the quick resentment in Chief Petty Officer Wilkin's voice. 'We'll go forward, sir, if that's your order. We don't want to give any excuse for trouble, that's all.'

'Quite right.' Gregory's tone became charming at once. 'You have acted wisely in remaining here. What is the situation on the Lower Deck?'

'Bad, sir! The eighteen men what was in irons 'as been released without instructions. I 'ave already reported that to Lieutenant Broughton, but 'e told me to do nothing till 'e'd seen the Commander. There's that there Stoker Crowder amongst them—'e is the centre of the trouble, 'im and that Leading Seaman Nobes; a regular sea lawyer 'e is with more education than's good for 'im. They'd both have been put off at Chatham before the ship went to sea if the Captain 'ad 'ad 'is way.'

'And how is the temper of the men generally?'

'Not good sir! they're a bit excited tonight but they're a fine lot of lads in the ordinary way, and we'd soon get 'em quietened down if only we could keep these ringleaders out of it.'

'Well, that's what we're going to do. I have no doubt you P.O.s understand how unsettled conditions are, but I've thrashed the matter out with your Commander and as my men seem to be involved as well, he has asked me to assist him in dealing with the situation.'

'Ay, ay, sir.'

'Now follow me,' Gregory moved towards the hatchway, but Sergeant Thompson, well fortified by whisky, slipped in front of him.

'By your leave, sir?'

'Very good, sergeant.' Sallust followed his senior N.C.O. quickly down the iron ladder.

'Party!' yelled the sergeant with all the strength of his

well-exercised lungs, as he reached the Mess Deck; 'Party —'Shun!'

Gregory looked round. For the moment he could hardly see through the blue haze of tobacco smoke, but after a moment he took in a long narrow compartment with scuttles on both sides—dark now except for the reflection of the deck lights on the flying spray which constantly hissed past them. Rows of wooden tables, scrubbed to an almost unbelievable degree of whiteness, were hitched to the ship's side, supported at the midships end by thin iron rods which hooked into slots in the deck. At these tables, seventy or eighty men were crowded together. Evidently the mess deck was never meant to hold such a number, but khaki figures here and there were wedged between the blue serge of the sailors. Some of the latter, stokers and engine-room ratings, were naked to the waist or covered with grease and perspiration. Along the tables in front of almost every man reposed a big tin mug, and as Gregory noted it he rightly assumed that the spirit room had been broken into. At the far end a small group was gathered; the lack of space made a platform impossible, but directly Gregory's glance pierced the smoke-laden atmosphere he realised that this group, consisting of five sailors and two soldiers, comprised the ring-leaders, and that it was with them that he would have to deal.

At the sergeant's order there was a quick shuffling among the tables; the soldiers, almost to a man, came smartly to their feet, many of the sailors followed—slower to take up the word but obviously still respectful of authority. Yet at several tables there were little knots of men who remained seated, looking guiltily away from the General for the most part, but with anxious faces—half-frightened and half-sullen. The ringleaders at the far end of the Mess Deck remained seated to a man.

For a moment, only the sound of the sea, the pulsing engines and an occasional clang on the steel deck broke the stillness. In his left hand Sallust held a lighted cigarette, and he puffed at it slowly while sizing up the situation. Then in a quiet, level voice he spoke:

'Why are you men not turned in?'

A giant of a man who sat in the centre of the far group sprang to his feet; Gregory guessed him to be Stoker Crowder.

'What's it to do with you?' the big man thundered, 'you're not our officer!' A mutter of approval untraceable to any individual, but clearly perceptible, ran round the deck.

'What have you done with our Bloke?' shrilled a small, ferret-faced man who was sat beside the stoker.

'Leading Seaman Nobes,' thought Gregory, and his guess was confirmed when Chief Petty Officer Wilkins stepped out from behind him:

'That's enough of that, Nobes,' said the P.O. heatedly. 'We're now on a special mission an' the General 'ere 'as explained everything to the Commander so it ain't for the likes of you to start gettin' uppish!'

Absolute silence greeted the Chief Petty Officer's words, and Gregory added sharply: 'You hear that men? At the moment, I am in a position to give orders here and I mean to stand no nonsense.'

The men at the nearer tables shuffled awkwardly and looked at their boots. This quiet Army Officer was obviously not to be trifled with, but Nobes had a reputation to maintain.

''Ear that?' he shrilled: 'oo's this blinking soldier to order us abart, eh?'

The sailors muttered, looking angrily at their erstwhile companions in khaki.

'Look at 'im!' screamed Nobes; 'in 'is brass 'at—'e's the sort wot grinds the faces of the poor! Wot did I tell yer abart my cousin in the army—tied 'im to a gun wheel they did—jus' cause 'e overstied is leave w'en 'is old woman was 'aving a kid.'

'That,' rapped out Gregory, 'is a lie. Field Punishment No. 1 was abolished in 1915. Come here, you—or do I come and fetch you?'

For a moment Leading Seaman Nobes shrank back behind his large companion; then feeling so many eyes riveted upon him, came slouching out towards Sallust, a leer upon his face, a half-burnt cigarette dangling from his lip.

'Leading Seaman Nobes?' questioned Gregory smoothly.

'That's me,' the ferret-faced man nodded.

'You were under arrest until this evening. No order has been given for your release.'

Nobes shook his head, and blowing through his cigarette with a smirk, puffed the ash off on to the deck.

'You will surrender yourself at once to the Chief Petty Officer, said Gregory. 'Quick march!'

The sailor did not move an inch. He only grinned a little sideways at the crowded tables, half-closing his eye in the suggestion of a wink. A distinct titter showed the general appreciation of his humour.

'You refuse to obey me?' Sallust snapped out the words.

Nobes nodded with silent insolence.

'All right.' Gregory's tone was silky now: 'You realise that the country is in a state of war, and that for the maintenance of general discipline it is my duty to make an example of you?'

''Ark at 'im!' said Leading Seaman Nobes: 'just 'ark at 'im!'

Gregory's left hand still held the cigarette. He smiled faintly, almost as though appreciating the humour of the crowd at the amazing wittiness of Leading Seaman Nobes. His right hand closed upon the butt of his automatic; in a flash he had advanced into the centre of the compartment within a yard of Nobes, and in the same instant the weapon was levelled at the Leading Seaman's head.

Arty Nobes was twenty-nine years of age. He had light brown hair and rather pale blue eyes; his mouth was large with mobile lips, which may be taken as a sign of generosity or of looseness of character—the two very often go together. His nose was short and freckled, his hands better cared for than those of the majority of his shipmates.

Early in life Arty had associated himself with those discontented elements in his home port whose avowed objective was the downfall of what they termed 'the bloody capitalist.' He was married to a very decent woman a year or two older than himself who was a good hand at cooking him a dish of steak and onions; she secretly kept a scrap-book of those photographs which appeared in the daily press chronicling the many activities of the Royal Family. She had often told him with a cheerful unbelief that sooner or later his political opinions would land him in jug. He also contributed small regular sums towards the rent of a small, plump-breasted young woman who occupied a room in the back streets of Harwich. He had one daughter aged five, and was a teetotaller.

As the flash came, the upper half of Arty's cranium lifted like the lid of a box. The human head is apt to react that way if the frontal bones are struck in a certain spot by a bullet fired at close range.

Arty pitched forward, and Sallust stepped back. The comparatively small amount of grey matter which had constituted the brain of Leading Seaman Nobes, spilled upon the spotless deck.

14

Mutiny at Sea

The smoke drifted away from the barrel of the automatic in a little eddy. The report in that confined space had been so shattering that the silence which succeeded it was almost frightening. Only the sound of the water swishing past the scuttles and the rumble of the engines continued unabated. Then Gregory spoke:

'This man has died, not through his folly alone, but largely through your encouragement. Every man of you here is partially responsible. See to it then, that, by encouraging others, you do not compel me to make further examples. Sergeant!'

'Yes, sir.'

'Order your men to their quarters.'

'Fall in,' bellowed the sergeant and the troops quickly separated themselves from among the sailors. Even the red-faced Brisket and Saunders of the protruding teeth, who were among Stoker Crowder's group, suppressed their sullen looks and stepped hurriedly into place.

'Party, 'Shun! Right turn—up the 'atch. Quick March!' Most of the soldiers were little more than boys and few had ever seen a man killed before. With white scared faces they filed past Gregory to the upper deck.

'Chief Petty Officer!'

'Yes, sir.'

'Have this cleared up.' Gregory nodded toward the body of Arty Nobes, and stood there grimly silent, while the remains of the leading seaman were carried away and the deck swabbed down. He then addressed the sailors.

'Now, men, wherever this ship may go, one thing is certain, it must finally return to a naval port. If you continue with your duties satisfactorily until then, I will recommend to your Commander that in view of the very terrible example which I have been compelled to make, he should take no further action against any of you. If you make further trouble, however, bear in mind that your court martial and punishment are inevitable.'

As he turned on his heel, the C.P.O. called the sailors to attention again, and after a last stern glance round Gregory left the compartment.

He had no regrets about the swift action which had so suddenly terminated the existence of Arty Nobes. The fact that he had no right to issue orders to anybody, or to the uniform he wore, hardly occurred to him. He was living for the time being in the part which he had created for himself, and he knew that although many people in his situation might have shirked such a terrible responsibility and endeavoured to restore order by half-measures, the result would almost certainly have been failure. At least he had put an effective stop to the threatened outbreak, but as he breathed in the sharp salt-laden air of the upper deck again, he wondered grimly for how long.

He answered Harker's challenge from the upper bridge and with Kenyon and Rudd at his heels ran up the ladders to join him there.

'Where's Broughton?' he asked in a sharp whisper.

'Here.' The American nodded towards the darkness over his shoulder. 'I'm mighty sorry but I had to knock him out.'

'Hum! What happened?'

'He started an argument at once when I showed up again instead of Fanshawe. Then we thought we heard a gun go off and that settled the matter. He dived for the ladder so I hit him hard. Only thing to do I thought.'

'Quite right. It's the devil, though, having to rough-house these officers. It's certain to drive the loyal men into the arms of the mutineers, and they're a pretty nasty lot. The shot you heard was mine; I had to out one of the ringleaders.'

'Say! that's bad.'

'Only thing to do. If I'd climbed down it would have meant open mutiny, and if I'd shot to wound we should have had the whole pack on top of us. Now the next act is to slow her up and about ship. The helmsman still thinks Broughton is up here I suppose?'

'Yes; with it blowing like this he wouldn't hear a thing.'

'Right!' Gregory turned to Kenyon. 'Think you can imitate Broughton's voice, Fane? Mine's too deep and the chap below us in the wheel-house would notice Harker's accent.'

'I'll have a shot if you like.'

'Good man; look, there's the voice pipe.'

Kenyon leant over it. 'What shall I say?'

'Not so close, you fool. Now, just say "put the telegraphs to half speed".'

In a voice that Kenyon would never have recognised as his own he gave the order. 'Repeat, sir,' same the answer of the Quartermaster below.

' "Put the telegraphs to half speed," ' Kenyon said again, and Gregory stroked his lean cheeks with quiet satisfaction as he heard the reply gongs ring.

'Hard a' port,' he whispered a moment later, and when the order had been repeated the long destroyer slowly made a big half-circle with a great churning of waters.

'Steady,' Gregory ordered. Kenyon reiterated the command, and they headed once more to the southward.

'That will do for the moment,' Gregory nodded. 'When we come opposite the North Foreland Light again I'll set another course to pass outside everything and then head down mid-channel. We must keep our eyes skinned for shipping but fortunately there's little enough of that about these days.'

'Did you put those other men who broke prison behind the bars again, General?' Harker asked suddenly.

'No. To be quite frank, I didn't dare risk it. I'm pretty certain their leader's got a gun. He was playing with something devilish like it when I first went below—and a few more of them may be equipped in the same way. If they had once made a rush for us we should have been downed in no time so I had to take a chance on the moral effect of outing one.'

'Don't you figure there'll be more trouble before morning then? I'd bet a hundred bucks to a nickel they're in conference again by now.'

Gregory laughed a little bitterly. 'I wouldn't take you even for a nickel, and I've been thinking of the best plan for holding the ship till morning. Once daylight comes we'll start in on the general round-up, but it's a question of hanging on till then.'

'How about shifting all the troops aft?' Kenyon suggested.

'No. I'd thought of that but unfortunately they are not all reliable. Brisket and that other chap were on the revolutionary committee, you saw that yourself, and after the hot air they've heard this evening a lot of the others may have been won over.'

Harker nodded. 'Well, what's the drill then?'

'Go down and see Sergeant Thompson. Tell him that I don't want any but real tigers about the bridge, and that he's to pick a dozen of the best N.C.O.'s or men, then bring them up here with as much ammunition as they can carry. Now, what about your lot?'

'All for King and country; they wouldn't be Greyshirts else.'

'Good, that gives us another seven. Tell Thompson to borrow rifles for them from the men who are left below. Excuse to the men they are to be taken from: rifle drill for the Greyshirts first parade in the morning. It's a bit thin but it's better than nothing and you'll be behind Thompson if there's any trouble.'

'Right, I'll see to it, General. What about this lad here?' Harker indicated the dark form of Broughton which lay stretched out behind him.

'He'll be coming round in a moment I suppose.'

'I doubt it; he hit his nob on a stanchion as he fell, poor chap, so I reckon he'll be under for some little time.'

'Never mind, we'll look after him; you get below and fetch up the Praetorian Guard.'

Kenyon was kneeling beside the Naval Lieutenant. He looked up at Gregory as Harker moved away. 'His head's cut badly, and he's bleeding like a pig.'

'Is he? We must get him below then. I don't mind killing mutineers or rioters, but I hate this business with the officers; they're only decent fellows doing their proper job.'

'If we carry him down the ladder the Quartermaster will see that we've laid him out and then the fat will be in the fire.'

'That's true, but we must get him down somehow.'

'What abart them there signal 'alyards,' suggested Rudd

who had been standing quietly in the background. 'Can't we 'itch 'im on to them, sir, an' lower 'im aft of the bridge darn on to the deck?'

'Splendid; that's the idea. Come on, give me a hand to lift him up. You slip down to the deck, Fane, and we'll lower him to you.' Gregory seized the unconscious sailor.

They tied the halyards firmly under his armpits, but just as they were about to put him over the rail, the Quartermaster's voice came weirdly to them from the pipe amidships.

'Damn,' muttered Gregory, 'hang on a minute and I'll see what it is.'

Rudd supported the Lieutenant while the General strode over to the tube. A moment later he was back again. 'That infernal Quartermaster is asking for his relief. I daren't send for the C.P.O. or he'll want to know what's happened to his officers. Quick, heave this chap over, hang on to the rope now, we don't want to break his neck.'

Broughton was lowered in a series of jerks to the waiting Kenyon and then Gregory turned back to Rudd. 'Nip down to the wheelhouse. The Quartermaster is certain to know that there has been trouble forward, tell him that owing to that he cannot be relieved at present. If he kicks and wants to speak to his officer stick your gun in his ribs and make him carry on. Harker will be back in a minute with the men.'

'Ay, ay, sir.' Rudd ran lightly down the ladder.

'Fane,' called Gregory in a sharp whisper leaning over the rail.

'Yes.'

'Have you got him off the line?'

'Yes, just finished.'

'Can you get him to the wardroom on your own?'

'I'll manage somehow.'

'Right! Tell the girls to look after him and bathe his head. Come back as soon as you can, and bring the Lewis guns with you; I had them stowed under the settee.'

'All right.' Kenyon slid his arm under the legs of the sailor, and gripping his wrist hoisted him over his shoulders in a 'fireman's lift.' Then he staggered aft and down the hatchway to the wardroom.

He was greeted by a flood of breathless questions from Ann and Veronica, and after he had laid the Lieutenant on the table he told them roughly what had happened, suppressing Gregory's extermination of Leading Seaman Nobes.

Veronica bent over Broughton. 'What have you done to the poor sweet?' she cried angrily as she saw the ugly wound on the side of his head.

'Silas Harker had to knock him out and he hit his head on an iron stanchion as he fell. Sallust says you are to bathe that cut and take care of him.'

'Of course we will, but where can we get some water?'

'One of the cabins I should think.' Kenyon was hurriedly pulling the Lewis guns from under the settee and Veronica looked over at him sharply.

'Where are you off to with those things, Galahad?'

'Taking them up to the bridge; General's orders.'

'Fee-fie-fo-fum, I smell the blood of an Englishman!' she said suspiciously. 'Are you about to enliven us with a little war?'

'I hope not. Just a precautionary measure.'

'I don't like the look of victim number two at all,' said Ann. 'Can't we get him off this hard table?'

'I'll lift him on to the settee if you like,' Kenyon volunteered.

'No, carry him along to his own cabin, he'll be more comfortable there, and we can wash his wound properly if there's water handy.'

'I must get these things up on the bridge.'

'Oh, we'll take the arsenal for you, if you'll carry him.'

'Right!' Kenyon handed over the Lewis guns to the two girls and pulled the recumbent sailor on to his shoulders again. They followed him out of the wardroom and along to Broughton's cabin where Kenyon laid the wounded man in his own bunk. Then he turned with his finger on his lips.

'For goodness' sake don't make a noise,' he whispered, 'I think Cousens lives next door, and if we wake him it will only mean more trouble. Sallust will probably be able to tackle him quietly once he's got control of the ship.'

Ann nodded silently and stepped over to the basin. Veronica was already pulling one of the Lieutenant's best white shirts out of a drawer to make a bandage.

Kenyon collected the guns again and turned for a second in the doorway. 'When you've done what you can for him, don't stay here. Get back to the wardroom, and to be on the safe side lock yourselves in—though there's not likely to be any trouble this end of the ship.'

Back on the bridge he found that Harker had already assembled his Greyshirts, and to the troops on the forecastle Gregory was giving quick instructions. The Chart-house on the lower bridge was to be used as a guard-room where two-thirds of the small force were to doss down for the night. The remaining third were being posted as sentries; a screen of four abaft the bridge, Sergeant Thompson and Rudd at each extremity of it and two more men towards the bows in case of a surprise attack from forward. Rudd was busy at the moment serving out a stiff tot all round from various bottles, which, with his amazing nose for the whereabouts of supplies, he had collected.

They were back now with the North Foreland Light abaft the beam, and Gregory, after a quick look at the chart, set a new course, which he knew to be roughly accurate, although for the time being he was unable to make allowance for the tide.

The Lewis guns were mounted, the ammunition carried up, and it seemed that no more could be done for the moment when the Chief Petty Officer appeared. Gregory spotted him coming up the port ladder to the bridge and hastily blocked his way by running down a few steps to meet him.

'What is it, Wilkins?' he inquired.

'I was about to report to the Commander, sir.'

'He's busy on the upper bridge—so I'll take your message.'

'I think I'd better go up, sir—there's more trouble forward with the men.'

'I see. Well the Commander has asked me to take measures for the protection of the bridge with my troops so you'd better let me know what is happening.'

'There's another meeting, sir, an' I don't like the looks of things at all.'

'All right, you'd better remain with us, but go and fetch Petty Officer Sims first, we need all the reliable men we can get.'

'It's a bit difficult, sir. They've made him attend the meeting. Half a dozen of them cornered him, and I think he reckoned it would be more than 'is life was worth to refuse.'

Gregory grunted angrily.

'And what's more, sir,' added the C.P.O., 'the magazine keys is missin' from the board. I wanted to report that to the Commander.'

'I'll tell him. You stay here and keep your eye on the forward hatch.'

'Ay, ay, sir.'

Gregory went up the ladder again and walked over to look at the gyro compass. The Quartermaster was still carrying on his duties at the wheel with an imperturbable face. A soldier with a fixed bayonet, however, now stood behind him. Silas and Kenyon were talking together in low voices. In a few words Gregory told them about the forcible detention of Petty Officer Sims.

'Let's go and get him out,' said Harker promptly, but Sallust shook his head.

'No, I'd like to but we should be mad to go and put our heads in the noose again. They won't do him any harm if he does what he's told—and if there is going to be trouble I prefer to fight on my own ground.'

For some minutes they stood talking together while the destroyer ploughed its way evenly at half speed through the tumbled seas. The night was dark and still and no sound came from the forward quarters, which, Gregory agreed with Harker, was a bad sign. They knew that the sailors had access to the rum ration and if they had been singing it would have been a better omen. The stillness of the crew constituted a silent menace and his rudimentary knowledge of the ship's topography caused Gregory constant anxiety as to what might be going on below decks. Suddenly one of the forward sentries challenged.

A figure had risen from the forward hatch. There was a short consultation and then Petty Officer Sims was led up on to the bridge.

Gregory could see at once that the man was badly rattled and throughly ashamed of the part he was being forced to play, as he stumblingly excused himself for acting as the messenger of the mutineers. 'Rudd,' he called.

'Ay, ay, sir.'

'A tot of something for Petty Officer Sims.'

'Certainly, sir, 'ere we are.' Rudd hurried forward with a bottle and an enamel mug.

The Petty Officer swallowed the proffered beaker at a

gulp. 'Ha, that's better, sir,' he sighed, drawing the back of his hand across his mouth.

'Out with it, Sims,' said Gregory. 'What's happening now?'

'There's been another meeting, sir. That devil Crowder is making trouble among 'em, and they've sent me with what they call terms.'

'Terms, eh!' sneered Gregory. 'Never mind, let's hear them.'

'The First Lieutenant's to alter course to Harwich—most of them's Harwich men, and they want to get home, not knowing what's happening to their families. If he'll take the ship in they promise not to molest him or the officers or you and your men, and they'll set you all ashore; but if you won't sir——'

'Well?'

'They say they'll shoot the lot of you, and run the ship in themselves.'

'Thank you.'

'I'm to take back the reply, sir.'

'There is no reply, so you will remain—that is unless you prefer to return to them.'

'No, sir, no,' replied the Petty Officer hastily, 'I sticks by my officers and you.'

'Good man—you'll find the Chief Petty Officer on the port ladder; better park yourself with him, I'll go and let the Commander know that you are safe back with us again.'

'Thank you, sir.'

The ship slithered on into the darkness West-South-West with occasional spray lifting over her bows as they cut through the waves. Gregory kept a watchful eye on the compass but all was silence once more on deck. Then something happened—for the second he hardly realised what, but a sudden absence of vibration told him that the ship was easing down.

He swore softly beneath his breath.

'What'll this mean?' asked Harker.

' 'Fraid they've got control below,' Gregory answered softly. 'We shall know in a minute.' He stood by the binnacle peering intently at the compass in the guarded light of the hood.

For a few moments the ship swung silently, rolling a little in the trough of the waves. Then the propeller started to thud again and the bows of the vessel veered slowly towards the East.

'Ship not answering to the helm, sir,' reported the impassive Quartermaster, and as they watched the lubber's point it swung from West-South-West to North-Eastward, then steadied.

'They've got us,' muttered Gregory, 'they've set a course for Harwich as near as they can.'

'But surely the ship is controlled from here?' said Kenyon.

'Yes,' Sallust made a wry grimace, 'in the ordinary way, but obviously they have disconnected the fore bridge steering, so now we can't do a damn thing.'

'Can they steer her from below then?'

'Looks ter me as if the matloes is usin' the after control position, sir,' volunteered the Quartermaster.

As he spoke the thresh of the screws increased, and soon the destroyer was forging ahead to the North-Eastward with all the power of her 30,000 horse-power engines.

Gregory snapped his teeth together angrily. 'These devils will run me out of the oil I need if they mean to maintain a pace like this. We've got to get that after-steering position—they'll slow her down if we can secure that, or at all events we can turn her again the way we want her to go. Hullo, what's that!'

A commotion was going on amidships, and a struggling group arrived at the foot of the starboard ladder. It was Lieutenant Cousens, angry-eyed and hatless, in the grip of two flushed sentries.

'Tried to break through, 'e did, sir, and wouldn't reply to the challenge,' spluttered one of the Tommies.

'What the hell's going on here?' demanded the N.O.

'Good Lord! I'd forgotten all about you; we've been up to our neck in trouble ever since dinner,' Gregory said with a trace of amusement in his voice. 'Let him go, men. Come up on the bridge, will you, Mr. Cousens?'

The ruffled sailor jerked his tie back into position and stamped angrily up the ladder after Sallust, who led him to the deserted starboard side of the bridge.

'Now what the devil's been happening in the last watch and where's the Commander?' Cousens demanded.

'I'm sorry to say there's been a mutiny,' said Gregory.

'Yes, that's plain enough, but where are the First

Lieutenant and Broughton, that's what I want to know?'

'Prisoners, unfortunately, in the hands of the mutineers. They rushed the bridge and collared them both, while I was trying to quell the trouble on the lower deck.'

'The devil they did—they darn near got me, too. When I left my cabin I went to the wardroom to get my cocoa before taking over, and there were the matloes with both the magazine hatches up and passing arms out on deck through the after ammunition hand up hatch. They chased me out on deck and your sentries damn near stuck their bayonets through my ribs.'

'Well, if they've got to the magazines we're in for real trouble; they've got control of the after-steering position too, and disconnected the forward steering-gear.'

'I guessed that from what little I saw on deck. Of course I'm in command here until we can get the Commander released—but I'd be glad to have your views on what you meant to do, sir.' The sailor was regaining his breath and his temper. The furrows which ringed Sallust's mouth deepened into a smile as he noted the 'sir' and the ease with which his story had got over.

'I had meant to send one of my officers with a detachment of men to endeavour to regain control of the after part of the ship,' he said slowly, 'but since you've turned up perhaps it would be better if you took the job on yourself. It's much more likely that the mutineers will listen to one of their own officers—you may be able to persuade them to stop this idiocy.'

'That's true. Anyhow I'll have a cut at it.'

'Good! I can let you have eight men. I must keep the rest to man the Lewis guns. We'll cover you with them if it comes to a fight and you have to retreat.'

Sallust called Harker over to him and gave instructions. The troops were turned out from the chart-house and the Lieutenant went aft with eight of them. The remainder lined the bridge, peering anxiously into the darkness.

All except the navigating lights had been put out on the deck and only the reflected glow from the scuttles on the rushing waters afforded any illumination. The ship raced swiftly through the foam which swished and rustled with a continuous quiet hissing noise against her sides, while Gregory strained his tired eyes into the shadows.

The parley aft was brief. Cousens addressed the men,

but Crowder gruffly told him to get back forward and mind his own business if he valued his skin. The Lieutenant raised the rifle which he had taken from one of Sallust's Tommies but there was a sharp crack. Private Brisket who stood by Crowder had seen the motion and the N.O. pitched forward shot through the chest.

There was a sudden crash of shots as the troops replied and other mutineers joined in. Sallust's men were hopelessly outnumbered; another fell, and the remainder bolted, scrambling and tumbling back towards the bridge.

'Ready,' sang out Gregory. He paused a moment, giving the Lieutenant's party time to get clear, then as the mutineers surged forward he bellowed: 'Fire!'

The machine-guns opened and the troops joined in with their rifles, aiming for the dark smudges of shadow that slipped from cover to cover on the after deck.

Above the din came a scream and then a blasphemous curse.

'Cease fire,' ordered Gregory; he had no wish to waste his ammunition and knew that he had taken toll of the enemy.

For a moment there was silence and not a movement to be seen. Then a spasmodic fire was opened by the mutineers from their shelter behind the funnels and torpedo tubes.

'Get down,' barked Gregory, and as the bullets came spattering against the superstructure of the bridge its defenders flung themselves upon the deck. Sallust alone re-remained upright, miraculously immune from the bullets as he continued the direction of operations.

Kenyon felt a slight perspiration break out upon his forehead at this, his first experience of being under fire, and with one hand pushed back his rebellious auburn hair; with the other he instinctively fumbled for his cigarettes.

'For Gawd's sake put that out, sir,' came a hoarse whisper as he struck a match. It was Rudd crouching beside him in the darkness and in some strange way he felt comforted.

Gregory's voice came again: 'All ranks! pick your marks. Three round rapid—Fire!'

The kneeling figures rose and suddenly there was a crashing blast of fire. The bullets snapped and rattled as they hit the steel deck and the after part of the ship was subjected to a rain of lead. Yet even as it ceased the return fire leapt out again.

There were numerous casualties now on both sides, and the groans of the wounded were mingled with the screams of pain as the bullets found a human mark.

At Gregory's orders the machine-guns opened once more, pouring another belt apiece into the darkness amidships. They gibbered and chattered like street drills gone mad, while their leaden stream clanged and whistled as it struck and ricocheted upon the metal fitments of the ship.

Then from the starboard quarter there came a blinding flash, a shrill screech a few feet overhead, and almost instantly the crack of an exploding shell.

Kenyon crouching on the bridge, caught a glimpse of Sallust's face. The muscles about the mouth had tightened suddenly with the swift realisation that any moment might bring annihilation to them all. The mutineers had manned one of the two-pounder Pom-Pom anti-aircraft guns, and turned it on the bridge.

'All ranks—concentrate on flash—rapid—fire!' came the General's last desperate order, but it was too late.

A scorching sheet of flame leapt up on Kenyon's left, accompanied by a thunderous, ear-splitting detonation. The bridge rocked beneath him as he was flung sprawling to the port end. Even the ship seemed to shudder for a second as it ploughed its way through the sea. Another followed and another, at hardly a second's interval. The night was livid with a blinding series of explosions, the air foul with the acrid, choking fumes.

When they ceased the deck-house had almost completely disappeared, the binnacle and telegraphs were a twisted mass of brass and copper, while a hundred cries of pain and triumph seemed to rend the air at the same moment. Pandemonium had broken loose.

'Abandon bridge,' yelled a voice above the din. 'Come on, now—make it snappy. All hands on the fo'c'sle, they won't be able to shell you there.' It was Silas Gonderport Harker, who had taken charge on the silence of the General.

Kenyon struggled out from beneath Chief Petty Officer Wilkins who had been flung on top of him. The sailor's leg had been broken at the thigh by a flying fragment of shell and he was whimpering pitifully. As Kenyon raised his head the whimpering ceased, the body twitched and lay still.

'I got ter get Mr. Sallust,' croaked a hoarse voice and Kenyon turned to find Rudd still beside him.

'No good,' he gasped, 'he'll be dead for certain, and they'll be putting more shells into that deck-house in a second. Get off this blasted bridge, while there's still time.'

'Not me, sir, 'e's my officer an' I ain't goin' without 'im.'

'All right—I'll help you,' muttered Kenyon thickly.

Cries, shouts and groans came from every side as they crawled along the bridge. The canvas screens had caught fire and lit the tumult in a lurid glare, the sickly smell of fresh-spilled blood came strongly to their nostrils. The survivors were tumbling over one another in their efforts to get down the ladders.

The chart-house, when they reached it, was a shambles. Half a dozen twisted bodies lay with mangled limbs and white distorted faces; Gregory was among them, his left leg doubled unnaturally back beneath his body, a trickle of blood running from one ear. They dragged his limp form from among the others without pausing to see if he was alive or dead, and lugged him between them to the port ladder.

' 'Arf a mo', sir; bung 'im on my back,' cried Rudd, pausing when he was half-way to the deck.

'Right—you carry him—I'll protect your rear.' The precaution was not unnecessary for the mutineers were already running from cover forward to the burning bridge, sniping at the retreating soldiers as they stumbled towards the fo'c'sle.

Zip! A bullet pinged past Kenyon's head and flattened itself upon a steel projection, another seared through his sleeve and catching a stanchion ricocheted with a loud whine into the sea.

Rudd staggered along under his burden. A rifle cracked in front. One of Harker's men had mistaken them for the attackers.

'Don't fire,' yelled Kenyon, 'it's Fane and Rudd.'

'Attaboy,' sang out Harker. 'Thank God you're safe; seen anything of the General? My, but you've got him here; great stuff!' In another moment willing hands were relieving Rudd of his load.

Harker was already preparing a new position in the bows. Kenyon had no chance to see how many men had survived the débâcle of the bridge, but from the dark forms moving swiftly about him he gathered that there must be at least a dozen. With a sudden feeling of relief he found that he still had the old-fashioned service revolver that Gregory had procured for him that afternoon, stuck in the borrowed belt, then an appalling thought flashed into his mind.

They were cut off from the women—Ann and Veronica were marooned aft and must have fallen into the hands of the mutineers.

15

With Women on Board

The two girls had turned their whole attention to Lieutenant Broughton the moment Kenyon left them.

'What an awful gash,' said Ann as she cut away the hair surrounding the wound with a pair of nail scissors.

'Can you wonder!' Veronica was tearing a shirt into rough strips for a bandage. 'It was that elaphantine American who hit him, and he must weigh twenty stone if he weighs an ounce.'

'Yet he doesn't look fat somehow.'

'No, just sheer bigness. He's a nice creature, I think.'

'Yes, I love that lazy good-natured smile of his. Hello! What's happening now?' Ann ceased dabbing at the sailor's wound and straightened up.

'We've stopped, lovie.'

After a moment the propellers started to thud again and it was obvious that they had increased their speed.

'There's that light flashing.' Ann nodded at the scuttle. 'It was on the other side before, so we must be going north again.'

'Perhaps Napoleon-Mussolini has had an inspiration. Thinks Iceland would be more shattering for us than the Cannibal Isles.'

'No, Gregory loathes the cold and you can trust him to think of his own comfort.'

Veronica supported the Lieutenant while Ann applied the bandage. Then they settled him as comfortably as possible in his bunk.

'I don't think there is the least chance of his coming out of this coma for hours,' Ann remarked.

'Then we might as well get back to the wardroom. One of us can come and have a look at the poor boy every now and again.'

Veronica led the way down the passage but paused, frowning suddenly when she reached the wardroom door.

'What is it?' asked Ann.

'Goodness knows, my sweet. Someone has opened up a couple of trapdoors in the floor and another in the ceiling. Kenyon, I suppose, getting more things for King Sallust—but he might have shut them down again before he went on deck.'

They settled themselves on the settee and were silent for a little, then Ann said suddenly: 'Do you think we'll ever get to the West Indies?'

'Why not? The boy friend in the brass hat seems a determined enough person. I should triple lock the door and throw the key out of the window if he manifested any desire to become amorous, and I wouldn't feel quite safe even then.'

Ann chuckled. 'No, if I know anything about Gregory he would be waiting underneath the window to catch the key.'

'Yes, and to be truthful, my dear, I should probably wait until he turned up before I threw it out!'

'Really! Do you mean that you have fallen for him then?'

'No—not quite. But I always have been attracted by the type of blackguard who has brains and guts providing they have a sense of humour and the decencies.'

'I like to listen to him, but I should hate him physically.'

'Would you? Well, I'm afraid I'm a shameless hussy,' Veronica confessed. 'That wolfish look plays the devil with the back end of my brain. One might get hurt but I bet that man knows how to make love.'

'Yes, but not the kind of love that appeals to me. I'm a simple soul just liking to be cuddled and cuddle in return—for ages and ages and ages. It's laziness, perhaps, but it's the sort of thing I'm always wanting from the right kind of man.'

'No, you're just deliciously normal, my sweet, and if I wore trousers I should be just crazy about you as Kenyon is—but I'm just a nasty vicious slut—God! What's that?'

A rifle had cracked above their heads. Others followed.

'The mutineers must be trying to get possession of the ship,' Ann gasped.

'Oh, Hades! What idiotic fools men are!'

'Gregory will stop them.'

'Oh, darling, of course he will,' Veronica's words were almost drowned in the clatter as the machine-guns opened from the bridge, 'but I was thinking of the men in general. Why can't they all be sensible and go to bed instead of trying to kill each other.'

'It would be ghastly if the sailors did get control of the ship.'

'They wouldn't dare to touch you and me.'

'Wouldn't they?' Ann disagreed quickly, and for a few moments they sat in strained silence while the shots rattled and thudded above.

'Oh, my God! What's is happening?' Veronica clutched wildly at the curtains across the scuttle above the settee to save herself from being thrown to the floor. The two-pounder Pom-Pom had just been brought into action overhead.

Ann went white, and clapped her hands across her ears in an effort to shut out the series of terrific detonations from the shells which were being poured into the bridge. The ship seemed to shudder through its whole length. 'Do you—do you think we're going to sink?' she whispered.

'We'll be drowned if we do.'

'Why, can't you swim? There will be boats I expect if we can get to them.'

'Yes, but we might so easily be trapped down here.'

'No.' Ann pointed at the after munition hand-up hatch which still remained open in the deck above. 'We could climb out through there.'

The Pom-Pom ceased fire. The machine-guns were silent, and only the sound of intermittent rifle fire came to them as they stood together peering anxiously up at the hatch.

Suddenly they heard a voice bellowing harsh orders, the

thudding of many feet as the mutineers streamed forward, and then the noise of the conflict drifted away to the other end of the ship.

They sat down again, this time at the table, staring at each other in strained, nervous silence, and wondering miserably what could have happened to their men.

Ann sniffed. 'Can you smell burning?'

Veronica wrinkled up her arched nose. 'Yes, I suppose they've set this filthy ship on fire, and now we'll all be burnt to death.'

'Unless we blow up. It's run with oil, I expect.'

A loud hammering sounded on the lobby door.

'Who's that?' cried Veronica.

'Open this door,' boomed a voice.

'Who are you?'

'Never you mind. Open this door—d'you hear?'

'It's the sailors,' whispered Ann. 'Oh, if only Kenyon hadn't left us.'

'We can't. It's locked on the outside,' lied Veronica sharply.

'Stand aside then,' roared the voice, 'or you'll get hurt.'

They drew away to the far end of the wardroom. There was a loud report, the lock was shattered by a pistol bullet and the door swung open. Crowder, the gigantic stoker, naked to the waist, his great hairy chest glistening with sweat and blood, shouldered his way into the room.

Behind him came Private Brisket, a sly grin on his red flushed face, a steel helmet dangling from one hand, a rifle in the other. A mixed crowd of soldiers and sailors stood peering from the doorway.

'Get up on deck, boys, an' keep the party busy for'ard; we'll be with you in a minute.' Crowder flung the order over his shoulder and the crowd dispersed. Then he advanced on the two girls, eyeing them with a cold speculative look.

'Well,' asked Veronica evenly, 'what do you want?'

'Ter take a look at you an' see if there's any officers here.' Brisket leered at Ann, 'Well, big eyes—wot's your name?'

'Croome,' she replied in a low voice.

'Croome, eh! Well, let's 'ave the other arf.'

'I don't think that concerns you.'

'Don't it, my gal. I'll teach you to keep a civil tongue in

yer head before I'm done. I've 'ad me eye on you ever since we pulled you aht of that restaurant place in Jamaica Road.'

The colour had drained from Ann's face, but she kept her gaze fixed boldly upon the man's small hot eyes and stood silent, her back against the table.

'Tasty bit of goods, ain't she?' Brisket's remark was addressed to the big stoker, but his eyes never left Ann's neat figure. His mouth was working queerly.

'Hadn't you better get back on deck?' Veronica suggested, seeking to create a diversion; 'we don't want any fighting in here, and there will be if the officers come down.'

Brisket turned a contemptuous eye on her. 'Speak when yer spoken to, Skinny Lizzie—unless you want ter get my fist in yer ugly mug.'

'I'm the Bloke on this ship now,' Crowder added as he moved towards the door. 'Most of the officers is dead and the rest soon will be. Come on, Brisket.'

''Arf a mo'—what's the 'urry.' The soldier put down his steel helmet on the table, and with a sudden movement reached out, his fingers closing on Ann's breast.

'Oh!' She gave a little cry of pain and jerking herself away knocked up his arm.

He stood there leering. 'Might 'ave a bit more on yer. I likes 'em plump meself——but you'll do. D'yer know where ter find the Chief's cabin?'

Her eyes blazed at him but she did not reply.

'If yer don't I'll show yer. Might as well start as we mean to go on, eh ? You'd best get along there an' tidy up; make it all nice and comfy fer yer new lord an' master. then wait till I got time to come an' attend ter yer.'

Ann swallowed hard. She was nearly choking with revulsion and loathing for this shallow-skulled, red-faced burly brute whose quick eyes were stripping her clothing from her body as he spoke. The knuckles of her hands stood out white and hard as she gripped the edge of the table behind her for support.

'Don't you go gettin' sullen now.' A threatening note crept into Brisket's voice. 'You'll find me easy enough ter live wiv if yer take it pleasant without no fuss, but wiv wimin oo's uppish I sez treat 'em rough, an' if yer starts puttin' on any of the la-di-da stuff, you'll get a darn good 'iding—see?'

'Come on,' said Crowder impatiently, 'you'll have plenty o' time to amuse yourself when we've scuppered the rest of the bunch.'

'If you are the Captain, I appeal to you,' cried Veronica. 'For God's sake use your authority—stop this man insulting Miss Croome and take him out of here.'

Crowder lurched back from the door and faced her; hands on hips, his enormous biceps standing out like cannon balls beneath his grimy skin.

'See here,' he said thickly, 'we're running this ship now, an' my right 'and man's entitled to 'is pleasure if 'e wants it. The officers have had their innings I'll be bound, an' we mean to have our turn—make up yer mind to that. You may be skinny, but I like yer spirit so I'll attend to you meself later on. In the meantime there's work to be done on deck. Come on, Brisket.'

'Righto, Capting. I'll be with yer, but we might as well sample the goods.'

As Crowder left the wardroom Brisket seized Ann round the waist and flung her across the table, forcing her down beneath him while he sought to press his lips on hers.

She screamed and struggled, twisting in his grip and beating wildly at his face with her clenched fists, but he only gave a guffaw of laughter and his hot mouth fastened greedily upon the soft flesh of her neck.

Veronica snatched up the decanter, with the idea of smashing Brisket over the head, but Ann was jerking her face from side to side with such rapidity as she strove to free herself from the soldier that Veronica feared to hit her by mistake; slamming it down again she dashed out of the room.

Ann gasping and shuddering still endeavoured to fight Brisket off. An awful nausea seized her as she felt the sharp bristles of his chin rasp against her flesh, and the smell of his pungent breath in her nostrils, but her eyes were staring wide with blazing anger, and with a sudden snap her sharp teeth met, as she bit viciously into his ear.

With an obscene curse he jerked his head away and struck her savagely in the ribs.

'You ruddy bitch—I'll learn you.' Then as she cowered away he raised his fist to strike her in the face.

'Stop that you!--d'you hear!' roared a new voice, and Fanshawe came bounding into the room. He had recovered consciousness more than an hour ago but remained, bound, gagged, and seething with rage, in the pantry until Veronica had the inspiration to release him.

'Gawd! it's the Capting,' Brisket leapt away from Ann and stooped to snatch his rifle from the floor.

'Drop that, you little swine.' The Lieutenant-Commander gripped a wine bottle by the neck and his blue eyes were cold with fury as he made a terrific swipe at the crouching soldier's head.

'Blast yer—yer murdering devil!' Brisket jerked his head aside but the bottle caught him on the upper arm just as he lunged at the officer with his rifle. The bayonet slipped past Fanshawe's ribs and buried its point with a thud in the panelling of the wardroom.

Next second the two men had crashed to the floor, the bottle shattered and they rolled over and over striving to grab each other by the throat, while Crowder, who had caught the sounds of the struggle in the passage, came pounding back through the lobby.

The stoker stood hesitant in the doorway of the wardroom, his revolver raised, but fearing to shoot the wrong man in the *mêlée*. Suddenly the officer came out on top. With his left hand he had the soldier by the throat, and with his right was dealing him quick slashing strokes in the ribs and belly. Brisket choked and groaned as every hammer blow descended on his aching body.

'Stop!' screamed Veronica, 'stop!' as she flung herself on Crowder, but it was too late. His revolver flashed, there was an ear-splitting report in the confined space of the wardroom, and at the same moment the Lieutenant-Commander sank down on his antagonist, shot through the brain.

Brisket crawled from beneath him and staggered to his feet. His face was purple, his eyes bloodshot, half-mad with pain and rage he grabbed at Ann again. In quick agonising gasps she had recovered her breath while they had been fighting and now swung the decanter at his head with all her force.

Then without warning came a sudden grinding crash. For a moment the deck of the wardroom seemed to lift and then plunge down again. Brisket was flung off his feet;

Ann's blow missed his skull but caught him a glancing blow across his left cheek and eye, then she pitched forward on top of him. Veronica and Crowder struggling together in the doorway fell in a tangled heap.

The ship seemed to hesitate for the fraction of a second and then soughed on again at full speed. Crowder scrambled to his knees and thrusting Veronica from him, stooped to grab the pistol he had dropped, but as he did so there came a heavy thud. With startling suddenness a man dropped into the wardroom from the upper deck through the after ammunition hatch. Swift on his heels another followed.

'Kenyon,' gasped Ann. 'Oh, Kenyon,' but he pushed her roughly aside and held the stoker covered with his gun. Petty Officer Sims, who was beside him, gripped the moaning Brisket by the neck.

Crowder was still kneeling on the floor, and had Kenyou arrived a second earlier he would have had him at his mercy. As it was the stoker's revolver was in his hand again and pointed upward at the middle of Kenyon's body. For a moment they remained, rigid, glaring into the barrels of each other's pistols.

'Stalemate,' panted Kenyon. 'If I fire, your gun will go off and get me. If you fire my finger will contract on the trigger and I'll get you—how about it?'

'You're right.' Crowder came slowly to his full height.

'Lay your gun on the table and I'll put mine there too,' Kenyon lowered his pistol a fraction to encourage the leader of the mutineers. Then watching each other like cats, the two men put down their weapons, and stood one either end of the long table.

'What have we 'it?' demanded Crowder.

'We've been slap through a drifter.'

'Gawd! The poor blighters!'

'Do you think the ship is damaged?'

'What, the old hooker! She'd go through a drifter like a slab of butter, but we may have sprung a plate or two.'

'How can we find that out?'

'I'd better nip forward with some of the lads and have a looksee.'

In the sudden anxiety that they might be about to sink, both had momentarily allowed the mutiny to take second place, but they were brought back to it by Kenyon saying:

'Do you realise that the forepart of the ship is in our hands?'

'I know that—an' I'm wondering how you ever got aft.'

'Crawled through your men in the dark with Sims here. It was he who put me up to the dodge of coming down the hatch, but how about making certain that the ship *is* all right?'

'Well, I can't go forward if your people are going to snipe at me, can I? What do you say to a bit of a truce?'

'Why not?' Kenyon drew himself up. 'I'm willing and you seem a sensible sort of chap; can't we agree to stop this slaughter altogether?'

'Yes, if you're prepared to accept me as Captain of the ship.'

'No, I can't do that. Your men would murder the General if they got hold of him, and I'll be frank with you, I'm scared for the ladies too. Even if you are giving me a straight deal, could you guarantee to protect them from a mutinous crew?'

'I couldn't, and I wouldn't have time to try.'

'Well, that's straight, anyway.'

For a moment there was silence while the two men considered the situation.

'Look here,' said Crowder suddenly, 'there's more of us nor what there is of you—so I'll get you in the end—won't I?'

'The odds are certainly in your favour.'

'Well, when I have, the hooker'll be mine, won't it?'

'What's left of it; we may be damaged now.'

'Then I'm game to meet you 'alf-way. We're makin' 'Arwich so I'll let you have a boat an' all the gear and you can 'op it for the nearest spot of mud.'

'All of us?' asked Kenyon quickly.

'Yes, all of you. An' to be honest I'd a sight sooner have the women out of it. If we kill your lot off there'll only be trouble among the men as to who get's at 'em first.'

'What about the badly wounded who've been fighting on our side?'

'Any who's not fit to be moved I'll take care of and put ashore later—they'll be treated same as those who've copped it in our bunch.'

'You'll give us food and drink, and let us take our arms, ammunition, and Lewis guns?'

'Yes, them's the terms; I've no love o' killing for killin's sake, an' if you clear out it'll save life on both sides.'

Kenyon eyed his man for a moment. 'No tricks?'

'No, I'm a man o' me word.'

'All right. I agree to your terms.'

Crowder nodded, and picking up his pistol stuffed it in his belt. 'It'll be a bit o' time yet before we make 'Arwich, would you like to join your crowd on the fo'c'sle—or will I send them down here?'

'A heavy spray was coming over the fo'c's'le when I came down,' said Kenyon slowly, 'so I think the ladies had better remain here and I prefer not to leave them again. Perhaps it would be best if you took Sims forward to explain to Mr. Harker what we have arranged, then he can come down or stay there as he likes. You'll accept Stoker Crowder's word that it's all right, won't you, Sims?'

'Ay, ay, sir,' the Petty Officer agreed. 'I'll just close down this hatch though before I leave you in case someone takes a fancy to have a pot at you from the deck while we're away.'

'I'll shoot the first man wot tries any monkey tricks,' said Crowder gruffly. 'Come on, Sims, let's put a stop to that scrapping; they're still at it on the for'ard deck.'

'If Mr. Harker elects to stay up there you might ask him to send me down a couple of men, will you?' Kenyon added. 'I'd like some help to clear up this.'

Fanshawe's dead body lay on the deck and a puddle of blood had trickled from his head. Brisket was crouching in a corner whimpering and groaning as he rocked to and fro, his hand clasped to his injured eye. The stoker pulled him to his feet and half-led, half-carried him out, throwing over his shoulder to Kenyon: 'I'll send a couple o' your chaps unless the lot comes down.'

Sims, having secured the hatch, followed him from the wardroom and Kenyon was left alone with the two girls. Ann had sunk down on the settee and was weeping pitifully upon Veronica's shoulder. She had kept her nerve through the ordeal with Brisket but now that it was over all restraint had left her. She clutched the elder girl desperately while large tears welled from under her eyelids and coursed silently down her cheeks. Her small body shook with the stress of her emotion.

Kenyon, who knew his sister more intimately than most

of her closest friends, was well aware that her cynical irreverent humour was only an outer armour against the world, but even he was amazed by the soft natural phrases she used to soothe Ann's terror and distress.

A few moments later Rudd and his satellite the Greyshirt, Bob, appeared. The former grinned at Kenyon.

'Mr. 'Arker's compliments, sir, an' 'e sends 'is congrats on the Peace Treaty. An' there ain't no serious damage to the ship. Bein' 'is size 'e'd be certain to float all right, 'e sez, but 'e always did 'ate water.'

Between them they removed the Lieutenant-Commander's body and cleaned up the wardroom. Rudd produced a bottle of brandy from the pantry and Ann was given a strong tot, after which her sobbing ceased and she lay with closed eyes against Veronica's shoulder.

For a seemingly interminable time the ship raced on into the darkness, while they sat, silent and disconsolate, weighed down with the horror and futility of the bloodshed which had taken place that night.

At last Crowder reappeared and told them to come on deck. They filed up the ladder for the last time, the stoker leading with his revolver drawn, and as they made their way forward the mutineers on the deck shambled aside to let them pass with sullen glances. In the bows they found Gregory propped up against the capstan.

'How is your Majesty?' Veronica inquired. She could not resist the gentle sarcasm.

He smiled up at her a little grimly in the darkness. 'Lucky to be alive, I suppose. The shellburst knocked me out, but miraculously I escaped further damage except for a twisted leg.'

Crowder's husky voice broke in behind them. 'Now if it's all the same to you I'm going to drop you here. See over there? That's the Sunk Lightship winking now—an' that's the direction of 'Arwich. Nigh on fifteen mile it 'ud be, but if the men put their backs into it you should be there for breakfus'.'

'Right, carry on, Crowder,' said Gregory tonelessly.

The lurching form of the stoker disappeared in the shadows. Silence fell on the little group by the capstan while the thresh of the screws sensibly diminished and the destroyer eased down. The periodic flash from the Sunk appeared, a friendly note in the darkness, but as the ship heaved to in a gentle swell they felt a moderate breeze which had sprung up from the south-east, and Petty Officer Sims remarked that he thought it heralded a threat of fog.

The sailors were busy turning out the whaler. The falls ran easily, and at a curt order from Crowder she was slipped with a barely perceptible splash. The party collected with their rifles at the ready, and marched aft with Harker leading. Sallust and a man who had a bullet through the calf of the leg was supported on each side, and followed the girls in the centre of the remaining troops; Kenyon brought up the rear.

Harker and Sims climbed into the boat which was gently tossing alongside. They made a rapid survey of the stores and reported all satisfactory. The girls, the wounded, the ammunition and the Lewis guns were lowered, then the rest of the party went over the side, Kenyon remaining alone for a moment with Crowder at the rails.

He pointed past the lightship and said: 'You are certain that is the direction of Harwich?'

'Sure of it—I got a wife and kids in 'Arwich,' the stoker added thoughtfully.

'Have you?'

'Yes, an' I'm real anxious about them—not that the old lady can't look after herself—but still——'

Kenyon glanced at the man curiously. A few hours before he had been prepared to murder anybody—he had in fact shot his own Commander, for what Kenyon supposed he considered his rights and principles; now, he was as human as anybody else and anxious about his wife and children.

'Well, I hope they're all right,' he said. 'So long.'

'So long,' repeated the big man. 'Best o' luck,' and Kenyon slipped over the side into the waiting boat.

As the boat shoved off, the oars were got out by the soldiers and Greyshirts who were sitting amidships, and pulling slowly, they passed under the stern of the destroyer, being momentarily caught up in the wash from her powerful screws as she forged ahead again.

From the low altitude of the boat the flash of the Sunk did not show so plainly. A tenuous mist seemed to be rising from the sea and borne on the south-easterly breeze, wisps of fog began to obscure their vision.

'I don't like the looks of it,' muttered Sims who had the tiller.

Gregory, seated next to him in the stern, glanced back towards the ship, but with amazing swiftness it had already been swallowed up in the rapidly rising mist. The men were pulling as well as their inexperience allowed towards the flash of the Light Vessel, but it was only visible hazily now, for the great banks of chill grey fog seemed to be closing in all round. Ten minutes later that too had disappeared.

Rudd relieved Sims at the tiller in order that the Petty Officer might get out the compass. For some minutes he fumbled with it and muttered to himself anxiously, then setting it down he said in a low voice to Gregory: 'I'm sorry, sir, but this compass has had a biff; it's out of action.'

Gregory nodded quietly: 'I see; we're out of the frying-pan into the fire then—adrift in the great North Sea?'

'I fear that's so, sir.'

Suddenly the hideous wail of a banshee echoed out over the desolate waste of the fogbound waters. I was Rudd who had broken into his other aria: 'A Life on the Ocean Wave.'

16

Latitude 51° 49′ N. Longitude 2° 06′ E.

'Oh, shut up,' moaned Gregory.

'Sorry, sir,' Rudd ceased his serenade abruptly. I forgot you were *'ors de combat.'*

'This compass,' said Kenyon, 'can't you make it work, Sims?'

The P.O. had just unscrewed the top and removed the card. He shook his head. ''Fraid not, sir, the pivot's broken.'

'What'll we do then?' Harker asked.

'God knows. Let the men row gently but don't tire them. When daylight comes we'll get our direction from the sun. For the Lord's sake let me rest till then.' Gregory closed his eyes wearily.

Veronica made a pillow for his head with some coats and laid him out at full length on the bottom boards in the stern, while Kenyon and Silas checked up the occupants of the boat.

Besides themselves, the girls, Gregory, Rudd, and Sims, there were Sergeant Thompson with a lance-corporal and six of his men, one of whom had a head wound, and another a bullet through his leg; also five Greyshirts, including Rudd's henchman, Bob, who sat in the bow of the boat with his arm in a sling. The party numbered twenty all told, therefore, of which four were disabled and two were women.

The boat was a long, five-oared whaler so they were not unduly overcrowded. Sims had the tiller and Sergeant Thompson acted as look-out in the bow. The pulling was jerky and uneven owing to the men's lack of experience with boats, but one or two had done a little sculling and Kenyon and Silas decided to take turns at stroke.

Counting out the wounded and the women there were just enough of them to form two complete crews; Kenyon with the Tommies, Rudd for steersman and Sergeant Thompson as look-out making one watch; and Silas with his Greyshirts, Sims and the lance-corporal the other. Once these arrangements had been made, Kenyon's party took first turn at working the boat.

It would have been stupid to exert themselves, since they only had a very vague idea where they were or in which direction they were going, and Kenyon did not attempt to do more than keep the whaler gently moving. Instead, by a monotonous repetition of 'In-Out—In-Out' as the men dipped their oars he endeavoured to coach his crew into keeping some sort of time.

Gradually the darkness lightened but the mist lay heavy and thick about them, not even a glimmer of sun penetrated to the sea and no sound of sirens, indicating other shipping in the vicinity, reached them. With slow and wearisome regularity the oars rattled backwards and forwards in the crutches while the wavelets lapped and chuckled under the stern. The heavy seas of the night before had subsided into a gentle swell and the grey-green waters seemed to rise rhythmically before them in huge low mounds, only to slip away again and mount to fresh heights in their wake.

When full daylight came they suffered the illusion that the mist was lifting, since from the stern it seemed that they could see several lengths ahead, but they soon realised that they had only discovered the general density of the fog, and their length of vision did not alter as they advanced into the curtain of chill greyness which shut out light and sun. A dree, eerie feeling of loneliness and uncertainty stole over them, engendered by the silence and mystery of these seemingly impenetrable yet opaque walls of gloom. Even Harker's resilient cheerfulness was temporarily dampened and all of them were cold, hungry, and exhausted from lack of sleep.

Those who were not rowing crouched, dejected and miserable, in the bottom of the boat. The man with the injured leg groaned now and again. Gregory tossed in an uneasy sleep. Ann and Veronica, huddled together on one of the seats in the stern, sought to conserve what little warmth they could under a tarpaulin which had been found for them, and the oarsmen were half-asleep as they swayed monotonously backwards and forwards at their task.

They had been rowing for the best part of an hour and a half when Silas leaned over to Kenyon:

'What about a spell?'

Kenyon nodded wearily. The boat rocked a little as they ceased to ply their oars and the crews changed over, then the men who had been relieved settled down as comfortably as they could on the hard bottom boards and nodded into sleep.

Rudd thought of examining their supplies and suggesting breakfast, but two-thirds of the grey, drawn faces about him were sunk in deep slumber. It seemed no kindness to rouse them from their brief oblivion to a knowledge of the cheerless uncertain prospect. Next moment the thought had drifted from his mind and he too was asleep.

Ann woke from a fitful doze as Kenyon sat down beside her. 'How are you feeling?' he asked softly.

'Pretty miserable—I'm so wretchedly cold,' she whispered, but she gave him a sleepy smile.

Very gently he slid his arm along the gunwale behind her shoulders and her head slipped down on to his chest. As he drew the corner of the covering more closely round her she closed her eyes, and wriggling into a more comfortable position dropped off again. Fagged out as he was and aching in every limb the moments were too precious for him to lose them in unconsciousness, and he remained, half-dozing but never lapsing from the joyous knowledge of her nearness to him, all through Harker's spell.

With the idea of warming up his Greyshirts, Silas set a quicker stroke, but soon found it necessary to ease down and teach his squad to regularise their swing from Kenyon's example. Time wore on, and as the sun rose higher in the heavens the greyness lightened, but no rift on any side in the all-pervading murk.

Kenyon was recalled from his half-dreaming state by Silas placing a large hand on his shoulder, and saying amiably: 'What about it? Your turn now, I reckon.' Another hour or more passed.

He shivered, the damp chill of the mist seemed to have penetrated to the very marrow of his bones, then he pulled himself together and gently resettling Ann, who was now sleeping soundly, took the oar. The crews were already changing places and soon his party had settled down again into a long monotonous stroke. Almost unconsciously he noticed that his men were rowing better for their short training, then the thought of food came to him, but it was too late to think of that for the moment now. He could not leave his oar, and Silas was already curled up in the stern sheets next to Petty Officer Sims, his broad chest rising and falling in the long respirations of deep and healthy sleep.

Rudd sat huddled at the tiller again, his blue eyes alert and watchful. He grinned at Kenyon, showing his uneven teeth. 'Tike yer 'oliday on the Broads this summer, eh, sir. Travel by Moonshine Line—kids under six travels free—an' if yer got a dozen yer get a cokernut.'

Kenyon's lips parted in a quick smile. 'I only wish we were on the Broads. Ever been there?'

'No, sir, but me uncle's brother-in-law were drowned there, so I knows a bit abart it.'

'How was that?'

'Well, 'e were a red-'eaded man, sir—an' beggin' yer pardon, with no reference to yerself—'e were apt to fly off the 'andle a bit quick if yer know what I mean.'

'Yes,' Kenyon agreed, slightly mystified.

'An' 'e 'ad an upsydisy wiv a lock-keeper wot wouldn't let 'im through 'is lock.'

'Why—did he refuse to pay?'

'No it weren't that, but George were a bit of a Socialist, more fool 'im—tho' we shouldn't speak ill of the dead, an' 'e couldn't see why 'e should wait fer a private yacht ter come through from the other side—that's wot started the argument. Then the lock-keeper starts gettin' personal abart 'is missus—my uncle's sister as was—an', they bein' on their 'oneymoon thet properly riled poor old George, so 'e ups in the boat to give the lock-keeper a piece of 'is mind when unfortunate like 'e steps on the end of 'is oar.'

Kenyon quickly suppressed a rising chuckle and looked appropriately grave.

'An' the oar come up like a jack-in-the-box an' 'it poor old George on the 'ead.'

'Dear me!'

'Yuss—knocked 'im arse over tip, if you'll pardon the words, an' 'e never come to the surface no more.'

'That was appalling luck, especially on his honeymoon.'

'Yuss,' agreed Rudd philosophically, 'but me uncle's sister 'ad twins all the same.'

'Did she get the King's bounty?'

'No fear, sir—that's triplets.'

Kenyon swayed backwards and forwards at his oar while Mr. Rudd, having discovered in him a willing and intelligent listener, entertained him with a variety of those views which a close acquaintance with men and things had impressed upon him.

At none o'clock Kenyon woke Silas, who opened his enormous mouth in a gigantic series of yawns and then demanded a cigarette before he took over, his own supply being exhausted.

'Cigarette, sir,' exclaimed Rudd, 'why, 'ere you are, I got enough to larst us even if we goes ter China,' and he produced a tin of a hundred from one of his bulging pockets.

'Thanks, boy—were did you get these?' Silas puffed at the Balkan Sobranie contentedly.

'I made 'em out of the Officers Mess in the ship, sir; 'tisn't right them Bolsheviks should be left wiv decent cigarettes although I prefers gaspers meself. Still, I thought they might come in handy. Mr. Gregory's a rare one for 'is Turks.'

'What about some food?' suggested Kenyon when he had been relieved of his oar.

'Righto, sir. If Mr. Sims'll take charge of the *Mayflower*, I'll 'ave a look at the eats.'

Sims took over the tiller again but he leant forward towards Kenyon. 'I'm afraid we're a long way off course, sir.'

'Are we? Well, that's not surprising in this wretched fog.'

'You see it's this way, sir,' the Petty Officer lowered his voice. 'The Sunk isn't more'n twelve miles from the shore and so we ought to have sighted land a couple of hours ago if we was makin' dead for it, and even if we was swept out of our course a bit by the current, we ought to have made landfall by now.'

'Well, what's the best thing to do?' inquired Kenyon.

'Give the men a spell, sir, they can do with it, and we may be rowing further out to sea for all we know. We can keep a sharp look-out for shipping—an' the sun may break through later in the day.'

'That's sense,' agreed Silas. 'Come on, boys, ship your oars.'

Rudd had pulled an oblong box from under the seat and was examining its contents critically, 'My! this ain't the larder of the *Aquitania*,' he said softly. 'Where's that ruddy Bob—Bob where are yer?'

'Here I am, sergeant.'

'What d'yer do wiv them stores I give yer ter take care of?'

'I left them on the ship, Mr. Rudd. I put them down when the lady was bandaging my arm, and I forgot to pick them up again.'

'Streuth,' muttered Rudd to Kenyon. 'These kids don't arf make yer sick. Anyone ud think 'ed lorst 'is blooming 'ow d'yer does instead of 'aving a blighty in the arm. Any'ow we'll 'ave to make do wiv what they give us.'

'What is there then?'

'Biscuits, a lump of meat, some tea wiv nothin' ter cook it on, an' a bit of cheese.'

'All right, the biscuits and cheese will do for the moment.'

They were hard, unsweetened ship's biscuits and the cheese was mouse-trap cheddar. Not a particularly appetising breakfast for people whose nerves had been stretched to the utmost limit of endurance all through the night, and who had then spent some five hours crouching in an open boat chilled to the marrow by sea mist; but the men put a good face on it and gnawed away at the broken bits of flour and water.

' 'Ow abart a nice cup of corfie, sarg?' one of them called cheerfully to Rudd.

' 'Ow abart it, son! Like me ter bring it up to yer bedroom, eh?'

A little ripple of laughter went round the boat.

Kenyon looked across at Veronica, who was cheerfully attacking the iron biscuits with her sharp white teeth. 'How are you feeling this morning, long legs?'

'Grim, my sweet, grim! But I suppose this early rising is good for one, it's the first time I have eaten any breakfast for years.'

He nodded and turned his attention to Ann. There were dark shadows under her eyes, and her face looked pale and drawn, but she caught his glance and smiled.

'Well, I've always hated getting up in the morning but I'd rather be here than on that beastly ship. Hello, Gregory's awake!' she added as she caught his quick eye examining their faces from the bottom of the boat.

'Have been for some time,' he murmured.

'How is the leg?' she asked, bending over him.

'Aching like hell, but my head's better and that's what matters. Where's Rudd?'

' 'Ere we are, sir.'

'Right. Give me a hand up on to the seat.'

With Kenyon's help he was lifted up and made comfortable by the tiller.

While they were finishing their meagre breakfast they discussed the situation, and then for a time sank into silence, each one privately considering the unpleasant possibilities which might arise. They were adrift in the North Sea, perhaps many miles from shore. If the mist failed to lift all day and night came on before they could sight land, winds and tides which they had no means of assessing might carry them a hundred miles from their assumed position off the Suffolk coast, and then it might be days before they were picked up. Their supplies were extremely limited and another night at sea without proper food or warmth was a thing to dread. The fog showed no signs of dispersing. It clung and pressed about them, muffling even the sounds of their voices as it hemmed them in.

The forenoon dragged by, each hour seeming the length of half a day. They talked in subdued voices, or dozed again between the thwarts. Veronica displayed a marvellous cheerfulness and kept Gregory amused by her witty chatter, but Ann, chilled to the marrow and shaken occasionally by slight shivering fits, could only assure them that she was quite all right, and hug her frozen limbs in silence. Kenyon and Silas chafed her hands, arms, and feet between them, but the shock of Brisket's assault the night before in the wardroom seemed to have sapped her vitality and left her body temporarily incapable of resisting the rigours of their situation.

At midday Kenyon suggested the issue of a further ration but Gregory would not have it. He pointed out that they had breakfasted less than three hours ago and that it was essential to conserve their limited supplies. At one o'clock he made the same reply to Rudd who had been in the bows talking to Sergeant Thompson and came aft with a similar suggestion. Every one of them was hungry now, having had nothing but a few mouthfuls of dry biscuit and a wedge of cheese since the previous night, but he stuck to his decision.

A little before two Sims pointed to the heavens. 'The sun, sir, or I'm mistaken.'

'Where?' asked Kenyon quickly. The vague chill greyness above and about them did not seem to have altered, but Gregory nodded.

'You mean the lighter patch: are you sure?'

'Certain, sir. The mist'll clear in about half an hour I should say, but it's enough to give us a rough direction now. It'll be near four bells, won't it?'

'Yes.'

'Well, it's on the port beam so we must've been on a north-westerly course unless we've been going round in circles. Shall I take over the tiller now, sir, being more used to this sort of thing?'

'Do.' Gregory moved futher along. 'Whose spell is it?'

'Mine,' said Silas getting out his oar. 'And now we've got something to go on we'll put some ginger into this pocket Ark. Come on, boys.'

The course was altered by about forty-five degrees towards the bearing of the sun, and the Greyshirts cheerfully enough put their backs into the rowing. Half an hour later Sim's prediction was fulfilled, the mist broke into banks and patches, the sea began to sparkle and the sun came through.

'In-Out, In-Out,' Harker urged his crew, and now that they had had rest and a little practice they managed to shift the boat along at quite a decent pace.

Gregory had himself inspected their scant provisions and now ordered the issue of a small ration of meat and biscuits to all hands with about a quarter of a mug of water. He still felt it necessary to exercise the strictest economy, and so with this frugal late lunch, chewing the tough cold meat to extract its goodness and spitting out the residue, they had to be content, but now the sun was shining everybody felt more cheerful.

The men roused themselves from their lethargy and began to crack jokes; the others in the stern discussed the possible places at which they might land, from Scarborough to Southend, and speculated vaguely once more as to what might be happening in London.

By three o'clock all traces of the mist had vanished. A wide expanse of shimmering sea lay all about them still rising and falling in a gentle swell. Of land there was no sign, but Sims cheered them with the statement that it might not be very far away since their low level on the water gave them such a limited horizon. No masthead or smudge of smoke, above the grey-green wash and where the waves melted into one another, broke the skyline, and for all indications of other human life they might have been a thousand miles out on the wide wastes of the Atlantic.

'What about a bit of a sing-song, sir?' suggested Rudd.

'Fine, just the thing. Go ahead,' Gregory agreed.

'Come on, mates.' Rudd waved a grimy hand. 'All-ter-gether now.'

'Pack up yer troubles in yer old kit bag,
an' smile boys smile,
Pack up yer troubles in yer old kit bag,
an' smile boys that's the style,

Wot's the use o' worryin', it never was worth while,
So-o-o-o-o Pack up yer troubles in yer old kit bag,

an' Smile! Smile! ! SMILE! ! !'

A hesitating support greeted the first line, the second was taken up more generally, and by the last everybody had joined in to the full extent of their lungs.

'Na, then, let's 'ave it again. All-ter-gether now!' and at the second attempt the rolling chorus thundered out across the seas.

After that the self-appointed master of ceremonies kept them going without ceasing, varying his programme from the bowdlerised edition of *Mademoisclle from Armentieres* to the sobbing sentimentality of *Roses of Picardy*.

The sun was high in the heavens, glaring from a bright blue sky, and soon the men at the oars began to feel the heat. Then to everybody's astonishment, Ann, who felt better since the coming of the sun, suggested a swim.

'You can't,' said Kenyon, 'you've got no bathing dresses.'

'Never mind. Rig us a shelter at the back of the boat and Veronica and I will undress behind that.'

'But how will you dry yourselves?'

'Sunshine and knickers,' said Ann promptly.

'No, it can't be done, if you cling on behind it will stop the way of the boat.'

'Don't make yourself out more of a fool than you are, darling,' Veronica chipped in with acid sweetness after a swift glance at Ann. 'Do as you're told.'

'Oh, I see,' he said lamely, and with a collection of rifles and coats he proceeded to erect a small partition shutting off the last few feet of the whaler. Ann and Veronica disappeared behind it and when they emerged again some twenty minutes later they both looked considerably more cheerful.

In the meantime the troops had relieved the Greyshirts and were pulling with a will. Sims had gone forward in the hope that they might soon descry the first glimpse of the coast, yet Kenyon's spell came to an end and Harker took over once more, but still no trace of shipping broke the horizon and no clouds ahead suggested land.

All through the long afternoon the strong sun blazed down on the backs of the oarsmen. Their muscles were aching from the unaccustomed exercise, their hands were chafed and blistered, but they still swayed backwards and fowards in monotonous rhythm. The sun was causing acute discomfort to other members of the party too.

'Jolly for sunbathing, but not like this, my dear,' as Veronica expressed it to Ann, for they had no shelter and whichever way they turned it seemed to beat down upon their bare necks; their faces, unprotected by hats, were already turning an angry red.

When Kenyon's party went on again, Sims, having handed the tiller over to Rudd, leant towards Gregory. 'There's something wrong, sir, I'm assured of that.'

'Oh, how do you mean?' asked Sallust.

'Well, I won't say Crowder didn't act in good faith when he said he put us off by the Sunk, but how's the likes of him to know one light vessel from another, and their course was only guessed at anyhow. If it was the Sunk we should see land by now even allowing that we was on the wrong track this morning. If you ask me, sir, it was the Galloper Light we saw, and not the Sunk at all.'

'I see, and how far is that from the shore?'

'Twenty-five miles, sir, or maybe more, we was a bit to the north-east'ard of it when they dropped us.'

Gregory nodded. 'What sort of speed do you reckon we can make an hour?'

'Three knots, sir, that 'ud be good for scratch crews like this.' The Petty Officer stroked his chin and looked at the General thoughtfully.

'Three knots, eh?' Sallust repeated. He was reckoning up quickly their probable distance from the coast. Over twenty-five miles meant an eight-hour pull at least. They had started with the break through of the sun at two and it was just on six o'clock, so they might have covered half the distance. Daylight should last till about nine, just long enough for them to pick up the coast line before the sun went down, and another hour to pull. But that was only providing that they had not increased their distance from the land by rowing in the wrong direction for three hours or more in the early morning. If they had, darkness would close down again before they picked up the coast, then it was probable that they would row round in circles again all through the night—a grim prospect. Yet there was nothing he could do about it so he sat there in the stern massaging the muscles of his leg and puffing away interminably at Rudd's looted cigarettes.

Gradually the sun sank towards the horizon, its slanting beams lighting up the tired faces of the men. For more than twelve hours now, apart from the forenoon interval, they had been rowing turn and turn about. Their mouths were parched and dry, their palms hot and aching, their backs weary with the strain, but wherever they turned their eyes there still remained the unaltered prospect of the gently heaving sea. Long banks of cloud were gathering in the west and for a little time those in the stern were entertained by the glory of a magnificent sunset, but Gregory and Sims who were whispering anxiously together again knew that it was the last glimpse of their friendly smile. In a great ball of fire the sun sank into the restless tossing waters beyond the bow.

'Think we'll be able to keep our course?' asked Gregory.

'I doubt it, sir.' The Petty Officer shook his head. 'But if it's a clear night there'll be a moon and stars. They'll help us to get back on it.'

Unfortunately as the twilight deepened, great masses of cloud seemed to be piling up from the west, obscuring what little light still remained in the sky, and half an hour after sundown black night had come upon them.

The double crews stuck uncomplainingly to the toil, relieving each other at set times, but there was no longer any strength or elasticity in their stroke. They did little more than pat the water with their oars despite Kenyon's and Silas's encouragement. The night of fighting and the long day in the boat had fagged them utterly.

At eleven o'clock Gregory ordered a further issue of rations. More of those evil biscuits, another wedge of cheese and a swig of water. It had turned chilly again and Veronica and Ann huddled together once more under their tarpaulin. Sallust refused to lie down, but sat, poker-faced and silent, in the stern.

Rudd started another sing-song, but gay choruses and marching songs were conspicious by their absence. Sad, lilting tunes followed one another with unbroken regularity. *Annie Laurie, A little Grey Home in the West* and *Mother Macree* took the place of *Tipperary* and *Three Men Went to Mow*. In an attempt to raise their spirits Rudd called for individual talent, starting with a raucous rendering of *Do we love our Sergeant-Major?* sung to the travesty of an ancient and popular hymn. Veronica, who had no voice at all, surprised them by a gallant attempt at *Sur le Pont D'Avignon,* but although she could not sing herself she adored music, and she was rewarded for her pains by the discovery that one of the Greyshirts was an ex-opera singer, so after a little persuasion she had the strange pleasure of hearing a first-class baritone pouring forth the clear notes of the Toreador Song from *Carmen* into the echoing silence of a desolate sea. No one had the temerity to follow so excellent a performance and by midnight the whole party were sleeping, or silently endeavouring to still the cravings of their empty stomachs.

Sims was nodding in his seat when Gregory roused him. 'Isn't that a light off the starboard bow?'

The Petty Officer started up. 'Why, yes, sir.'

'Is it a lighthouse or a vessel, do you think?'

'That I wouldn't like to say, sir, but we'd best pull towards it.'

Orders were given to the weary crew, and the boat headed again in a new direction. The man at the bow, now worn out with his exertions, occasionally caught a semi-crab and, topping the wavelets, sent a sheet of spray into the stern. Gregory cursed him mildly but knew that the man's blunders were unintentional. Kenyon was bandaging his blistered palms with the tail of his shirt which he had torn away. Veronica was feeling sick but feared to rouse Ann who had dropped off to sleep.

'I got a feeling that's Orford Ness Light, sir,' said Sims after another half-hour had slipped by. 'We'll make the coast quicker if we put her over to port a bit, for we should be south of that.'

'Very good,' agreed Gregory. 'Do as you think best.'

'If I'm right, sir, we've been drifting down the coast for some little time.'

The new direction taken with the light on the starboard bow, the duty crew, unutterably weary now, tugged at their oars. No sound broke the stillness but the gentle swish of the waters and the rhythmic rattle of the oar looms in the crutches.

After a time Kenyon stood up to take over again, he had ceased by this time to count the number of spells that he had done, but looking forward he saw a line of whiteness in the gloom and at the same moment a cry came from the bow.

'Something ahead, sir.'

All but the sleepers peered into the darkness. It was the

surf breaking upon a shallow beach, and as the boat slid forward, the exhausted crew leaning on their oars, a black mass became visible.

'All together,' sang out Gregory, and with a sudden access of energy the Greyshirts began to pull again.

Sims hastened forward and was the first to jump ashore. Several others followed, plunging knee-deep into the water as the boat grounded on a shelving beach of shingle. The remainder stretched their cramped limbs and climbed out one by one.

'Pull her ashore,' Gregory ordered, 'we may want to use her again later,' and after two or three heaves the men succeeded in running the whaler up out of the water.

In groups of three or four they stumbled up the beach, the loose pebbles slipping and slithering beneath their feet. When they reached the top the faint starlight from one quarter of the heavens gave a little help as they looked about them. The shore seemed to curve away on either side without any sign of habitation.

'We'll try to the right,' said Gregory, 'must strike something sooner or later, but first let's get clear of this shingle.'

The pebbly foreshore seemed to stretch interminably inland, hummocks and dips of slippery stones alternating like the waves of a solidified sea, but at last they became firmer and interspersed with small tussocks of coarse grass. The party turned right and trooped wearily along the last embankment beyond which it seemed that the sea never penetrated.

Ann was almost dropping with fatigue but Kenyon had his hand under her arm and was leading her forward into the darkness. Silas was helping Veronica, and Gregory, limping painfully now, was at the head of the party, leaning hard on the shoulder of the faithful Rudd, but suppressing a groan at every step. With bowed shoulders the non-commissioned officers and men brought up the rear.

Suddenly a dark blotch loomed up before them. 'Martello Tower,' Kenyon and Ann heard Gregory mutter, and a moment later the whole party were standing in a group beneath it.

They had not got a torch between them but the lance-corporal produced a box of matches; they found the doorway and Gregory followed him inside. In the faint light the walls were hardly perceptible, but the floor seemed reasonably clean and even.

'All right,' he said to Rudd, 'we'll doss down here for the night. Fetch 'em in.'

Everybody was too completely exhausted to grumble at the lack of bedding. In the light of the remaining matches they sorted themselves out and scattered round the walls. The two girls sat down on the hard floor; they had never felt so unutterably tired in their lives before. Kenyon was near them and he glanced at his wrist-watch as a match flickered on the far side of the tower.

'It's a quarter past two,' he said.

'When? What day are we now?' asked Veronica.

'Let's see, we left London on Friday, didn't we? Well, it's Monday then.'

'Gosh!' she exclaimed rolling over on her side, 'never, ever, at any time, have I been away for such a ghastly week-end.'

Gregory's cigarette glowed faintly in the darkness. 'Yes,' he said slowly, unaware that the whole of his audience were now sound asleep, 'but the trouble *is* that we have failed to make our getaway. We're back in England—after all.'

17

Strange Sanctuary

Dawn came and found the whole party still sunk in heavy slumber. The pale light filtering through the narrow door did little more than lessen the musty darkness in one segment of the tower, and their many hours of exertion, anxiety, and distress had utterly exhausted every one of the survivors. It was well after eight o'clock before the first stirrings among the men showed signs of returning consciousness.

When they awoke it was with no sense of tired limbs refreshed after healthy sleep. They were stiff and sore from a night spent upon the hard concrete without bedding or blankets, chilled through by the damp atmosphere into which the sun never penetrated, and gripped instantly by the sharp pangs of unsatisfied hunger.

Silas looked round the great, circular, vault-like chamber. His eyebrows, which Veronica had likened the day before to *circonflexe* accents, rose, giving a comically Robeyish expression to his large pink face, as he turned to Kenyon.

'Where in the world have we got to now?'

'This is a Martello Tower,' Kenyon replied. He was hopefully but quite uselessly trying to comb back the rebellious auburn curls with his fingers.

'And what would that be?'

'An old fort. There are dozens of them dotted along the East Coast of England, and the South Coast too. They were built when Napoleon threatened to invade England with the army of Boulogne in 1802.' Kenyon rose stiffly to his feet and followed Gregory who was limping towards the door.

Silas smoothed back his thin, rather fine hair over the bald spot at the back of his head and, following them out into the morning sunshine, looked up at the old tower with interest. It stood solitary and grey upon the edge of the shingle, windowless and severe, its sides sloping inwards towards the top; rather like a vast sand castle that some enormous child had deposited upside down out of a gargantuan bucket; the strange relic of military activities in a former age.

Gregory was studying the landscape. Half a mile of rolling shingle separated them from the sea, and to the south the long curving beach swept uninterrupted to the horizon. Behind them spread a mile or more of low, desolate marshland, intersected by watery dykes, then further inland rose gently sloping wooded hills.

They walked round to the north of the tower and Kenyon gave a quick exclamation of delight. The same curving beach of shingle stretched away to infinity before them, and the same low marshlands, but some three hundred yards on a little eminence between the two stood a single row of fishermen's cottages. 'Breakfast,' he added briefly.

'We'll hope so,' Gregory agreed.

'Where would you think we are, General?' Silas inquired.

'God knows, but we'll soon find out.' He settled his impressive cap at a rakish angle over one eye.

Ann came towards them from the tower, pale dishevelled, but smiling. 'This is Shingle Street,' she cried. 'I've often picnicked here.'

'Have you, my dear,' Gregory turned to her quickly. 'And where does Shingle Street happen to be?'

'Suffolk; it's only about five miles from my old home at Orford.'

'I see. Sims was right about that light then. At all events we're a healthy distance from Harwich.'

'Oh, miles and miles,' Ann agreed. 'The nearest town of any size is Ipswich.'

'How far is that?'

'About fifteen miles as the crow flies, but you'd have to cross the river Deben and there isn't any bridge unless you go round by road and then it must be twenty or more.'

'Good! We're not likely to have any trouble from that quarter then. Fane, will you take half a dozen men and reconnoitre the hamlet; see what they can do to help us with supplies.'

'With the greatest possible pleasure.'

All the men had come out of the tower now and were stretching their cramped limbs in the sunshine. Kenyon picked half a dozen lads and set off with them along the foreshore, but evidently their presence had already been noticed by the locals, for as they advanced a small crowd came out to meet them. Several fishermen in dark blue jerseys, an anaemic-looking youth in plus fours and a little tubby man with an ancient boater set at a jaunty angle on his round head. The latter seemed to be the spokesman of the party.

Kenyon explained briefly how they had fetched up the night before and were in urgent need of food. The tubby man gave him a whimsical look.

'So's lots of people or my name's not Solly Andrews.'

'Well,' said Kenyon persuasively, 'there are only about twenty of us and we had practically nothing to eat all day yesterday so we should be awfully grateful if you could help us out.'

'What do you say, Jan?' Mr. Andrews looked at a tall fisherman with bright blue eyes and a face tanned coffee brown by constant exposure to wind and sun.

'There's no lack of fresh fish and plenty more where they come from.'

'Well, there you are,' said Mr. Andrews; 'fish if you want it and water to wash it down, but nothing else mind.'

'That suits us splendidly.'

'Right, best bring your party down to the hotel, and I'll tell my girl to put on some whiting and a few herrings.'

'Hotel?' repeated Kenyon in mild surprise, glancing quickly at the single line of twenty or thirty low houses.

'Yes, the Anchor; that's my house and has been these twenty years. I'll be setting up the tables up in the garden.'

'Thanks, Mr. Andrews, it's very good of you. With a smile Kenyon turned away and a few moments later he was reporting the good news to Gregory.

The remnant of the small force was paraded and marched down to the inn, Ann and Veronica following fifty yards behind since the latter declared that she would allow no one to see her until she had had a bath.

'I feel completely leprous, darling,' she announced to Ann. 'Somebody ought to give me a bell so that I can warn them of my coming.'

'What nonsense,' Ann protested, shaking back her short, dark, tangled curls. 'We may be a little untidy, but look at those awful stubbly beards on the faces of the men.'

'Sign of virility, love, and you'd be all right in your birthday suit; everybody would simply adore you, but I become a perfect hag without the amenities. My face must be like the Gorgon's head at the moment, and every male would be frozen in his tracks at the very sight of me.'

'What'll that thing be?' Silas asked Gregory on the way to the hotel, nodding at a low, round, flat-roofed concrete structure perched on a slight ridge of rising ground halfway across the marsh. A narrow slit like the elongated mouth of a pillar-box gave it the appearance of a stumpy, grinning head peering towards the sea.

'Oh, just an old machine-gun emplacement.'

'Really! But who'd put a thing like that in this god-forsaken spot?'

'The army,' Gregory laughed. 'The whole country round here is peppered with those pill-boxes; you'll find them even miles inland. They were put up in the German invasion scare of 1916.'

'Is that so? Well it certainly brings home to a stranger

like me how near you really are to the Continent of Europe. We're apt to overlook that in the States.'

'It's a darn good job nobody wants to invade us now,' said Gregory thoughtfully. 'We should be caught properly on the hop.'

When they arrived at the Anchor they found two buxom fresh-faced girls and a busy lad laying up long tressle tables on a square fenced-in lawn behind the inn. It was a jolly little place; two broad bow windows set in the house and painted, like a porch, a brilliant green, suggested the quiet homely comfort of long winter evenings with good fires burning, and big tankards of Mr. Tollemache's best beer. The proprietor bustled out, a pleasant smile on his face.

'Well I never! To think I should live to see a real live General as a guest of my house,' he cried as he caught sight of Gregory's hat, 'but it's strange times we're living in.'

Gregory limped up to him. 'It's very good of you to give us a meal at all with things as they are, but you must let us pay you whatever's right.'

'Keep the money, sir.' Mr. Andrews gave a short laugh. 'What good is it now? There wasn't a tin of biscuits to be bought in Ipswich Saturday; no, not for a five-pound note.'

'Things are as bad as that, eh?'

'Worse, friend, worse, and the people spreading over the countryside like a flight of locusts. We're in luck's way being off the map like this or they'd eat us out of house and home.'

Gregory led the little man on to talk of his last visit to the town, and listened with sombre interest to the account. Andrews, it seemed was the only man in the community who owned a car, and he had gone to Ipswich in the hope of obtaining groceries. He found the shops all shut, while police and Greyshirts patrolled the main streets of the town, and long queues of people waited patiently before the Government depots for their rations, the delivery of which had been delayed owing to the breakdown of the railway services. There had been riots on Friday night, and the poorer suburbs were in a ferment. In fact, when he was trying to leave the town again, bricks, bottles and stones had been hurled at his car, smashing the windows and the windscreen, and only by driving recklessly through the demonstrators had he escaped. The road towards Woodbridge had been thick with hungry people seeking shelter and food in the outlying villages, and as Andrews described the long procession of vehicles, vans, carts, cars, and even perambulators, piled high with furniture, bedding and more precious household goods, it reminded Gregory with terrible vividness of the refugees retreating westward along the poplar-lined roads after a big German advance in France.

'Would you go in again?' he asked. 'I mean, if it is necessary to make a reconnaissance?'

'Not me,' said Mr. Andrews fervently. 'Not for a thousand pounds I won't; and I couldn't if I would for that matter. I'd hoped to get the gas for the car, but there wasn't any so it died on me back on Sutton Common, and I had to walk the last five miles home.'

Gregory smiled. 'There must be hundreds of thousands of cars abandoned by the roadside by now. What a chance for the car bandits, eh?'

'Ah! if they had the gas,' laughed Mr. Andrews, 'but a thousand atmospheres would be worth more than a Rolls today. Come on now, sir, here's breakfast, and eat hearty. You never can tell when you'll see another square meal.'

The men had already sorted themselves out and stood round the two long tables, which had last accommodated a crowd of noisy trippers, and Gregory needed no urging. With Veronica and Ann on either side of him he took his place at the top and they sat down to the dishes of fine fresh fish.

'Boiled, they are, miss,' Mr. Andrews apologised, leaning over Veronica's shoulder, 'but none the worse for that and I must keep what little fat we've got for other cooking.'

'They're delicious,' she declared heartily. 'What fools people are to make such a fuss about blue trout; if herrings cost as much they would be three times as expensive because they've got ten times the flavour.'

'Well now!' declared Silas, 'I do think Lady Veronica's arithmetic is just marvellous. I couldn't have worked that out in a month of Sundays.' His blue eyes twinkled merrily at her out of his round expressive face, and they all joined in the laughter.

When the meal was over Gregory led three rousing cheers for mine host of the Anchor, and after many expressions of goodwill, marched his queerly assorted company back to the Martello Tower.

The men were sent down to the beach for a bathe under Sergeant Thompson and Petty Officer Sims, while Gregory called a conference of the officers. Ann, Veronica, and Rudd were asked to attend *ex officio* and the party settled themselves upon tufts of coarse grass in the sunshine, some fifty yards to leeward of the tower.

'Now,' said Gregory, 'we must discuss our future plans. As you know it was my intention to take you all safely out of England but my luck didn't hold, so here we are back again in this unfortunate country where everyone is about to starve to death or go mad. The question is, do we stay here where an inscrutable providence had seen fit to park us, or do we advance upon a port in the hope of securing another ship?'

'We haven't been lucky with ships,' murmured Kenyon, 'and we *are* lucky to be here at all.'

'Unless you can procure a private yacht of at least a thousand tons with a skipper and crew who adore you, my dear, this child sits on the beach until it is all over,' said Veronica firmly.

Gregory smiled. 'You assume that it will be over then, in—say a week or a fortnight's time?'

'I haven't the faintest idea, but nothing will get me on a warship again until the King holds his next review at Spithead.'

'You prefer to face the very real possibility that civilisation is breaking up and England going back to the dark ages?'

'Yes, O man of valour! I'm prepared to walk naked about the beach if need be, but I'm not going on a warship.'

'This ship business,' said Silas suddenly. 'Why did you choose a naval boat? Surely a trader would have been easier to get away with in the first place, and a whole heap easier to control once you were on board.'

'In order to be able to say "Stand and deliver" at the Azores or to other shipping when our supplies of food and fuel ran low.'

'Well, it certainly was a great idea, and with fifty good men behind you it might well have come off, but we've nothing like the same chance now, so I'm for taking a tip from the big Willie with the brown face. There's plenty of fish in the sea, let's stop here and eat them.'

'What's your view, Ann?' Gregory smiled, noting that a touch of colour was creeping back into her lovely face.

'No more ships for me, thank you,' she said promptly; 'and anyhow I'm quite near my home now.'

'I don't see how that will help you, or us. However, what do you say, Rudd?'

'I'm for doin' jus' what you think best, Mr. Gregory, sir. I don't doubt but we'll manage all right.'

'Yes, but I'd like to have your opinion all the same.'

'Well, if that's your wish, sir, this is 'ow it seems to me. Mr. 'Arker there, if 'e'll excuse the expression, said a mouthful. Wiv invalids an' ladies—pardon me, Miss—'ow are we goin' ter get another ship? But if we stays put in this 'ere tower we could 'old it against the 'ole blinking Army if we wants to, an' speakin' for meself I've 'ad worse vittals than those we 'ad fer breakfast many a time, so wots the matter with a bit of a 'oliday by the sea?'

Gregory nodded. 'Well, you all seem pretty unanimous against any further attempt to leave the country, although frankly if I thought there was any reasonable chance of capturing a sea-worthy ship, I'd take it, whether you came with me or not. I can see some sort of decent future for myself if only I could get to a black man's country where the climate's good and the food abundant, but I can't see any here. In a week or so the people from the towns will have permeated the whole countryside and then it will be dog eat dog. Once our ammunition is exhausted we shall stand no better chance of surviving than the rest, and if we do, it will be to drag out a miserable existence through a bleak East Coast winter on a diet of herring. However, there is no prospect of a ship at the moment, and as Rudd says, we can hold the fort if we're attacked by any starving rabble, so we had best dig in here for the time being. Now I'm going to have a talk to Sergeant Thompson about the men.'

'One moment, General,' Silas raised his pointed eyebrows. 'Are you banking on our friends in the village feeding us all the time?'

'They don't imagine that they are going to at the moment, but, of course, they will.'

'Does that mean that King Sallust is going to do his buccaneer act again?'

'No, I hope that won't be necessary. There are many ways in which we can be useful to the locals and earn our keep. The gift of our protection alone is worth a lot at a time like this.'

Silas looked up in admiration. 'Give them your protection in exchange for fish, eh—you're a marvel. Al Capone would have gone all green with jealousy if he had ever heard about you.'

Gregory grinned back. 'Well, at least I'm adaptable. If I can't be King of the Hebrides, I certainly mean to be King of Shingle Street, and that before the day is out.'

'Sure,' drawled the American, 'and what do we do now?'

'Sit in the sunshine while I see Thompson, and discuss the future with the Mayor and Corporation.' With a little laugh Gregory moved away.

'Kenyon,' said Ann quietly, 'I want to talk to you.

He looked up catching his breath a little as he met her eyes. 'Righto, let's walk down to the shore.'

Side by side they strolled across the little valleys of shingle, the pebbles jumping and sliding under their feet until they reached the last ridge above the gleaming line left by the turning tide.

As they sat down Kenyon felt a nervous apprehension, the tension was almost visible between them now, then slowly, awkwardly, Ann broke the silence.

'This has been an incredible experience, my dear, and I shall never forget you, as long as I live.'

Something seemed to sink in the pit of Kenyon's stomach as though he was falling in a rapid lift. 'What on earth do you mean, Ann?' he managed to say.

'Only that, although I was stupidly angry with you at the time, I do realise that you saved my life by dragging me out of London, and I wanted to thank you before I go.'

'Go!' he echoed with dismal foreboding, 'go where?'

'To Uncle Timothy at Orford. It's only five miles away, you know, and I must see what has happened there. I'm naturally anxious about him.'

'But you won't stay there, will you?'

'Yes, if everything is all right.'

'You'd be safer, much safer here with us.'

'Why, it's such a quiet little place I don't suppose for a

minute that it's been affected any more than Shingle Street, and it's my home. The people there have known me all my life and would never dream of doing me any harm, besides——'

'Besides what?'

'Well, I don't want to see you again—for a long time.'

'But why, Ann, why? What have I done? I know I behaved like a fool in London, but everything seemed to happen so quickly. My head was bung full of the election when I met you, and before I saw you again we were right on the verge of the crash. I hadn't a thought of marrying anybody, and was only living from day to day, just wondering what was going to happen to us all. I loved you before that night in Grosvenor Square, you know that, but I hadn't properly woken up to it, and because I hesitated a second you're holding that against me. Surely you're not going to turn me down because of that?'

Ann sat silent, staring at the countless spangles of dancing sunshine which flickered on the sea. In her heart she knew she loved him, and she was fighting a bitter battle with herself. If she had been certain that Gregory was right and everything was going sky-high she would not have hesitated, the trimmings of civilisation were not essential to her happiness, and she would have remained cheerfully, joyfully adapting herself to a new and primitive existence, where she would cook and fend for Kenyon while he snared game or gathered shell-fish from the beach; and both would laugh together over silly stupid things till dawn dimmed the camp fire, then sleep, his curly head pillowed upon her breast, far into another day. Ann, perhaps, was more bitterly disappointed even than Gregory that their fortunes had not carried them to Southern Seas. There it would all have been so simple—but here the old problems remained.

Kenyon had taken her hands in his and was kissing the small grubby palms while he went on pleading fervently for her to stay, but she could only mutter: Don't, my dear, don't,' and stubornly shake her head as she visualised the actual possibitities.

If Gregory was wrong, and, after a period of violence, order was restored again, where would she be if she had married Kenyon in the meantime, as he was pressing her to do now? That streak of pride in her which took the form of queer inverted snobbery, revolted at the thought of the position she would occupy. His wife, but not quite of his world. If only all the women were like Veronica, but they weren't and she was tortured by a vision of their subtle slights, aimed at her but lodging in Kenyon's heart and therefore causing her a hundred times the pain and mortification.

He could laugh over it now and call her 'a precious little fool with absurd notions about people she did not know,' but would he laugh after a year or so if they went back to Grosvenor Square? If she married him and then lost him she thought it would kill her, and her resolve not to let him see her true weakness for him made her harsher in her refusals than she knew herself. Yet despite the pain in his face she was determined not to give way and chance spoiling his life by a surrender to this passion scarcely yet a week old.

She even refused to allow him to accompany her to Orford saying that she had already spoken to Gregory who had promised her Rudd and two men as an escort for that afternoon.

For an hour he reasoned, and finally, driven by the ill success of his arguments, bullied; but her firmness shook him, and as he talked on, reverting again to tender expostulations at her hardness, he began to be conscious of a horrible feeling of futility, that whatever he might say or do she would not alter. His awareness of it sapped the logic from his contentations and the passion from his pleading, so that after a time he found himself stupidly repeating the same phrases over and over again, and at last, by sinking into a miserable silence, he acknowledged defeat.

'My dear, I'm sorry,' she said, 'terribly sorry, but it is far better that I should go away, and that five-mile trudge with a parting at the end of it would be a miserable business, you must see that.'

'All right,' he agreed a little suddenly, then with a quick movement he drew her to him. 'Kiss me, Ann, kiss me; we shan't have a chance later on.'

She pressed his face back gently, terrified that if he kissed her she would fail at the last and let herself go. 'I—I'd rather not, Kenyon. Oh, well, if you want me to.'

He hesitated for a second, and then as she assented

crushed her in his arms, but her lips had none of the soft warmth that has made his senses rock in Gloucester Road, they were firm, cold and unresponsive. With a little sigh he put her from him, and she turned her face away to hide her quick relief that he had not tried her resistance higher.

A few hours later he watched her small, almost childish, figure as she stepped rapidly along between the tall soldiers. All four grew smaller and fainter until they were gradually merged into the green and grey of the foreshore towards the north.

He turned away to find Veronica beside him. 'I wish she hadn't left us,' she said suddenly. 'Do you remember, there was death in her cards that night I told them at Grosvenor Square?'

18

The King of Shingle Street

True to his boast, Gregory concluded a highly satisfactory understanding with Mr. Solly Andrews that evening, by which he became virtually the dictator of Shingle Street, and at the same time responsible for the lives and well-being of the whole community. Then he set himself with tireless energy to provision and fortify the place against seige, which he felt certain they would be called upon to sustain from the starving multitudes of town workers who would sweep the country, picking each village clean.

During the days that followed, every man, woman and child who were not employed in augmenting their supplies, laboured at the fortifications which he threw up; and once they understood the grim menace of the furtive strangers whom Gregory's sentries were already turning back from the outskirts of their area, they worked cheerfully enough; joking and laughing as though they were assisting in the erection of some strange fair for a super Bank Holiday.

His main objective was to make the place impregnable and self-supporting so that whatever horrors might befall beyond the wooded hills that ringed them in, they might live secure and in plenty for many months, or even years, if need be.

Silas was set to build a strong redoubt at the north end of the village and with his machine-gun party took up his residence there. Gregory continued to occupy the Martello Tower which must prove the natural keep of the fortified enclosure, and Kenyon, now made Town Major, moved with Veronica to the Anchor.

All four messed at the inn, Mr. Andrews handing over his private sitting-room to them for the purpose, and after the first night the jolly little landlord became by invitation a member of the Mess.

The day after their arrival was mainly occupied by making the first dispositions, and after dinner that night Gregory outlined his plans.

'Hell's bells!' exclaimed Veronica when he spoke of remaining there for months or years; 'what a prospect!'

'Sorry you're bored.' He gave her a quick, sidelong glance, 'but later I hope to have more leisure to entertain you.'

Her curved eyebrows went up as she puffed at her after-dinner cigarette; two a day was the ration now. 'Is that a promise or a threat?'

'Shall we say a desire,' Gregory answered smoothly, and for once Veronica was left without an apt reply. Then he turned to Kenyon: 'You and Silas will take out parties tomorrow. Four men apiece should be enough. Move off at eight o'clock, and scour the country for five miles around, one to the south and one to the north. Visit the nearest farms, make a note of all provisions, live stock, fruit and crops, then get back about four o'clock to let me have all the information that you can. On Thursday we'll start in to clear up everything we can lay our hands on while the going is good.'

'Do you mean that you're going to rob these poor people of anything they have left?' Kenyon asked in a shocked tone.

'My heart bleeds for them,' Gregory smiled with mocking cynicism, 'but my stomach craves for fresh meat—or will do before long. So I fear it has to be. By the by, keep your eyes skinned for a bull and if you find one don't take any chances on it being there the following day, but bring it back with you.'

'You're going in for raising cattle then,' Silas remarked.

'Yes, the sooner we start a home farm the better. Cows, pigs, sheep, geese, chickens; we'll need them all if life is to be made bearable.'

Solly Andrews shook an admiring head. 'It was a lucky tide for Shingle Street that washed you up on the beach, if I may say so, sir.'

'Well, I hope you're right,' Gregory laughed. 'Who's for bed?'

Silas stood up slowly. 'I've no objection if you're all for it, but not requiring a deal of sleep I'd be happy to take a stroll along the shore first, if Lady Veronica felt that way.'

Gregory just caught the twinkle in Veronica's eye before she lowered her lids and said demurely: 'I'd adore to, Mr. Harker.'

'That's fine.' He held the door open for her and threw a casual good night over his vast shoulder to the others.

Secretly she was tremendously intrigued. Gregory's interest in her had been patent from the beginning, but Silas had never shown anything more than the genial good nature that seemed to radiate from his large person to all about him.

He led her down to the fringe of the beach where the rollers thundered ceaselessly upon the shingle, without attempting to start a conversation, and vaguely troubled by his silence she said suddenly:

'The waves are a natural orchestra, aren't they? We might be listening to the overture of the "Flying Dutchman".'

'Yes, or Beethoven. It must have been like this when he wrote the "Moonlight".' He nodded at the bright August moon riding high in the heavens, and added slowly: 'It seems natural somehow to transmute these long dark shadows and the shimmering of the waters into sound.'

She looked at him curiously. 'You're musical then; I don't know why, but somehow I feel I might have guessed.'

'Yes, it's half my life—by far the better half—and I knew we had that in common from the way you watched that fellow singing in the boat.'

'Did you? But tell me about the other half. What do you do in normal times, Mr. Harker?'

'I?—oh, I'm in Steel,' he replied laconically.

'Were you over here travelling for your firm when the trouble started?'

'I wouldn't say that exactly, the firm's got a London office on this side.'

'Oh, you were here permanently then?'

'No, just looking round, but maybe you wouldn't have heard the name of Harker in connection with Steel before.'

'What!' Veronica exclaimed, 'are you *the* Harker?'

'Surely. If you have ever heard of anyone named Harker in Steel, I think it would be me.'

'Of course; how stupid of us not to realise that before.'

'Well, now, why would you?' he protested with a little laugh. 'I'd hate to go around with "Millionaire" placarded on my back.'

'Yes, but your other name, Gonderport, ought to have given us the clue, if we hadn't been so busy wondering how long we were going to remain alive; and you must admit it's surprising to find a Captain of Industry who rows boats and digs trenches as cheerfully as if he had been used to it all his life.'

'Believe me, Lady Veronica, this is the first decent holiday I've had in years.'

'Holiday!'

'Yes, it's as good as breaking prison to get away from the sort of life I lead. Stenographers, balance sheets, and big business folk chasing me all the time, and every ten minutes: "This'll be your call, Mr. Harker. Mr. Harker, I've got your office on the wire. Mr. Harker, you're wanted on the Transatlantic line." The same thing goes on even if I'm at Deauville or down for a bit at my favourite home in Atlanta, Georgia, for what the folk on the news sheets call vacation. For once in my life, too, I was dead certain that no one was after me for my money, and you've no idea what a joy it is to be taken at my face value by people like your brother and the General, without having to wonder just what they want to sting me for.'

Veronica nodded. 'Looked at that way a millionaire's life must be pretty grim, but how in the world did you metamorphose yourself into an officer of Greyshirts?'

'Easy,' he chuckled. 'I tumbled to it pretty early in the game that there was real trouble coming and I figured that every live man would have to take a hand some way in the cause of law and order, so I had a talk with an old friend of mine that I met way back in the War. He just insisted that I must be an officer and fixed it for me; so when the crash came all I had to do was to walk right out of Claridges and get into a suit of dungarees.'

And you honestly mean to tell me that you are enjoying this incredible party?'

'I do; but you're not really unhappy, are you?'

'Not really. In fact I might be quite enjoying it too, if only I could see my hairdresser and buy a few things for my miserable face.'

'Now isn't that queer—' she could see his cherubic smile in the bright moonlight—'ten days ago I could have gone right off and bought you a whole beauty parlour if you'd felt that way, now I can't even buy a ten cent cigar for anyone; but why worry, you don't need those things, you're just lovely as you are.'

'Mr. Harker!' Veronica's voice was not a protest, but a faint, delicious mockery.

'Have a heart now,' he protested quickly. 'I may have lost my fortune but I've still got my first name; it's Silas.'

'Well, Silas, do you know what I think about you?'

'No; but I'd give a heap to learn.'

'You haven't got it dearie; but I'll tell you all the same. You're some fast worker.'

'An' you're sure the Katz pyjamas,' he laughed, copying her idea of Bowery American idiom.

'Sez you?'

'Sez me—an' *how*.'

'Is that a fac', big boy?'

'It certainly is.'

'Tra-la-la, well, some dew and some don't—so let's get back to the ballroom.'

'What's that?'

'Oh, just a very antiquated joke, my dear; but seriously, I think you're a grand guy and I like you lots.'

'That's good to hear—er—Veronica!' He casually drew her arm through his and they began to stroll back up the beach.

'You may think so,' she said after a moment, 'but I'll tell you something. Silas. I'm a cad from cadville, so be sensible, laddie, and don't waste your time on me.'

'Thanks for the warning, but I'm not just out of the egg myself.'

'Why? Are you heavily married or something?'

'I have been—and divorced, but that was when I was a kid pilot in the War days. We were all mad then and it didn't last a year.'

'But that's æons ago; surely you haven't been lying fallow ever since?'

'Not exactly, but I've been mighty cautious these last three years. I near as damnit got hooked by a girl in Boston; she had all the virtues and was daughter to a rich man who ran his local church, but I caught her selling my market tips and got out in time; since then I've been extra careful.'

'My poor friend, how easily you brainy men get stung.'

'Yes; I might have known she looked too good to be true.'

'Like me?' Veronica paused on the doorstep of the inn.

'No.' His slow smile came again. 'You're not good; but I'll bet you're true.'

Her ripple of laughter echoed up the stairway as she softly closed the door of the Anchor.

On the following day the exploring parties set off before Veronica was up so, after attending to the wounded who were progressing favourably under her somewhat spasmodic care, she spent the morning attacking a huge heap of mending which she loathed, but which Gregory had insisted on her undertaking as payment for her keep. After lunch she deliberately played truant and wheedled an old salt into taking her out for a few hours in his boat. By the time she got back Kenyon and Silas had returned, and both had a tale of woe to tell.

They spoke of deserted farms and frightened people who had fled at their approach. Kenyon had seen one poor woman and three children obviously murdered, a gruesome heap lying where they had been flung in a manure pit. A few of the farm houses were already looted and their contents left scattered about the rooms in wild confusion, while on the moors inland, the startled hares had given place to frightened humans, crouching in ditches here and there, scared and suspicious of each other. The few that they had caught and questioned could tell them little, except that nothing would induce them to return to the terror of the towns.

Only one piece of possible good news came out of these

expeditions, and that was Silas's discovery of the Hollesley Labour Colony, which lay some two miles to the north-west of Shingle Street. It comprised a considerable settlement of town dwellers who had been transferred in previous years to the land, where they occupied small but pleasant houses and were peacefully engaged in fruit and dairy farming. Their principal official had failed to return from a visit to London early in the crisis, but under the leadership of an early colonist, whom Silas reported to be full of ability and sense, they had organised themselves to preserve order in their own district and resist encroachment.

Gregory felt that such neighbours might prove a blessing if they could be induced to trade the fruit and eggs which they had in abundance for Shingle Street's surplus of fish, and made up his mind to visit their leader as soon as more urgent matters had been attended to; but the general report of the state of the countryside made him more determined than ever to secure all the provender he could without further delay.

In consequence Kenyon was dispatched early the next morning with a party of six soldiers and six villagers, to collect all that he could of the remaining stock from farms which he and Silas had marked down the day before.

It was a heartrending experience and one that set a severe strain upon his loyalty. As a boy, like others of his class, he had snared many a plump pheasant on the neighbouring lands that marched by Banners out of sheer devilment, but to rob old women of their chickens in broad daylight is apt to turn the stomach of any decent man. Yet he knew that if they did not hang together and obey Gregory's orders, given in the interest of them all, they would surely die.

With a heavy heart he watched his men harness the scraggy horses into commandeered wagons at the nearest farms, and by ten o'clock a procession of five vehicles were winding their way behind him through the peaceful lanes.

At each house they visited he witnessed the same heart-breaking procedure, women in tears and sullen, cursing men. Whenever he could, he dealt mercifully with them, taking in quantity only from those who had comparative abundance, and consoled a little by the knowledge that, had he refused to undertake this foray, another might have been sent who would perhaps have dealt far more harshly with the unfortunate country people.

As the day wore on their loads increased. One wagon contained chickens under a net, another pigs, a third a fine stock of flour from a mill, a fourth ducks and geese, the fifth all sorts of miscellaneous provender; but the farther they advanced inland the more frequently they came upon batches of stragglers and the bolder these became. At first the little parties of two and threes only pleaded with him to give them food and followed for a short distance before despairing of succour from his convoy but, later, larger parties advanced threateningly from scattered coppices by the wayside and only the sight of the soldiers' rifles kept them from attacking.

When he arrived at Shottisham he encountered real trouble. A farmer had followed them two miles on foot, shaking his fist and shouting curses at them for the seizure of two of his pigs. To Kenyon's annoyance the man raised the village against him and the locals, hurriedly concluding a brawl in which they were engaged with some town roughs, joined forces with their late enemies and set on his convoy. The farm carts could not be galloped so he halted them as close together as possible in the wider portion of the village street, and then stood up in an endeavour to pacify the crowd, but a shower of stones soon put an end to his peroration.

Obviously there was only one thing for it; but he warned his men to fire high, and a volley shattered the silence of the sleepy street. For a moment turmoil reigned and the eighty or more people who composed the crowd fled in all directions, but with the sudden realisation that no one had been hurt they regained their courage, and under the leadership of the angry farmer made another rush.

Kenyon knew that his dozen men would be overwhelmed in two minutes if he hesitated any longer and that, hate it as he might, the outcome depended upon himself, so he drew his pistol and shot the farmer neatly in the thigh.

With a yelp of pain the man rolled over in the gutter, while the crowd stopped dead, overawed by this sudden display of determination. Swiftly Kenyon seized upon the ensuing silence.

'Take warning!' he shouted, 'or my men will put a volley

in the middle of you. Up against that wall, quick now!'

In a rapid shuffle they obeyed, pressing near each other for shelter as they huddled against the barn he indicated.

He ordered down his troops and lined them up with rifles at the ready: 'If any of you move a step, you're for it,' he announced tersely to the cowering crowd, then, determined to punish the villagers for their attack rather than loot any more of the miserable scattered farm dwellings, he sent his half-dozen Shingle Street handy-men into every house in the place to commandeer all that they could lay their hands on.

Two more carts had to be requisitioned for the extra load, which consisted of a fine miscellaneous haul including the entire supply of drinks from the village pub, which were discovered to have been hidden in a hen house, and a most welcome find of some three thousand cigarettes.

With a parting threat, that if any of the wretched inhabitants moved a foot before his last wagon was out of sight they would get a volley, Kenyon turned his convoy about and headed once more for Shingle Street.

Silas was sent out on a similar errand the following day, but Gregory, suspicious that his Lieutenants were too soft-hearted for the business, set out himself on Saturday with a squad of twenty men.

Just before midday Silas abandoned his herculean labours on the Redoubt and went in search of Veronica. He found her, dressed in a suit of borrowed overalls, busy painting three enormous notice boards in the garden behind the inn. They bore the legend, WAR DEPARTMENT —ENTRANCE FORBIDDEN, and were being made at Gregory's orders for erection, one about a mile inland on the road up into the hills and the others on the foreshore half a mile or so to the north and south of the village. In his view, the English being such law-abiding people, the sight of them with a sentry pacing up and down nearby would be sufficient to prevent isolated tramps, or even small parties of fugitives, from advancing nearer to Shingle Street.

'Would you do me the honour to have a little lunch with me today?' Silas inquired blandly.

'My good man,' Veronica jammed her paint brush back into the pot, 'don't we always feed together in this infernal pub, and it looks as though we shall until I'm grey.'

'No, this is a little private party I'm throwing at the Ritz-Carlton, Shingle Street; do come.'

'O.K., big boy,' she said a little mystified. 'Lead me to it,' and pulling off her overalls which concealed her long slim legs in a pair of borrowed shorts, she strolled along beside him to the Redoubt.

Rudd greeted them in the big dug-out which Silas had constructed for himself; it seemed that he had been borrowed for the occasion, and he was busy arranging a mass of cottage-garden flowers on a carefully-laid table.

Veronica sniffed an appetising smell. 'Don't that make yer hungry, miss?' grinned Rudd.

'It certainly does! Produce the ortolans, friend.'

Silas settled her comfortably in a chair and the meal began. Fresh lobster, roast duckling and green peas, followed by a dish of nectarines and washed down with a bottle of Moselle.

'How did you do it?' she laughed as Rudd served the coffee and Silas produced fresh boxes of cigars and cigarettes. 'That's the best lunch I've had in the hell of a time.'

His round face broke into a puckish smile. 'There are plenty of lobsters on the coast and if you treat the fishermen right they're first-class boys. As for the rest, didn't Gregory send me out raiding yesterday? The party occured to me when I struck a good-sized private house.'

'Well, I give you full marks, Silas.' She stretched out a hand across the narrow table, and he laid his own great paw gently on it.

'It's comforting, somehow, to eat a Christian meal again, but what wouldn't I do with you if I had you in New York.'

'You never know,' mused Veronica.

'No, I guess you never know,' he repeated and they smiled quickly at each other.

Silas went out to set his men to work after their midday spell and then returned to keep Veronica company, declaring that in the last six days he'd done enough work for a dozen men, which justified him in taking a holiday.

They laughed a lot, finding immense amusement in their different lives and the strange fate that had brought them together on this undreamed-of-shore.

The afternoon sped by all too quickly, and they were

still together when Gregory returned from his foray. His men were grim and silent, evidently hating the work which he had imposed upon them, but his haul was far larger than that made on either of the two previous days and told the tale of many a ravished farmstead.

Not yet content he sallied forth again on the Sunday, this time with a different squad of men, and returned once more in the evening, tired, morose, and poker-faced, but with a long line of loaded wagons. Between them in the four days the countryside for miles around had been swept bare of every living thing except the starving humans whom he now reported to be living on their cats and dogs; but Shingle Street was provisioned against an indefinite siege. With fish, meat and poultry in plenty the inhabitants could survive the most rigorous winter almost in luxury.

All he required now was fruit and fresh vegetables, so on Monday, having carried out a rapid inspection of the fortifications which were growing apace on the lines he had laid down, he set out as his own ambassador to Hollesley.

Mr. Merrilees, the elected representative at the Labour Colony, received him a little suspiciously at first, but soon became friendly. He was a small, nervous, bearded man, and his somewhat bigoted enthusiasms provided much material for Gregory's cynical sense of humour, yet Gregory took care to conceal his amusement with that urbane manner of which he was such a master.

The labour movement, the Wesleyan Church, and the British Empire were the trinity of gods which governed Mr. Merrilees's existence, but he was not above killing a chicken and cooking it for a Brigadier-General.

'Not that I approve of the Military,' he hastened to say. 'I'm a pacifist myself, for the burden of war ever falls heaviest on the working man, but all soldiers are the servants of the Government and represent the King, who is a fine man if ever there was one—long may he be spared to us!'

'Amen,' said Gregory, marvelling at the quaint philosophy by which his host had arrived at this loyal wish. Then after the fashion of all potentates, whatever the manner of their arising, they fed first and got down to business afterwards.

In Merrilees, when he had explained his project, Gregory

found a willing trader, but one who knew how to drive a hard bargain. An agreement for the exchange of commodities proved a simple matter, but with all the tenacity with which he had fought against wage cuts in the past, Merrilees now demanded shelter for his people within the Shingle Street fortifications in the event of a concerted attack by the starving workers from the towns.

This Gregory was loath to concede since in a time of crisis it would mean his having to support a number of useless mouths who could no longer make a return for their keep, but eventually a compromise was reached. Merrilees was to place thirty of the fittest men in his community permanently at Gregory's disposal forthwith, to be trained in the use of arms and apprenticed to the fisherman's craft, so that they would be a present help and an additional support, in case it should become necessary to receive the whole Labour Colony into the sanctuary of Shingle Street.

When the treaty was concluded, Merrilees puffed thoughtfully at his pipe, filled with dried herbs, with which he was already experimenting and looked across at Gregory from beneath his bushy eyebrows.

'What's your opinion of the trend of things, General?'

The corners of Gregory's mouth drew down into an ugly bow. 'Pretty black,' he confessed. 'It seems to me that the present civilisation is doomed utterly. Railways, planes, motor-cars, newspapers, are only words now; for all practical purposes they have ceased to exist. Even the wireless which might have kept us in touch with things, has broken down. It's ten days since the broadcasting stations have been silent, which means beyond any shadow of doubt that the mob have triumphed over any form of organised Government. It means the survival of the fittest, and for those who do survive, back to the land in almost primitive conditions.'

'I'll not agree to that,' Merrilees protested. 'We're passing through a terrible upheaval, I'll grant you, but the people will adjust themselves to changing conditions and the innate sanity of the British working man will prove the ultimate salvation of the country.'

'Perhaps—he's a fine fellow, but it's difficult to keep sane on an empty tummy. I see no remedy short of divine manifestation and I think we can count that out.'

'You're wrong there, General. The Lord shows His will in strange ways at times, and like as not it will be in a movement of the common people.'

Gregory nodded silently, forbearing to voice his own conviction that race movements and mass urges, either to sound policies or madness, had for their inception fundamental reasons which al owed no place for a benign or angry God.

'Besides,' Mr. Merrilees went on, 'there must be other groups like ours scattered all over the country, whose leaders are getting into touch for the general benefit like you and I today.'

'Here and there,' Gregory agreed, 'but you forget the great industrial centres. I can do with vegetables and you can do with fish, but neither of us would swap a rabbit for a railway train, so the poor devils in the towns stand no chance, and the troub e is that they are in the great majority. Tell me what do your people do if they fall sick, ordinarily?'

'There's the hospital at Ipswich.'

'True, but from all reports nobody's life is safe there any more. What do you intend to do with them in the future?

'I hadn't thought, but why do you ask me this?'

'Because it is our greatest danger. People are killing each other in the towns already, some are dying as we sit here, in attempts to loot; others in trying to defend their property. Soon there will be thousands dropping by the wayside from sheer starvation. It is too much to hope that even a tenth of them will receive proper burial, and it is August, remember. The bodies will decay in the hot sun.'

'Yes, I take your meaning.'

'Disease will spread like wildfire, perhaps even plague will deve'op and sweep the country like the Black Death in 1348. What do you mean to do if some of your people begin to sicken?'

Merrilees bowed his grey head. 'It is a terrible picture that you paint, General. What can one do but try to nurse them back to health?'

'I'm sorry,' Gregory leant over the deal table, 'perhaps I'm looking on the black side.'

'No, we must face facts and you have spoken of a terrible possibility.'

'Then to save the majority we must sacrifice the unfortunate, you see that, don't you?'

'What is it that you would have me do?'

'Isolate ruthlessly. It sounds brutal, I know, but we've got to do it for the sake of our respective people. Select a house a good mile from your Colony. I will do the same. The sick must be sent there to fend for themselves; if their relations care to accompany them, that is their look out, but there must be no communication and no exception to the rule.'

'But they'd die there without aid or comfort, man!'

'Maybe, but if you were sick yourself, which would you rather do; stay and endanger your companions, or take a chance of pulling through alone?'

The elderly man regarded him out of sad eyes. 'Why that's a simple problem, General, as you know yourself. It's these others that I'm thinking of.'

'Well, we ask no more of them than we would be willing to give, and as leaders we should be prepared to enforce our judgment; otherwise we are not fitted to be leaders.'

'Ah, it's a hard thing you ask, but you are right.'

'Then from tomorrow I think each of us should hold a morning inspection. Every man, woman, and child should be present; and if any are sick they should be given rations, but they must go. Is that agreed?'

'Yes, it shall be as you say; and may the Lord have mercy upon us all.'

A quarter of an hour later Gregory took his leave, and with a puzzled look upon his careworn face, the ageing fighter of many battles in the good cause of a fair wage for a fair day's labour, watched his retreating figure as, lean and panther-like, his shoulders curiously hunched, he swung away into the distance.

On his homeward journey Gregory encountered two incidents which seemed to bear out his gloomy prophecy. First a dead horse lying at the roadside. Obviously the poor beast had recently been hamstrung, and from its still steaming haunches neat strips of flesh had been removed, while from the bracken a hundred yards away a thin spiral of smoke ascended. He did not doubt that certain very hungry persons were there gleefully awaiting an impromptu meal. The second might have proved his undoing had he been less well prepared. Three men with gaunt, strained faces, from which the eyes bulged large and unnaturally bright, leapt from the bushes at a turning in the lane and set upon him with silent animal ferocity. He felled the first with his loaded crop and flinging himself back against the bank covered the others with his automatic. They fell into a miserable whining about their ravenous hunger, and in a sudden access of pity he flung them the emergency lunch which he had carried with him to Hollesley; yet, turning from them as they fought for the parcel in the road, his clear intellect, rejecting compromise, told him that he wou d have done them better service had he put a bullet through their brains.

The sentry at Veronica's newly-erected notice board reported when Gregory reached it, that he had had a trying day. On one occasion he had actually had to fire over the heads of a party of intruders before he could scare them away; so on the last mile into Shingle Street, Gregory resolved that his guards should be trebled, and two men apiece from his new Labour Colony levies set to support each of his armed sentries. It was evidently no longer safe to leave them in such isolated positions on their own.

That night at dinner Gregory told them of his conversation with Merrilees and his agreement to shelter the population of the Labour Colony if they were attacked, but Kenyon shrugged his shoulders.

'I can't see what either of you are worrying about,' he declared. 'We may have to deal with a few poor starving wretches that any well-fed man who is callous enough could drive off with a stick, but the refugees from the great centres aren't organised, so what earthly harm can they do to us?'

'No, but those who survive soon will be,' Gregory prophesied grimly. 'The strong men are probably forming Workers' and Soldiers' Councils now, and to keep the life in their bodies they'll take anything they can lay their hands on before we're through. I haven't thrown up these entrenchments to keep off tramps and derelicts, but an organised attack upon a definite source of supply. Our only hope then will be to make it so hot for them that they will leave us alone and go for easier game until they settle down, with an enormously reduced population, to new conditions. Then we may be able to make a deal with whatever powers there may be.'

Silas laughed suddenly. 'You'll be a Kommissar-General before we're through.'

'Well!' Gregory smiled back at him, 'I've no rooted objection to Kommissars providing I'm one myself. Care for a stroll, Veronica?'

She smothered a fake yawn. 'Why not, O reincarnated Vicar of Bray.'

'You think I change coats too quickly, eh?' he asked directly they were outside.

She laughed. 'My dear, if only some of papa's old cronies could see you in your present get-up!'

'They're probably all dead by now, so what's it matter?'

'Not two hoots in hell, General, dear. If you choose to become an acrobat and get yourself up in tights, it's all the same to me.'

'You're no fool, are you?' he exclaimed.

'No dearie, I certainly am not.'

'This way.' He suddenly pulled her arm and turned inland behind the houses. 'The surf makes so much noise you can't hear yourself speak; and the shingle's hellish hard to sit on.'

'So we're about to sit are we?'

'Yes, unless you prefer to go back to the pub; I should not dream of protesting against your decision.'

'And you're no fool either, are you?'

'Yes; if I'd had any sense I'd have shot another half-dozen of those bloody mutineers, then we'd be running south from the Azores by now.'

'Don't kick yourself unnecessarily. You put up a pretty marvellous one-man show.'

'Not too bad, but I ought to have done better. How's this?' Gregory pointed to a gently-sloping grassy bank.

'I've seen worse in my career of crime.' Veronica stooped to sit down.

'Half a minute, it may be damp,' he warned her as he slipped off his tunic and spread it out for her to sit on.

'Thank you, Sir Walter; but what about you?'

'I shan't die that way,' he laughed, and pulled her down beside him.

'You're a queer bird, aren't you?' she said after a moment.'

'Yes, I suppose I am, but so are you for that matter.'

'*Touché*—and birds of a feather!'

'That's about it, but honestly I should go mad if you weren't in this party.'

'Liar!'

'No, I mean that.'

'Tra-la-la! so you say.'

'It's a fact, but I wonder why it is that women always see the main issue of a thing so much clearer than the average man. Kenyon can't chuck off his stupid public-schoolboy morality, Silas is so damned soft-hearted he thinks I'm a devil from hell; Thompson and the troops still believe me to be a Brigadier so "theirs not to reason why"; Andrews is only interested in the welfare of his people, and good old Rudd follows me blindly, never pausing to think at all. Not one of them really appreciates that although I could clear out on my own tomorrow I'm staying here to fight their battle as well as my own. You're the only one in the whole party who may protest at times but, given a reason, understands and approves my actions.'

'Perhaps that's because woman always consider the man so much more important than the principle.'

'That's about it; and in this instance I'm the man, aren't I?'

'Your grammar, my sweet, is appalling.'

'Does that matter?'

'Not a nickel in hell!'

'Good for you; are you comfy?'

'Yes.'

'I'm glad of that because I now propose to kiss you.'

'Well,' she turned her face up to his in the moonlight. 'I'm glad of that because it will intrigue me to see if you are as great a lover as you are a leader of men.'

19

Death in the Cards

The first ten days at Shingle Street had seen the transformation of that quiet hamlet into a pulsing centre of strange and seemingly unconnected activities: the second saw them take form and cohesion. Regular convoys were proceeding between the village and the Labour Colony. The small fishing fleet was organised on Naval lines the men electing, at Gregory's suggestion, the most experienced among themselves as Commander and Lieutenant. They ordered sailings in accordance with weather and tide, while Petty Officer Sims augmented the flotilla by supervising repairs to boats that had long been out of service. The majority of farm carts, now no longer needed, were knocked to pieces, and from the material a jagged but stout palisade erected behind the village under the lee of the houses. Into the compartments of this great corral the live stock were herded, safe from the rigours of the coming winter or the depredations of desperate men who might slip past the sentries under the cover of night.

The fortifications were now almost completed and a long line of breastworks linked the Martello Tower on the south with Silas's redoubt to the north, screening the whole village and the stockaded enclosure upon the landward side. Gregory well knew the weakness of his defence to be his limited armaments. Only thirteen men with rifles had survived the debacle of the *Shark*, and his pistol and those of Silas, Kenyon, Sims and Rudd would be of little use except at close range. He still had his three Lewis guns, however, and leaving those in charge of picked troops, passed on the rifles to some of the ex-service men in his Labour Colony levy. He had also acquired eight shotguns and several hundred cartridges on his forays into the interior, and formed a special squad to bring these into action if an attack was pressed to within the limits of their range, so he hoped to be able to put up a performance which would lead an enemy to think that the garrison was far stronger than it was in fact.

However, he placed his confidence far more in rendering the place almost impossible of approach, and for that purpose raked the village from end to end for suitable material. Wireless aerials, now silent and therefore useless, flagstaffs, wood fencing, iron palings, obsolete fishing nets. Every box, barrel, and wicker basket in the place to be filled with shingle and inserted in the breastworks. Old potato-sacks and tarpaulins were filled with earth, and he even demolished several sheds to utilise their corrugated iron roofing for revertments.

Entrenchments were dug and emplacements thrown up,

fields of fire cleared for the Lewis guns and these rendered doubly difficult of approach by a hundred ingenious devices. Tangles of wire and netting, pieces of board with long nails driven through them and scattered broadcast in the long grass to stab the feet of running men, and lines of pits with pointed stakes set upright in them, but cunningly concealed by rushes and dried turf.

Veronica meanwhile, slim and boyish in her borrowed overalls, worked at her mending in the August sunshine, or, when she could, sneaked off to sun-bathe in a sheltered dip of the beach that she had found, continuing in the evenings her dual flirtation.

She felt that she liked the big American the better of the two; he never pestered her, but placid, smiling, efficient, always seemed to be at her side when wanted, and she grew to know him better she came to appreciate more and more the immense and kindly tolerance of his simple straightforward nature. He was widely travelled, deeply read, a distinguished *amateur* of music and at some time or other he seemed to have met nearly all the really important people who had influenced events, a month—no, it seemed to her a year—ten years ago, in that other, now so distant and orderly, existence. Yet he seldom spoke of the influence he had wielded and only little by little did she become aware of his vast interests.

Gregory on the other hand treated her in a fashion she would have resented from any other man. He forced her to fulfill her daily quota of the mending that she so detested, as ruthlessly as he made his soldiers dig; stalked off to bed immediatley after dinner when he felt that way inclined, hardly troubling to throw her a casual 'good night', yet such was his magnetism that when he uttered an abrupt 'Come on—let's walk,' her resistance seemed to crumple and with a half-guilty, half-defiant glance at Silas she would gaily respond 'Why not?' and accompany him to the grassy bank behind the stockade. He was as great a lover as he was a leader of men, when he chose to devote himself to her. His crisp intellect was a continual delight and he confided in her alone, often days in advance, every new plan as he devised it for their better security and comfort. He knew too, instinctively it seemed, just when to caress her and when to refrain; so that his passion never irked her, and she began to crave the deft touches of his masterful hands. She wondered sometimes what would have happened if they had met in normal times and felt, that if he had insisted on it, she might well have abandoned Grosvenor Square for Gloucester Road.

Some nights he would neither go to bed nor make love to her, but set off alone on long tramps, penetrating far inland and often not returning until dawn. No one else was allowed outside the fortifications on any pretext, so their news of the outer world was confined to such rumours as he chose to pass on to them after these solitary expeditions. However, he spoke little of them, except to state that conditions in the interior were growing more and more terrible and the roving population desperate to a primitive degree, until at the end of the third week of their stay he told them that he had good reason to believe that a Communist Government had been established in London.

'What effect is that likely to have on us?' Kenyon inquired.

'The disruption has been too great for it to have any at the moment,' Gregory replied slowly; 'and it is doubtful if it can last for more than a week or two. If the old order couldn't feed the people how can the Communists? Yet it is the danger that I have feared all along. Similar groups may gain control in places like Ipswich, and while they last they will endeavour to secure any sources of supply which are left for their own maintenance, regardless of the remainder of the people. Our state of plenty here must be known for miles around by now, and it is to protect us from a proper organised attack that I have thrown up all these defences, my automatic and a loaded crop would have been good enough to scare off anything short of a multitude without arms.'

'Do you think we'd be able to defend this place against troops then?' Silas asked.

'Yes,' Gregory declared firmly; 'the surrounding marshes form a natural barrier and all the ordinary approaches are now so skillfully protected that I am prepared to hold Shingle Street for the Shingaleese against all comers. They won't have any artillery and nothing short of shell fire could drive us out of here.'

During all his days of labour at the entrenchments and palisades, Kenyon's thoughts had never been far from Ann. Had he supposed her threatened by any danger, he would have set out for Orford instantly, but Rudd had reported her safe delivery into the hands of her delighted uncle with a wealth of fluent detail. He reported that the leading citizens of Orford had formed themselves into a committee to deal with any emergency and that, just as at Shingle Street, a plentiful supp y of fish could be relied upon to keep the small population from any danger of actual starvation. The little town was shut away from the industrial areas and great trunk roads by miles of desolate heath and sparsely-populated farm lands, so there seemed little imminent risk of invasion by hunger marchers; feeling her to be secure, Kenyon had flung himself whole-heartedly into the work alloted to him in the early days of their arrival.

As time wore on the urge to see her again was strengthened by a desire to reassure himself about her safety, and in the second week he spoke of it to Gregory, but the General reasoned with him.

'Hang on for a day or two,' he begged. 'Ann's no fool and if there is any trouble at Orford she's certain to seek shelter here. I simply can't do without you, even for a day, until Shingle Street is straightened up and my plans completed.'

'Perhaps she would like to now but is afraid to face the journey with all these toughs on the roads.'

'Nonsense, Kenyon. They wouldn't attack a woman; it's food they are after, and anyhow, she knows the district like the back of her hand, she could easi y come by by-paths if she wanted to.'

'All right,' Kenyon agreed reluctantly, his uneasiness quieted for the moment by Gregory's reasonable hypothesis, but as the days passed he began to worry again. Orford might have its watch committee, but the town possessed no military strength, so how could they resist the growing bands of hungry desperadoes who were pressing daily nearer to the sea? Despite the hard labour on the fortifications which left his body tired each night, and should have ensured a sound healthy s'eep, he could no longer quieten the wild and horrible misgivings which filled his brain. His imagination began to play havoc with his nerves and night after night he tossed and turned sleepless with anxiety until the paling of the stars.

When Gregory spoke of the possibility of organised

attack, therefore, he could bear it no longer but declared his intention of visiting Orford on the following day.

The General shrugged his lean shoulders. 'If you want a holiday by all means go; it's Sunday tomorrow, anyway, and now we have broken the back of our job we might as well reinstitute the ancient custom of the Seventh day. The men will get stale if they're not allowed a break now and then.'

'Good. Then I'll set off first thing tomorrow.'

'As you wish, but I wouldn't fret yourself. I was in Orford a few nights ago and the place was perfectly peaceful. You'll find a picket at the approaches to the town, but I expect they'll let you through when you mention Ann's uncle. I had to dodge them, of course, but that was easy at night because I have the sort of eyes which can see in the dark better than most people's.'

Kenyon had already consulted Rudd on the best way of getting to Orford and knew it to be a longish journey. True it was no more than six miles as the crow flies but the River Butley, only a tiny stream at low tide yet with formidable mud banks on either shore, cut off direct approach from the south-west. He must strike north, cross the stream three miles inland, and turn south-eastwards along the Woodbridge Road, a good ten miles in all; but one of the villagers possessed a bicycle and proved willing to lend it to him for the day, so on Sunday, despite dull and cloudy weather, Kenyon set off immediately after breakfast with his heart high at the prospect of seeing Ann again.

He stopped for a moment at the Labour Colony to exchange a few words with Merrilees whom he met just starting out to visit Gregory. The little man was highly elated at a report that order had been restored in Ipswich and a limited ration, procured from where he could not say, was being issued to the residents who had remained in the town; but his brief mention of a Workers' Council which was apparently in control caused Kenyon to discount the goodness of the news. Merrilees would naturally suppose them to be an honest body, similar to his old colleagues of Trade Union days, but if Gregory was right they would prove a greater danger to the countryside than the unarmed stragglers who infested the woods and moors at the present time.

One thing was certain: no such groups could possibly be powerful enough to reorganise the country with such a terrible upheaval still in progress, and the probability was that, after a brief local reign, they would disappear or develop into bandit formations, who wou d levy a regular toll upon the produce of the surviving peasants in their area, just as their predecessors had done in the dark ages.

With these black thoughts, Kenyon pedalled on through Capel St. Andrew, Butley and Chillesford. Here and there upon the roadside, even in these quiet lanes, he passed an abandoned motor-car or tradesman's van, and twice saw helicopters which had been forced to land in the open fields. Once he caught sight of some fifty people slouching along the road in his direction, and thinking discretion the better part of valour hid behind a hedge until they had passed, but for the most part the people that he saw seemed frightened of him and bolted into the bracken at his approach. Those whom he passed at close quarters showed faces gaunt and evil by lack of food.

Just after he reached the main Orford Road he got a nasty scare. A newly-erected bungalow stood at the roadside apparently deserted, but a big Alsatian suddenly leapt the wicket gate and came for him with gaping, slobbering jaws. Evidently the poor beast, maddened by hunger had taken on the semblance of his half brother the hunting wolf and famished, perhaps for days, was now grown bold enough to attack a man.

Kenyon was knocked spinning from his bicycle and rolled into the ditch, but the dog got his forepaw caught in the spokes of the front wheel so he had a moment to whip out his jack-knife, a souvenir of the *Shark*, and by the time the animal was free he was standing again, ready to meet its attack.

The dog howled pitifully as the blade went home between its ribs and Kenyon felt almost worse about it than when he had had to levy toll on the defenceless farmers, but it was absolute'y necessary, and as he mounted again he felt that he had had a lucky escape from being badly mauled.

'Orford could not be far now,' he thought, and the last few miles of the way thither, he began to be more than ever satisfied that Gregory was right about Ann's safety. The scattered farms grew more infrequent, alternating with long stretches of beautiful but desolate heath where little woods of pine and birch, or wide stretches of golden flowering gorse, broke the monotony of the rolling sweep of heather. A land that had known the imprint of the hand of man for centuries but one with which he had dealt kindly, never settling in his hordes to blacken it with smoke and grime. As the road narrowed Kenyon felt that in normal times one would not see a human being in a three-mile stretch, the way leading nowhere but to Orford and the sea. The last mile or so lay downhill through narrow twisting lanes and there was the little town sleeping in the sunshine as it had slept for centuries, cut off on the north by the great sweep of the Alde and on the south by the Butley from intercourse with its neighbours, its only method of communication the solitary inland road. He noted that it was even separated from the sea by a strip of water which he remembered to be the River Ore; a mile of marshland had to be crossed before the beach cou'd be reached, and there no stretches of fair golden sand lay spread to attract the tripper, but a hard steeply-shelving foreshore where the waves broke monotonously upon the pebbles. Ipswich might be barely a hundred miles from London and its population of eighty thousand people had enjoyed, up to a month ago, all the amenities of modern civilisation, but Orford, although only a further sixteen miles from the metropolis, was literally in the back of the beyond and the life of its inhabitants differed little in essentials from that of their predecessors two hundred years before. In the days of the Flemish weavers it had been a prosperous little port—now it was only a village. A few crooked streets with rambling houses and fishermen's cottages clustered about the great Norman Church; yet even that relic of bygone splendour was in partial ruin, the transepts fallen away, the main aisle only kept watertight for a limited number of parishioners. No railway station linked it with modern life, the nearest being at Wickham Market, seven miles away and only a branch line. Where in all England could Ann live more securely at such a time?

At the first houses four men with staves, and brassards on their arms, stopped him but one of them knew Ann so Kenyon was allowed to pass, having learnt from them that the Reverend Timothy Croome was not the incumbent of the parish as he had supposed, but lived retired at Fenn

Farm some way outside the town. The shuttered shops in the straggling square seemed no more strange than on a normal Sunday and turning to the right he took the road beneath the great eight-sided single tower of the Castle, which dominates the coast for miles around, out into the open country once more. After a little it faded almost to a track running parallel to the sea, and passing two small farms half a mile or so apart, he came to a solitary house which he knew must be his destination.

The track ended there and he propped his bicycle against the ramshackle gate, noting as he did so from the hill upon which the place was set, the broad mud flats of the Butley which cut it off so securely from the south and west. For a second he wondered if Ann would run out when she saw him, and if they would kiss, but his thoughts were chilled by the bleak appearance of the house. Its peeling paint and dilapidated exterior suggested straitened circumstances and, set in this desolate spot between the wind and sea and sky, the thought of easterly gales beating upon its jimcrack doors and windows leapt to his mind, and how cheerless the place must be when the grey mists crept up to it from the marshes in the winter.

He paused for a moment irresolute beneath the scanty foliage of a tree warped by the constant pressure of the wind. The house was silent as the grave; silent with a queer sinister silence that seemed to catch at Kenyon's heart. Why were there none of the little noises that spoke of peaceful habitation? Why no questioning bark—there should at least have been a dog. The iron gate clanged behind him with a dismal sound, yet no inquiring face appeared at the windows.

'Ann!' he bellowed, 'Ann!' but no small figure appeared to greet him. The house remained cold, a cheerless example of Edwardian architecture, grimly foreboding in its continued silence.

With a set face Kenyon hurried up the path. Something was wrong, he knew it with a horrible certainty as he pressed the bell in the absurd ornate porch which gave the place the air of a suburban villa that had gone a-wandering. Jarringly the peal shrilled through the house but no footsteps sounded in the hall. He pressed again but no stir or movement broke the following silence, now weighing like a cloak of dread upon his troubled mind.

He left the porch, stepped back to stare up at the windows and noticed for the first time that the curtains were drawn. Perhaps the place had been abandoned, yet somehow he did not feel that it had, a second sense seemed to tell him that there were people in the house. In search of another entrance he walked swiftly round the corner and coming at once upon an open window, thrust it up, pushed back the curtains, and peered into the dim recesses of the room.

The furniture was in keeping with the house, an Edwardian mahogany dining-room suite, heavy and tasteless. The remains of a meal lay spread upon the table, but Kenyon's thoughts were not upon the furnishings.

An elderly woman lay stretched on her face in the doorway, she was quite still—dead undoubtedly, and the dark matted patch in her grey hair showed that she had been struck down from behind. By the fireplace lay another huddled form, black clad, a clergyman—his white collar proclaimed the fact—but that was stained with blood, and the head hung back at a queer unnatural angle. Horrified but fascinated, Kenyon could not drag his eyes away from the white face and the red gash beneath—for the man's throat had been slit from ear to ear.

'Ann,' he called again, but his voice only came in a hoarse choking whisper, and still there was no answer.

20

A Beacon in the Darkness

For a moment Kenyon leant against the window-sill, almost sick with the fear he now felt for Ann, then, with an effort he pulled himself together and scrambled inside.

He stooped for a moment over the prostrate clergyman although he had no hope that his eyes had deceived him. The man had been brutally and abominably done to death. Next he turned to the woman and found her too, stiff and cold. It seemed the work of a maniac; then Kenyon noted that, although the knives and forks on the table remained unused, there was not a scrap of food left in the dishes, and he knew that men driven desperate by acute hunger must have done the killing. Staggering slightly he stepped across the body of the woman to the door.

It opened on a narrow hallway. A hat-rack showed him the position of the front entrance and two other doors stood on either side of it. He flung open the one on the right and poked his head into an ordinary country drawing-room. Chintz-covered chairs, a mantelpiece loaded with indifferent china, and a piano decorated with photographs. Closing it softly behind him from some instinctive reverence for the dead who lay so near he tried the other. That led to a small study, and a little pile of silver coins lying on the top of a cheap light-oak roll-top desk were evidence that the murderers had not broken in for money. Food was all that mattered. For a second Kenyon ran his eye along the shelves of worn books; most of them were on ancient coinage, evidently the dead man's hobby, and that seemed in some way to bring the tragedy nearer. Softly he closed the door.

A green baize curtain beyond the stairs caught Kenyon's eye and with the sudden thought that the murderers might still be in the house he drew his revolver and tiptoed towards it. Beyond lay the kitchen, orderly and tidy as the old woman must have left it, but the larder had been ransacked. A broken dish and fishbones scattered on the tiles showed the haste which the ravenous pack had made to satiate their hunger.

He crept back into the hall and peered into the shadows of the stairway. It was possible that they were sleeping off their debauch upstairs. Gingerly, and testing each stair before he trod upon it, he made his way up to the first floor landing. In the dim light three doors were visible and with sudden decision he stepped briskly towards the one which opened into the room above the study.

As he opened it a new tension gripped his strained senses. It was Ann's, he knew by the very scent of it before he had the door open a foot. The bright simplicity of the furnishings, so different from the rooms below, confirmed his thought a second later and then he looked towards the bed.

Ann lay there, a small dishevelled figure, huddled upon the outer coverlet, her head buried in the pillow. For a second he felt a restriction in his chest as though his heart had ceased to beat. Was she still alive? Perspiration broke out in pearls little of cold dew on his forehead as he stood crouched in the doorway. He wanted to run to her but his legs seemed paralysed and he could not move a foot. Veronica's prophecy came back to him, and with leaden fear that it might have been fulfilled he whispered again:

'Ann, darling, Ann!'

She did not move, but lay there horribly—unnaturally quiet. Then breaking through the invisible bonds that held him rooted he stepped across to the narrow room and put his hand on her shoulder. Still she did not stir but beneath the thin cotton frock he felt her flesh warm to his touch.

'Ann,' he spoke louder now, shaking her slightly, and at last she rolled over on her back.

'Kenyon!' The big eyes opened.

He covered his own for a second, wiping away the beads of sweat, and sank to his knees beside the bed.

She sat up suddenly, staring with wide distended eyes round the familiar room, then with a little gasp she flung her arms round his neck.

'There,' he soothed her, 'there, don't worry, sweet. No one shall hurt you now. I swear they shan't. Thank God you're safe!'

For some strange timeless interval they clung to each other, speechless instinctive creatures seeking to escape from the horror of a world that had gone insane. Cheek pressed to cheek, their only realisation was that they were together again, although about them mountains slipped into the sea. Her body shook with frightening, tearless tremors, but in his relief at finding her alive, it was his eyes which filled with tears.

'Kenyon?'

'Ann dearest.'

'Have I gone mad or is it really you?'

He pressed the little body in an even stronger grip, seeking to assure her by sheer physical force of his actual nearness.

'Yes, really, Ann darling, and we're both alive and well.'

She laughed then, but her laughter had a queer jarring note bordering upon the unnatural. For a moment he feared that her brain had given way.

'No nonsense,' he said sharply. 'You must try and pull

yourself together, and tell me what's been happening here.'

She stopped then, as suddenly as she had begun, and drawing away put her hands upon his shoulders. As she stared at him her eyes were strangely bright and the pupils horrifyingly enlarged.

'Are they—are they really dead? Or did I see it in a nightmare?'

He nodded slowly. It was impossible to conceal the truth, and she shivered slightly.

'Oh, it was horrib e, Kenyon!'

'Where were you?' he asked gently.

'Outside the window. It was before dinner last night, I had gone up to the hill. I used to do that every evening. Just sit and gaze towards Shingle Street, thinking of you, and wondering if I'd ever see you again.' She spoke simply and naturally now, caressing his hair with her hand. 'I came back in the twilight and what it was I don't know, but something made me look in at the dining-room window as I passed, so I saw it all.'

He took her other hand and kissed it as she went on: 'Poor Agatha was just coming through the door as I looked in; her eyes suddenly seemed to start out of her head and she fell forward on her face, then I saw the men! There were five of them and their faces were horrible, they sprang over her body and set on Uncle Timothy, and one of them snatched up the carving knife, but I couldn't look away. I simply couldn't. Oh, Kenyon!'

It was a wail rather than a cry and again he pressed her to him while her body quivered and shook with great choking sobs, yet he was glad to see her cry for he knew that tears, would bring her relief, and after a desperate fit of weeping she looked up again.

'Then—then I realised that if they saw me they might kill me too—so I ran, just wildly out into the heath among the gorse and bracken, and when I was breathless I flung myself down in a deep ditch where the long grass hid me. How long I lay there I don't know. It must have been hours I think, for the dew had fallen and I was shivering with cold when I did screw up courage to come back. My teeth were chattering, I couldn't keep them still, but when I crept in through the back door, the men were gone, then in the dining-room I—I saw them both.'

She burst into a fresh fit of sobbing at the awful memory,

and for a little time Kenyon strove unsuccessfully to comfort her, but at last she choked her tears back and concluded her story.

'First I thought I'd go to Orford, but my legs simply would not work so I thought I'd better rest for a little until I felt able to face the journey. I crept up here and lay on the bed crying desperately for I don't know how long, and then I suppose, oh, it sounds awful, but I was simply dead beat, and I must have dropped asleep.'

'Thank God you did,' he answered fervently. 'It probably saved your brain.

'But, Kenyon, what shall we do?'

'Why, get back to Shingle Street just as fast as we can.'

'I can't, dear; there'll be the funeral and all sorts of things to see to.'

'Well, we must arrange all that as best we can, but I promised Gregory that I'd be back this evening and nothing will induce me to leave you here another night.'

She smiled rather wanly. 'You haven't changed much, have you?'

'Listen, darling I'm not threatening to carry you off as I did before, but you must see this time that it's really dangerous for you to stay behind on your own.'

'Oh, I wouldn't stay here. I've plenty of friends in Orford who would take me in.'

'Perhaps, but what guarantee have you got that the same awful thing isn't going to happen again, and to you, in a week or so's time?'

'How can I go, it's impossible until after the funeral.'

'Then that must be this afternoon.'

'Kenyon! It's not decent!

'Why, surely you're not afraid of what people in the town will say, are you?'

'Of course not.' Ann shrugged impatiently. 'It is respect for them—I—I loved them, Kenyon.'

'Steady, darling.' He put a supporting arm about her shoulders as she choked back her tears. 'Don't you think that they would wish it themselves, Ann? They'd be the very first to urge it, if it meant your safety.'

She nodded wearily. 'All right, if you can arrange it.'

'Good, we'd better go into Orford at once then, I'll leave you for a moment while you put a few things in a bag.'

Downstairs he applied himself to the grim task of laying the two poor battered bodies side by side and covering them decently, yet even beneath the sheets he unearthed for the purpose the Reverend Timothy gave rise to gruesome thoughts. One knee, bent under him, was held firm by *rigor mortis* and defied all Kenyon's efforts to force it down. At last he was compelled to leave it, a grotesque and faintly terrifying proturberance still cocked ceilingwards beneath the linen.

He had only just finished when Ann came down, and after rummaging for some straps in the cupboard under the stairs, they attached her suitcase to the back of his borrowed bicycle and set off for Orford.

The Vicar's wife, whom Ann knew well but had never liked on account of her dictatorial manner, proved in this emergency a truly Christian woman. After their first words she would not allow Ann to talk of the tragedy, but made her lie down upon her bed, produced aspirin and fine china tea which she valued more than gold dust from her own limited store, and insisted that all arrangements should be left to herself and Kenyon.

Her husband was another of those who had been caught away from home at the time of the outbreak, so Orford was without a vicar; but a local colleague had promised a service for that evening and she suggested that he should be asked to officiate at the interment of the Reverend Timothy and his housekeeper, at the same time.

Kenyon soon learned from her that the little town was by no means so secure as he had supposed. At the outset of the trouble the local farmers had marched in and wrecked the bank, burning the ledgers that contained particulars of their overdrafts, derisively calling upon the manager, who had sought to protect his company's property, to telephone 'Head Office' and see what they meant to do about it. The Watch Committee had restored order, and the head of it was a retired Colonel, a capable organiser, but a martinet, many of whose decisions were resented by the locals, and a Communist Party had been formed among the poorer classes which was likely to revolt against his authority at any moment.

The village undertaker was sent for, and the verger, but neither expressed surprise at this hasty burial of a well-known local character. Both had been called on in these last few weeks to deal with a rush of their melancholy business which neither had ever known before. Even to this seeming sanctuary the terror was creeping closer day by day and a ready outlying farms were no longer safe from the murderous hunger raiders, so they accepted the tragedy at Fenn Farm almost as part of the gruesome daily business which they had come to know.

Later, in an effort to cheer him, the Vicar's wife led Kenyon out into her garden, but the dahlias and golden rod could not draw his thoughts from the long queue of people that he had seen earlier that afternoon in the Square. Not a cigarette or pipe had he seen among the men, and the faces of the women were filled with strained anxiety as they stood patiently waiting for their meagre rations; some distance away a group of men wearing red armlets had been hustling three miserab'e-looking fellows towards the lock-up; invading townsmen, he had no doubt, caught in the act of housebreaking or some nefarious business on the outskirts of the town.

Now he was regarding Orford with very different eyes to those with which he had viewed it in the morning. It seemed only a matter of a week or two before the Colonel and his committee must be submerged under a wave of Bolshevism, and for the first time Kenyon admitted to himself that there was real justification for Gregory's policy of ruthlessness to any but their own community. Only behind those well-p'anned and well-provisioned defences at Shingle Street was there any real hope of survival in this dissolution of England which was now affecting even its remotest parts.

At half-past six Ann and Kenyon accompanied the Vicar's wife to the ancient church. All regular parisioners had gathered for the service and, in addition, many townspeople who had learned of the Reverend Timothy's tragic death.

The visiting clergyman was an e'derly man of unusually fine physique, stooping slightly in the shoulders but with a handsome leonine head on which the silver hair swept back from the broad and lofty forehead. His eyes were large, intelligent and kindly, and the fine tenor of his voice would have attracted 'arge congregations had he been the incumbent of a wealthy parish. In a few simple sentences he passed from the subject of the newly-dead to an address upon the present situation, urging his listeners upon a course which would ensure their spiritual, and might ensure their bodily, preservation.

He proceeded to cite the conduct of his own parishioners as an example. At the beginning all had been filled with fear at the approach of these terrifying and unknown dangers which were creeping in upon them, but a few, and those by no means the most regular attendants at his church, had come to talk with him about measures for their safety; and, in what seemed to him almost a miraculously short space of time, a strange understanding had come to them that if they would only believe in Our Lord and Saviour, no fear should ever trouble them any more.

Hard-headed business men, and farmers who all their lives had been wrestling every penny from each other, had put their avarice behind them and spoken to others of their conversion, so that soon the whole village had come, in this great emergency, to see the light.

He went on to describe the new life and hope that had permeated his community. How each morning they gathered for a simple service to ask a blessing and a guidance for the labours of the day, and met each evening to render thanks for their preservation; while their need being greater than his, it had even been necessary for him to lend his own Bible to poor people who lacked that blessing, that they might read at home the wonderful message which all had learnt at school, but so many forgotten in the turmoil of modern life, yet which stood as a timeless beacon, unflickering, undimmed, in the growing darkness of a changing world.

'Of what value is property any more?' he asked; 'God in His goodness has given us many blessings, but in our folly we have abused them, hoarding where we had opportunity, striving against each other for a greater share than our necessities warranted, and waxing fat and slothful upon the labours of our weaker brethren. Now, in His infinite wisdom He has chosen to change the order of things that we may see them in their true perspective and live more nearly in accordance with His will. The fruits of the earth remain with us and the fishermen may still go down to the sea. There is no reason, once the crisis is past, why any man should starve, but once more the money changers have been thrown out of the temple and humanity given a new chance to accept the simple, straightforward teaching which Christ laid down nearly two thousand years ago for the guidance of mankind.

'Death and destruction are upon every side,' came the clear clarion note of the silver voice, 'yet that is only because we have been bound up with ignorance and evil for so long. No man who truly believes upon our Saviour can raise his hand against another, and although everyone will be called upon to make some sacrifice of worldly goods, how infinitesimal is that sacrifice compared to the ineffable peace and joy which comes to those who live daily according to the Word, strong in the knowledge that the divine love is about them, and certain that whatever may befall, their blindness has been lifted from them, so that when their eyes are closed to this life on earth they will be the joyous recipients of the eternal salvation in the life to come.'

It was the most vital sermon that Ann and Kenyon had ever heard, and with the people of Orford they stood silent and awe-struck, so that the passion of the afternoon was gone and the terror which had assailed them in the morning.

Silently, with lowered eyes, they followed the creaking farm wagon which carried the coffins to their last resting place and after the final rites set out, with new hope in their hearts but little knowledge of what lay before them.

21

Gregory 'Reaps the Whirlwind'

Kenyon had been anxious to get Ann safely back to Shingle Street before dark, but that was impossible now. It was already seven-thirty when they started off up the hill out of Orford, and he knew that they would have to tramp a good portion of the way for, in this undulating country, he could only carry her on the step of his bicycle where the gradients were favourable.

They made fair going until they reached the forked roads in Watling Wood, but there they were delayed for a little by a curious incident. A lanky man in a battered bowler planted humself in the middle of the road and asked where they were going.

'To Woodbridge,' said Kenyon promptly.

'Then you have our permission to proceed,' replied the queer individual.

'Oh? Oh, thanks!' Kenyon murmured with some surprise.

'Don't—er—mention it to the Cardinal,' added the other.

'What?' inquired Ann.

'I find him a little difficult, you know,' the stranger waved his cane gaily and then leaned forward in a confidential attitude. 'He is a little puffed up with the success of our Army at La Rochelle.'

'I quite understand,' agreed Kenyon with a soothing note in his voice. 'It must be very difficult for you.'

'True—true, but not for nothing are we called Louis the Just, and the Bishop of Luçon has proved his worth.'

'I am certain that he appreciates the confidence of his master,' declared Kenyon, for after such a day he could not resist the temptation to indulge his humour with this curious acquaintance.

'You are a person of understanding,' was the quick response. 'What a pity that you are not noble. If you were we would nominate you for the Order of the Golden Fleece. Our brother of Spain has just sent us a couple.'

'Fortunately,' said Kenyon, 'I happen to possess the necessary quarterings.'

'In that case we must certainly think of you, but can we persuade the Cardinal? That's the thing. De Richelieu is always after these windfalls for his own cronies—and he's so devilish plausible. We have hardly been able to call our soul our own since that terrible trouble with poor Cinq Mars.'

'Yes, that was a dreadful business,' Kenyon shook his head, 'but with your gracious permission we must proceed.'

'Of course, of course. We too must ride on. La Villette tells us that he has raised a fine stag in the forest of St. Germains, and as the Cardinal will not be back until tomorrow evening—you understand.'

Kenyon politely raised his hat, and setting the battered bowler more firmly on his head, that strange wraith of a vanished sovereignty disappeared into the lengthening shadows of the Suffolk lane.

'Poor sweet,' said Ann. 'Who did he think he was, dearest?'

Louis XIII of France, I imagine, though God knows why!'

'Stark staring mad, of course.'

'Yes, these troubles must have sent him off his head, unless he is from the Ipswich Asylum. When they could no longer feed them they probably turned the inmates loose.'

'How ghastly.'

'I know, but let's not talk of it. There'll be a good dinner, and everyone so pleased to see you when we get to Shingle Street; I only wish the light would last a little longer though.'

Already the sun had set behind the trees, but the afterglow lit their way as they pushed on to Chillesford, where Ann suggested that they could save a mile by turning off down the track through the marshes, which would bring them out at Butley Priory.

By the time they reached the road again dusk had fallen, and now made bold by the coming darkness the human wolves who infested the countryside began to leave the hiding places where they had lurked during the day. Some accosted Kenyon, whose progress with Ann behind him on the bicycle was slow, casting envious glances at her suitcase, suspicious that it might contain food, but he warned them off with a flourish of his pistol. Others slunk quickly back into the hedges on their approach, fearful that Kenyon, with his superior physique, might have a mind to prey on them.

The cottages that they passed were either dark and deserted or, if inhabited, showed it only by chinks of faint light through heavily-boarded windows behind which the owners lived a state of seige, yet in the second hour of their journey the road was rarely free of sinister-moving shadows.

Only Horsley Heath now remained to be passed before they reached the friendly Labour Colony, and another half-hour should see them home, but night had fully fallen, and when Kenyon was forced to dismount at a rise in the road both were filled with apprehension. Somehow the lonely stretch of common land seemed so much more likely to hold hidden danger than the friendly hedgerows which they had left behind, and it was easy to imagine every bush to be a crouching enemy.

Strange, whining voices came out of the darkness every now and then, and once the sounds of a violent quarrel. Ann's arm was through Kenyon's and her hand clasped his as they trudged up the hill, yet at each unaccustomed sound from behind the gorse on either side she shrank nearer to him in sudden fear and, as he caught the note of soft padding footsteps in their rear, he urged her faster towards the hi ltop, suddenly apprehensive that they were being followed.

'Who goes there?' A sharp voice cried as they breasted the rise.

'Friend!' said Kenyon, automatically.

'You come here, then,' said the voice.

Kenyon drew his weapon and, passing the push bike to Ann, stepped a few paces forward. Three men advanced out of the darkness to meet him.

'Where be ye a-goen' to?' asked the man who had challenged.

'Hollesley,' declared Kenyon.

'Oh! then just you come and see the boss.'

Ann made ready to run for it and Kenyon moved a little nearer to her, but the following footsteps had stopped, and turning they saw two other men waiting silently behind them.

'Look here!' Kenyon protested.

'Now then,' countered the first man, 'you be a-goen' to have a word with the boss; come on now!'

For a moment Kenyon was tempted to shoot the fellow where he stood, but four others were near enough to rush him and one of them gripped Ann by the arm. 'Take your hands off,' he said sharply.

'All right—all right,' the offender protested. 'I ain't a-goen' to do no harm.'

Four more men joined the group and Kenyon felt that it would be a risky business to start a fight now that they were surrounded. He might shoot a couple but how could he protect Ann in the *mêlée*—better be tactful and after having been searched for food they would probably be allowed to proceed. 'As you like,' he agreed with a shrug, 'but it's late and I'm in a hurry.'

'Foller me,' the man who had first challenged them turned on his heel and led them through a small coppice and out onto the open heath while the last four arrivals followed.

'Cattermole,' called the leader as he halted on the lip of a shallow dell, 'do you want to have a look at two folk a-goen' to Hollesley?'

And Kenyon, peering over his shoulder, saw that two hundred or more men and women were seated in the hollow, their faces shadowed or illuminated alternately by the flickering flames of a small bonfire. From what little he could see he judged them to be agriculturists, farm labourers and the like, accompanied by their women. Then a tall man in gaiters and a yellow waistcoat came up the slope towards them.

After a sharp glance he nodded to his lieutenant. 'Bring them down to the fire, Rush, we'll see 'em better there,' and, the men behind closing in, they were hustled forward into the dip.

The ragged people crouching round the blaze regarded them with scant interest, most of them were busy on a meal of roots and vegetables which they were eating with their fingers from still-steaming pots.

Kenyon was questioned by Cattermole who seemed to distrust his well-fed appearance, but was obviously only out to secure further supplies of food, and after Ann's suitcase had been searched it looked as if they would be allowed to go on their way again, until Rush suggested to his leader: 'Better keep 'em with we till by and by, hadn't us? Or they might let on to what's up——'

Even then it is probable that no harm would have befallen them if a stout red-faced man had not glanced at Kenyon curiously as he stumbled past them to the fire.

He stopped dead in his tracks and thrust his face nearer, then suddenly he cried: 'Blow me if this 'ere chap ain't one o' they hisself!'

'What's that!' snapped Cattermole and in a second a score of figures had crowded round them.

'E's one of they,' declared the farmer angrily, 'him an' his khaki boys took a dozen hins an' a pig off me three weeks ago—I'll swear to he and no mistake.'

A growling murmur ran through the hollow-eyed throng as they pressed nearer, and when a rasping voice cried:

'Hang 'un then,' the cry was repeated from a dozen throats: 'Yes, hang 'un—hang 'un!'

Too late Kenyon realised his crass stupidity in not having forced a passage in the road. Gregory would have done so, even at the price of killing half a dozen of these poor devils but, like a fool, he'd stopped to parley and now it looked as if his reluctance to shoot down unarmed men was likely to cost him his life.

Even now it was Ann who urged him into action as she clutched his arm and whispered fiercely: 'Shoot, Kenyon! Shoot! It's your only chance!'

'Run for it then—I ll follow if I can.' He thrust her from him and pressed the trigger of his gun.

Rush had caught her words and flung himself on her as she spoke, and with a sudden wrench she twisted from his grip and, ducking uner the arm of another man, fled up the slope.

The man in front of Kenyon gave a gasp and, clasping his hands to his stomach, sank to his knees. The revolver cracked again and another livid spurt of flame lit the darkness. The red-faced farmer let out a howl of pain and, tumbling into the heather, clutched at a shattered knee cap, but the others were upon him before he could fire again.

A heavy cudgel caught him on the shoulder, a piece of wood with a nail driven through the end descended on his upper arm, and as he stepped back, bashing sideways at a nearby face with the butt of his pistol, another cudgel came down upon his head.

His weapon was wrested from him and with the blood streaming into his eyes he fell half fainting to the ground. Someone kicked him savagely in the ribs, and a second blow on the head as he lay gasping in the heather made him see a horrid succession of bright stars and circles until blackness supervened and he lost consciousness.

Only the efforts of the gaitered Cattermole saved him from being kicked to death there and then, but he stood over Kenyon's prostrate body and drove off his followers with an angry snarl.

'Stop it, you fools,' he shouted, 'He'll be more use to us alive than dead—and you can always hang him later.'

With surly looks they reluctantly gave up the lynching, and instead tied Kenyon's hands and feet, then left him.

By that time he was beginning to come round. Vague

thoughts of Ann in Gloucester Road and the Mid-Suffolk Election came to him, but as he struggled feebly to sit up the full realisation of his wretched position flooded his mind.

He lay very still then, reasoning that no crowd, however maddened by fear and hunger, ever hanged an unconscious man. To be a really sporting event the victim should be dragged screaming to the gallows, or at least be sufficiently conscious to kick lustily as he is hauled off the ground, and Kenyon meant to postpone his threatened execution to the last possible minute.

Inch by inch, with the most desperate care not to attract attention, he shifted his position slightly so that he could see what was going on, and found that he was lying a little outside the circle of light upon the rim of the small natural amphitheatre. He searched the crowd swiftly for signs of Ann, but she was nowhere to be seen and he gave a sigh of relief at the thought that she must have got away, only a moment later realising with a new wave of distress that she, like himself, might quite possibly be trussed and lying hidden in the heather.

Cattermole stood near the blaze, his arms akimbo and his hat perched well upon the back of his semi-bald head. He was addressing the gathering in short sharp sentences, and as Kenyon listened, he caught both the trend of the speech and the reason for the crowd's violent hostility to himself. The last rousing sentences came clearly on the night air.

'Didn't they?' he cried with a challenging note. 'And what right have they to do that? None say I! Not under law or reason, soldiers as they may be. Property is property and if a man's no right to keep the hins what he's bred—what rights *has* he got I'd like to know? It's every man for himself these days, not to mention the wife and kid's he's got to fend for. So, if you're game to back me up I'll lead the crowd of you down to Shingle Street and we'll teach these thieving soldiers a thing or two. There's not many of them but there's a lot of us, and if we stick together we'll be having a square meal that we've a right to before the morning.'

Loud shouts of approbation greeted the conclusion of Cattermole's impassioned oratory, and Kenyon let his aching head sink back in the heather while a host of new thoughts struggled with the pain for supremacy in his mind.

These were wretched people whose homes they had robbed and looted, now banded together and planning a bloody revenge. He must warn Gregory! But how could he? His own skin needed saving first and of that there seemed little enough hope. The cords which bound him were cutting into his flesh already and he knew from his first efforts to free himself when still half conscious that his bonds had been tied with savage tightness. His friends at Shingle Street would be surprised and massacred—but no, it was far more likely that Gregory's sentries would rouse the garrison, and this unwieldy crowd, surging forward in the darkness, be mown down by the blast of the machine-guns, or caught as they fled in the treacherous pits and nets.

Both alternatives were horrible to visualise but Kenyon had little time for further speculation. A burst of cheering came from the dell and two men running up the bank seized him and pulled him to his feet.

He kept his eyes fast shut and tried to make himself a dead weight, but someone flung a pannikin of water in his face and his eyes flickered open at the shock. It was useless to pretend any longer that he was still knocked out.

His feet were untied and with his arms still bound behind him he was pushed roughly into the centre of the crowd.

'We're going to Shingle Street,' said Cattermole briefly—'they've got arms there—haven't they?'

'Yes,' said Kenyon, 'plenty. So unless you all want to get killed, you'd better keep away.'

'That's my business—how about sentries?'

'Yes, they've got sentries too. You'll never take them by surprise. For God's sake be warned in time.'

'You can keep your warnings. What's the password?'

'There isn't one.

'Naturally you'd say that, you thieving, murdering swine, but I'll unloose your tongue. Bring me a faggot, Rush.'

Rush pulled a long branch from the blazing pile and Cattermole took it from him: 'Now, are you going to talk?'

'I can't,' protested Kenyon, 'there is no password.

You'll be met by the ordinary challenge—that's all.'

'Hold him, chaps.' As Kenyon's arms were seized from behind, Cattermole thrust the lighted end of the faggot against his chest. He flung back his head in quick recoil, choking as the stench of burning clothing filled his nostrils.

'I can't,' he gasped again, struggling violently with his captors as the sharp pain seared his chest. 'If I said "stale fish" you might belive me, but there *is* no password.'

Cattermole removed the brand and nodded with slow understanding. 'Al right,' he muttered, 'I reckon that's the truth, but what's the most likely spot to get through the sentries, eh?' He advanced the red-hot piece of wood again threateningly.

Kenyon, the water starting from his eyes, sought wildly for some sympathetic face among the crowd, but their famished features showed only grim approval of their leader's tactics and a hard, gloating amusement.

'Don't be a fool,' he protested, 'if I tell you, what guarantee have you got that I'm not lying; and they'll shoot you down whichever way you try to rush them.'

'Well, you'll be the first to get it in the neck if that's the truth so you'd best take us the safest way,' Cattermole laughed with a bitter, scornful savagery. 'Why else d'you think I saved you from being lynched on the hill there? Come on, chaps, who wants red meat for supper!'

It was useless to argue further. Maddened by hunger the mob were prepared to take any risk and were as clay in the hands of their determined leader. With an answering shout they followed Cattermole from the dell as he pushed Kenyon before him, jabbing him in the back with his own pistol.

Muttering and cursing as they stumbled in the darkness the whole party streamed across the heath and out on to the road, then in a straggling body they set off towards Shingle Street.

As he trudged along, the unwilling head of the procession, Kenyon racked his brains for a way out of his dilemma. There were by-paths through the marshes by which he could lead these maniacs so that they would get very near the defences before the challenge came, but that would be a sheer betrayal of his friends, yet there was no prospect of escape if he did otherwise and his whole soul revolted against the thought of a sudden and violent death.

In twenty minutes the short journey was accomplished; he stood again with the salt breath of the sea filling his lungs and heard the murmur of the surf upon the beaches. Only a few hundred yards in front lay Gregory's outposts.

'Which way now?' came a sharp whisper. 'And remember you'll get all that's left in this the moment your people open fire—that is if you can't stop 'em. Now march!' Cattermole thrust the revolver into the middle of his back again.

'To the left,' he gulped, 'it will be easier there,' and he felt the hair prickling on his scalp as he lead them deliberately in the direction of Silas's Redoubt, the strong point in Gregory's whole system of defences.

A sickening fear filled him that when the time came his courage would ebb away. Wedged in front of the party he would stand no earthly chance of surviving the murderous hail of bullets which would sweep across the open fields, and if by some miracle he did, Cattermole would shoot him from behind.

As they advanced across the seemingly endless field a light wind rustled the tall grasses. No sign of life came from the fortifications, invisible in the pitch blackness relieved neither by moon nor stars, and for a moment it flashed into Kenyon's mind that perhaps after all the garrison would be taken by surprise. It would mean life to him, but what of the others, and Ann might be among them now for there could be no doubt that she had got clean away. At every second he expected to stumble into one of the stake-filled pits—the sentries *must* be sleeping. Then a tiny bell tinkled in the distance, someone had stumbled over one of Gregory's alarm wires and instantly the challenge rang out:

'Halt! who goes there!'

'Friend,' rasped Kenyon.

'Halt, friend, and give the countersign!'

Even in the second of horror and dismay, his gorge rising in a sickening fear, Kenyon found himself admiring Gregory for the faultless training of his little band. There was no trace of hesitation in the swift reply.

With a superhuman effort he braced himself. Then with all the force of his lungs, he yelled: 'I am Lord Fane but captured by the enemy—Guard, turn out!'

A single rifle cracked, then with a savage will to live he kicked out violently behind and flung himself flat, dragging the two men who held his pinioned arms down with him.

His heel met solid flesh—there was a grunt and then a deafening report as the pistol went off behind his ear. Next second the whole emplacement had leapt into flame. Silas was in action.

Kenyon kneed one of his captors in the belly and kicked the other in the face, stood up, staggered, fell again while the bullets sang and whistled overhead. Screams, curses, blasphemies came from the miserable people caught in that open field of fire so skilfully planned by a brilliant tactician. He jerked himself to his knees only to flop head foremost into a muddy ditch. He wriggled out and lurched up the steep bank, catching his feet in one of the treacherous, low-lying nets and sprawled his full length, howling with pain as an upturned nail penetrated his thigh. Groaning, he wriggled free of it, scrambled up once more and blundered on, uncertain of his position yet instinctively trying to avoid those horrid, stake-filled pits. A bullet, searing like a red-hot iron, ploughed through his shoulder. Another streaked through his hair, then suddenly a voice came sharp and clear only a few yards ahead: 'Cease fire' and on a lower note but quite distinct: 'They must have had enough by now. It may teach them to stick to their blasted ship.'

Sobbing like a child, Kenyon swayed towards the dark figure. It was Gregory, calmly directing fire from the parapet. As he fell against the earthworks Rudd, catching a glimpse of him, leaned forward with levelled pistol, then thinking better of it, seized him by the collar and dragged him in.

'Made a prisoner, eh?' Gregory's voice was cold. 'Best shoot him and have done—we've no use for useless mouths in Shingle Street.'

But Rudd had felt the cords that secured Kenyon's arms and pulled him over on his back. He stopped for a second to peer into the begrimed and bloody face, then he stood up.

'Lumme, if it ain't our bloomin' Lord.'

'What!' snapped Gregory.

'It is, sir, Mr. Fane 'imself, or I'm a Dutchman.'

Then Gregory was kneeling beside him in the trench, his

arms were free again, and Rudd was holding a flask of spirits to his lips.

'Well done, Fane! Well done!' Gregory repeated over and over again with an unaccustomed tenderness in his voice. 'Thank God you got away. I suppose those blasted sailors caught you on your return trip?'

'Sailors,' gasped Kenyon, spluttering as the fiery spirit burnt in his throat, 'what sailors?'

'Why those damned mutineers of course. The *Shark* anchored off here this afternoon and sent a landing party. They want to collar our supplies.'

'These aren't sailors,' Kenyon stammered. 'You've been massacring those poor devils of farmers that we robbed.'

'Easy now,' Gregory threw an arm about his shoulders. 'It's their own damn fault if they're fool enough to attack us here. The only people I'm scared of are the mutineers—you see they've got guns.'

At that moment there was a dull boom to seaward, a flash, and almost instantly a livid explosion on the beach a few yards short of the Martello Tower.

22

'The Strongest Shall Go Down into the Pit'

'It's this little upsydisy wot we bin havin's woke 'em up, sir,' Rudd declared.

'That's about it.' Gregory stared through his night glasses out over the darkened waste to seaward; 'seeing us attacked they thought it a good time to join in.'

The clouds which had obscured the sky were travelling fast, and through a partial break some stars now lessened the blackness with a faint uncertain light.

The destroyer was just visible, a jagged outline low in the water, less than a mile from the shore. A flash came from her bow, another dull boom followed and almost instantly the crack of the shell as it landed in the marsh beyond the tower.

'They're bracketin' on the Albert 'All,' said Rudd.'

'They shouldn't need to,' Gregory grunted, 'but even if they're amateurs they're devilish dangerous with that gun. We must evacuate the tower at once—give Lord Fane a hand—come on!'

With Rudd's aid Kenyon limped down the trench; his shoulder had gone numb but his thigh was hurting badly where the nail had caught it, his chest was smarting, although he had been little more than singed, and his head seemed to open and shut with every step he took.

Gregory paused for a moment further along, where Silas was leaning against a traverse, hands in pockets, near a Lewis gun.

'Keep a look out this side,' he warned him, 'but it wasn't a landing party—only some farmers, and I should think they've had their belly full.'

'If that's so I'd best go out and see if Fane's among the wounded.'

'That's nice of you, Silas,' Kenyon stumbled forward, 'but by a miracle I got through.'

'My hat! Then there's a God in heaven yet.' The big man's voice came warm and cheerful as he gripped Kenyon by the arm.

'Don't,' moaned Kenyon. 'For God's sake—I'm hit.'

'Sorry—brace up, old chap—but tell me, did you see the kid, or did they pinch you before you got to Orford?'

'What, Ann! Yes and I was bringing her back with me, but we were separated—I—I'd hoped that she was here.'

Gregory shook his head. 'No—I'd know of it if she'd turned up on her own.'

'Then she's lost somewhere out on these cursed moors,' Kenyon passed his hand across his throbbing forehead wearily. 'Oh, God! I'm sick with worry for her.'

'Take a pull,' Silas tried to comfort him. 'She's full of pluck so she'll make Shingle Street some time before the morning.'

A third explosion sounded from the beach and Gregory turned away quickly. 'Come on, Rudd, that Martello was never built to resist modern shells—once they get the range they'll pound the place to pieces.'

He climbed out of the trench and with Rudd's aid Kenyon followed. Three minutes later they were in front of the Anchor.

'Is Veronica in?' Kenyon asked Gregory.

'I expect so.'

'Then I'll get her to patch me up—feel about all in.'

'That's right, I expect you need a meal as well. Get Andrews to cook you something and open up one of his remaining bottles. If you feel fit enough you may be able to give us a hand later.' With a quick smile Gregory hurried on into the darkness.

Andrews stood in the porch of the inn watching the bombardment. 'Why, sir, we'd given you up for lost,' he exc aimed as he saw Kenyon.

'Had you—well, I'm back again, thank God. Where's my sister?'

'You'll find her in the sitting-room. I tried to persuade her to come out here and see the fireworks—but she wouldn't. Still, I mustn't stay here talking when you've had no supper. I'll get the girls to cook you something.' With a friendly grin on his chubby face the little man went off towards the kitchen whi.e Kenyon pushed open the sitting-room door.

Veronica lay back in a low arm-chair, her feet cocked up on the fire guard, showing a long length of leg, browned by three three weeks' exposure, to excellent advantage. She was reading and did not turn her head but gave a little gurgle of laughter.

'Andrews, isn't Dickens too divine—do you think people ever really made love like that?'

'I don't know—or care.' Kenyon closed his eyes and dropped on to the sofa.

'Darling!' At the sound of his voice she cast the battered volume on the floor and jumped to her feet. 'Oh, Kenyon, we've been worried stiff about you. I couldn't even watch the fighting for fear you were mixed up in it somewhere outside the camp—so I've been trying to sink myself in David Copperfield.'

'I was,' he murmured. 'They damn near killed me too.'

Instantly Veronica was beside him, her long fingers tenderly investigating the cuts upon his head, and the wound which still ebbed blood in his shoulder. 'My poor lamb, what have they done to you—I'll get some water to bathe that horrid place.'

As she left him Kenyon sank back on the pillow, his bodily distress momentarily submerged, now that he had time to think coherently again, in fear for Ann. She must have escaped when he was captured but what had happened to her since? Perhaps she was lost and crouching in some ditch, desperately frightened by those ghoul-like creatures who prowled the lanes, or worse, she might already have fallen prisoner to some gang of roughs. He knew that men had become crazed by their misfortunes; morals and all sense of decency had been flung aside, so it was hideously possible that these men turned brutes might seize upon any diversion which offered even temporary forgetfulness of their hunger. His tortured brain began to visualise the drama that might be proceeding in some lonely wood if half a dozen of them came upon a lovely girl alone and unprotected—fine sport for the night, to satiate at least one appetite.

His terrible forebodings were cut short by Veronica's return. She bathed his wounds and sought to comfort him, as he told her of events at Orford, the return journey, and his fears for Ann.

No bones seemed to be broken in his shoulder, and by the time she had bandaged the gash and plastered up his head, his supper was on the table. His anxiety had driven away all appetite but she forced him to eat it, telling him meanwhile about the arrival of the destroyer.

'Crowder's not with them,' she declared, 'he and a dozen others took the second boat and made for Harwich. For a time it seems they've been playing pirate up and down the coast, raiding the smaller places for supplies, and now they want to take possession here.'

'How do you know all this?' Kenyon asked dully.

'Gregory got it out of them this afternoon at a sort of pow-wow. They sent a boat ashore.'

'I wonder that they thought it worth while risking their skins.'

'Worth it, my love?' She took him up quickly. 'Twelve hundred chickens in the poultry farm, and a hundred head of cattle in the corral; Gregory adopted no half-measures when he turned cattle-thief.'

'Yes—I suppose so, but what happened at the parley?'

'They said at once that they meant to land a party and seize all our stock.'

Kenyon nodded. 'I suppose Gregory threatened to turn a machine-gun on them if they didn't sheer off at once.'

'Got it in one, my sweet, but luckily for them they were

halfway back to the ship before Silas arrived with the arsenal.'

'I wonder they didn't attack the place right away.'

'No, they flagged a message saying that they would give Gregory until nine o'clock tomorrow to capitulate, and that if he wouldn't they'd blow the lot of us to hell, but he was afraid they might start in on us tonight.'

'I see, that's why you were all up and dressed when I came on the scene then!'

Every few moments a deafening explosion punctuated the conversation with clock-like regularity, and Kenyon, his nerves keyed up but feeling a different man after his meal and Veronica's attentions, decided to go out and see how the sailors' marksmanship was progressing.

On the doorstep of the inn with Andrew and Veronica beside him he watched the bombardment. As they opened the door a shell pitched at the foot of the tower and even from that distance they could hear the whine and rattle of pebbles, as they sang through the air and bounded along the beach. The next shell fell slap on the roof of the old fortress, bursting with terrific impact and hurtling lumps of stone in all directions.

'Put out that ruddy light,' cried a voice they recognised as Rudd's from further along the foreshore, and a few moments later he loomed up out of the darkness beside his master.

'It looks like a hectic night at the Albert Hall.' Veronica used Rudd's nickname for the Martello which they had all adopted.

'Yes,' Gregory agreed grimly. 'If they keep this up for half an hour the place won't be even fit shelter for the chickens in the morning. I got all our stores but we've lost poor Thompson.'

'Is—is he dead?' Veronica hesitated.

'Yes—a fragment of the third shell caught him.'

'What filthy luck—such a decent fellow too, but couldn't we do something?' Kenyon stepped forward from the doorway. 'I'm pretty groggy still, but I'm game to have a cut at them.'

'I'm afraid there's nothing we can do against shell-fire, that's just the devil of it.'

'Couldn't we man a boat with a volunteer crew and a couple of Lewis guns? Under the cover of the darkness we might get near enough to wipe out the men who are serving that gun.'

'Stark lunacy, my dear chap. They'd sink us before we got a hundred yards.'

Shell after shell burst upon the ancient tower with reverberating thuds which seemed to shake the very ground beneath them. The starlight showed a great crack which had appeared in one side of the fort, and large lumps of stone slipped and tumbled to the ground after each explosion. The strong point in their defence which Gregory had counted impregnable, was being pounded to a heap of ruins.

Suddenly the firing ceased. They waited in the doorway with strained, breathless anxiety—two minutes, three—four—five—then a long finger of bright light flashed up to the clouds, circled slowly and, descending, was brought to bear upon the village. Hovering for a second here and there, the searchlight picked out every detail of the foreshore and, as it moved on, the little group at the entrance of the inn were momentarily blinded by its powerful glare.

'Hell!' exclaimed Gregory pushing the others into the hallway. 'With that damn thing they'll be able to pick us off like rabbits—this is even worse than I bargained for.'

The beam swept slowly back and forth, strong depths of shadows playing about its edges but revealing all within its circle with the vivid brightness of full day; then, as it passed on, its late discoveries sank again into the unnatural blackness of an even deeper night.

There was a sharp whine, a rending crash, and then the rumble of falling masonary.

'Next door but one,' cried Kenyon.

'Come on—out you go,' Gregory pushed Veronica before him and they stumbled through the back entrance of the inn. Shouts and cries came from the neighbourhood of the demolished house and further off the sound of people running. Andrews's maids were already on the lawn, one of them was screaming in a fit of hysterics.

'Stop it—d'you hear?' Gregory seized and shook her roughly.

'Can't we—can't we help them,' hazarded Veronica.

'No, if they're not dead they soon will be. Come on, all of you.' Still gripping the girl by the arm he hurried them round the corner of the stockade, but Andrews stopped and turned.

'What is it?' muttered Kenyon.

'My money. I'm not going to leave my cash for others.'

'Don't be a fool,' snapped Gregory. 'What earthly good is it to you?'

'You never know.' At a quick trot the little man started back towards the Anchor.

'Hurry then,' Gregory called after him. 'There'll be another in a minute,' but his warning came too late. There was a blinding flash, the small hotel seemed to stagger for a second and then, as though some giant invisible hand had crushed it flat, it disappeared into a shapeless heap of debris, leaving a black empty gap between its neighbours.

Andrews had been halfway across the garden. They saw him stagger for a few steps like a drunken man and then slip down into a pathetic little heap.

Kenyon dashed back to him and raised his head, but a lump of flying brick had caught him on the forehead and killed him instantly.

'Oh, Gregory, I'm hating this.' Veronica's grip tightened on his arm.

'Of course you are.' His voice thrilled her by its tenderness. 'But you'll stick it, won't you? I've got to run this beastly show and it will be hell for me if you break down.'

She nodded quickly. 'I'll be all right—don't worry about me, sweet—just do your job.'

'Thanks.' He smiled in the darkness as they stumbled on. 'This last month may have been hell for some people but I've enjoyed it more than any time in my life. We've had a lot of fun, Veronica.'

'Yes, darling, we've had a lot of fun.'

Kenyon, his wounds throbbing afresh from the exertion, caught them up. 'Are you going to evacuate the village?' he panted.

'Not except as a last measure. I must protect the Shingleites as well as I can, and how could I do that once they're outside the fortifications—think of all these women and kids straggling about in the darkness.'

'Yes, the farmers would set on us again for certain; there were a good two hundred of them, and that one burst of machine-gun fire couldn't have laid out more than twenty or thirty.'

Gregory led them swiftly towards the Redoubt, where Rudd, who had run on ahead, was already assembling the villagers. Silas came out to meet them. 'All quiet, General,' he reported laconically.

Kenyon gave a brief, strained laugh.

'This end I mean,' the American amended. 'They seem to be making the village a pretty lively little hell.' As he spoke another shell came over crumpling up two fishermen's cottages.

'Yes. The inn's gone,' Gregory informed him.

'Any casualties?'

'Sergeant Thompson and poor old Andrews, and half a dozen more I expect by now.'

'That's bad—I wouldn't give a dime for our chances here either if they turn their little pop-guns on us.'

'Nor I,' Gregory agreed. 'A direct hit would go plump through the roof of any of these dugouts. I wish to God we'd had proper engineers' materials to make them with; still they are better than nothing.'

Silas made Veronica comfortable in what he called his 'parlour' while the other women and children were packed into the larger dugouts, and the fishermen, scattered through the trenches, miserably watched the destruction of their homes.

The single line of houses was now burning fiercely at one end, shell after shell crashed into the remaining buildings, and still the malevolent eye of the searchlight picked out fresh targets for the merciless gun.

'Wonder why they keep it up like this,' Silas muttered. 'They know we can't reply to them—it seems stupidly vindictive to create such senseless havoc.'

'Drunk, I expect,' Gregory replied tersely. 'Once some madman started in on us when the farmers attacked, the rest began to glory in the fun. That gun's like a new toy to them now they are able to blaze off as much stuff as they like at real targets.'

'Well, there won't be much left of the place when they come ashore to drive the cattle off in the morning.'

'Unless they come tonight. They can't have seen much red meat themselves in the last fortnight, so they may if someone thinks of chops for supper.'

'What'll you do if they turn that darn gun on to us here?'

'Evacuate—only thing to do—but I dread it with all these

civilians to look after.' Gregory flung a glance over his shoulder. 'Where's Fane? Oh, there you are. Look here, the three of us had better arrange the order of our going if we are forced to quit.'

While the three of them went into conference, Veronica, her nerves strung to the highest pitch, sat fiddling with the papers on the table in Silas' dugout. Suddenly the drawing of a woman caught her eye. She moved the candle nearer and saw at once that it was a portrait of herself—a beautiful thing, showing her lying on the beach, her hands spread out behind her, her legs stretched to their fullest extent and crossed. The toe of one of her shoes was turned up and in the drawing she was smiling at it pensively. A characteristic attitude of her, but how clever of Silas, she thought, to have caught it. She rummaged among the papers and found others, nearly two dozen of them and all of her in different positions. She realised then with a little catch in her throat that every waking moment he had spent there must have been devoted to making these charming studies of herself.

Gregory was just a lovely madness of course; the old tag came into her mind 'Man cannot live by caviare alone,' and Gregory was caviare. Quite marvellous if you liked that sort of thing, and Veronica did: 'We are a couple of rips, my dear,' she had told him once, 'and we wouldn't be otherwise for a million pounds,' she remembered how he had chuckled mightily—but Silas——

'Like 'em?' said a voice behind her and she looked up to see him in the doorway.

'I'm a brute to look but I think they are divine.'

He adjusted the blanket carefully over the entrance and took the drawings from her. 'Just a little hobby of mine,' he said quietly. 'I felt they'd be good to have if we got separated.'

'You're a dear, Silas—how's the war?'

'Not so bad considering it's one-sided, but the General's scared they'll turn that gun on this place.' He carefully folded the drawings and tucked them in his tunic.

The dugout seemed to rock as a new concussion demolished the last house their end of the village. 'It'll be sheer murder here if Gregory's right,' he added.

'I see,' her fingers drummed nervously upon the table. 'It looks as if we're for it then?'

'Not quite, I've got a proposition I want to put up to you.' His eyes held hers, kind and firm.

'Well—let's hear it then.'

'It's this way. One woman's easier protected alone by a man who's useful with a gun, than she is with a whole crowd; so if we get out together now there's a chance for us. If we run into the farmers we'll be for it mind, but I mean to strike south along the coast, out of this area that Gregory's made so hellish hostile. Even then we'll be up against everyone who hasn't had a meal in days, but as long as they're only in batches I'll bluff them or shoot my way through. It's a better prospect to my mind than staying here, so if you'll trust me I want to take you out of here right away.'

For a second Veronica was silent, then she shook her head. 'I'd trust you, Silas—anywhere, but we mustn't let Gregory down. I know it is unofficial and you've a perfect right to clear out if you like, but you are one of his officers in a way.'

He smiled quickly. 'Don't fret your sweet heart, Gregory and I fixed that between us.'

'What—he agreed?' Veronica's delicate eyebrows went up in astonishment.

'Yes, what else would you expect—you ought to know Gregory if anyone does.'

'Why do you say that?'

'You can't kid me, Veronica; I don't go about in blinkers, and I know pretty well how things stand between you and him.'

'Yes,' she said slowly, 'I'm glad you do, and he's just the sort of adorable blackguard who can be trusted to do the proper thing. He would pack me off with you if he thought it would save me, even though he knows that you are in love with me.'

'That's it, we've only got one idea between us, and that's your safety.'

'Silas, it's dear of you, but I think I prefer to stay and see it through.'

'Why?'

'All sorts of silly reasons.' She took his large brown hand in hers. 'There are Gregory and Kenyon, not to mention that divine idiot Rudd—we've all been in this from the beginning so I don't think it's quite fair to scuttle now.

Then if we go I shall be depriving them of at least one good fighting man—hush, now, don't interrupt—and on top of that wherever could we go? So let's all stick together—understand!'

'Yes; it's like you to say that.'

'No dearest; it's just laziness really. I loathe walking, and the prospect of being raped by starving farmers attracts me not at all.'

'Just as you say, Veronica.'

'I'll tell you what we will do though. If we do have to clear out you shall be my special defender, and I'll stick to you like a limpet.'

'That's fine—we'd better leave it at that then.' With a nod Silas left her and went out to join Kenyon.

Gregory was pacing slowly up and down the parapet seeking to give confidence to the fishermen, labour colonists, and troops while keeping a wary eye upon the bombardment which continued with horrible regularity. Rudd sat opposite, perched on the parados. As Gregory passed he turned his back and a faint glow showed him applying a match to his pipe.

'Where did you get that?' asked Gregory curiously.

'Saved it for a rainy day, sir.'

Gregory moved on, a faint smile twitching his thin lips. He would gladly have given any chances of the survival of his immortal soul for a packet of cigarettes, but he had smoked his last three days before.

The searchlight shifted. Gregory flung himself flat and Rudd slipped off the parados. With a roar that reverberated and echoed in the hills a mile away the eighty-pound shell burst upon the earthworks. Every sort of filth with pieces of wood and corrugated iron revetments sailed high in the air, and then descended with a series of dull thuds upon the trenches.

Kenyon, half-dazed, staggered in the direction of a dug-out from which came cries and groans. He knew that a score of women must be entombed there by a ton of earth. A kneeling figure rose before him—it was Rudd. 'Blarst them swine,' came a hoarse whisper. 'I bin an' lorst me bleedin' pipe.'

Gregory forced his way past them towards the crater. 'They've found us,' he shouted above the din. 'We must clear out now—and quick. Get the men together.'

He came on Silas round the corner of the traverse frantically digging at the entrance of the collapsed dugout with his mighty hands. 'What the hell are you doing here?' he thundered.

'She wouldn't go—bless her.'

'Oh, hell! Why didn't you make her? Never mind, leave this to me—get hold of her quick as you can and stick to her. We'll strike up the North beach; tell Kenyon.'

A fisherman and a soldier arrived with spades, and under Gregory's directions attacked the buried entrance with fierce determination. Rudd came hurrying up to help and was the first into the hole when it had been uncovered. He reappeared a moment later and a white-faced woman peered from the opening.

'Come on, Missis,' he called; 'give us yer 'and and don't be frightened, Ma—it's only like goin' through the roly-poly at the circus. Ever bin ter Sarthend?'

She extended her arms and they pulled her through, the others followed weeping, or with terror in their faces. One poor creature just before the last had to be forced through the hole. She bit Rudd's hand as he tried to help her and staggering to her feet, clawed at the fisherman; the shock of the explosion had cost the unfortunate woman her reason.

'Christ! That's torn it!' Rudd slipped to his knees. He knew enough of shell-fire to judge where a projectile would pitch, and by the short sharp scream low overhead, he knew that within a fraction of time another would burst just beyond the trench where Kenyon was endeavouring to get the crowd into some sort of order.

As the falling debris rattled down he popped his head over the parapet. 'Mr. Fane's copped it, sir,' he gasped, 'an' there ain't a ninepin in the bunch lef' standin'.'

'All right—you carry on,' Gregory's voice was quiet but there was a note of sadness in it—a grim acceptance of fatality.

'Very good, sir.' Rudd scrambled obediently out of the trench. 'Na then, chaps—no shell falls in the same place twice—take an old soldier's word fer that an' show yer-selves—some of yer. We're abart to start on a 'iking tour.'

Almost at once shadows began to stir and creep hesitatingly towards him. 'That's ther spirit,' he sang out lustily: '*Coorage mons onfongs* as they sez in the French—

old soldiers never die. 'Oo wants to see sunny Suffolk in the rain!'

Many forms remained still or groaning on the ground, but the rest came forward in increasing numbers, and when Gregory arrived Rudd had mustered the remainder.

'Armed men to the front,' ordered the General sharply, and eight or ten stepped from the uneven ranks, but he noticed sorrowfully that Kenyon was not amongst them.

'Now, follow me. Quick march!'

As they set off towards the shore Silas hauled Veronica out of the trench. He had kept her there until the last possible moment now that the destroyer was actually shelling the Redoubt, but no sooner were they standing together on the parapet than he flung himself flat, pulling her down beside him. Another shell screeched like the grinding brakes of a tramcar, and burst, causing the ground to shudder beneath them. They struggled to their feet again and, choking from the fumes, ran side by side after the straggling column of survivors.

When they were within twenty yards of its tail he caught her arm. 'No hurry now,' he urged. 'Till they get into open country we'll be safer here behind them.'

Once the main party reached the beach Gregory turned north. The gun continued to fling its high explosives into the Redoubt at intervals, but otherwise there was no sound except the scrunching of the pebbles beneath their moving feet for several minutes. Then without warning a single shot rang out ahead.

'On the ground all of you!' came the swift command. 'Ready with your rifles there!' and instantly the party flattened themselves upon the shingle, scuttling for any dip or runnel which might afford them greater protection.

Silas and Veronica dropped together and as the unknown enemy to their front opened a rapid fire, he clutched her to him, burying her head beneath his chest in an effort to shield her more effectually.

Gregory's order came clear and strong: 'Aim for their flashes. Fire!'

'Silas, what is it?' Veronica's muffled voice was hardly audible above the crackling of the musketry. 'Have we run into the farmers after all?'

'No, they've got no arms. This must be a landing-party from the ship.' As he spoke that staccato note that they had grown to know and dread, the horrid rat-tat—tat-tat-tat-tat-tat-tat of a machine-gun, struck upon their ear-drums.

Veronica gasped as a flying pebble struck her on the leg and shrank closer to him.

'It's them all right,' he added. 'I wish to God I could get you out of this,' but even as he glanced over his shoulder seeking a way of escape, final calamity swept upon them. The beam of the searchlight shifted, slowly, relentlessly, from the wrecked village, across the now blasted Redoubt, and came to rest upon them as they lay in little crouching groups half-buried in the shingle; its fierce blinding light throwing every man and every movement into sharp relief before the enemy.

The machine-guns were silent for a second, and then burst out anew trained now upon the writhing figures, their bullets clicking sharply on the stones or thudding dully as they found a human mark.

'Oh, hell!' groaned Silas, 'this is sheer bloody massacre.'

A man in front leapt up with a sudden scream and then dropped down again; another sprang up to run and fell with half a dozen bullets in his back. A small boy, with a seemingly charmed life, jumped to his feet and, head down, fists doubled, pelted up the slope into the safety of the darkness. A woman followed but fell before she had gone five yards, shot through both legs.

Suddenly the firing ceased. For a moment Silas waited, then cautiously he lifted his head from the cold stones. Clear in the relentless light beyond the rows of bodies Gregory was standing upon a mound waving a large white handkerchief above his head.

Silently but profanely Silas cursed himself. By following Gregory's party on to the North Beach at a little distance he had thought to use them as cover until he and his precious charge were free of danger from the farmers. Now they had been caught by the landing party from the *Shark*.

Bitterly he regretted that he had not stuck to his former plan of heading south, but to suggest running for it now was to risk instant annihilation.

As he watched, Gregory walked slowly towards the enemy.

'Had enough?' asked the leader of the mutineers sternly as he came forward to meet the defeated General.

'Yes,' Gregory's voice was even, but the scar above his eyebrow showed a livid white; 'don't think you've beaten me though, we haven't fired a dozen shots the whole evening, and I would have fought you for a year if you hadn't had that blasted gun.'

'Fortune o' war,' said the sailor grimly.

'Yes, and I want the honours of war.'

'Not likely,' came the quick reply. 'You should ha' surrendered when you were asked this afternoon; now you bin an' killed four of my men your crowd are for it, an' make no mistake!'

'Not for myself,' said Gregory gruffly, 'you can do what the hell you like with me, but leave these poor fishermen out of it, and the handful of soldiers whose only crime has been to obey my orders!'

'Officers excepted?'

'Yes—one's dead, and the other is a couple of miles away by this time.'

'All supplies an' livestock must be handed over to us, I'll shoot anyone who hides so much as a rabbit.'

'Yes, you're entitled to the spoils of victory.'

'All right, it's the officers an' cattle I come to get, so I'll accept your surrender.'

'Thanks, I'm grateful.' Gregory extended his automatic, holding it by the barrel, and the sailor's hand closed over the butt.

So, with the searchlight playing on the scarred and weary survivors, the burning village in the background, and the defences, which they had worked so hard to perfect, lying in ruins about them, ended the uneven battle of Shingle Street.

23

The Terrible Journey

After her sharp tussle Ann stumbled through the heather and bracken, terrified each moment that a restraining hand would fall upon her shoulder, but Kenyon's desperate resistance held their assailants until she was well away and, once assured of her escape, she threw herself panting into a ditch near the coppice.

For a little while she feared that they might search for her with torches, but the sounds of fighting ceased and, peering cautiously from her hiding-place, she could see no moving forms between her and the camp fire that lit the dell, so she crawled out and gave a low whistle.

No answering note came from the surrounding moor and after repeating the experiment once or twice she decided that Kenyon must have been captured. For a moment the idea of trying to fetch help from Shingle Street occurred to her but, even if she could reach it, would Gregory be willing to send a force sufficiently large to cope with this big gathering, and was Kenyon still alive?

Her fingers plucked feverishly at the strands of coarse grass as she thought that he might be already dead, and she realised at once the necessity of finding out what had happened to him before endeavouring to reach Shingle Street by herself.

She began to creep forward slowly and carefully, fearful that the snapping of every twig might mean discovery, and after ten minutes of cautious manœuvring managed to reach a position some ten yards from the backs of the nearest men, where she could see the hollow.

Kenyon was nowhere to be seen, and for a little she was filled with new hope that he might have escaped in a different direction to herself, but the bonfire interfered with a large section of her view so that she could not be certain.

A little man with fair lank fair hair and eyes that glittered fanatically in the firelight was haranguing the crowd. Ann could not catch all he said but snatches of his discourse came to her borne on the night air: 'Our brothers black, white and brown—An era of new Freedom—Already the towns are organising——'

The man nearest her spoke in a gruff voice to his companion, a frail-looking woman. 'They ain't organisen' Communist though.'

'Ain't they, Jim?'

'No; too sensible be half.'

'What be 'em a-doen' then?'

'Blow me if I know, but the chap I spoke to on the road

today say as how the Mayor were back an' the Greyshirts a handen' out vittals from the Town Hall.'

'Think o' that now; in Ipswich do 'ee mean?'

'Yer—and other places too!'

'Don't 'ee believe that,' cut in another labourer, ''tis a Soviet what's been set up—it be true about the vittals, though only for the townsfolk—they 'on't part with any for the likes o' we!'

'Well, if it do be the Communists that be a wonderful pity!'

'What the 'ell's it matter 'oo it be so long as they stop a-murdering o' each other; seein' as the old lot let us down so bad, I'm all for given' the others a chance.'

'England won't never go Bolshie; happens us'll be all dead afore then.'

'If you fared as hungry as what I do, you'd go Bolshie all right; ain't you a commen' on this party tonight?'

'That be different thing; they stole my horse and tumbril, not to mention the hins and eggs. It be only human nature to want your own back.'

'You be right,' said the woman. 'Fair's fair, as I allus do say.' The agitator sat down and Cattermole took his place. With feverish impatience Ann listened to his speech, for until they made some move she had no means of ascertaining if Kenyon was still among them and every now and then she shuddered at the thought that he might be lying murdered in a nearby ditch.

At last in a storm of applause Cattermole ceased speaking and then Kenyon was dragged down the bank. Her intense relief at finding him still alive was soon submerged in shuddering dismay as she saw them press the burning branch against his chest. Unable to bear it any longer she closed her eyes and rocked with misery, but when she opened them again the whole crowd were on their feet and struggling away up the far slope.

She had followed enough of Cattermole's speech to gather their intention, but she had little thought to spare for Shingle Street; Gregory would deal with an attack by such a rabble with horrible efficiency. Kenyon was all that mattered and she must keep as near to him as possible. With that one central fact dominating her distraught mind she crept after the farm people and, seeking all the cover she could from the sides of the road, followed them down to the coast.

At the turn of the road where it debouched from the trees and curved across the marsh, she remembered an old concrete pill-box and, finding it without difficulty, slipped inside. The long slit in the front of the musty little circular chamber commanded the village and its approach, so, from it, although the whole scene was shrouded in darkness, she was able to watch for the crisis which she felt was imminent.

The Redoubt was a quarter of a mile away but she heard Kenyon's shout that gave warning of the attack and next moment the rapid tattoo that heralded the butchery. Stray bullets ripped through the branches overhead and a couple thudded on the little concrete fort, then the firing ceased abruptly. The stricken field was mercifully covered by night, but the dark curls clung damp about her temples at the thought that Kenyon must be somewhere among those panic-stricken, shouting people. Then there was a dull boom to seaward and in the flash of the following explosion she caught a glimpse of the Martello Tower.

For what seemed an interminable time she watched the shelling and then the silhouette of the village, black and sharp against the revealing searchlight, while little running figures gesticulated to one another. One by one the houses seemed to leap into a blinding sheet of flame as the projectiles struck them, and then disappear, so that the remnant of the burning hamlet began to take on the appearance of a row of black and jagged teeth which were being steadily extracted.

The gun took a new angle, and the shells fell nearer to the fields where Ann believed Kenyon to be dead or wounded. She wrung her hands helplessly together, and at every fresh detonation a shudder shook her from head to toe. For hours it seemed she had been crouching there, sending up little muttered prayers that the holocaust should cease, but there was no indication of its speedy termination. The searchlight shifted to the north but, owing to the shelving beach, she was spared the sight of that last desperate attempt of the survivors to seek safety; she only heard the renewed rattle of rifle and machine-gun fire and then a sudden silence.

For another quarter of an hour she watched, fearful that at any moment the fighting might break out again, then by the dancing light of the flames she saw figures moving freely about the wreck of the village and crawled from her shelter.

If Kenyon was dead she felt that it mattered little what happened any more, but if he was still alive she might yet be able to aid him so, taking a deep breath of fresh night air, she set off towards the Redoubt.

The going was not easy in the darkness; deep ditches half-filled with water and stinking mud intersected the fields of long coarse grass and, having fallen once, cutting her hand badly on a rusty nail, she did the last hundred yards on hands and knees until she was among the victims of the fighting.

Someone stumbled near her and she realised that others were seeking friends among the more seriously wounded who had been unable to crawl away. Then lights appeared a little distance to her left and she saw that a group of men were carrying those still living in rough stretchers towards the village. She stood up suddenly with fresh hope, feeling how senseless it was to stay there listening to those pathetic voices calling for the missing. In the darkness she would stand little chance of finding Kenyon, but if he was still alive he would be carried down to the beach with the others.

Trailing a group of stretcher-bearers she made her way down to the foreshore, and saw that two camps had already been formed. The farmers and the fisher-people were now mingled together and, a little apart, stood some fifty sailors from the ship. At the sight of the mutineers she drew back quickly with a sudden horrible memory of Crowder and Brisket, but they were busy about the bonfire that they had lit across which they were hoisting a spitted pig. Then she caught sight of Gregory hunched on the shingle, his arms tied behind his back.

Veronica was kneeling by him adjusting a rough bandage to his head, and a little way behind them sat Silas, also bound. Rudd was there too, some way away and half-obscured by the fringe of shadow. His hands were free, she noticed, but the bulging pistol holster which had always decorated his hip was missing, and as the flame flickered for a second, lighting his face, she saw a miserable and hopeless expression upon it.

For a moment Ann thought of going to them, but her

fears for Kenyon overcame every other impulse and she turned away towards the larger gathering. They too had heaped a fire and by it some men were busy dismembering a horse. Although she knew little of the situation Ann judged from this that the sailors were the masters in this partnership, and to placate their unsought allies had parted with this indifferent portion of their spoil rather then be compelled to drive them off.

Mud-stained and bedraggled as she was there was little chance of her being recognised as Kenyon's companion of earlier in the evening, so she threaded her way in among the men to a spot some distance from the fire where the long line of wounded were being deposited. Some lay unnaturally still and silent, others were twisting and groaning in their pain, but she peered furtively at each in turn and came to the end of the row without finding Kenyon among them.

'Happen you're looken' for a friend?' As the man behind her spoke she started guiltily, but his voice was sympathetic and kind, so recovering herself quickly she replied:

'Not—not exactly—but I was wondering what happened to the tall man they caught up on the heath.'

'Happen you be meanen' him that give the alarm. The officer chap; 'ooldn't that be him they're a-setten' down now?'

He pointed a grimy finger towards the other end of the row and Ann recognised at once the long-limbed body which was being laid beside the others. The firelight caught the auburn curls, no longer smoothly-brushed but rumpled now and clotted with dried blood.

She hastened over to him, her new acquaintance following. 'Is he—is he dead, d'you think?' she managed to stammer.

The man peered down at him. 'It fare to me he'll live all right. They 'ooldn't trouble to bring him in else, but anyways these fellers be shooten' all the officers come mornen'.'

'Are you certain; how do you know?' Ann's voice held a sudden sharp note, half-fear, half-challenging refusal to accept the statement.

'Waren't you here ten minutes agone?' the man looked at her curiously. 'The furrin' looken' sailor who fare to be the boss told all of us we they meant to sail again come sun up, and after that us 'ooldn't have no more trouble with any o' they thievin' soldiers hereabouts.'

'I see; then that settles it.' Ann hardly recognised her own voice, it came so strange and harsh although she strove to make it sound as natural as possible.'

'I be rare vexed for they,' said the man slowly, 'but I reckon they'd have done the same to the others, come to that.'

Ann nodded, she was past all speech and could only visualise her wounded Kenyon, kindly Silas and the ever-defiant Gregory, being massacred upon the beach in the cold morning light.

As the man moved away she looked furtively after him and then stooped to Kenyon. Despite the blood she could find no wound upon his head, perhaps he had been thrown against another casualty; his arm had fallen from a sling and she replaced it quickly, noting the flesh wound in the shoulder that Veronica had bandaged. Apart from that he seemed to be unhurt and he was breathing regularly, so she guessed that the explosion from a shell burst had knocked him out.

Another man paused near to her, it was Rush, and suddenly fearful of being recognised she hastened away into the darkness of the beach, but a gruff voice brought her to a standstill: 'Not this way, Missie; your supper's a-cookin' on the beach.'

A broad-shouldered sailor leaning on a rifle barrel barred her passage, so she turned away without protest, veering off towards the still smouldering houses, but another sentry farther along also turned her back and then she realised that they were posted in a circle guarding the approaches to the corral that held Gregory's fine collection of poultry and live stock, about which Kenyon had told her on the way from Orford. The idea flashed into her mind and out again, for it mattered little to her who secured this wretched provender. Her whole anxiety was centred in the prisoners, so she struggled across the now deserted fortifications and, gaining the open marsh, sat down to think.

As she rocked backwards and forwards, torn with a terrible distress, her natural urge was to risk discovery, but get back to Kenyon and remain with him, to face whatever the dawn should bring, yet all her sound practical common sense revolted at the thought of final surrender. Alone among the little band that had set out from London she remained free. Surely she could use her freedom in some way to help the others.

For half an hour she sat, her head in her hands, her brain absolutely incapable of coherent thought, tired, miserable, dejected, unable to think of a single way in which she might bring them succour or relief, then like a thunderclap the words of the agitator in the dell: 'Already the towns are organising,' came back to her.

She recalled the ensuing conversation, with its mention of the Mayor being back in Ipswich and the issuing of rations by the Greyshirts, word for word. If only she could get to Ipswich they would be sure to help her, and she might yet be able to save her friends.

No sooner had the thought come to her than she was on her feet, angry with herself for the time that she had already lost by not having grasped the full implication of the news before, yet moving cautiously, terrified that she might be stopped and questioned; for now she was quite convinced that upon the retention of her freedom hung their only hope.

Every shadow seemed a menace and every sound a threat. Even the grounding of a rifle butt or the calling of the sentries to each other caused her fresh alarm. With quick stealthy steps she headed inland until she had passed from the lingering glow into the darkness of the marshes.

The ground soon began to give her trouble. Uneven, boggy in places, or sown with Gregory's man-traps for the protection of the Martello Tower, which lay in ruins to seaward. Then, clear of the defensive belt at last, she ran up the slight incline only to pause breathlessly at the top visualising suddenly the tremendous task she had set herself.

Ipswich was sixteen miles away, she would never be able to do it after her journey with Kenyon and the strain to which she had been subject the previous night; yet she hurried on, assessing the chances as she went.

They had left Orford at seven-thirty, two hours at least must have been spent upon the way, another hour between their capture and the first attack on Shingle Street; that then would have been somewhere about ten-thirty. How long had it lasted, from start to finish? an hour perhaps. Then she had waited in the pill-box for a bit, hung about the bonfire on the shore looking for Kenyon among the wounded—and then wasted more time stupidly doing nothing. It must be twelve-thirty at the least, and sixteen miles would take her a good five hours. She could not hope to arrive in Ipswich before six o'clock.

Too late, she decided. Aeroplanes and cars could hardly be running again yet, so soldiers or police would have to rely on horses and bicycles. By such means it would take them a good two hours to get to Shingle Street and the sunrise would be about six. Unless she could reach Ipswich by four o'clock they would arrive too late.

Suddenly a new plan came to her, the cross-country route. If she took that it would save her at least four miles, but it meant crossing the River Deben.

In normal times there was a ferry boat at Ramsholt and in an emergency the ferryman could be dragged out of bed, but would he still be at his house, Ann wondered. Perhaps, starving like the rest, he had wandered farther towards the coast or back into some town. She would never be able to swim the Deben—a quarter of a mile of water with treacherous muddy banks.

She paused for a moment by a solitary farmhouse, leaning against the low stone wall, breathless already from the pace at which she had come, and miserably undecided which road to take—the track leading north to Melton and Woodbridge or the lane to the left through Alderton to Ramsholt. Then, with the swift realisation that her only hope lay in taking a chance on being able to cross the river, she turned down the lane; to go by Woodbridge meant certain failure on account of time.

With that vital factor of time pressing upon her brain she broke into a run and covered the next half mile in seven minutes. Then she slackened into a breathless, shambling trot.

All question of what reception she was likely to meet with when she got to Ipswich, and if the authorities would be willing to undertake her friends' relief, had passed from her mind. The one thing that mattered was to get there at the earliest possible moment, for she had already convinced herself that, if she could only stay the course, troops, police and Greyshirts would be sent dashing to the rescue.

A voice hailed her out of the darkness. With swift fear, no longer for herself, but that she might be held up or stopped altogether, she burst into a fresh spurt and ran again as fast as her short sturdy legs could carry her.

The houses of Alderton came into sight and she checked, approaching them at a quick cautious walk, fearful that she might be set upon, but her alarm had no foundation; the village was silent, ghost-like and untenanted, for all its inhabitants were congregated on the beach at Shingle Street tearing lumps of fresh roast horse between their teeth.

Two more miles yet to the ferry and even that was only a little over a third of the distance she had to cover. If she was ever to reach Ipswich she must conserve her strength so she moderated her pace and settled down into a steady dogged trudge.

Another mile and the road sloped upward toward the hills that held the Deben to its banks. The pebbled surface, rarely used except for motor traffic in the summer, was rough and tiring to her feet. Grass grew on either side, creeping towards the centre of the track, so Ann abandoned the road for the grass and found it better going. At length she breasted the rise and, stumbling slightly, slithered down the steep descent, the broad bosom of the river plain before her in the starlight.

There lay the ferry, an old broad-bottom punt, and on the right the tall bleak house, an inn where trippers came in the summer-time, filling the small tea garden with their noise and clamour. Now it was silent, dark, apparently unoccupied.

Panting a little she regained her breath and shouted. There was no reply. Again she called, then, desperate, picked up a pebble from the road and flung it at one of the first-floor windows. The glass splintered under the impact, and the pieces tinkled to the unseen floor with a melancholy sound, then silence descended on the little cove once more.

The landlord, his family, and the ferryman were gone, where, heaven knew. Impatiently for a moment the small agitated figure on the foreshore waited, and then abruptly turned away.

With quick steps she hastened on to the short broad 'hard' that jutted out into the river. Great posts of wood, rotting under the pressure of time and sea, held the banked earth together, except in one corner where the mass had crumbled and a gap showed plain between the surface, beaten down by generations of trampling feet, and the decaying pillars at which the tide sucked and gurgled.

The river being in flood it occurred to Ann for one moment to swim it, but she knew the treacherous mud banks on the farther side that the night concealed. She would be trapped for certain in the slimy ooze.

The ferry lay there in the starlight but Ann knew that her slender arms would never be able to cope with the great heavy pole, or steer the ancient barge safely to the other side; once she got out into the stream she would be swept seaward by the tide.

In desperate haste she began to scan the other boats for one that might be suitable. Most of them were inaccessible, being moored out in the river. Yachts and motor-launches rocked gently in the tide, lonely and forgotten now in the stress of terrible events, but kept there for the week-enders who, in happier times, forgot their business worries during the hours they sailed, or chugged gently, down-river, along the coast, and up the reaches of the Orwell or the Stour. A dinghy swung at the stern of all the larger boats but not one of them was within Ann's reach.

She stamped with impatience at the thought that in such a place there must be something in which she could get over if only she could find it, and hurriedly retraced her steps to the landward end of the hard. Her eye lit on a battered rowing boat half sunk in the mud. She paused by it a moment and hastened on, its planks were rotting even if she could prise it from its sticky bed. Then on a shelving beach of pebbles above the mud she saw a dinghy, queerly lopsided but lying high and dry. Next moment she had seized the painter and was dragging it towards the water. Her sense of flying time, upon every moment of which Kenyon's life might hang, lent her added strength, and with a superhuman effort she managed to get it launched.

The sculls had been left beneath the thwarts, and the boat was hardly rocking in the water before she had them out and in the crutches. With a sharp left-handed stroke, she swung the nose towards the opposite shore, and then with all the weight of her strong shoulders pulled towards it.

Five minutes later she had shipped her sculls and was scrambling out into the ooze that fringed the farther bank. It sucked and plopped as she struggled through it but she was on to the coarse grass a minute after landing, leaving the dinghy to drift out on the tide.

With renewed courage she ploughed her way up the rising ground and over the thick heather. The brief respite on the hard and the use of different muscles in rowing had eased her legs and rested her feet a little. The river too had been her principal anxiety, now she had succeeded in crossing it the remainder of the journey depended only upon sheer dogged endurance.

At last, with infinite thankfulness she struck a road and, leaving the uneven ground, turned north along it for half a mile until she came to a cross-roads that she recognised. There she turned left but with a sinking heart, for she knew that she had barely accomplished half her journey, and that a solid seven mile tramp still lay before her.

It seemed hours and hours since she had left Shingle Street and her head was burning with fatigue. As she trudged on she became half-delirious and began to sing, strange breathless snatches of half-forgotten tunes, hymns, choruses and nursery songs, that she had learnt in Orford when she was a little girl.

She broke off suddenly, impelled from sheer fatigue to sit down and rest by the wayside. Slipping to her knees, she leaned against a bank and lay there for a few moments panting heavily, while she tasted the supreme pleasure of relaxing all her limbs. Instantly a great drowsiness came over her, with a little flicker her heavy eyelids closed, and the great weight of sleep bringing relief to her utter weariness, pressed down upon her.

That would have been the end of her pilgrimage had not a sudden picture blazed in her half-conscious brain. Kenyon, with the burning brand pressed against his chest! She started up with a muffled scream, those devils were going to hang him—no, he was to be shot tomorrow—today—when the light came in the morning. Wide awake again now she struggled to her feet, and pressed on down the road, running a few paces and then dropping back into a staggering walk.

She wondered vaguely how much farther she had to go and, knowing the country well, she would easily have recognised any bend or turning in the daylight; but now that she could only see hedged fields on one side of her and heath on the other, her brain would no longer take in the significance of the gradients and dark coppices. At last another cross-road loomed up out of the darkness, and the place was unmistakable even in her weariness. It was a little north of Brightwell and on one corner of it stood a signpost, but she did not trouble to peer at it for she knew its legend; it read, 5¼ miles to Ipswich.

Five and a quarter miles still to go. She felt that she would never be able to do it. Her feet were aching, galled and blistered about the heels. The road seemed to waver in front of her, closing up then broadening out before her with a horrible sickening motion. She swayed as she walked, lurching from one side of the road to the other, and failed to see the faces of the starving prowlers who peered at her from the hedgerows every now and then. Furtive, soundless, they watched her pass and then slipped back into the shadows for she carried nothing, not even the smallest packet that might contain food, and seemed to be as destitute as themselves.

It was not until he was actually upon her that she saw the man who sprang from the roadside and seized her arm.

What could have urged him to attack her is past conjecture. She obviously had no food about her and even less of beauty. Her dark hair hung in matted locks; her face was puffed and swollen. The mud of the Deben clung about her feet and blackened her arms up to the elbows; smears of it disfigured her face where she had sought to wipe away the perspiration and her mouth hung open in an ugly contour, but as she swung terrified to face him she saw that his eyes were glowing bright in the darkness with the horrible glare of insanity.

She screamed and with a sudden access of strength wrenched her arm free, then slogged him again and again with her clenched fist in the face. For a second he stood there, a look of stupid amazement in his eyes, his arms dangling foolishly, then he tripped and fell backwards in the roadway.

Ann screamed again and, forgetful of her weariness, ran and ran until she was clear of the hedgerows and out once more upon the open heath. There she collapsed and fell into a ditch, lying sobbing for several moments.

Rocking from side to side, moaning a little from acute bodily distress and terrified that she might fall asleep, she began to massage the aching muscles in her legs, then recognising a cottage opposite suddenly realised that she could now be no more than three miles from her goal.

As she got on her feet something rustled in the bushes at her rear, only a stoat or rabbit perhaps but, terrified by her recent experience, she dashed off down the road.

She was drunk now, drunk with terror and fatigue, but somehow she staggered on, every thought blotted out from her exhausted brain but that they meant to burn Kenyon unless she could reach Ipswich in time.

Suddenly she realised that she was no longer walking through open country. Houses were upon either side. Her mind cleared for a space, and she shook her head violently from side to side. Then as she looked round she knew that she could not be dreaming. The electric tramwires were overhead.

This was Ipswich, but the suburbs seemed interminable and her feet like leaden weights as she dragged them one after the other. There were lights ahead and she groped on towards them but, when she was only a few yards from the barrier which they illuminated, all strength seemed to leave her and, pitching forward on her face lay gently moaning in the gutter.

A man came forward and, stooping, gripped her by the arm. He shook her roughly and pulled her to her feet.

'You can't stay here,' he said sharply, 'you must go back where you came from unless you live in the town.'

'Communists,' muttered Ann, 'they're going to burn them.'

'Eh! what's that?' he questioned with a quick glance. 'Where have you come from?'

'Shingle Street,' she flung at him with a desperate effort. 'They'll be burnt alive unless you take me to the Town Hall.'

'All right, pull yourself together, it isn't far.'

Ann remembered nothing of the last part of her journey. Her mind was blank until she stood, supported by the man who had found her and another, before a bald man at a desk in a bare, ill-lighted room.

He pressed her for her story, but her memory and even her power of speech had almost gone. 'Communists, Mutineers, they'll burn them alive if you don't send help, Shingle Street—Shingle Street,' was all that she would mutter over and over again.

Limp and utterly exhausted she sagged upon the arms of the two men until at a gesture from their superior they led her to a chair, where she flopped inert, her head lolling forward on her chest.

'Send for the Colonel,' said the bald man, and with infinite overwhelming relief Ann knew that her task was accomplished. She dozed for a moment, but just as she was going off again the thought of time flashed into her mind once more. How long had she been, and could the rescuing force reach Shingle Street before dawn.

Jerking up her head, she gazed round the room, and through dull eyes saw the face of a big white clock. Yes, she had done it, the black hands stood at a quarter to four. She had taken only three hours and a quarter to do that terrible journey.

She smiled then, wanly but happily; with horses or bicycles they would easily get to Shingle Street before six.

Next moment the door opposite to her opened, the bald man stood up deferentially at his desk, the others came to attention and a khaki figure entered. He stood there staring into her face for a second and then he stepped forward.

'Well I never! if it ain't little big eyes turned up again!' and she found herself staring into the blotched unhealthy face of Private—now Communist Colonel—Brisket.

24

The New Justice

For the moment Ann's state of collapse saved her. Utterly overwhelmed by the appearance of Brisket and all that his new authority portended, after the continual stresses which she had sustained in the last thirty hours—she fainted.

Despite her forlorn and bedraggled appearance he still

regarded her with a lecherous stare from one small hot eye; the other, which she had injured three weeks before, remained hidden under a black shade.

'Take 'er away,' he said suddenly, 'over to the 'otel opposite an' give 'er a bed in one of the guarded rooms. She's an old frien' of mine, is big eyes, an' I'll enjoy a little talk with 'er ter-morrer—'op to it.'

The other men jumped to obey his order and Ann was carried out, across the square and up the stairs of a small commercial hotel which had been taken over by the Ipswich Soviet. They pushed open the door of a small bedroom, flung her on the bed, and left her, locking the door behind them.

She moaned a little and came out of her faint, but hardly regained consciousness; the room was dark, her muscles at last relaxed and almost instantly she fell into a deep, dreamless slumber.

'Wake up,' shouted a voice, 'wake up, will you,' and feeling her shoulder violently shaken she groaned, then opened her eyes to stare round the strange room lit by the afternoon sunshine.

Momentarily she remained dazed, then the details of her desperate but useless venture came back to her.

'You're wanted,' said the man who had woken her, 'come on now.'

With an effort she slid off the bed. Every bone in her body seemed to be racked with shooting pains, her throat was dry and parched, her head splitting. As she caught sight of herself in the mirror of the cheap dressing-table, she gave a little gasp. Her clothes were torn and mud-stained, her hair a matted tangle, her eyes red-rimmed and swollen. Picking up a towel from the washstand she dipped it in the water jug and began to dab her face but the man pulled it away from her.

'No time for that, Colonel wants to see you,' he said sourly. Then he pushed her before him from the room, down the narrow stairs and out into the square.

The streets were nearly empty but over at the Town Hall there was considerable activity. Thirty or forty men, some in khaki, but mostly in civilian clothes, and all with a bright red sash crossing their bodies from shoulder to hip, stood leaning on their rifles or passing to and fro. Evidently a selected guard ready to deal with any emergency which might threaten the new local Government. A small group of them, obviously a detachment of cavalry, stood by a dozen horses, and as Ann was led over to the building she noticed that a line of despatch-riders stood ready by their bicycles while one or two others were arriving and departing in apparent urgency.

Inside the Town Hall was swarming with people. Messengers were constantly coming and going, men with set important faces carrying bundles of papers hurried from room to room, and a motley throng, who seemed to have no particular business but whom Ann supposed to be adherents of the new movement, blocked the hallway, stairs, and passages.

Her captor forced a way through them, up the staircase and along a corridor, then he poked his head into a room, muttered something, and drawing back thrust Ann inside and slammed the door behind him.

With sick apprehension she saw that Brisket, seated with his legs crossed in a big arm-chair, was the sole occupant of the room. A slow smile lit his heavy face as she appeared in the doorway.

'Well, big eyes,' he greeted her, 'feelin' better for yer nap?'

Youth, a healthy body, and eleven hours of complete oblivion had certainly restored Ann's bodily well-being to a considerable extent, yet having slept in her clothes and been allowed no opportunity to bath or wash, she was feeling incredibly stale, stiff after her supreme effort, and weighed down to an unutterable degree of sadness by the fate which she had been unable to avert from Kenyon and her friends.

'I'm all right,' she answered dully, 'although I think I could have gone on sleeping for a week.'

He nodded. 'You'll soon pick up agin, don't you fret. An' I tike my 'at off to yer fer that sportin' effort of yours to sive yer pals. 'Ave a pew?' He pushed a chair towards her with his foot.

She sank down in it and passed her hand across her eyes. 'It wasn't much use, was it?' she said wearily.

'Wot's the odds,' he said, trying in a queer uncouth way to comfort her. 'They were for it any'ow. Only a question of time 'fore we mopped 'em up.'

Her long lashes trembled towards the dark hollows beneath her eyes. It was only now coming home to her that she had failed completely. Kenyon, dear Kenyon, to whom she had so stupidly denied a declaration of her love, was dead; and Uncle Timothy, and Agatha, and Gregory, and Rudd, and that funny good-humoured American, and the gay, generous-hearted Veronica too perhaps. It seemed that she had not a single person left to care for in the world. The tragedy was so complete that she hardly thought of her own position, once more at the mercy of this loathsome soldier whom she hated and despised.

'You'll go up before the beak as a reactionary o' course,' he broke in on her sombre thoughts, 'but don't cher worry abart that, I'm not their commander 'ere worse luck, though if I plays me cards right I soon may be, but I got influence all right, an' plenty of it. They got to consider Colonel Brisket in their little game, so you leave it to yours truly; 'cause I'll tell yer, even if you did biff me one, I got a bit of a pash fer you, big eyes.'

Slowly the full significance of her appalling plight filtered into her mind but it was too numbed to respond by flaming anger to his covert offer, only a sullen determination to kill herself rather than satisfy his cravings caused her to mutter: 'You can't blackmail me, or force me to do anything I don't want to.'

'I know that,' his single eye narrowed with sudden cunning. 'I want yer willin', understand? I've tried aht the other gime these lars' three weeks an' it ain't worth the candle, so I'm aht to treat you right from the beginnin', see?'

'Whatever you do it will make no difference,' she cried with sudden spirit.

'But I got influence,' he argued. 'I'll be the King pin in this ahtfit 'fore I'm much older, an' you can be the Queen bee if you be'ave decent, strite, I'm tellin' yer.'

'I don't care what you've got,' she responded doggedly.

'Don't cher?' He leaned forward quickly, determination in every line of his strong coarse face. 'Then what abaht that red-'eaded feller you was sweet on, I saw yer googling at 'im when 'e wasn't looking that afternoon we was 'anging orf the Margate coast. If you'd be matey I could get 'im off as well as you.'

'Kenyon!' she swung round on him, 'is he still alive?'

'Yes o' course, if that's 'is nime! *Shark's* orders was ter land a party fer drivin' the cattle in, an' ter bring the orficers back fer trial and execution. She made the Orwell rhand abart midday an' sent the prisoners off in boats.'

'But, but,' she stammered, 'do you mean that the destroyer was sent from Ipswich?'

'Yus, we cruised around for a bit makin' the villages on the coast corf up enough fish fer us ter live on, but we was runnin' out of fuel so we brought 'er up the river far as we could an' threw in our lot wiv this new Soviet. I 'ate ships meself so they give me a job on the Committee but, knowin' abart all the cattle wot the General pinched orf the locals, they filled the *Shark* up wiv oil an' sent 'er rahnd ter tike it orf 'is Mightiness.'

The door was flung open and a grey-haired man pushed his head inside. 'Court's sitting, Colonel, and they'll want that woman directly—will you send her down?'

'I will.' Brisket rose slowly to his feet as the door closed again and thrust his chin forward peering into Ann's strained face. 'Na! wot abart it?'

A hundred new thoughts and emotions were coursing wildly through her brain. They were not dead, but here in Ipswich, and this man had it in his power to save them. How could she let them die?

She closed her eyes to shut out the eager watchful stare with which he was regarding her.

'All of them?' she said after a moment. 'All of them?'

'No, the Court 'ud kick at that.'

'All of them,' she repeated thickly, 'or I won't do it.'

He was silent for a minute then he nodded. 'All right, there'll be a rumpus I expect but I'll fix it some'ow, though only postponement of the sentence mind, I'll keep 'em on the strings as guarantee you treat me fair.'

'I can't,' she wailed suddenly springing to her feet. 'I can't. How can you ask me to knowing that I detest you?'

'You'll get over that,' he laid a heavy hand on her shoulder, 'but you're going through it anyway, see? Just think it over when you get dahnstairs. I'll tell the orderly to wite in Court so as you can send 'im up ter me if you're prepared to tike it cheerful fer the sike of gettin' off yer pals. But ter-night's the night, mind, any old 'ow—fer you an' me.'

He struck a hand bell and placed her in charge of the orderly, who marshalled her through the press of people down the stairs and into the lofty chamber on the right of the entrance hall.

It was the Court-room, empty now of the public and the Press. Only one man sat at the long lawyer's table, and on the magistrate's bench were two men and one woman, seated beneath the red flag which had replaced the royal arms of England.

In the dock stood Gregory, still in the uniform, now ragged and torn, of a brigadier, his face unusually pale, his head bandaged. Silas stood next to him, his enormous bulk seeming to dominate the group, then Veronica, her eyes half-closed, her hand on Silas's arm. Beyond her Rudd, in a slouching attitude picking his uneven teeth with a scrap of paper, and lastly Kenyon, stooping slightly, his left arm still in a sling. About them stood the only other occupants of the Court, a little group of soldiers.

Ann gave a half-articulate cry and ran towards them as they greeted her appearance with amazed ejaculations, but the orderly caught her shoulder and jerked her back: 'Steady you,' he growled.

The voice of the man who occupied the centre chair on the bench came, smooth, cold, and passionless: 'Is this the woman who came from Shingle Street early this morning?'

'Yes; this is her,' the orderly nodded.

'Put her with the others in the dock.'

Two men with rifles held slackly in their hands stepped aside and Ann was pushed past them next to Gregory. One of those rare bewitching smiles lit his bloodless face. 'Hello, Ann.'

'Hello, Gregory,' she murmured, but the greetings of the others were cut short by the President of the Tribunal.

'You will please be silent,' he said sharply.

As in some awful nightmare Ann stared at him. He was frail, elderly, grey-haired, clad neatly in a worn dark suit. A straggly beard covered an undeveloped jaw but his forehead was broad and lofty, his eyes large, pale and almost hypnotic in their power of penetration. He leaned forward and addressed them.

'All of you, including this woman who has just been admitted to the Court, are proved enemies of the New Order. You have without warrant robbed defenceless people of their only means of sustaining life, and on many occasions committed acts of banditry. The Government is now the people, and all property theirs to distribute in the most equitable manner; but when called upon to surrender your stolen supplies to the people's representatives, you were guilty of armed resistance which caused loss of life: you men are therefore enemies of the State and the women have aided and abetted in your crimes. It is my duty to order your execution. Have any of you any reason to state why the sentence should not be carried out?'

'You are neither magistrate nor judge,' Gregory cried quickly. 'What right have you to sentence us?'

'I have been appointed by the Committee to dispense the New Justice in this area with full powers of life and death,' the bearded man answered slowly. 'I fear that is the only answer which I can give you.'

'We haven't even had a trial,' Gregory broke out. 'You'll swing for this before you're done.'

The Chief of the Tribunal shrugged. 'Such men as you are dangerous to the New Order. Your rank of General alone would justify me in condemning you.'

'New Order be damned!' The white scar which lifted Gregory's eyebrow stood out angrily. 'We've been trying to keep the peace, not break it; and what authority have your Committee got to order killings?'

Quiet, restrained, sad almost, the Soviet judge answered patiently: 'Their authority is derived from the Central Committee in London. From the beginning it was recognised by all sane men that the old Goverment had failed in carrying out their first duty to the people—the protection of their lives and livelihood. Five days ago the New Provisional Goverment was recognised.'

'By whom?' snapped Gregory.

'By the People, the final authority upon which any Government must base its power if it is to survive. By the will of the People the Glorious Revolution has been accomplished, and now their only hope is to bide absolutely by the decrees of the Central Committee. For the safety of the nation and to avoid further bloodshed, all declared reactionaries must suffer the extreme penalty—therefore I condemn you.'

It was so obviously useless to protest further against the decision of this cold fanatic that Gregory gave a little shrug and with a queer twisted grin, directed as Silas, fell silent.

'You fools!' cried Veronica suddenly. 'We are for law and order every bit as much as you; surely you see that.'

The woman on the bench, grey, fifty, lean-faced but fine-featured, stared at her with hard, cold eyes. 'Is one of these men your husband?' she asked silkily.

'No; I have not got a husband.'

'But you have lived with one of them perhaps?'

'What is that to do with you; my body is my own to do as I like with.' Veronica's nostrils were quivering with furious anger.

'True, and the freedom of women to choose their own path of life without disgrace is one of the first things which the New Order will establish, but as a doctor of psychology, I can speak as to the results of such associations. The laws of nature are unalterable and a woman's thoughts are always coloured by those of her male partner for the time being. Your refusal to answer my question implies an admission, so you are doubtless contaminated by their theories and must pay the price.'

Veronica's voice came in a quick harsh sneer. 'Then I hope it amused you to live with a lawyer who had a secret lust for murder.'

'Get rid of 'em,' growled the great gross man with beady eyes who constituted the third member of the Court. 'Get rid of 'em, we're wasting time.'

As the President nodded and turned to the guard to order their removal, Ann leaned over and spoke in a sharp whisper to the orderly. If she was to suffer the last degree of torture in Brisket's arms that night, at least she might try and save the others.

'One moment,' Kenyon addressed the Chief of the Tribunal, as the orderly hurried from the room. 'I don't want to argue, but I've got a favour to ask.'

'Let me hear it then,' the man waved the guards aside.

'It's this. I don't question your authority—you've won, that's all, but in every Court that's ever sat there is one right which is never denied to any prisoner who is to die.'

'Well—what is it?'

'Marriage before execution; I wish to marry this lady here.' For a second he smiled at Ann. 'Can that be done?'

'It is an old custom, useful only to secure the transfer of property,' said the President. 'The abolition of private ownership and the fact that you are both to die makes it useless here.'

'Nothing can be useless which gives mental joy, however brief,' declared Kenyon firmly.

'All right then. I grant your request since it is in accordance with the established customs of humanity. But I fear you must be content with civil marriage. There can be no priest.'

'That doesn't matter; where can it be done?'

'Here,' replied the President quietly, 'and now. Under the New Order a simple declaration made before this court will be binding upon you both. Is the woman willing?'

This new development threw Ann into a fresh torment of indecision. How could she refuse Kenyon when she loved him so much, she would have said yes gladly with all her heart if they had been free or both about to die. If she refused he would think her utterly heartless; for how could she explain. Yet how could she marry him and commit adultery that very night?

With growing amazement he saw her hesitation and watched her lowered lids. Then slowly she raised large dark tear-dimmed eyes. 'I—I can't, Kenyon,' she murmured. 'I'd like to, dear, but—but Brisket's here, so I've promised—I've promised, he's going——'

Her voice was drowned by the rattle of the rifles as the soldiers came to attention on Brisket's entry. Stocky and powerful he strode to the centre of the Court. 'The execution of these people's ter be postponed,' he declared loudly.

'What's that?' The President stiffened in his chair. 'By what authority?'

'By mine.'

'But . . .'

'I'm a member of the Committee, ain't I?' Brisket thrust his chin out aggressively at the magistrate.

'Your interference with the course of justice in intolerable,' the bearded fanatic cried angrily.

'I got me own way o' doin' things—see, an' you keep a civil tongue in yer 'ead or there'll be trouble.' With a threatening glare Brisket motioned to the guard: 'Remove the prisoners. Come on, big eyes; you come wi' me.'

In a second Kenyon had sized up the situation. Ann had made a bargain with this brute to save their lives. With a flaming face he leapt from the dock, and as the soldier stretched out a hand to take Ann by the arm, hit him a tremendous blow beneath the chin.

Brisket, taken off his guard, went crashing on the ground. Kenyon, his left arm wrenched from the sling, dived at him as he fell and caught him with both hands by the throat. The soldiers flung themselves upon him, but Rudd and Silas had both joined in the scuffle; with his immense strength the latter gripped two guards by their collars and cracked their heads violently together.

One soldier loosed off his rifle and there was a splintering of glass. The magistrates were shouting from the bench. The doors burst open, more soldiers and an excited crowd rushed in. For a few moments a wild tumult reigned in the well of the court, but when at last order was restored, and Kenyon dragged, panting, back into the dock, Brisket remained a crumpled heap upon the floor. His head had cracked like an egg in his fall against the solid dais.

The crowd stood there for a moment gaping at the body from which life had passed so suddenly, but the soldier who had fired the rifle was exclaiming, 'One of 'em's got away; after him, quick!' and dashed out of the room. He alone had seen Gregory leap to the tall window on the first sign of trouble, and dive through it to the lane which ran along the side of the Town Hall.

A detachment was sent in pursuit of the flying Gregory, Brisket's body removed, the court cleared, and then the President looked sternly at the figures in the dock. 'If there had ever been any doubt in your case, this murderous attack upon a loyal officer of the New Order would serve to condemn you a hundred times.'

'The swine! he asked for it,' Kenyon panted.

The Chief of the Tribunal smiled a little grimly. 'Perhaps—such men are necessary to restore order, but their morals do no honour to our Cause, and his interference for some private reason was unwarranted.'

'Then let's get back to where we left off,' said Kenyon promptly.

'You still ask for this marriage?'

'Yes, I am no less condemned than I was before.'

Ann felt as though a great weight had been lifted from her shoulders. Even if they were all to die she had escaped that unspeakable degradation. Willingly she gave her hand to Kenyon and in a few short sentences the ceremony was performed.

Silas bent over to Veronica, as the others signed on the first page of a new ledger. 'You know,' he said, 'it would make me very happy too.'

'What's the use, darling?' Veronica sighed.

'Well, tell me,' he pressed her. 'Just say we'd met in ordinary times—would you—would you have thought of becoming my wife?'

Slowly she turned and faced him. 'Yes, Silas, I would have married you. You're the only man I've ever met who has all the interests I really care about, who is kind to the verge of stupidity, yet strong enough to prevent me making a fool of myself.'

'Then let's, Veronica; it's great to know you really care that much, and it may be stupid sentimentality, but I'd like to have you Mrs. Gonderport Harker for any hours we've got.'

'Why, darling, if you want me to,' her voice cracked suddenly and two large tears trickled down her face. She rubbed them away impatiently, and gave a rueful smile. 'What idiots we are, my dear; but never mind.'

So they, too, were married, and it fell to Rudd to claim another privilege. 'I've always 'eard,' he stated loudly, 'that them 'as was due for a 'anging got a good square meal at the lars'.'

'Waste,' thundered the fat man on the bench, but the President upheld Rudd's submission and ordered an issue of rations to each of them when they had returned to their temporary prison. Then he ordered their removal.

On his way out Rudd paused before the bench and in a low voice again addressed the President: 'Er—you'll excuse me, Guvnor, but 'ow long 'ave we got, if yer know wot I mean?'

'About three hours, was the soft reply. 'Executions take place at seven o'clock in the morning and the evening.'

'Coo-er! that ain't long, is it. Couldn't yer make it termorrer? It's me birfday, an' it 'ud be a kind o' celebration ter go out on what they calls yer natal day.'

'No, that is impossible.' The Chief of the Tribunal shook his head. 'Other reactionaries are constantly being arrested and your place of confinement will be needed for them.'

'Orl right, Guv'nor.' Rudd moved to follow the rest but

threw a parting shot over his shoulder. 'I 'ope it keeps fine for yer when they bumps you off; an' they *will,* yer know, sure as me favourite dish is winkles.'

An armed escort piloted them across the square, into the little hotel where Ann had spent a portion of the night, and the morning, then up the stairs to the first floor drawing-room, where they were locked in and at last able to talk freely.

'Well, we're for it all right,' Silas announced grimly, 'but you certainly are an extraordinary people. That magistrate managed to give me the impression that he had a real right to deliver judgment on us, he was that serious about it.'

'Yes, we're orderly enough,' Kenyon agreed, 'even in a revolution; it's in the blood, I suppose, but that's what makes it so horribly final. They'll take us out of this place on the tick of seven o'clock and shoot us with the same precision as if they were serving a summons on us for not having paid the dog licence.'

'Kenyon,' said Ann suddenly, 'we haven't got long—kiss me.'

She was still so overwrought that she could think of nothing but his presence and her escape, the others were shadows moving in the room, and as they turned away she clung to him with pathetic passion.

Twenty minutes later their food arrived. Two potatoes apiece boiled in their jackets, a hunk of course light brown bread and an apple each. Rudd came away from the window where he had been staring out into the square. Veronica rose from her new husband's knee where she had been endeavouring to keep up a cheerful flow of banter, and Kenyon and Ann ceased to stare at each other stupidly upon the sofa.

They had not tasted food for the best part of twenty-four hours so, despite the fact that they might not live to digest the meal, they set to almost ravenously, while Ann recounted her adventures and they told her of their trip crowded together in one small cabin of the *Shark*, in which they had been brought from Shingle Street to Pinmill on the Orwell.

After they had fed they fell silent, only the monotonous tread of the sentry as he paced up and down outside the door was audible.

'Silas, is there *no* way that we can get out of this place?' Veronica demanded suddenly.

He looked a little hopelessly around the old-fashioned hotel drawing-room. It was a low-ceilinged room of moderate size filled with indifferent furniture. A spindle-legged writing-table stood between the windows, and a geranium plant on a pedestal occupied one corner. Anti-macassars of coarse lace draped the arm-chairs and sofa, the wallpaper was a hideous shade of green, and cheap prints of sentimental subjects hung on long wires from the picture-rail. There was one door only, and the sole outward sign that the place had been converted into a prison was a network of barbed wire across the windows. Silas shook his head: 'I'm afraid not, honey.'

'If you call me honey I shall scream,' she exclaimed wildly and began to pace nervously up and down the room.

Rudd stood again by the window keeping an anxious, facinated eye upon the hands of the clock opposite. Kenyon and Ann had returned to the sofa and once more a strained unnatural silence fell upon the room.

'What's the time?' asked Veronica suddenly breaking the tension.

'Jus' turned 'arf pars' five, Miss,' reported Rudd.

'I wonder,' she said slowly, 'if Gregory got away.'

'You bet 'e did,' Rudd's belief in his master's capabilities remained unshakable.

'Yes,' said Kenyon from the sofa a little bitterly, 'he would be the one to get out in the end; I expect he'll walk to London and turn Kommissar after all.'

'Well, good luck to him if he does,' Veronica took him up sharply.

'Oh, rather,' he agreed heartily, 'and if he did I'll bet his first action would be to secure an order of release for us; the only trouble is that even Gregory couldn't get himself made a Kommissar in the hour and a quarter we have to go.'

'I wonder what *is* happening in London,' Ann said ruminatively.

Kenyon squeezed her hand. 'It's much the same as here I expect.'

'Then there is a chance that things will settle down again.'

'After a bit perhaps, but first there will be wholesale

shootings. It wouldn't be so bad if the chaps like that magistrate could keep control, the trouble is that the extremists like Brisket always get the upper hand in every revolution after the first month or two, and massacre the moderates. Once that happens it may be years before the country recovers.'

'The English are very conservative,' Silas put in. 'It wouldn't surprise me any if there were a counter-revolution.'

No one contradicted him and they sank into silence again, too busy with agitated thoughts of their approaching end to enter into argument.

'What time is it now?' Veronica asked again after a little in a nervous, high-pitched voice.

'Few minutes ter six, Miss,' Rudd muttered from his post of observation at the window.

'God!' Kenyon groaned, forgetful of Ann for the moment. 'We've got another hour of this.'

'Try not to think of it, my darling,' she smiled at him. 'I wish we could know if there is going to be a counter-revolution though.'

Silas heaved his bulk out of the arm-chair. Despite his apparent calmness he was desperately worried for Veronica, yet he could think of no way to engage her mind and quieten her restfulness. 'I wish a darn sight more that this radio was working,' he remarked, laying his large hand on the switch. 'If only we could tune in to a band it might cheer us up a little.'

Tick, tick, tick, the instrument responded with its rhythmic note.

'Good God! it is,' exclaimed Kenyon, bounding to his feet, 'That's the metronome.'

For a full minute they all stood staring at it in astonished silence, and then a clear resonant voice impinged upon their listening ears, coming to that drab, old-fashioned room out of the vastness of the ether:

'This is London calling.'

25

The Devil Rarely Gets His Due

They stood with strained expectant faces, their eyes riveted upon the instrument, while the voice continued slowly and distinctly:

'I am not a professional announcer, listeners will please overlook any faults of delivery. I will, however, speak as clearly as possible for this message is of vital importance.

'As you are aware the Broadcasting Service has been suspended for nearly a month and doubtless you will have assumed this to be due to sabotage; actually, the wrecking of all stations throughout the country was deliberate and carried out, under the instructions of the late Government, by the principal executives before abandoning their plant; it being the policy of the Government to prevent facilities for propaganda falling into other hands.

'During the first fortnight in August a reign of anarchy swept the whole country. Many deaths are reported from all quarters, and owing to a complete breakdown in the distribution of supplies, the prospect of starvation drove an ordinary law-abiding people to unheard-of acts of savagery.

'Desperate efforts have been made however to cope with the vital questions of feeding the population, and if listeners will faithfully carry out the instructions which I am about to give there will be no further danger to any member of the community from lack of food.

'On the breakdown of the late Government only one political body in this country was sufficiently organised to offer any prospect of stability if they were placed in power; I refer to the Communist party. For many years this party has been increasing in numbers, intelligence and strength. They have watched the gradual decline of confidence among the people in the succession of so-called National, Socialist-National, and finally United British Governments, convinced that a time would surely come when the nation would turn to them in some great crisis as the only body offering a clear-cut break from the old tradition of muddle, compromise and imcompetence.

'This party was very highly organised, and every member

of it fully instructed as to his duty when the expected crisis at last came; it is therefore not surprising that, on the fall of the late Government, the power of this party came to be felt very strongly, particularly in the towns, where its following was considerable.

'Faced with the country rapidly dissolving into a state of anarchy a very large proportion of the people naturally rallied to this cause, which offered the only obvious means of restoring law and order.

'Many of the principal towns of England, Scotland and Wales accepted the authority of the local Soviets a short time after the dissolution of the late Government and, although the street fighting was bitter and severe, London acknowledged a provisional Communist Government five days ago.'

'There you are darlings, just what Gregory told us, and what the greybeard said in the Town Hall,' Veronica shrugged impatiently.

'Shut up!' snapped Kenyon, 'oh hell! the battery's fading out.'

The voice had grown weaker as they leaned anxiously nearer to the instrument. Silas twiddled the knob but atmospherics intervened and they could only catch snatches of the announcer's speech here and there.

'Failure of foreign support . . . unable to redeem pledges . . . Manchester leading the way . . . two days and nights of massacre . . . first successes . . . three causes mainly contributing . . . dispatched by aeroplane . . . wonderful response by the United . . . recovery under new . . . food ships now . . . feeling of Empire never more strongly demonstrated . . . Canadian offer to admit . . . South Africa under this . . . difficulties of . . . enrolled at once . . . severe blow to Provisional Government . . . forces of the Prince Regent entered London at 3.15 a.m. this morning . . .'

'Good God!' cried Kenyon; 'do you understand? There *has* been a counter-revolution!'

'Listen, listen!' muttered Ann, 'what did he say? read what?'

'Something about a proclamation,' Silas turned the knob again, the instrument crackled, hooted, and buzzed, then the voice of the announcer came clear, loud and dominant once more:

'. . . has ever strained the heart of this great Empire, yet I am proud to say that never in their long history have the English speaking peoples given a finer demonstration of their power to unite together for the preservation of freedom and justice in the darkest hour.

'For years we have been drifting powerless in the grip of an effete system of Government. His Majesty knew it, I knew it, and the best brains in this country, who now constitute my council, knew it; moreover, in the last twenty years, I have made it my business to gather the opinions of men and women of every shade of thought and feeling in the country, rich and poor alike, and I am aware that many thousands of them realised it too, yet I was powerless to intervene.

'Had I made any premature attempt to save the country from the crisis which I foresaw I should have been instantly accused of seeking a dictatorship, thereby seriously prejudicing the goodwill of a large section of the community when the crisis came.

'I have never sought a dictatorship, and I give my assurance that as soon as law and order have been re-established throughout the country, I shall cease to act as a dictator. In the meantime however His Majesty's condition being too grave for him to bear the strain of such a crisis, the last act of the legally constituted Government was to surrender supreme power into my hands; to refuse it would have been a cowardly neglect of my duty as your Prince.

'Parliament will reassemble in due course, for it is as much a part of the Constitution as the Sovereignty itself, and time has proved that a Constitutional Monarchy is the form of Government best suited to the British people.

'But when it reassembles, it is my intention to urge upon it the passage of bills which will make it a different body to that which we have known for many generations. Firstly, I shall propose that hereditary Peers resign their right to sit by descent alone, and that for the future they be represented by certain members of their own order elected amongst themselves. By this means the best elements among the aristocracy will be retained and the Upper Chamber disembarrassed of those less useful.

'Secondly, that the House of Peers be strengthened to twice its remaining number by new members; men of proven worth who have served the country well in every walk of life, yet who would never prostitute themselves to enter politics by throwing out promises, impossible of fulfilment, to an ill-informed electorate. These will be elected in varying proportions by the newly constituted Upper and Lower Houses, Dominions Parliaments, Councils of Crown Colonies, and on the personal nomination of the Sovereign.

'By these measures it is hoped that a body of men may be gathered together who will represent in achievement, integrity, and intellect, all that is finest, not only in Britain, but in our Empire beyond the seas.

'To such a body we could well restore the ancient powers of the Upper House, while the Lower will remain, not as it has come of late years to be, a manœuvring ground for ambitious party leaders, and wielding an authority far beyond its rightful place in the Constitution, but an elected body to voice the opinion of the people and a stepping-stone for men of talent to the Upper House.

'There will be in future no Prime Minister. That office was created solely on account of the difficulty which William of Orange experienced in speaking and understanding the English language. It is the rightful prerogative of the Crown, and, should His Majesty's condition continue to improve, as we pray it may, he will once more assume the Sovereign's ancient position at the head of the Council table. In the meantime I shall continue to act on his behalf.

'I come now to the greatest step which has so far been taken to bring prosperity back to this dear country of ours. It is a policy which should have been developed long ago, but only this great crisis made possible the removal of opposition in the domestic politics of the Dominions and inter-colonial rivalries. I speak of the redistribution of the population throughout the Empire.

'At home we are faced with the tragic figures of the unemployed, while in our Dominions and dependencies there are stored enough fertility and wealth to give abundance to all the Empire's peoples. Emigration in the past has been difficult and expensive: families going out from this country have gone alone to face hardships and, in the remote parts, possible danger.

'In the early days of this crisis I used my personal influence to dispatch a number of Royal Air Force machines to various destinations, and in them sent trusted friends who knew my purpose to act as my ambassadors.

'The response to my appeal by our kindred overseas has been magnificent beyond words, and a unique example of their love for the Mother Country.

'They have agreed to open their vast territories to us, and vast tracts of fertile land, at present difficult of access, are to be brought into cultivation in many portions of the globe.

'New towns and cities are to be built which will offer employment in every type of industry. Free passage will be given to all who are willing to emigrate and accommodation on arrival in these new State-owned towns at moderate rentals deducted from subsidised wages, leaving a margin sufficient to ensure a decent standard of living.

'Emigrants will be asked to sign on for three, five or seven years, and during that period they will be guaranteed a minimum wage according to their employment; special allowances in addition will be paid for wives, children and dependents. Full particulars of this great emigration scheme will be published and broadcast throughout the country.

'I ask then for five million volunteers; men and women who have the courage to go upon this great adventure, and lighten the burden which is upon us at home.

'I appeal especially to the unemployed. For years now many of them have lead a tragic and humiliating existence. If they remain here their lot cannot be bettered, at least for many years to come. If they go forth in the spirit of their ancestors a useful self-respecting life, in which they may once more hold up their heads, awaits them.

'I want *five million volunteers,* and if they will come forward they may count themselves the saviours of the country.

'And now I would urge upon every one of you, whatever your age or circumstance may be, the absolute necessity in this great crisis, the worst of which is now happily over, to stand firm in the cause of law and order. Not to do so is to betray your own family and friends to a renewed, and perhaps final, anarchy. It is therefore the duty of every freeborn man and woman in this country to obey fully and loyally such decrees as shall be issued for the protection of the State upon my Sovereign authority. God bless you all.'

There was a brief pause and then the announcer's voice came again:

'This proclamation was issued from Windsor at four o'clock this afternoon under the signature of the Prince Regent.'

'By jove, he's done it!' exclaimed Kenyon, 'and he's the only man in the kingdom who could have pulled if off.'

Silas nodded as he switched off the loud speaker: *'Five million volunteers,* eh? d'you think he'll get them?'

'Why not?' Veronica laughed a little hysterically; 'they got five million volunteers to offer themselves for a killing before conscription was brought in during the Great War, and this applies to women too. He'll get them easily once it becomes the patriotic thing to do!'

'It's amazing that your Colonies should agree to this scheme, though,' Silas hazarded.

'They'll benefit too.' Kenyon began to pace up and down: 'Look at Australia, a vast continent with a population something less than that of London. They could lose a couple of million people there! Take some absorbing perhaps, but with new towns being built and Government organisation it could be done. Redistribution of population, eh? and a new bond to knit the Empire together. By God! he's cutting at the root of the trouble!'

'I wonder how many people heard the broadcast?' said Ann suddenly.

An immediate soberness descended on them all and Rudd lurched over to the window; 'Not many,' he said tersesly, 'can't 'ave bin.'

'No,' Silas added, 'it was pure chance that I happened to switch it on, the damn thing's been out of action for a month, there won't be one in ten thousand listening in to-night.'

'But they can't shoot us after this!' Veronica clutched him by the arm, 'they *can't!'*

'They may. Ipswich is Communist still and will be perhaps until the morning.'

'It's twenty-five pars' six by that there clock,' announced Rudd.

'Good God! only thirty-five minutes to go.' Kenyon ran

to the door and hammered on it. 'If we tell the guard what's happened he may pass on the news.'

'He won't believe you, darling,' Ann shook her head miserably.

The sentry opened the door and in a quick spate of words Kenyon poured out the news from London.

'You can tell that yarn to the marines,' said the fellow morosely, and slammed it shut again.

'What about breaking out?' cried Veronica.

'We'd all be shot, sweet, just as surely as we would have been an hour ago,' Silas told her.

'But we can't let them murder us now!'

'We'll put up a fight when they come for us,' he assured her with a quick glance at the window; 'but I only wish someone would start a riot here. Other folks besides us must have heard that radio somewhere in this town.'

'Then they'll have to make it snappy, sir,' Rudd threw over his shoulder, 'it's twenty ter seven now!'

'This is intolerable,' exclaimed Kenyon; 'to think our side is on top again yet we're to be killed off in twenty minutes' time; it's fantastic!'

'I know!' Ann's face brightened, 'let's ask to be taken before the Magistrate again.'

'That's it—that's it.' Kenyon began to bang loudly on the door.

The sentry opened it a foot and thrust an angry face in; 'What the 'ell is it now?'

'We want to be taken back to the Magistrate,' Kenyon begged.

'Aw, shut up, can't you. He's busy and you've had your turn. Be quiet now!' The man jerked the door shut again with a bang.

Rudd's face was glued to the window. Orderlies on horseback and bicycles continued to arrive at the Town Hall; a little group of the new Red soldiery sat on the steps, their rifles handy, but laughing and joking over a game of cards in the late afternoon sunshine.

The gross bulky man who had made the third member of the Tribunal came hurrying out of the building; he looked furtively to right and left, then set off at a quick pace up the street. Rudd glanced at the clock again. 'It's a quarter to seven,' he said anxiously. 'We'll be for it unless someone does something pretty quick.'

As he spoke a small body of Greyshirts came round the corner, the leader held a long white paper in his hand. At their appearance the guards on the Town Hall steps grabbed their rifles and scrambled to their feet. Rudd threw up the window and leaned out, his head pressed against the barbed wire mesh.

'Silence!' cried the leader of the Greyshirts. 'If you shoot us it will be murder. I am about to read a proclamation by the Government in London.'

'Thank God!' Kenyon breathed, 'it's the message on the wireless.'

The Greyshirt held up his paper and began to read in a loud voice. The armed men on the steps shuffled uncomfortably; in some mysterious fashion news of the development had spread. A crowd of people surged out from the Town Hall, and the Square, which had been almost empty a few moments before, began to fill like magic. From every side-street figures ran to block the wide open space.

'Hell!' exclaimed Veronica.

'What is it?' whispered Ann.

'That filthy woman who was on the bench.'

Then they all saw her; tall, haggard, wisps of grey hair blowing about her face, she forced her way towards the troops of the local Soviet. As they watched she issued a swift order; two men shook their heads and backed away, but the rest obediently raised their rifles.

The reader of the Proclamation hesitated, faltered, stopped. For a second an unearthly silence filled the square, then the woman's voice came fierce and shrill.

'Shoot!'

There was a rattle of shots. A groan went up from the crowd; three Greyshirts dropped from sight, but their leader still stood unharmed. With a sudden shout he flourished the Proclamation and charged up the steps.

'Down with the Reds,' bellowed Kenyon. 'Long Live the Prince!'

A hundred faces in the crowd turned to stare at the windows whence this clarion call had come, and another voice took it up. 'Down with the Reds! Come on, chaps—foller me!' It came from a burly carter in a leather apron.

The cry was taken up on every side. A little phalanx of blue-clad policemen had appeared from somewhere and, with an inspector at their head, were thrusting their way towards the Town Hall.

The reports from the rifles of the Red soldiers echoed sharply again. The Greyshirt leader fell backwards, shot through the head, but the rest were fighting at close quarters seeking to wrest their weapons from the guards.

A solitary rifle cracked from a window at the side of the square and the woman who had urged on the Communists clutched wildly at her chest, her mouth dropped open as though to shriek, then she pitched forward under the feet of the struggling mob.

'It's jus' turned seven o'clock,' said Rudd.

Next minute a body of Communist cavalry came charging out of a side-turning into the crowd. Two were pulled from their saddles, a third fell from his horse, struck on the head by a brick, but the rest cleared a wide lane through the mass and, turning at the far end of the square, galloped at full tilt again into the shrinking, struggling mob of people.

The troops on the steps poured another volley into the fleeing pedestrians, and in another minute the square was empty except for the Soviet soldiers and the wounded.

'Blimey!' exclaimed Rudd bitterly, 'if we ain't sunk after all.'

Kenyon nodded sadly. 'I'm afraid that was our last chance, and they may come for us any minute now.'

'No,' cried Ann. 'Listen! What's that?'

The sound of wild cheering came from somewhere out of sight along the street. The mob surged back into the square, and in their midst a lorry nosed its way into view.

'Troops!' yelled Veronica shrilly. 'Hell's bells! we've won!'

A machine-gun stuttered, checked, and then burst into a violent chatter. The horses of the Red cavalry reared, plunged and fell: another lorry came into view, a third, a fourth, a fifth—all packed with khaki figures. Under the death-dealing zip of the machine-gun bullets the Soviet infantry fled, jostling and fighting among themselves to be first through the doors of the Town Hall.

Careless of the barbed wire at the windows the prisoners leaned out waving and shouting wild encouragement; then Rudd's voice came above the din. 'There 'e is—I knew 'e'd come back fer us. Go on, sir—give 'em 'ell!'

'It *is*—it's Gregory!' Veronica cried, almost off her head with joy.

As he caught Rudd's stentorian shout Gregory, still in his tattered khaki, the golden oakleaves on his scarlet banded hat now frayed and grimy, looked up from the leading lorry and waved a smiling greeting. Ten minutes later he was with them in the room, answering a hail of excited questions.

'I could't have done it if you people hadn't given me the chance to get away,' he told them, 'and finding out the real situation was a bit of luck, the rest was dead easy.'

'Tell us, tell us!' Veronica insisted.

'Well, when I got into that lane beside the Town Hall I knew I was certain to be hunted through the streets if I was spotted in this rig-out, so I shinned up a fire-ladder and scrambled over the roofs as hard as I could go, but I slipped on a loose slate and pitched, feet foremost, through a skylight—that's where the luck came in!'

'Go on,' urged Ann. 'Go on!'

'Be patient, pansy face,' he chaffed her; 'the place happened to be the temporary hiding place of an Ipswich policeman. He wasn't in his uniform of course, but as soon as he saw me he came out of his shell and he was a remarkably intelligent chap. He joined a secret organisation, composed mainly of reliables in the old force, early in the troubles, and with half a dozen others had been keeping an eye on things here, and then passing on his reports to people higher up for transmission to Headquarters at Windsor. Naturally I had been racking my brains as I came over the roofs as to how to get you out of it, but this chap had all the dope about the Counter-Revolution having taken place this morning; and he said that having secured the great industrial centres they would be mopping up the other towns tonight. I didn't dare to wait though, and when he told me he felt certain loyal troops would be in Colchester already, I borrowed his push-bike and beat it. I was chivvied through the streets before I got out of the town but the rest was easy.'

'Easy?' echoed Veronica, raising her eyes to Heaven.

'Yes.' He smiled with his old air of superb self-confidence; 'I flung my weight about a bit and, seeing all my blood-stained bandages, they thought me no end of a tiger so I go away with half a company.'

'Won't you get into awful trouble now that the Government is restored?' asked Kenyon anxiously.

He laughed gaily; 'No, *Old Soldiers never die*. I'm just going over to the Town Hall to see that the job has been properly completed, then I propose to shed the purple, and as the song has it, gently *Fade Away*.'

They followed him downstairs and at the entrance to the hotel he turned and smiled at them. 'You'd better stay here for the moment, I won't be long.' Then he shouldered his way into the press.

For a few moments they stood on the pavement watching the cheering jostling crowd, then Veronica seized Kenyon's arm and pointed to another lorry that was slowly entering the square.

'Look, look! on the box!' she cried, 'there's Alistair!'

'Why, so it is, old Hay-Symple by all that's wonderful.'

'Alistair you brute!' shrieked Veronica; 'I adore your ugly face, come here!'

Major Hay-Symple heard her shout, looked his amazement in seeing her there and, jumping down, pushed his way towards them. As he stepped on to the pavement Veronica flung her arms round his neck and Kenyon thumped him on the back; but he took it all quite calmly, surveying their ragged clothes and the unshaven faces of the men with mild amusement. His own attire was as faultless as if he had just come off the parade ground; his firm chin seemed newly shaven, and his moustache was brushed stiffly upward as of old.

'My dear, where have you been, I'm terribly glad to see you,' he smiled affectionately at Veronica.

'Oh, everywhere,' she waved her arms, 'all over England, and Scotland too I think!'

'By jove!'

'But tell us,' she urged, 'what's been happening, we've only heard the Proclamation on the wireless.'

'Well really, I don't know,' he stroked the fine brown moustache. 'We've just been carrying on, most of us. It's all been done from Windsor; we occupied Maidenhead for a few days, ordered there you know, then last night we were ordered back to London, and there you are.'

'You maddening person, surely you were in the fighting?'

'Oh, rather, if you call it that, but of course it was of no value as experience to a soldier, beastly work and the men hated it as much as we did.'

'Hark at him!' Veronica appealed wildly to the darkening sky. 'To hear you talk anyone would think that there had never been a revolution at all!'

'Oh, well, there was a nasty patch in the middle of last week but the sailors did most of the—er—laying on of hands, if you know what I mean!'

'The sailors? but I thought they'd all mutinied?'

'There was a little trouble with them in the earlier part, but when things began to look really sticky they turned themselves into special police.'

'Well done the Navy!' laughed Kenyon.

'Yes, good show, wasn't it? But tell me about yourselves quickly because I've got a job to do.'

'Darling,' gasped Veronica, 'it's been too thrilling, first we were nearly all murdered in the East End somewhere, but we were rescued and taken on board a destroyer—' She paused suddenly as Gregory appeared from behind Silas's broad back.

'Hullo!' exclaimed Hay-Symple sharply.

'Hullo!' replied Gregory with a queer twisted grin.

'By God! you're the bogus Brigadier,' cried the Major, thrusting his way past Veronica. 'The crook I've been sent from Colchester to get; you're going to be court-martialled my fine fellow—and shot!'

26

September Moon

'Don't be a fool,' Veronica burst out; 'Gregory's been marvellous, we should all have been dead a dozen times if it hadn't been for him.'

'I'm sorry,' Hay-Symple shook his well-groomed head. 'You don't understand the enormity of the thing. It would have been bad enough if he had only dressed himself up in a uniform he had no right to wear, but to divert half a company of troops at a time like this is treason of the blackest kind, and, of course, the moment you mentioned a destroyer I tumbled to it that he's the chap who got away with a platoon and the *Shark* a month ago. I was ordered to follow him up from Colchester and arrest him, and I shall.'

'You can't!' stormed Veronica, 'you can't.'

'My dear I'm sorry, terribly so if he's been decent to you, but you must realise that plain murder is nothing to what he has done.'

'But you don't really mean to shoot him, do you?' Kenyon asked in a shocked voice.

'Not personally.' Hay-Symple beckoned to some of his men. 'But my orders are to take him back to London for court-martial, and there's no doubt about the verdict or the penalty. He will undoubtedly be shot.'

As Hay-Symple's soldiers surrounded him Gregory began to laugh, quietly at first, then louder, until he rocked where he stood, shaken by gargantuan bursts of laughter.

'I see nothing humorous about it,' said the guardsman acidly.

'Don't you? I do.' Gregory sighed as he wiped the tears of mirth from his eyes. 'First I'm to be shot by mutineers because they thought I was an officer; then by Communists because they thought I was a King; and now despite the fact that I've regained this town for the Government, by you, because I've got myself up in your stupid fancy dress. If that's not funny . . .'

Hay-Symple's face turned a darker shade of red. 'You will refrain please from insulting His Majesty's uniform.'

'Go to hell, you brainless idiot,' cried Gregory with a sudden burst of fury.

Veronica flung herself between them. 'Don't take any notice of him, Alistair,' she pleaded, 'he's overwrought; we've all been through the most appalling time.'

'Then make him keep his tongue between his teeth.'

Gregory shrugged. 'I didn't mean that personally; it's just that I loathe your type.'

'There, my dear,' Veronica begged, 'do try and forget that you're a professional soldier for a moment. We're all *alive,* Alistair, and that's what really matters. How can we get back to London?'

The guardsman gave her half a smile. 'I've no desire to quarrel with this chap, only to hand him over to the proper authorities. As for London—I've got to take him there, so

I can take you too, if you like; that is if you don't mind going in the lorry?'

'Of course not! And you'll take the others as well?'

'Yes, I don't mind.' He glanced round quickly and his eye fell on Rudd. 'Who's this man?'

'Batman to the General, sir,' said Mr. Rudd.

'Oh, you're the minor crook, are you? Well, I'm glad we've roped you in,' he swung round on Gregory. 'You see, it happens that, quite apart from this business at Colchester, I heard all about your first exploit from the Colonel whose men you trundled off with. He's a particular friend of mine, and he'll be better pleased to see you shot than to get another bar to his D.S.O.'

'Will he?' sneered Gregory, 'he's a fool then, he'll never live this story down, you know. "The Colonel whose troops were marched off by a civilian, in a hired suit from Clarksons!" I'd hush the whole thing up if I were you.'

'And let you off scot free? No thank you. In due course you're going to get it in the neck, my friend, so you'd better make up your mind to it. Are the subalterns from Colchester still here or have you sent them off to the War Office with another fake message?'

The ex-king of Shingle Street laughed. His furious anger at being caught had given way to his habitual philosophy. This earnest soldier was more a matter for amusement than abuse. 'You'll find them in the Town Hall,' he said cheerfully, 'a nice pink-faced youth, and a tall spotty one; Spotty is the senior, but the cherub's got more brains!'

'Thanks.' Hay-Symple nodded to the escort. 'Put these two men in the back of the lorry while I go across and see that things are all right. You others had better make yourselves as comfortable for the journey as possible.' He turned and thrust his way into the crowd.

When he returned they were all settled among the half-dozen privates on the sacking in the back of the vehicle with the exception of Veronica; despite Silas's protest she had elected to take the only place that would be vacant on the driver's seat. Hay-Symple climbed up beside her.

Slowly the lorry turned and edged through the seething mass of people. The whole population of the town seemed to have congregated in the square and principal streets; they were singing, cheering, and carrying soldiers, Greyshirts and policemen shoulder high as they swayed and rocked before the Town Hall. From the windows men were making speeches which had no chance of reaching their enthusiastic audiences, others were waving Union Jacks dragged forth for the occasion.

At last the lorry crawled into Fore Street, likewise crammed with people and, passing along it at a snail's pace, reached the less congested end where it was able to put on speed and take the London Road.

When they were clear of the town Alistair Hay-Symple turned to Veronica. 'The Prince makes his official entry tonight.'

'What? Of London? How positively thrilling; shall we see anything of it?'

'We might. I have to report to Wellington Barracks and that's only a stone's throw from Buck House as you know.'

'My dear, how *too* marvellous. But listen, Alistair; you've just got to let Gregory Sallust go. Arrange it so that it looks like an escape if you like. I'll never speak to you again if you do hand him over to the authorities.'

'Sorry, Veronica,' his voice was kind and sympathetic. 'I can understand in a way that you think he's a bit of a tiger but that doesn't alter the fact that he has twice got hold of troops, who might have been needed very urgently elsewhere, under false pretences. It was absolutely criminal and he's got to take his medicine.'

Veronica stood up in front of the lorry which was now rattling along at a good pace. 'All right,' she said firmly, 'if you feel that way you're no friend of mine. I prefer to travel with the troops.'

'Steady, steady,' he urged, catching her by the arm and pulling her down; 'I'm only doing my duty and that's got to be done.'

'I don't care a hoot in hell for your filthy little duty, and I'm going to travel in the back of this pantechnicon. Now, pull it up and let me get out.'

'Veronica, darling, don't you see that I can't help myself.'

'Help? *You!*' Veronica gave a sudden angry laugh. 'You wouldn't raise a finger to save your own mother from drowning if your Colonel said you were to march half a dozen men to the baths!'

'Veronica!'

'Yes, I mean it. You're weak and narrow; hidebound by this fossilised code which orders you to kill a man whose boots you are not fit to lick!'

'Damn it, be fair. *I* don't want to kill him; if he's in a mess it's his own rotten fault.'

'But you admit that they'll shoot him if you hand him over?'

'Yes, they've got ample powers under the National Emergency Act, and this is a case for shooting if ever there was one.'

'Then I beg of you, Alistair, to let him go.'

'I *can't,*' exclaimed the unfortunate soldier, goaded beyond endurance; 'and it's rotten of you to ask me! I couldn't do it even if you promised to marry me—and you know it!'

Veronica gave an angry snort. 'I wouldn't marry you in a thousand years! what's more I'm married already.'

'Good God! do you really mean that?'

'Yes, I do, and I haven't sunk to sitting beside the common hangman yet, so pull up at once, d'you hear?'

With a sullen nod Hay-Symple ordered the lorry driver to slow down, but when they came to a halt he climbed out himself; 'Stay there,' he flung at Veronica, 'I'll send the other female along to keep you company.'

'Thanks, but I'd rather have my husband, he's the largest man in the back!'

The driver cast a glance of mingled fear and admiration at this wrathful lady, then smothered a grin as Hay-Symple climbed in behind and Silas took the vacant seat.

Ann was sleeping with her head pillowed on Kenyon's knee; Gregory sat, hunched between his escort, with Rudd beside him, their backs against the fore-part of the wagon. The wretched Major sank down beside Kenyon.

'Veronica's crazy!' he snapped, as the lorry started off again.

'Always was,' replied Kenyon lightly.

'First of all she tells me she's picked up a husband, and then she wants me to let this blackguard escape who tried to march off with the troops.'

'Tried?' Kenyon's voice was cold. 'Did, you mean, and he's a damn' fine sportsman. I'd rather serve under him than any of you hidebound professional warriors any day when there's real trouble about.'

'Oh, shut up! I know my job as well as most people.'

For a time they fell silent. The lorry rattled and clanged through the narrow lanes to the west of Colchester, Hay-Symple having decided that it would be quicker to avoid the towns. The driver was getting every ounce out of his engine, and there was little danger that they would run into other vehicles as these were still almost non-existent.

'What was it really like in London?' Kenyon asked after a while.

'Bloody!' replied the soldier tersely—'absolutely bloody! but the troops put up a first-class performance.'

'What really happened?'

'God knows! I don't. Each of us only saw our own little bit of it, and personally, I thought the whole lot of us were for the high jump a week ago; but H.R.H. has been quite marvellous. It seems he had the whole party taped before it even started.'

'It's wonderful the hold he has on the affections of the people.'

'Well, he's earned it.'

'He has, but what's going to happen now?'

'Ask me another. All sorts of rumours are flying about; the banks are to be taken over by the state they say, and anybody who can prove their bona-fides will be able to get loans, to develop property or business, on fantastically easy terms.'

Kenyon grunted. 'That sounds all right, but what about private overdrafts? My people have always treated me damn well but I bet I'd never get a penny from the state without security when I'm hard up!'

'That's true, anyhow, it's only a rumour, and another is that the great Industrialists have sunk their differences and are to pool the interests of their own trades in the future, rather like the old City Guilds did centuries ago I gather, each bunch to supervise and foster their interests for the common good. There is one bit of good news I'm pretty certain about though, I had it from a chap who is on the Prince's staff; He means to kill D.O.R.A. as dead as mutton, and the liberty of the individual is to be restored. Even our seaside places may be worth a visit in a year or two, and the tax is to be taken slap off beer!'

'Yo-Ho for Merrie England!' Kenyon laughed. 'Come on Alistair, tell me more.'

'The whisky duty is to be reduced as well, and gin to somewhere about the old standard. They say it will bring in a far greater revenue and support home industries to boot. Overboard with all these fool restrictions, Empire Free Trade at last, and protection of the things we make ourselves, seems to be the line of country they mean to take.'

'And Government by Mandarins,' added Kenyon.

'Yea, like China, but the devil of it is they're so apt to be corrupt.'

'You won't find that here, and it's the finest form of Government in the world when they are straight.'

For another hour they discussed rumours and possibilities while the lorry bumped and jolted its way towards London. Here and there figures stepped out into the road, begging a lift and food or, if they had heard the news of the re-established Government, giving a cheer at the sight of the soldiers. Abondoned cars, tradesmen's vans, and every sort of conveyance littered the sides of the roads as they drew nearer to the capital.

Silas, on the box beside Veronica, was holding her hand in his, almost oblivious of the journey as he told her of his favourite home in Georgia, and his orange grove spread among the lakes and lagoons on the Florida coast above Miami.

At last they entered the Southend by-pass, and a few miles further on came to Camden Town; here they met the first crowds. In type they were the same mixed multitude who would have kicked them to death a month ago, but now their whole bearing was absolutely different. Laughing and waving to the Tommies, they made way for the lorry with ready cheerfulness.

'Ever been to the Zoo, darling?' Veronica asked as they passed the North End of Regent's Park, 'if not I'll take you one day.'

'I've been,' he smiled, 'and it's a poor show to what I'll take you to see in Central Park.'

'That's quite enough from you, my boy. You've got to learn from now on that England has the largest and best of everything, and also that little something that others haven't got!'

'I'll bet they haven't got the largest Zoo,' grinned Silas;

'can you hear any little lions aroaring now, or the dog-faced apes chattering on Monkey Hill?'

'Now you speak of it I can't,' she confessed.

'Of course you can't, honey—they've all been eaten long ago!'

'Silas you idiot, of course you're right, but if you call me honey again I'll eat *you*—get that?—eat you alive!'

'Eat on, honey,' he squeezed her hand. 'It would be a marvellous death.'

At the top of Baker Street they met a long column of sailors.

People were lining the pavements eight and ten deep to watch them pass, and the naval men seemed to be the heroes of the hour; but as they advanced they realised how terribly the upheaval had stricken London. Smashed shop windows, now temporarily boarded over, showed on every side. On one corner of Portman Square a whole great block of flats had been burnt right out, and only the twisted girders showed clear against the sky. The streets were dark and strangely mysterious, not a single standard threw its arc of brightness in the dim half light of the summer night. Only the principal cross-roads boasted flares—relics of an orderly London when special precautions were taken against fog.

Selfridge's windows lay gutted and empty, but a small army of men were already clearing away the wreckage preparatory to refitting at the earliest possible moment. In Oxford Street a vast crowd overflowed the pavements and spread across the roadway. The traffic was still practically nil only an occasional car carrying a Government official on urgent business or a line of vehicles loaded with sailors, police, Greyshirts or troops, crawled through the crowds who made way for them with cheerful badinage.

On the west side of Grosvenor Square Hay-Symple halted the lorry and, getting down, walked round to Veronica. 'Want to get down?' he inquired, but she shook her head.

'No, ducky; I want to see the fireworks so you may as well take us with you. Half a minute—Silas and I will come in the back now, then we shall all be together.' Her rancour at the guardsman's determination that Gregory should pay the penalty of his exploits had subsided. Old friend as he was, she realised now that it would have been easier for him to cut his throat than to grant her request.

Ann had woken up, and smiled with some of her old merriment as Silas lifted Veronica bodily over the side. 'Do you remember the dinner we cooked in the kitchen?' she laughed, nodding her head towards the east side of the square as the lorry moved on again.

'The night you slid down the drainpipe? Do I not, my dear! We'll all go back and cook another in an hour or two.'

'If there's anything left to cook,' laughed Kenyon.

'Oh, we'll find something—but darlings, I'd forgotten.'

'Forgotten what?'

'Why, it's Ann's job to say if she'll have us now!'

'What the deuce do you mean?' Hay-Symple cast a curious glance at Ann, whom up to that moment he had hardly noticed.

'Let me present you, Alistair, to my lovely sister-in-law—Major Hay-Symple—Lady Fane.'

'You're joking, Veronica! . . . I'm sorry. May I offer my congratulations and all that?'

'Thank you.' Ann sat up suddenly on her pile of sacking. 'But it wasn't a real wedding, was it?'

'It was,' said Kenyon firmly, 'you shall have another with orange blossoms and all the trappings just for fun if you like, but if you try to call it off I'll fight you in the Courts!'

'Oh, darling—' she gripped his hand impulsively and the golden eyes shone with love and laughter. 'I surrendered long ago really, and I'll never fight anywhere again.'

'I won't give you a chance,' said Kenyon with a little sigh.

'Now,' Veronica interrupted briskly, 'does your ladyship receive this evening or am I to be cast out of the ancestral home?'

'You stupid, of course I do; what's more I'll cook another dinner for you if you can find the food.'

'Leave that to me,' said Silas promptly. 'I'll find the food all right now money's worth something again in this old town.'

Veronica gave him a swift glance. 'Of course, I'd forgotten that too, you're simply lousy with money aren't you?'

'I can raise enough to buy half a dozen eggs,' he

chuckled, 'or the Koh-i-noor diamond. You've only to say if there's any little thing you're wanting any time.'

As they talked the lorry had been moving slowly through the crowds that filled Park Lane, but at Hyde Park Corner they found a solid jam. It took a good half-hour and all Hay-Symple's persuasion, with the assistance of Kenyon and the good-humoured Silas, before they managed to crawl inch by inch across the open space and enter Constitution Hill.

That thoroughfare was black with people edging and pushing to get nearer to Buckingham Palace, before which a vast throng was already gathered in expectation of the Prince's arrival.

'We'll never do it,' said Hay-Symple.

'Get as far as you can,' urged Veronica, 'we may be able to see something if we can only get as far as the corner.'

They made another two hundred yards in the next twenty minutes and then the pressure of the crowd compelled a final halt. The lorry was still in Constitution Hill, but almost at the bottom end, and the side of the Palace lay on their immediate right, strangely dark and silent. Only three windows showed any light, and those not the glare of electricity, but the soft, subdued glow of old-fashioned oil lamps. They could not see the Palace frontage but, by straining over the hood of the lorry, the first floor balcony jutting out in front of the State apartments was just within their line of vision.

'We shan't see a thing after all,' moaned Veronica.

'Yus we shall, Miss,' Rudd, who was standing up between his guards, assured her, 'that's the balcony wot the Prince'll come out on I'll bet a tanner. That's where the King an' Queen come aht on the declaration o' the lars' Great War. I was in the crush meself that night, so I know!'

A murmur like the surging of a great sea came up to them as they gazed over the heads of the enormous multitude. Thousands upon thousands of people stood, jammed together, hemming them in. Behind them Constitution Hill was now impassable and the crowd overlapped, hundreds deep, into Green Park. In front, line upon line of white upturned faces stretched away, unbroken but for the memorial to Queen Victoria which stood out like an island before the Palace, fading into a greyish blur where thousands more stood massed together.

Shoulder pressed to shoulder, stretching out of sight, they packed the Mall to Admiralty Arch.

Occasionally there were bursts of cheering, and now and again sections of the crowd lifted up their voices in a patriotic song. Women hung fainting in the tight-wedged mass, yet the pressure was so great that, while it prevented them from being carried away, it also saved them from being trampled underfoot.

The troops were bandying jests with the people near the lorry who clung to the sides of and occupied the bonnet. Gregory alone remained seated, hunched in a corner now at the back. Veronica left the others who were crowded near the hood and slipped down beside him.

'Fine party, isn't it?' he said, smiling at her in the darkness.

'You poor darling; it can't be much fun for you.'

'Oh, I don't know, it's good to think you're all safe out of it anyhow and that the country is going to be all right.'

'But I'm frightened for you, Gregory.'

'That's nice of you, my dear.'

'Listen. Herbert, my father, went to Windsor at the outset so he must be all right, and he's got tremendous pull in a quiet way. He's a great personal friend of the Monarch, who seems to have turned the corner now, and we can count on him to do everything in his power to get you off.'

'No,' he shook his head, 'intercession would only mean imprisonment, and I couldn't bear that.'

She gripped his hand suddenly and, leaning forward, whispered rapidly in French.

He gave a low delighted chuckle. 'You're a great woman, Veronica, but even if you did cling on to Hay-Symple, and Silas and Kenyon joined in, I could never get away. Look at the crowd—it's impossible to run on people's heads!'

'But my dear, we can't just let you die like this!'

'Oh, they'll out me I haven't a doubt, and I suppose I deserve it looked at from their point of view. Still—I'm not unhappy; "I've taken my fun where I found it and now I must pay for my fun." Kipling wrote that, didn't he?'

A renewed burst of cheering came from afar, but this time it did not slacken. Borne on the night wind it grew and grew, rushing in a vast wave of sound from Buckingham Palace Road to the gathered thousands before the Palace.

Veronica scrambled to her feet and saw that every face was upturned to the sky. The bright pointed fingers of the searchlights had flashed out while she was talking to Gregory and, caught in their glare, a dozen aeroplanes hovered overhead. A second dozen followed and a third; then came the wingless racing helicopter of the Prince. The searchlights concentrated upon it, shutting out the following squadrons of fast planes, as it sank easily and gracefully until lost to view, descending to its landing ground behind the Palace.

'Isn't this just grand, honey?' Silas flung his arm round Veronica's shoulder. 'Isn't it just too marvellous for anything.'

'Yes, honey,' she agreed, 'it is,' and, side by side, they stood staring at the Palace. There was nothing to be seen but the myriad upturned faces, yet the thunderous cheering continued unabated for the Prince must now be somewhere in the building; then there was a sudden lull in the roaring of the crowd. For a moment or two they swayed and muttered; then an arc lamp flared into life, throwing the first floor balcony into a dazzling patch of light.

A solitary slim figure stepped upon it. He wore no uniform, but, with the simplicity beloved by the English people, a suit of well-worn plus-fours. Curiously informal in his gestures he stood there bowing—a little jerkily, and smiling a pleasant friendly smile as he acknowledged the deafening plaudits of the crowd.

The mighty roar of sustained cheering seemed unending as it issued from those thousands of throats, but gradually it took a lower note and, merging into strange harmony, welled up again with renewed volume upon the pæan of the National Anthem.

As the last bars reverbrated against the walls of the Palace, Ann squeezed Kenyon's arm and pointed: 'Look, darling,' she cried, 'do you remember that terrible prophet —his month has run!'

Then Kenyon, looking upward saw, bright and clear above the Palace, the slender sickle of the September moon: 'My blessing', he drew her closer, 'we've come through Black August so, God willing, we'll have many moons together now.'

The Prince was holding up his hand for silence and, gradually, the cheering subsided; then he spoke, his voice faint but clear from the loud-speakers.

'I thank you from my heart for this great demonstration of loyal feeling. With your support I now have every confidence in the complete recovery of our country, and it is my joyous duty to announce the formal restoration of law and order.

'From tonight the ancient laws for the protection of life and property will be administered with the utmost severity against all who seek to retard recovery by breaches of the peace; but, since many thousands have been led to criminal actions contrary to their nature by the stream of late events, I proclaim a general amnesty and free pardon for all such, in the heartfelt hope that they may become once more loyal and responsible citizens.'

'Gregory!' Ann cried, pulling herself away from Kenyon.

'You're free—free!' shrieked Veronica.

'How perfectly splendid.' Kenyon hastened over to the prisoners.

'Yes,' Silas's cherubic smile spread over his broad face, 'I felt certain he'd get out of this jam somehow.'

But Gregory was gazing at his faithful henchman and familiar; 'I'm thundering glad,' he said huskily, 'the thought of what they might do to you is the only thing that's really been giving me hell on this journey.'

'*Old soldiers never die,* sir,' said Mr. Rudd.

The Prince had gone in but the thunderous cheering brought him out again. Once more he returned—bowing, smiling, waving a cheerful hand, yet they simply would not let him go. Five times more he appeared upon the balcony before he finally withdrew.

The great concourse of people would not disperse. Gaunt—hungry—knowing full well that tomorrow, and for many weeks to come, they would have to face life and all their individual difficulties, upon a meagre ration; perhaps to reconstruct their whole manner of living, or turn their steps from the known ways of the city to strange territories across the seas, they still remained for a new hope was born that night in England. The Prince Regent, idol of a still great and virile nation, would lead them yet into a new prosperity.

Their voices merged again into a solemn wave of sound, unrecognisable at first, yet taken up with the speed of wildfire, until the words of the famous hymn rang out clear and strong:

'Land of hope and glory—Mother of the free
How shall we extol thee—who are born of thee
Wider still and wider—shall thy bounds be set
God, who made thee mighty—make thee mightier yet
God—who—made—thee—mighty
MAKE—THEE—MIGHTIER—YET.'